The Ca[t] WHO Cracked A COLD CASE

L T Shearer has had a lifelong love of canal boats and calico cats, and both are combined in *The Cat Who Caught a Killer*, a one-of-a-kind debut crime novel. The series continues with *The Cat Who Solved Three Murders* and *The Cat Who Cracked a Cold Case*.

By L T Shearer

The Cat Who Caught a Killer
The Cat Who Solved Three Murders
The Cat Who Cracked a Cold Case

L T SHEARER

The Cat Who Cracked a Cold Case

PAN BOOKS

First published 2024 by Macmillan

This paperback edition first published 2025 by Pan Books
an imprint of Pan Macmillan
The Smithson, 6 Briset Street, London EC1M 5NR
EU representative: Macmillan Publishers Ireland Ltd, 1st Floor,
The Liffey Trust Centre, 117–126 Sheriff Street Upper,
Dublin 1 D01 YC43
Associated companies throughout the world

ISBN 978-1-0350-4381-1

1 3 5 7 9 8 6 4 2

A CIP catalogue record for this book is available from the British Library.

Typeset by Palimpsest Book Production Ltd, Falkirk, Stirlingshire
Printed and bound by CPI Group (UK) Ltd, Croydon CR0 4YY

MIX
Paper | Supporting responsible forestry
FSC® C116313
FSC www.fsc.org

The Cat Who Cracked a Cold Case

1

It was a twenty-minute walk from *The Lark* to the supermarket, but Lulu Lewis was glad of the exercise. She had been driving her narrowboat for the best part of six hours since dawn and needed to stretch her legs. They were just outside a small village about thirty miles to the south-west of Manchester. *The Lark* was on the Bridgewater Canal and it had been a spectacular day, and tiring. They had covered fifteen miles and had gone through three long tunnels. The longest was the Preston Brook Tunnel, which was over twelve hundred yards long and was so straight that she had been able to see daylight at the end all the way along. The tunnel wasn't wide enough for boats to pass each other, so boats heading north were only allowed to enter the tunnel during the first ten minutes of every hour; there had been a queue of half a dozen waiting to make the journey when Lulu had pulled up at the entrance.

After passing through the third tunnel, she had decided to stop for provisions. She had found a mooring spot with a supermarket just a mile away. Several other boats had clearly had the same idea.

Conrad wasn't so keen on walking and so he rode on her shoulders, attracting curious looks from anyone who passed by. It was unusual to see a cat perched on a person's shoulders, but Lulu had become quite used to it. He weighed barely anything and it was comforting to hear his soft purr in her right ear.

'I feel like salmon,' said Conrad as she carried him along the towpath.

Lulu had become used to the fact that Conrad the cat could speak, and that she was the only person that he would talk to. When he had first walked into her life and onto her narrowboat in Little Venice, the shock of finding out he could talk had almost made her faint. Now she took it in her stride. 'Salmon sounds good,' she said. 'Or sea bass.'

'Oh yes, sea bass would be nice. Can I change my order?'

'I hadn't realized that you had placed an order, but yes, of course you can.'

Conrad fell silent as a lady walking a golden retriever headed towards them. The dog spotted Conrad and its tail began to wag furiously. The woman pulled at the dog's lead and then her jaw dropped when she saw Conrad. 'Oh, my goodness. There's a cat on your shoulders.'

'Yes, there is,' said Lulu. 'He's a fashion statement.'

The woman stood still and tugged the dog back. 'That is amazing.'

Lulu stopped and smiled. 'He is an amazing cat.'

'I love his colours. What do you call a cat like that?'

'His name is Conrad.'

The woman frowned, then laughed. 'No, I meant what breed is he? I love his colours.'

Conrad was often complimented on his colouring, a mixture of black, white and orangey brown. The right side of his head was mainly black with a white patch around the nose and mouth, and the left side was brown and white. 'I call him a calico cat,' said Lulu. 'But people tell me that's an Americanism and that I should say he is a tortoiseshell. But there is nothing of the tortoise about Conrad.'

'Well, he is absolutely lovely,' the woman said. She looked down at the golden retriever. 'Isn't he lovely, Murphy?'

'Woof!' said the dog, straining at its lead.

'Oh, he talks!' said Lulu.

'Yes, he does,' said the woman. She patted the dog on the head. 'You love to talk, don't you?'

'Woof, woof!'

'Well, you and Murphy have a lovely day,' said Lulu, heading off.

'You too,' said the woman. 'Come on, Murphy.'

Conrad waited until the woman was out of earshot before speaking. 'A talking dog?' he said. 'Good grief, when did anyone ever hear a dog talk?'

'I was being polite.'

'And if a dog could talk, what could it possibly say? Throw me a stick? Feed me? Can I smell your butt?'

'Conrad!' said Lulu. 'What a terrible thing to say! That's practically doggist.'

'I'm not in the least bit doggist,' said Conrad. 'Some of my best friends are dogs. But conversationalists they are not.'

They left the towpath and Lulu checked her phone to make sure they were heading in the right direction.

'However did humans manage before smartphones?' Conrad asked.

'That's a very good question,' said Lulu. 'There are printed canal guides which would tell you everything you need to know about a canal and its facilities. People used them, I suppose. Or asked a local.' She held up the phone. 'This is so much easier.'

They walked down the road until they saw the sign for the supermarket. It was a Waitrose and Conrad's ears pricked up. 'Waitrose do sell the best sea bass,' he said.

'They do, don't they?' agreed Lulu.

Conrad jumped down from Lulu's shoulders when they reached the entrance. 'I'm sorry you're not allowed in,' said Lulu.

'You could say that I was your seeing-eye cat.'

'I don't think that would work,' said Lulu.

'Your emotional-support cat, then.'

'You definitely provide me with that,' said Lulu, 'but best you wait here. I won't be long.'

'Don't forget my Evian water.'

'As if I would.'

Lulu went inside and picked up a basket. She went to the wine section first and chose a bottle of Chardonnay that was on special offer, then added two bottles of Evian. The sea bass did look good and she chose two fillets, then picked up a bag of salad and some new potatoes. Dinner sorted, she bought bacon, six free range eggs and a loaf of bread. She was running low on tea and added a box of Tetley teabags. The fruit displays looked so inviting that she took some bananas, oranges and apples. The basket was getting heavy so she called it a day and headed to the tills. Her heart sank when she saw the self-service checkout machines, and her reservations were confirmed when she had to call for assistance to confirm that she was over twenty-five, but she persevered. She used two carrier bags to pack everything away, knowing that balance was important when you had a cat on your shoulders.

Conrad's tail swished when she came out. 'Woof, woof!' he said.

'You're not going to let this drop, are you?' said Lulu. She bent down so that he could jump onto her shoulders, then headed back to the canal.

2

The twin carrier bags had definitely been a good idea, but her arms were still aching by the time they reached the towpath. It was a gloriously sunny day with just a few wisps of cloud overhead. A narrowboat went by, clearly a live-aboard as the roof was covered with boxes, crates and two bicycles. There was a man in a flat cap at the stern and he waved. Lulu nodded and smiled. Canal folk were friendly people, there was no doubt about it. The narrowboat was called *Over the Hull*, a nice play on words. Lulu had bought *The Lark* from a retired teacher who had owned it from new and had bought it, he'd said, as a lark.

As they approached *The Lark*, Conrad's ears pricked up. 'Do you hear that?' he said.

'Hear what?' asked Lulu.

'A woman, crying.'

Lulu turned her head from side to side, narrowing her eyes as if that would somehow improve her hearing. It didn't. She could hear birds in the trees to their right, and off in the distance the sound of the narrowboat engine phut-phut-phutting, but no crying. 'I can't hear anything.'

'Well, you're not a cat, of course. Cats can hear things four or five times as far away as humans, and at much higher frequencies.'

'And it's a woman? Crying? You're sure?'

'Yes. I think she's on *The Kingfisher*.'

Lulu looked down the towpath. *The Kingfisher* was six boats away, dark red with gold trim and a line of solar panels across the roof. She still couldn't hear anything.

Conrad jumped down off her shoulders and padded along the towpath, his ears focused on *The Kingfisher*. He reached the narrowboat and stood there, tail twitching. Lulu caught up with him and finally she could hear a soft sobbing.

'She's very sad,' said Conrad.

'I can hear that.'

'We should do something.'

'Oh, no, you can't go intruding on someone's personal grief,' said Lulu. 'You have no idea what she's crying about. It could be anything.'

'Maybe we can help,' said Conrad. He jumped up onto the rear deck in a smooth, fluid motion, making almost no sound.

'Conrad, no!'

He ignored her and padded over to the double doors that led down to the cabin.

'No, you mustn't!' hissed Lulu, but she was too late: Conrad had already disappeared. Lulu sighed and put down her shopping bags, not sure what to do. If the woman was upset, it really wasn't any of their business. After Lulu's husband had passed away she had been inconsolable for days, for weeks, and for most of that time she had wanted to be alone with her grief. A large part of the grieving process was dealing with thoughts and memories and the feeling of loss, and you had to go through that alone. Yes, it was lovely to have someone with you who cared and who wanted to try to make things better, but some things couldn't be made better; some things just had to be dealt with.

The crying stopped and Lulu heard a muffled voice, a

woman speaking softly. Lulu really wasn't sure what to do. Narrowboat etiquette was that you never boarded a boat without being asked first. A bit like vampires, who also needed permission to cross a threshold. If she had been visiting a narrowboat friend, then she would have just called out, but Lulu had no idea who was on *The Kingfisher*. The decision was made for her when a white-haired lady appeared in the doorway, holding Conrad in her arms. 'Oh, is he yours?' said the lady. She was stick thin and wearing thick-lensed spectacles. Her long hair was tied back in a ponytail and she had a green quilted waistcoat over a Fair Isle sweater.

'I think I might be his,' said Lulu. 'I'm so sorry that he intruded. He has a mind of his own.'

'Cats do.' The woman was stroking Conrad behind the ears and he was clearly loving it, pressing his head against her hand. 'They walk their own path.'

'Conrad certainly does that.'

'Calico cats are almost always female, aren't they? It's a gene thing.'

'They are, but Conrad is a very unusual cat.'

'He's lovely,' said the woman, looking down at him. Her cheeks were wet from tears and her eyes were red.

'It's none of my business, but is everything okay?' asked Lulu.

The woman forced a smile. 'Not really,' she said. 'I'm a silly old woman, that's all.' She sniffed.

'Oh, I'm sure you're not,' said Lulu. 'My name's Lulu, by the way.'

'I'm Jessie,' said the woman. 'Well, Jessica really, but everyone calls me Jessie.'

'Do you like wine, Jessie?'

Jessie frowned. 'Wine?'

Lulu held up one of the carrier bags. 'I have a very nice Chardonnay.'

'Oh, I'm not sure,' said Jessie. 'I might not be the best of company.'

'Well, Conrad seems very happy in your arms, and I do so hate drinking alone.'

Jessie looked at her with tear-filled eyes, then slowly nodded. 'Chardonnay does sound good.'

3

The main cabin of *The Kingfisher* was lined with polished ash and there were two bench seats facing each other across a table. The galley was also ash with a small microwave, a built-in oven, a double hob and a Belfast sink. Lulu told Jessie to sit down and that she would pour the drinks. Jessie did as she was told, still holding Conrad to her chest.

'There are glasses in the cupboard above the sink, and a corkscrew in the drawer above the fridge,' said Jessie.

'Oh, these days I always go for screw-top bottles, they're so much more convenient,' said Lulu. She opened the cupboard and took out two large wine glasses. 'Do you have a dish I can use?'

'A dish?'

'For Conrad. I'll give him some water.'

'There's a bowl on the draining board. The blue one.'

Lulu thanked her. She poured wine into the glasses and Evian water into the dish. Lulu put the bowl of water in front of Conrad and then sat down facing Jessie. 'Well, cheers,' she said. She clinked her glass against Jessie's and they both drank. Conrad padded over to the blue bowl and lapped at the water.

'This is quite lovely,' said Lulu, looking around. 'What is it, a fifty-foot cruiser?'

'Fifty-two feet,' said Jessie.

'And you live aboard?'

Jessie nodded. 'It's been my home for more than fifteen years,' she said.

On the wall opposite the table there was a framed photograph of Jessie with a tall, handsome man with a movie-star smile. 'Is that your husband?' Lulu asked.

Jessie smiled. 'That's Johnny,' she said. 'He passed away five years ago.'

'I'm so sorry.'

'It was cancer.' Jessie shuddered at the memory. 'He hated being in the hospital, at the end. He really wanted to be on the boat, but . . .' She shrugged. 'I suppose we don't always get what we want.'

Lulu sipped her wine. 'Is that why you were crying?'

'Why I was crying? No. Well, sort of.' She sighed. 'I'm so stupid.'

'Why do you say that?'

'Because I was robbed.'

'Robbed? When?'

'Today. This morning. I don't really know.' She drank several gulps of wine. 'I'm just a stupid old woman, it's my own fault.'

'Please don't say that,' said Lulu. 'Why don't you start from the beginning?'

Jessie put her glass down. 'I've been moored here for a week now. It's such a nice place and there's a Waitrose not far away.'

Lulu smiled and pointed at her carrier bags. 'I know.'

Jessie laughed. 'Yes, of course you do. Anyway, yesterday evening a man came around, asking if he could borrow some sugar. He had moored behind me and I just said yes, of course. He came aboard, which was okay, but then he came down into the galley and I had a bad feeling about him. I mean, he was pleasant enough but his eyes were everywhere, looking at everything. But he was very complimentary and smiled a lot and I didn't want to be rude. I mean, you don't want to be rude to someone, do you?'

'Of course not.'

'He kept talking. He wouldn't stop. And all the time he was looking around. Eventually I said I had to use the bathroom – that was the only way I could get rid of him. Anyway, he left, and I forgot about it. Then this morning I went to the supermarket and when I came back . . .' Tears began to run down her face. Conrad walked across the table to her and she gathered him up in her arms and buried her face in his fur.

Lulu took another sip of wine. It was best to say nothing; Jessie would tell the story in her own time. Questions would just stem the flow.

Eventually Jessie straightened up and wiped her eyes with the back of her hand. 'My figurines had gone,' she said. 'He must have come back while I was out.'

'Did you lock your boat?'

Jessie shook her head. 'No, I didn't. I never do. You never think anyone will steal from you, do you?'

'Well . . .'

'I mean, canal folk are good folk, aren't they? That's what Johnny always used to say.'

'Where were the figurines?'

Jessie twisted around and pointed down the cabin. There was a shelf unit on the wall with several paperback books, a small vase and a few knick-knacks. 'They were on the second shelf. Two Lladró figurines.'

'Oh, Lladró,' said Lulu.

'You know about Lladró?'

'My mother-in-law used to collect them. They're Spanish, right?'

Jessie nodded. 'Their factory is in Valencia, these days. They've been in business since the fifties. Three brothers: Juan, José and Vicente Lladró. Johnny bought two pieces for me, for our first wedding anniversary. One is a milkmaid, the other is a shepherd boy with a lamb. He said they reminded him of the pair of us.' She smiled. 'He was right – it was the funniest thing. The milkmaid looked just like me when I was sixteen.'

'Are they valuable?'

'They are now, yes. Maybe five thousand pounds each. But it's not about the money. I don't care about the money.' Tears started to flow again and she cuddled Conrad. 'I am so stupid. So, so stupid.'

'Please, Jessie, don't say that. So what do you think happened to the figurines?'

'He stole them, obviously. The man who came to borrow sugar. He was sitting on the towpath, smoking, when I left for the supermarket. And when I came back, his boat had gone.'

'How long were you away?'

'An hour at most. I had coffee and I read the paper and I did some shopping.'

'And when you came back, did you notice straight away that the figurines were missing?'

Jessie bit down on her lower lip. 'No, I put my food in my fridge and made myself a sandwich and I ate it on the deck. It was only when I went back down into the galley that I realized they were missing.'

'And so how long has the sugar man been gone? Two hours?'

'Yes, about two hours. Do you think I should call the police?'

Lulu wrinkled her nose. 'I have to be honest, Jessie, I don't think they would consider a burglary a high priority. They would probably just give you a crime number to pass on to your insurance company. You are insured, aren't you?'

'I am, Johnny was always a stickler for insurance. But it's not about the money, Lulu. I just want the figurines. Would the police get them back for me?'

Lulu sighed. 'I'm sorry, Jessie, I really don't think they would even try. I used to be a police officer in London.'

'Really?'

'I was a superintendent. I retired some time ago, but even then things were changing and they were struggling for resources. These days it's even worse.'

'I was thinking that if they sent out a CSI team they might find fingerprints or DNA or something.'

'CSI is what they have in America. In the UK it's SOCO. Scenes of Crime Officers. Forensic investigators. But the police rarely send them out to burglaries. And even if they did, any DNA or fingerprints could be explained by the fact that he was there when you gave him some sugar.'

'Lulu, they have to do something – I was robbed.'

Lulu shook her head sadly. 'No, it's only robbery if someone uses force when they steal. Theft is when someone takes property without the use of force, and burglary is when someone enters a property illegally in order to steal property from it. So you were burgled. And the police regard that as a low-priority crime these days.'

Tears welled up in Jessie's eyes again and Lulu reached out to hold her hand. 'I'm sorry.'

'I miss Johnny.'

'I know you do.'

'I've been so, so . . .' She caught herself and didn't finish the sentence.

Lulu looked at her watch. It was almost two o'clock. If the man had left two hours earlier, he could be up to eight miles away already. It got dark about six-thirty, so in four and a half hours he would be able to cover another eighteen miles at most before it got dark. He didn't have time to reach Manchester that night. 'I have an idea,' said Lulu.

4

Lulu gently moved the tiller to the left and eased back on the throttle as she passed a line of moored narrowboats. She wanted to go as quickly as possible, but it was never a good idea to upset canal users. Although they were generally a friendly bunch, one thing that was guaranteed to upset them was a speeding boat's wake tossing their craft up and down. Canal etiquette meant that the engine was supposed to be cut back to a tickover while passing moored vessels. She looked at her watch. Sunset was about an hour away and there was still no sign of the blue and white narrowboat that had the word 'Blue' in its name. That was the best that Jessie could do by way of a description of the boat being used by the man she thought had stolen her porcelain figurines. *Blue Lagoon* or *Feeling Blue* or something like that. She really hadn't been paying attention, which is why she wasn't sure what style the boat was. But she remembered the colours and the fact that there was an electric scooter tied to the roof. With any luck, that would be enough for Lulu to identify the boat.

Jessie had been more descriptive when it came to the man who had come onto *The Kingfisher*. He had black hair and a beard and he was short – just a few inches taller than Jessie, who was only five feet four. He had been wearing a denim shirt with the sleeves rolled up and had a tattoo of a dragon around a knife on his left forearm. His boots were made by

Timberland and seemed to be new, and he was wearing green corduroy trousers. Lulu had been impressed by the amount of detail and Jessie had explained that she had been so nervous that she didn't want to look him in the eye and so had concentrated on looking at his clothing instead. Lulu had taken Jessie's phone number and promised to keep in touch.

'So what exactly is our plan?' asked Conrad. He was sitting behind her on the bench seat at the rear of *The Lark*.

'I'll play it by ear,' said Lulu. They passed the line of moored boots and Lulu increased the throttle to the maximum.

'But as you told Jessie, the police aren't going to be interested, are they?'

'I don't see that they'd mount an investigation into two stolen figurines, no. It's like shoplifting – you hardly ever see anyone charged with shoplifting these days.'

'But he might be stealing from lots of people. He could be a career thief.'

'He could be, yes.'

'I thought you said that canal people were good people?'

'They are, mostly. But there are bad apples everywhere.'

'Which brings me back to my original question. You need a plan, Lulu.'

'Well, I suppose I could talk to him.'

'Use your powers of persuasion to get him to give them back?'

'I suppose so, yes.'

'I have to say, that's not much of a plan.'

Lulu cut back on the throttle. 'Is that him?'

Conrad jumped up onto the roof, his ears swivelling in all directions, his tail up like an antenna. 'I don't see anyone.'

'Sorry, not him, the boat. The blue and white one.' She shaded her eyes with her hand. 'I can't see the name. Can you?'

Conrad padded the full length of the boat and stopped at the bow. He stared at the narrowboat, which was a couple of hundred yards ahead of them, then he ran back to her. 'It's *Blue Moon*,' he said. 'That must be him.'

Lulu eased back on the throttle. The *Blue Moon* was moored by the towpath. There was another narrowboat ahead of it, also tied up to the bank. It didn't appear to be a signed visitor mooring. Boats were allowed to be moored anywhere on the towpath side of a canal, for up to fourteen days. If there were no fixed moorings, all you had to do was hammer in a couple of spikes and tie up to them.

She eased *The Lark* over to the side and cut the throttle. She lifted the lid of the bench seat and took out two spikes and the mallet that she kept there, then grabbed the centre line and stepped onto the towpath. She quickly hammered one of the spikes into the ground then pulled on the line, leaning back to apply all her weight. *The Lark* came to a halt and she tied the line to the spike, then hurried along the towpath to the bow. She stepped onto the boat, grabbed the bowline and jumped back onto the towpath. She hammered in a second spike and tied the line to it in a matter of seconds, then straightened up to see Conrad standing on the roof, watching her.

'I wish I could help,' said Conrad.

'It's the advantage of having opposable thumbs,' said Lulu.

She went back to the stern, grabbed a third spike and attached the stern line. It had taken her less than two minutes to tie up *The Lark*. She'd had plenty of practice on the trip up from London and could almost do it with her eyes closed.

She put the mallet back in its box and closed the lid. Conrad padded along the roof to join her. 'Jessie said he had an electric scooter tied to his roof,' he said. 'I don't see it.'

'Maybe he's gone somewhere,' said Lulu. She took out her phone and tapped on the screen. 'There's a shop about a mile away. He's probably gone there. Come on.'

'Come where?'

'Surveillance.'

Lulu stepped off *The Lark* and onto the towpath, then bent down so that Conrad could jump onto her shoulders.

'What if he comes back?' asked Conrad.

'We're just out for a walk.' Lulu looked up and down the towpath. There was nobody else around. She started walking towards the *Blue Moon*. As she got closer she saw that the double doors on the rear deck had been secured with a padlocked chain.

'It looks as if he's security conscious,' said Conrad. 'Which is ironic.'

They reached the boat. Lulu peered in the first of three portholes. There was a galley with a sink full of dirty plates. The second and third portholes looked onto the saloon. There was a scruffy sofa against the wall and a couple of empty pizza boxes on the floor.

They heard the rattle of a bicycle and turned around to see a young boy pedalling down the towpath. Lulu stepped closer to the boat to get out of his way. He had wireless earbuds in his ears and a glazed look in his eyes as he whizzed by, missing them by inches.

'Idiot,' said Conrad as the boy cycled away. 'Some people are so inconsiderate.'

'He's a kid,' said Lulu.

'And I'm a cat,' said Conrad. 'You can't use your species as an excuse for stupidity.'

Lulu turned back to look at the *Blue Moon*. Midway along was a sliding window that looked onto the end of the saloon and the start of the corridor that led to the bathroom and the berth. The left-hand side of the window was fixed but the right-hand pane was open a few inches. Lulu peered in but couldn't see much. 'I could get in and take a look around,' said Conrad.

'No, it's too dangerous.'

'He's clearly not here. And there's no one else on the boat. I could have a look around and see if the figurines are there. Then at least we'd know.'

'We don't have a search warrant.'

'I'm a cat, remember. Cats are always getting into places we're not supposed to go. It's what we do.'

'You're the one who said your species wasn't an excuse—' began Lulu, but before she could say anything else, Conrad had jumped off her shoulders and slid through the gap in the window. She heard a dull thud as he landed on the floor. 'Conrad, are you okay?' she whispered.

'I'm fine. Just keep watch.'

Lulu stepped away from the narrowboat and looked around. A middle-aged couple in matching Barbour waxed-cotton jackets were walking towards her, an Afghan hound between them.

'Conrad!' she whispered. 'There's somebody coming!'

There was no reply. The couple with the dog were about a hundred yards away, deep in conversation. Lulu realized she couldn't just stand by the *Blue Moon*; they'd be sure to wonder what she was doing. She started walking towards them. They still hadn't noticed her but the dog had and it began to wag its tail. It was a beautiful animal with a thick, silky coat and long ears and dark almond-shaped eyes.

Lulu walked slowly and reached *The Lark* at the same time as the couple. The dog strained at its lead and tried to get to Lulu. She smiled at the couple. 'What a lovely dog,' she said.

'Thank you,' said the man. 'He certainly likes you.'

'He probably smells my cat,' said Lulu. 'Is it okay to pat him?'

'Of course,' said the man. He was in his sixties, grey-haired with a neatly trimmed moustache. 'He loves to be stroked.'

'Don't we all,' said the woman. She was a few years younger than the man, with greying hair. Lulu thought that even without make-up she looked stunning, with high cheekbones and sparkling blue eyes.

The man laughed and hugged her. Lulu smiled, but the display of affection made her realize how much she still missed her husband. The man looked a little like Simon, but Simon had been taller and better looking. She felt tears well up in her eyes and turned her attention to the dog. 'Oh, you are lovely,' said Lulu, stroking the back of its head.

'Are you local?' asked the woman. 'We haven't seen you before, have we?'

'I'm just passing through,' said Lulu. She nodded at *The Lark*. 'This is mine.'

'Oh, how lovely,' said the woman. 'Do you live on it?'

'I do,' said Lulu. 'Usually down in London, in Little Venice. I'm on a bit of a tour.'

'Oh, we love Little Venice,' said the man. 'We always go for a walk there when we're visiting Lord's.'

'My husband's cricket mad,' the woman said to Lulu.

'My one vice.'

'Well, I wish that was true,' said the woman. She looked around. 'Is your cat around?'

'Oh, yes, somewhere,' said Lulu. 'Anyway, lovely to chat with you, but I left the kettle on.' It was the best lie she could think of. She just wanted them to leave so that she could go back and check on Conrad. As she climbed onto the rear deck, they heard the whirr of an electric motor. An electric scooter was zooming along the towpath and Lulu's heart began to race when she realized it was the man from the *Blue Moon*. He was bent over the handlebars of the scooter, head down, his eyes narrowed against the wind. 'Coming through!' he shouted.

The woman pulled at the dog's lead and they all stepped off the towpath. The scooter shot by. The man had a carrier bag hooked over his left wrist. He was exactly as Jessie had described him – dark haired, bearded, wearing a blue denim shirt with the sleeves rolled up, green corduroy trousers and Timberland boots. As he went past, Lulu caught a glimpse of a tattoo on his left arm.

'Why do people think that is in any way acceptable?' said the woman. 'He could kill someone, driving at that speed.'

'They are so dangerous,' agreed Lulu. The scooter rider stopped at the rear of the *Blue Moon*, folded up the scooter and carried it onto the rear deck. Lulu stared at the sliding window, but there was no sign of Conrad.

'We should say something to him,' said the woman.

'I'm not sure that's a good idea, darling,' said her husband. 'He looked a bit manic, actually.'

The man attached the scooter to the roof of the narrowboat,

then started his boat's engine. A cloud of grey smoke belched from the exhaust. 'He's leaving,' whispered Lulu.

'A good thing too,' said the woman. 'We don't need his sort here.'

Lulu's heart was pounding as if it was about to burst out of her chest. Where was Conrad? What was he doing?'

'Come on, darling, or we'll be late,' said the man. For a moment Lulu wasn't sure if he was talking to his wife or the dog, but it was his wife who answered.

'We've plenty of time,' she said. She smiled at Lulu. 'Well, lovely to meet you, you enjoy the rest of your day.'

'You too,' said Lulu, just wishing that they would hurry up and leave. She looked over at the *Blue Moon* and bit down on her lower lip. The husband and wife finally walked away, the dog between them. Lulu had to fight the urge to run over to the *Blue Moon*.

The man on the boat unlocked the chain, opened the doors and took his carrier bag down into the cabin. Lulu could barely breathe. Would he see Conrad? And if he did, what would he do? Her hands began to tremble.

The dog was barking at the *Blue Moon*, its tail wagging like a metronome.

The man reappeared, closed the doors and then stepped off the boat and untied the centre line. He jumped back on, coiled the line and placed it on the roof.

Lulu stared at the sliding window. If Conrad jumped now, he'd be able to run along the towpath and there was a good chance the man wouldn't realize where he'd come from.

The dog's bark intensified and its owner was pulling hard on the lead. Lulu heard the woman's voice as she tried to calm the dog.

The man jumped back onto the towpath and untied the stern line, and carried it to the rear deck.

'Come on, Conrad,' Lulu whispered to herself. 'Now's the time to get the hell out of there. Jump. Please jump.'

The dog walkers reached the boat. It didn't look as if the woman was going to carry out her threat to say something to the man; they just walked slowly by as the *Blue Moon* pulled away from the bank. Lulu kept staring at the side window, willing Conrad to appear, but there was no sign of him.

She stepped back onto the towpath and hurriedly began to untie her lines.

5

Lulu's hand was trembling on the tiller and she was finding it hard to breathe. The *Blue Moon* was about three hundred yards ahead of *The Lark*, chugging along at three miles an hour. Lulu wasn't worried about losing her quarry: there was only one way he could go. It was Conrad she was worried about. Had something happened? Was he trapped? She was fairly sure that the man hadn't discovered that he was on board because he had only been inside for a few seconds to drop off his purchases. Would Conrad be able to jump out while the boat was moving? Could he swim? His swimming ability had never come up in conversation.

She kept her left hand on the tiller and used her right to open her Canal app. There were no branches ahead of her, it was a straight run through Altrincham and Sale and then on to Manchester city centre. It would be dark in about half an hour. Boats could drive at night – they were all equipped with headlights – but canal etiquette held that boats didn't drive after 8 p.m. so as not to disturb those who were already asleep. The thing was, of course, that a man who was happy to steal cherished heirlooms from a widowed old lady probably wouldn't care much about upsetting other canal users.

She had thought about phoning the police, but they would probably regard cat-napping as even less serious than burglary. And how could she explain the fact that she had watched the man drive his boat away, knowing that Conrad was on board? All she could do was follow the *Blue Moon* and hope that she would find some way of getting Conrad back.

The *Blue Moon* slowed and Lulu eased back on the throttle. Following a narrowboat wasn't on a par with tailing a car – some days you'd spend hours with the same boats in front of you and behind you. With a four mile an hour maximum speed, there wasn't much overtaking going on. Still, she didn't want to get too close. She didn't want to attract attention.

The *Blue Moon* was definitely slowing. She checked the app again and saw that they were coming up to a canalside pub. Lulu said a silent prayer that he was planning to stop there. A pub would be perfect, especially if he stayed for a drink or a meal.

Lulu pulled the throttle back to tickover. The *Blue Moon* was getting ready to stop. She steered over to the bank, grabbed her centre line and stepped off *The Lark*. She pulled back on the line and eased the boat against the bank, then realized that she had forgotten her spike and mallet. 'Rookie mistake,' she muttered to herself. She jumped back on the rear deck, opened the hatch and took out the mallet and two spikes.

By the time she had stepped back onto the towpath, the bow of *The Lark* had swung out into the middle of the canal and she hauled on the centre line to bring it back. She kept looking over at the *Blue Moon*. The man had moored his boat and was bent over the hatch, presumably padlocking the chain.

She bent down and hammered in a spike, then attached the line. When she looked up, the man was off the boat and walking purposefully along the towpath. Lulu hammered in a second spike and tied the bowline to it. She climbed back onto *The Lark* and peered at the man. The sun had almost sunk behind the horizon and it was hard to pick him out against the hawthorn hedge that ran alongside the towpath. She pulled out her phone and checked the app again. He was definitely heading in the direction of the pub.

She opened the hatch in the bench seat and took out her toolbox. She grabbed a bolt-cutter that looked as if it would be more than a match for the padlock. She grimaced. If she cut off the padlock, he'd know that someone had been in his boat. She hurried down into the saloon, pulled open one of the kitchen drawers and took out a small leather wallet with a zip down the side.

By the time she was back on the towpath, there was no sign of the man and she hurried towards the *Blue Moon*. There were three narrowboats between *The Lark* and the *Blue Moon*, all with their lights off. She stayed to the left, keeping clear of their lines.

When she reached the *Blue Moon*, she crept over to the sliding window. It was closed. She tried to push it open but it was securely locked. She put her hand up against the glass and peered inside, but there was no sign of Conrad. She turned and peered down the towpath. If the man returned while she was at the back of the boat, she wouldn't see him coming and he would catch her red-handed. She took a deep breath and stepped onto the rear deck. There was still enough light to see by. It was a cheap brass padlock and she was sure that the cutters would slice right through the shackle, but she wanted to get inside without him knowing, so she shoved the cutters in her pocket and unzipped the leather case. Inside were more than a dozen metal picks. She took one out and carefully inserted it into the locking mechanism. She wiggled the pick around, trying to feel the tumblers and push them into place. It had been a while since she had picked a lock and she wasn't sure if she would be up to it, but in less than thirty seconds the mechanism clicked and the shackle was ejected. She smiled. 'You've still got it,' she whispered to herself.

She removed the chain from the door handles and pulled the doors open. 'Conrad, are you there?' she whispered.

'Of course I'm here,' he said frostily. 'I'm locked in. Where else would I be?'

'Come on, quickly, before he comes back.'

'There's something you have to see here.'

'Can't you bring it with you?'

Conrad sighed. 'I suppose I could, if I had opposable thumbs. Come on, you need to see this.'

'Okay, okay.' Lulu peered around the side of the boat. The towpath was empty. She felt her way down the steps into the galley. Conrad was sitting on the sofa. There was a damp smell mingled with the aroma of stale pizza and old socks that made Lulu shudder. 'How could anyone live like this?' she said.

Conrad stood up and gestured with his chin at a black Nike backpack at the side of the sofa. 'Look at that,' he said.

Lulu bent down. The backpack was open and she immediately saw the two figurines inside. 'You found them!' she said.

'They would be hard to miss,' said Conrad. 'It's not as if he was hiding them, is it? But there's other stuff in there, too.'

Lulu carefully took out the figurines. There were several

framed miniatures in the backpack. They looked Victorian. Another frame contained four Penny Black stamps. There were three pieces of intricately carved scrimshaw – she couldn't tell if they were bone or ivory – and wrapped in a handkerchief were half a dozen rings and a gold charm bracelet. 'Jessie isn't the only one he's stolen from,' whispered Lulu.

'We should show this to the police,' said Conrad.

'Well, yes, but then we'd have to explain how we got on board,' said Lulu. 'Let's just take the figurines and go. We can report him to the police anonymously and let them deal with it.'

They heard footsteps on the towpath and both froze. Lulu's heart was pounding furiously. She looked at Conrad. He was staring at the sliding window, his ears twitching.

The footsteps approached the narrowboat and then a shadow flicked across the window. Lulu held her breath. If it was the man, they were trapped – unless they could make their way to the bow and get off that way. She started to move along the boat towards the bow but Conrad looked at her. 'It's okay,' he whispered. 'It's not him.'

'How can you tell?'

'This man is much bigger. And he's walking a dog.'

'You can hear that?'

Conrad sighed. 'I'm a cat, Lulu. I can hear frequencies up to sixty-four thousand hertz, which is about three times higher than you humans.' His ears continued to swivel around independently of each other as the footsteps moved alongside the narrowboat. Lulu heard a dog panting, and then she flinched at a series of short, excited barks. 'He can smell me,' whispered Conrad. The dog continued to bark and they heard the man chastising it. The barking faded as the man took the dog away from the boat. 'All mouth and no trousers,' said Conrad.

'Excuse me?'

'Dogs,' said Conrad. 'All that barking, all that aggression. Yet I've never met a dog that didn't run away howling if you give them a good box on the nose.'

'I never had you down as a fighter,' whispered Lulu.

'Only if my back is against the wall,' said Conrad. He tilted his head to one side. 'They've gone.'

Lulu gathered up the two figurines and put them in the pockets of her fleece. 'Come on,' she whispered.

She headed along the galley and up the steps. She stopped at the doors. In the distance she could see a big man with a German shepherd on a lead. She looked the other way. The towpath was clear. She stepped onto the rear deck and picked up the chain and padlock. Conrad jumped up onto the bench seat. 'You picked the lock?' he said.

'I did, yes.'

'How on earth did you acquire that skill?'

Lulu closed the doors and wound the chain through the handles. 'It's a long story.'

'Oh, I love long stories.'

Lulu laughed and padlocked the chain. She rattled it to check that it was secure, then stepped off the boat onto the towpath. She bent down so that Conrad could jump onto her shoulders, and then headed back to *The Lark*. 'It was years ago, when I was a DC.'

'A DC?'

'A detective constable. I was given a housebreaking case, one of the first where I was lead investigator. A man had broken into a house and found the owner unconscious on the floor. He'd done the decent thing and phoned for an ambulance, but he used his own mobile. I was given his name and address and told to bring him in for questioning. I was a bit nervous because the DC I was with was even less experienced than I was, but the guy was as nice as pie. He was Scottish, Willie McBride. He was old enough to be my dad and he happily agreed to go back to the station. He actually asked me how the old lady was, so it was obviously him who had made the call.'

'And how was she? The old lady?'

'She was fine. Well, not fine, obviously, as she'd had a heart attack, but she was on the mend and according to the doctors if Willie hadn't called for an ambulance, she'd have died. Anyway, we get to the car, a Ford Fiesta from the station pool. I'd been so caught up in what I was going to say that I'd left the keys inside. I felt like such an idiot.'

They reached *The Lark* and Lulu climbed on board.

'Willie was laughing, but then he went back inside his house and came out with this long piece of metal; he had the door open in seconds. He said it was the first time he'd broken into a police car. And that was the start of a wonderful friendship, as they say. I put in a good word for him and the Crown Prosecution Service agreed not to press charges. He was so grateful that he said if ever I needed a locksmith, to give him a call. Well, I kid you not, the very next day I locked myself out of my flat. I called Willie and he came around and let me in. I made him coffee and he gave me a crash course in lock picking. And a few days later a package arrived for me at the police station – my very own lock-picking kit.'

'And you're a bit of a Raffles, now, are you?'

Lulu laughed. 'Far from it. But I can manage a bog-standard padlock and on a good day I can open a Yale. My party trick used to be opening handcuffs with a paper clip.' She looked at her watch. It was a little after six-thirty. 'We should move on, just in case he spots that the figurines have gone.'

'Aye, aye, captain,' said Conrad.

6

There was a narrowboat moored ahead of *The Lark*, so Lulu pulled the throttle back to idle. Even ticking over, the thud of the diesel engine could be heard from half a mile away. She took a quick look at her watch. It was nine o'clock and it had been dark for more than two hours. She had switched on the searchlight on the bow so it was easy enough to see where she was going, but she knew that people hated to have their cabins illuminated when they were trying to get to sleep. The narrowboat bobbed up and down as *The Lark* passed it. Lulu could imagine the occupants cursing her and she muttered 'sorry' under her breath.

Lulu looked over her shoulder, half expecting to see the *Blue Moon* on her tail, but the canal was empty behind her. She really didn't enjoy driving in the dark, but she wanted to get as far away from the *Blue Moon* as she could. She pushed the throttle forward and *The Lark* picked up speed.

'Are you okay?' asked Conrad.

Lulu shrugged. 'I've been better.'

'You look tense.'

'We've just committed breaking and entering, Conrad.'

'You didn't break anything. You picked the lock, you didn't break it.'

'Well you can always argue that point with the judge,' said Lulu. 'We're burglars, Conrad. I've never been a burglar before.'

'We didn't steal anything. We took back what was Jessie's.'

'Another point you can argue before the judge.'

'Seriously, you are worrying about nothing,' said Conrad. 'What's that man going to tell the police? You stole what he'd stolen? And what about the rest of the ill-gotten gains on his boat?' Conrad shook his head. 'The police are the last people he'll talk to.'

'I suppose so.' Conrad was right, of course. But if the man didn't call the police, maybe he'd take matters into his own hands, and that might well be worse.

'You're worried that he might come after us,' said Conrad.

She looked at him in astonishment. 'Did you just read my mind?'

He chuckled. 'You keep looking over your shoulder and you're clearly worried. It doesn't take a Sherlock Holmes to guess what you're anxious about.'

'You are one smart cat.'

'It has been said. But seriously, you're worrying about nothing. He had left the boat before you came to get me. Other than the figurines, we left the boat exactly as we found it. And we were gone before he returned. He probably won't have realized that the figurines have gone, and even if he has, there's no way he could know that we've taken them. He didn't even see *The Lark*.'

Lulu forced a smile. Conrad was right. He usually was, about most things. But she would still be a lot happier once they weren't on their own. Stretford Marina was close by and she would be able to moor there overnight.

The headlight picked up another narrowboat ahead of them and she pulled the throttle back to idle. The lights were on in the saloon and two faces glared out at her as she went by, clearly resentful at their peace being disturbed. 'I'm sorry,' she mouthed, though she doubted that they could see her in the dark.

Her left arm was aching from steering and she had a throbbing headache, but finally she saw Stretford Marina ahead of her on the left. It was a private marina and she would have to pay to moor there, but there was safety in numbers. She looked over her shoulder for possibly the thousandth time. Nobody was following her. She smiled ruefully. The reason that nobody was behind her was because everybody else was following the rules. There was enough moonlight to see by, so she switched off her headlight.

Lulu slowed as she approached the marina, and guided *The Lark* into an empty bay. She killed the engine so as not to continue disturbing her neighbours, and stood looking back at the canal. Conrad jumped onto the roof and joined her, his tail twitching. There were more than a dozen narrow-boats moored, and another dozen or so pleasure craft.

'He's not there,' he said. 'There are no engines running on the canal.'

'Good to know,' said Lulu.

'You can relax now.'

'I suppose so.' She opened the doors and went down into the saloon. It was cold outside but the boat's central heating was on and the saloon was cosily warm. She put the kettle on the hob and lit it, but then had a change of heart and opened the fridge. She'd left the bottle of Chardonnay with Jessie but she had a half-full bottle of Pinot Grigio, so she took this out and poured some into a glass.

Conrad jumped up onto the sofa. 'We still have the sea bass to eat,' he said.

'We do, don't we? Shall I cook?'

'I'm happy enough to eat it raw, but I know you prefer your sea bass pan-fried with a little oil and a squeeze of lemon.'

Lulu laughed. 'You know me so well.' She poured some water into a bowl and placed it on the sofa next to him before she set about boiling some new potatoes and frying the sea bass in her favourite Le Creuset frying pan. She removed one of the fillets for Conrad before squirting some fresh lemon over hers. She added some rocket and tomato to her plate, then topped up her wine glass and sat next to him on the sofa. She clinked her glass against his bowl. 'Well, today was definitely an exciting day, wasn't it?'

'Life with you is never boring,' he said. 'For a moment today I was worried that I might lose one of my nine lives.'

'How many do you have left?'

Conrad chuckled. 'That would be telling,' he said.

7

Lulu woke at dawn. The first thing she did was go up on deck and look around. She stepped onto the wooden pier and walked along the line of narrowboats. There was a cold wind blowing across the marina and she was only wearing a sweatshirt and tracksuit bottoms; she shivered. 'Are you still worried that he'll follow you?' asked Conrad.

Lulu jumped. She hadn't heard him approach. Conrad grinned. 'Sorry,' he said.

'You move so quietly,' said Lulu.

'I'm a cat.'

'Yes, you are. I sometimes forget that.'

'And the answer to my question?'

Lulu looked uncertain. 'I don't know. Yes, maybe. But then he probably won't have noticed that the figurines have gone. And even if he does, he won't know that we were the ones who took them. I suppose it's my guilty conscience kicking in. We did break into his boat.'

'You picked his lock,' said Conrad. 'For which, kudos. And other than taking the figurines – which weren't his to start with – you left the place exactly as you found it.'

'I know. I know.' She went back into the galley and put the kettle on. 'Speaking of the figurines, I should give Jessie the good news.'

She picked up her phone and called Jessie. It took Jessie almost a minute to answer and when she did, she sounded out of breath. 'Hello,' she said hesitantly, and Lulu realized that she had been crying.

'Jessie, it's Lulu. Good news. We've got your figurines.'

'You haven't.'

Lulu laughed. 'We have. Both of them. And you are absolutely right, the milkmaid looks just like you.'

'In my younger days, perhaps. Oh, I can't believe this. Really, you have them?'

'I'm looking at them now,' said Lulu, which wasn't exactly true, but they were safe in a cupboard. 'Jessie, I'm planning on coming back your way in a couple of days, are you okay to wait or I shall I send them by courier or something?'

'Where are you?'

'I'm heading to the centre of Manchester. A place called Castlefield. I'm seeing a friend today and then I'll be leaving either tomorrow or the next day and heading your way. Are you planning on moving on?'

'No, I'll be here.'

'So why don't I bring them to you on my way back?'

'That would be lovely. Oh, Lulu, I really can't believe it. You're amazing. How on earth did you get them?'

'It's a long story. I'll tell you when I see you.'

'I shall cook a very special dinner for you and Conrad. It's the least I can do.'

'We look forward to it,' said Lulu, and ended the call.

'I bet she was happy,' said Conrad.

'Over the moon,' said Lulu. She looked at her watch. 'I'm going to shower and then we'll head into Manchester. But first I'd better go and pay my mooring fee. I don't want to be accused of trespassing.'

There was no one in the office, so she used her phone to

take a photograph of the marina's details. She could phone and pay by card later in the day. She heard the phut-phut-phut of a diesel engine on the canal and her breath caught in her throat. She looked over at the canal just as a narrowboat came into view. It was red and green and there were three bicycles and a row of black and white striped planters on the roof. 'Relax, Lulu,' she whispered to herself. 'You're jumping at shadows.'

She walked back to *The Lark* and poured Conrad a bowl of Evian water before going into the bathroom.

It took her less than ten minutes to shower and change, then she made herself a cup of coffee, started the engine and untied *The Lark*. Lulu always preferred driving in the early morning. There were fewer boats around and often it was as if she had the canal to herself. There was a thin mist over much of the water and she had pulled on an old skiing jacket, a red, white and blue bobble hat and wool gloves with the fingers and thumb cut off. Underneath the jacket she wore a thick pullover and baggy jeans.

Conrad kept her company, sitting next to her as she sipped her coffee with her right hand and guided the tiller with her left. Lulu resisted the urge to look over her shoulder as she was sure that Conrad would tease her for it.

The Bridgewater Canal took them into the centre of Manchester. Off to their left was the much larger Manchester Ship Canal, the thirty-six-mile waterway that linked the city to the Irish Sea. The Castlefield Basin was just three miles from the marina and it took an hour to get there. Narrowboats could moor for up to seventy-two hours in the Staffordshire arm of the basin, between the Bridgewater Canal and the Rochdale Canal. The arm split into two, like the horns of an antelope. Lulu found a free mooring on the right-hand section, close to the railway viaducts, opposite the Museum of Science and Industry. It was near a water point so, after tying up *The Lark*, Lulu used a hosepipe to fill up her water tank. She left the diesel engine running to charge the batteries while she carried out some basic maintenance. There were several groups of teenagers gathered on concrete steps shielded by cream-coloured tented canopies; the cloying sweet smell of cannabis wafted over.

'Shouldn't they be at school?' asked Conrad.

'They could be over eighteen,' said Lulu.

'That's almost ninety in cat years.'

'Yes. But you get nine lives.'

'So they say.' Conrad sniffed the air. 'Catnip for humans.'

Lulu chuckled. 'I suppose it is.'

'What is that place, where they're sitting?' asked Conrad. 'I assume it wasn't built as a cannabis-smoking area.'

'According to the canal guide, it's the Castlefield Bowl, an outdoor music and entertainment venue. It can seat up to eight thousand people. I don't think there's anything scheduled for when we're here.'

Trams rattled across the bridge at regular intervals as Lulu worked on *The Lark*. She hoped they didn't run all night. She checked the oil levels – everything was fine – then she checked and cleaned the engine. She made sure the bilge pumps were working and inspected the three batteries. The toilet would have to be emptied at some point but it was good for a few more days. When she had finished she took another shower, applied some make-up and changed into one of her favourite Karen Millen dresses, white with large poppies on it.

Conrad nodded his approval as she walked out of the cabin. 'You look beautiful,' he said.

'Why, thank you, kind sir.'

'Are you going somewhere special?'

'Lunch with an old friend.'

'Am I invited?'

Lulu laughed. 'Well, of course you are. You're my plus one.'

'Plus one? I like the sound of that.'

'Then let's go.' She slipped on a linen jacket and then bent down so that Conrad could jump up onto her shoulders. She went carefully up the steps and locked the door, then stepped onto the towpath.

A young woman was sitting on a wicker chair on the roof of the adjacent narrowboat. 'There's no need to lock up,' she called. 'Safe as houses, here. I come here every couple of weeks and I've never had a problem.' She had blonde hair tied back in a ponytail and was wearing denim dungarees.

'That's good to know,' said Lulu. 'It's my first time here.'

'Oh, I'm here lots,' said the woman. 'It's a nice place with lovely people. I come and go and never lock my boat.'

Her boat was a few metres shorter than *The Lark*, dark blue with gold trim. As Lulu drew level with the boat, she saw the name painted on the side. *Bee Happy*. There were half a dozen cartoon bees flying around the name. 'Oh, I love the name of your boat,' said Lulu. 'That's so funny.'

'It was my husband's idea,' she said. 'He's a copywriter. He does a lot of advertising work.'

'And you live aboard?'

'We do. Have done for almost five years. Sold our house and bought this. And we've never looked back. Davey – my husband – does a lot of freelance work and I'm a graphic designer. Digital nomads is what they call us. With a decent Wi-Fi set-up, we can work anywhere. What about you?'

'I'm retired,' said Lulu. 'Just pottering around with Conrad, most of the time.'

'That's lovely,' said the woman. 'And what a distinguished name. It's a pleasure to meet you, Conrad. I'm Laura, by the way.'

'I'm Lulu. Pleased to meet you.'

'Are you off somewhere nice?'

'Lunch with a friend,' said Lulu. 'A place called the Wharf. Do you know it?'

'Oh, yes, the Wharf is lovely.' She pointed off down the towpath. 'About a hundred yards that way. They do marvellous food.'

'Thank you so much,' said Lulu. She set off down the towpath. It was a gloriously sunny day with only a few wisps of cloud overhead. They walked over a bridge that crossed the Castlefield Basin, where only long-term mooring was permitted. A young man in a wetsuit was clearing weeds from around the propeller of a Dutch barge and tossing them onto the towpath.

'That doesn't look fun,' said Conrad.

'Part of the joy of owning a canal boat.'

'Do you ever have to do that?'

Lulu laughed. 'Sometimes,' she said. 'But I don't have to get into the water, I can lean over the side to clear the propeller.'

The Wharf was indeed just a hundred yards away from where they had moored *The Lark*, and over that hundred yards Lulu received half a dozen smiles and greetings from people who were surprised – and apparently delighted – to see Conrad riding on her shoulders.

Jane Mackenzie was sitting at an outside table, a glass of white wine in front of her and a bottle in an ice bucket at her side. Jane and Lulu had been friends since school, but back then she had been Jane Higgins. She hadn't lived far from Lulu in a council block on Edgware Road and they had often played together in the Paddington Recreation Ground, a large park on the edge of Maida Vale popular with dog walkers and joggers. Jane had married a couple of years before Lulu. Her husband, Clive, was a BBC television producer and for twenty years or so they had lived in Shepherd's Bush and he had worked at Broadcasting House in Portland Place, but then the BBC began regionalizing its staff and Clive was transferred to Manchester. Jane – a teacher – had hated the idea of leaving London, but they had no children and there were plenty of job opportunities for teaching in Manchester, so they moved. The two friends had kept in touch and Jane often met Lulu in London for lunch, or Lulu would take the train up to see her in Manchester. Over the years, Jane had grown to appreciate the city, though she always felt as if she was a misplaced Londoner; their lunches were usually spent with Jane asking countless questions to catch up with the life she felt she was missing. Now her face broke into a smile when she spotted Lulu, and she leaped to her feet. She was tiny, barely five feet tall in her heels, her hair dyed a vibrant chestnut colour and her skin tanned. She had sunglasses pushed back on her head and was wearing a blue and white dress that Lulu was fairly sure was Karen Millen. They had both always loved the designer.

'Lulu!' she exclaimed, and moved forward with her arms

outstretched for a hug. She stopped when she saw Conrad. 'Oh my God,' she said. 'There's a cat. On your shoulders.'

'This is Conrad,' said Lulu.

'He's amazing.'

'Yes, he is.'

They hugged and planted kisses on each other's cheeks. 'I wanted to sit outside, it's such a glorious day,' said Jane, gesturing at the table.

'Outside is fine,' said Lulu. 'Most restaurants don't like cats inside anyway.'

They sat down and Jane poured wine into a glass for Lulu. Conrad jumped down onto an empty chair and curled up, his nose against his tail. Lulu and Jane toasted each other and drank. 'I'm so glad you came,' said Jane. 'This is, what, only your third visit to Manchester?'

'Fourth. And this one is my first on *The Lark*.'

'I can't believe you sailed all the way up here.'

Lulu laughed. 'Well, you drive a narrowboat rather than sail it. But yes, it's my first time bringing *The Lark* here.'

A young waiter wearing a black shirt and jeans came over and gave them menus. 'Oh, I know what I want,' said Jane. 'Can I have the roasted cauliflower, chickpea and spinach burrito?'

'With mango chutney and coconut yoghurt?'

'Oh yes, please.'

The waiter smiled at Lulu.

'I'll have the baked hake with spring vegetables and new potatoes,' she said. 'And could you possibly put the tartare sauce on the side?'

The waiter grinned. 'Because your cat doesn't like tartare sauce?'

Lulu smiled. 'Exactly.'

'I quite understand.' He leaned closer and lowered his voice. 'Actually, I'll get the chef to do a separate fillet for you. With our compliments.'

'Oh, no, please don't go to any trouble.'

'It'll be fine. The chef is a big fan of cats. And he has a calico himself.'

'Well, that would be lovely,' said Lulu. 'Thank you so much.'

'I don't remember you having a cat when I last saw you in London,' said Jane as the waiter left.

'I didn't, back then,' said Lulu. 'He walked into my life – literally – after I'd moved onto *The Lark*. I was in the galley one day and Conrad strolled along the towpath and that was that.'

'And he doesn't have a collar?'

'A collar implies ownership, and I don't own Conrad. If anything, I'd say that he owns me.' She smiled. 'I'm just grateful that he came into my life.'

'Well, he's a lovely boy,' said Jane. 'And he goes everywhere with you?'

'He does,' said Lulu. 'And what about you? Do you think you'll stay in Manchester?'

'I'm not sure. Maybe I should get a boat like you. Just go where the spirit takes me.'

'It can be very freeing,' said Lulu. 'And every day is an adventure.'

'I bet,' said Jane. 'But how do you manage those lock things on your own? I'm assuming that Conrad isn't much help.'

'True, locks are much easier if there's two or three of you, but you can do them on your own. There's a lot of to-ing and fro-ing and climbing up and down, but it's perfectly doable. Why don't you come with us for a day or two? My sofa converts into a berth, so you could spend the night.'

'Let me think about that,' said Jane. She sighed and picked up her glass.

'Are you okay? That sounded like a sad sigh.'

'Oh, it's nothing. Nothing to worry you about, anyway.'

'Now I'm intrigued. Tell me.'

Jane sighed again. 'It'll sound stupid.'

'At least let me be the judge of that.'

'I've met someone,' Jane said.

'Oh, well, that's good,' said Lulu. She frowned. 'Isn't it?'

Jane was a widow. In fact, Clive had passed away exactly a year to the day before Lulu's husband, Simon, had died. Jane had gone through a very brief phase of referring to the two of them as the Merry Widows but neither had been in the least bit merry and she hadn't kept it up for long.

Clive had died from a massive heart attack while filming a documentary in Poland, and Jane had been distraught. She had flown over to bring back the body and Lulu and Simon had driven up to Manchester for the funeral. The Mackenzies' plan had always been to spend their retirement in their villa in Spain, but Jane didn't have the heart to move abroad on her own.

Lulu wasn't surprised that Jane had met someone; she was pretty and vivacious with a killer sense of humour. And years of teaching had given her a confidence that many men found attractive.

'It's fantastic,' Jane said.

'How did you meet?'

Jane shifted uncomfortably in her chair. 'One of those dating apps,' she said quietly.

'Really?' Lulu laughed. 'Swipe right, swipe left?'

'I wasn't taking it seriously. I was just passing the time, really. But his profile jumped out at me.'

'Young? Fit? Handsome?'

'Lulu, stop it! He's age appropriate, a couple of years older than me, actually. He has a George Clooney vibe, loves animals . . .'

'Enjoys walks on the beach and watching the sun go down.'

'I know, I know, the profile was every woman's dream. But we started chatting and I met him and . . . well, he's asked me to marry him.'

Lulu's jaw dropped. 'What?'

'He wants to get married. He says I'm the love of his life.'

'Jane, that's amazing. Congratulations. When did all this happen?'

'The proposal? Two weeks ago.'

'So when is the wedding?'

'I'm still thinking about it.'

'You've got doubts?'

'Not doubts, not really. I'm just . . .' She pulled a face and shifted in her chair again. 'Oh, Lulu, I don't know. I just . . . I know so little about him.'

'You talk, don't you?'

'Oh, yes. We never stop talking. We laugh, we joke, we talk about books, about movies, politics – everything. But I don't really know anything about him.'

'Then you need to ask the right questions.'

'I do. But . . .' She gestured helplessly.

'He's evasive?'

'No, not evasive. But he's light on details.'

'Tell me what you do know.'

Jane took a deep breath and nodded. 'Okay, so his name is Jeremy Connolly, he's retired but has investments, mainly in Ireland. He lives in Dublin, says that he's never been married, no children. He has a sister in Melbourne and a brother in Sydney.'

'So he's Australian?'

'No, he's English. Or Irish. He's vague about that, too. His parents died when he was young and the kids went to live with their grandmother. It wasn't the best of experiences and, as soon as they could, his brother and sister emigrated.'

'Is that possible?'

'They went on that visa programme that allows youngsters to work in Australia.'

'The working holiday visa?'

'That's it. They both married Australians and never came back. But Jeremy stayed in the UK. He started as a labourer on building sites and then got into property development. Now he owns a few commercial buildings and flats that are rented out.'

'It sounds like you know everything about him, Jane.'

'I've never met any of his friends, or his family. I've never been to his house in Dublin. He's just very vague about things.' She shrugged. 'It's hard to explain. I ask him questions and he answers, but his answers don't always give me the information I'm looking for. Not that I'm probing, it's not that, but sometimes talking to him is like grabbing at mist.' She frowned. 'Do you know what I mean?'

'Yes, I do,' said Lulu. 'I've interviewed people like that.

Many times. They talk and they talk and they talk but they end up telling you nothing.'

'That's it, exactly.'

'If you think he's holding something back, why don't you hire a private detective?'

'A gumshoe? Oh, I couldn't.'

'Actually, you could. Easiest thing in the world. Lots of former police detectives set up on their own after they leave the job.'

'Oh, but Lulu, that would be so . . . I don't know . . . sordid.'

'Nothing sordid about it.'

'But suppose he is Mr Right, how would it look when I told him that I'd paid a private detective to check him out? It would suggest that I didn't trust him, wouldn't it?'

'Jane, darling, if you did trust him then we wouldn't be having this conversation, would we?'

'It's not that I don't trust him.' She grimaced. 'No, you're right, of course. You always are, Lulu. The voice of reason in a world that's gone mad.' She leaned forward across the table and lowered her voice, like a spy about to betray her country. 'Could you help me? Could you, you know, make some enquiries?'

Lulu laughed. 'Jane, I'm not a police officer any more. And even if I was, I couldn't start checking up on people for personal reasons. That would mean breaking the Data Protection Act, if nothing else. Abuse of the Police National Computer is a very serious offence.'

'I suppose so.'

'Look, have you tried social media? Is he on Facebook or Instagram?'

'No. None of those. He says he thinks it trivializes life and I have to say that I agree with him.'

'You said he lives in Dublin?'

'Yes.'

'Does he have an address?'

'I can hardly ask him outright for his address, can I?'

'Tell him you want to send him something. What about his driving licence? Can you get to see that?'

'What are you suggesting? That I go through his wallet while he's in the shower?'

'Jane, you can't have it both ways. You can't check him out without, well, checking him out.'

'I don't want him to think I don't trust him. Lulu, please, can't you just . . .' She sighed. 'I'm being ridiculous, aren't I?'

'No, you've met someone new and you're apprehensive. That's understandable. What are you worried about – that he's been married before?'

'Oh no, that wouldn't really matter. Not if he was up front about it. I was married, Lulu, more than thirty very happy years, most of them. I'm not looking for a husband. A partner, maybe. Someone I can share my life with. The rest of my life, anyway.' She smiled and gestured at Conrad. He had started scratching his ear. 'Someone like Conrad. Someone I can go for lunch with, curl up and watch Netflix with, someone I can go on holiday with.'

'It sounds as if you have that already.'

'Yes, I do. But now he wants to marry me, and . . .' She sighed again and took another gulp of wine. 'I'm not rich, Lulu. Not *rich*, rich, anyway. Compared with the life my parents had, I am, of course. They lived most of their lives in that poky council flat with its damp walls and noisy plumbing. Now I live in a four-bedroom house that's worth half a million pounds, I have the cottage in Norfolk that Clive inherited from his parents, and I have the villa in Marbella that was Clive's pride and joy. I have money in the bank and Clive's share portfolio, and I get his pension and my teaching pension.'

'And you think Jeremy has his sights set on your money?'

'No, of course not.' She pulled a face. 'Well, the thought has crossed my mind, yes. He did propose very quickly, as if he's in a rush.'

'Does he know about the cottage and the villa?'

Jane nodded. 'We've stayed in both. He loves the villa. But who wouldn't? The pool is amazing. And the sea views . . . You never came out to the villa, did you?'

'We always meant to,' said Lulu.

'Simon would have loved it. And just down the road is this most amazing little tapas place. They do an albondigas en salsa that just melts in your mouth.' She looked wistful. 'Maybe I'm overthinking it all. It's just that he knows so much about me and I know so little about him.' She paused. 'Say I do marry him and then it all goes wrong and we divorce. He'd be entitled to half of everything I have.'

'Well, yes, unless you had a prenup – but you would also be entitled to half of everything he has.'

'Except that I don't know what he has. He might be penniless for all I know.'

'He doesn't pay for anything?'

Jane laughed. 'He's not a gigolo, Lulu. Of course he pays. Actually he pays for most things. He's very generous. He never lets me pay for meals and he always buys the tickets when we go anywhere. He talks about his investments, but I don't really know whether he has money or not.'

'Does that matter? If you're happy.'

'I don't care if he's rich or not. I enjoy his company, he makes me laugh, we have fun together.'

'And the sex?'

Jane's jaw dropped. 'Lulu!'

'Well, it has to be asked, doesn't it?'

'Does it? Really?' She chuckled and shook her head. 'The sex is fine, Lulu, thank you for asking.' She drank some wine to hide her embarrassment. 'You're terrible.'

'You see, if it's all as good as you say it is, there's nothing to be worried about. Just carry on as you are, enjoying each other.'

'Well, I would, but, as I said, Jeremy wants to get married.'

'And what about you, Jane? It takes two to tango.'

'I don't know. It'd be nice to grow old with someone.' She smiled ruefully. 'Grow older with someone, I mean.'

'And he's the one?'

'He's lovely, Lulu. He's everything a woman could want.'

'I sense there's still a "but" coming.'

'I don't know. Maybe. There's just this nagging doubt.'

'How long have you known him?'

'Three months. Almost four.'

'That's no time at all.'

'Jeremy says if it's right, it's right.'

'It sounds as if he might be rushing you, and that's not good.'

'No, it's not.' She looked up. 'You know what might be a good idea?'

Lulu smiled; she had a feeling she knew what was coming,

and that it was what the conversation had been leading up to. 'What?'

'Why don't you meet him? You can come to dinner with us tonight. At the house. Jeremy loves to cook.' She nodded at Conrad. 'And bring Conrad.'

'My plus one?'

'Exactly. You can both get to meet him and let me know what you think.'

Lulu raised her glass. 'Sounds like a plan.'

8

The blonde woman who had been sitting on the roof of the *Bee Happy* wasn't there when Lulu and Conrad arrived back at *The Lark*. The doors were still locked and *The Lark* seemed secure. She stepped onto the rear deck and undid the padlock to open the doors. 'I was hoping you would demonstrate your lock-picking skills,' said Conrad.

'I'm rusty, at best,' said Lulu. 'But honestly, there isn't much to it. You just jiggle the pick around until the lock springs open.'

She opened the doors and went down into the saloon. Lunch had been enjoyable, though most of the conversation had centred around Jane's new boyfriend. Lulu had agreed to go for dinner with them, but already she was having reservations. It hadn't been a social invitation: Lulu would be there to pass judgement on Jeremy, which felt a little dishonest.

'You don't have to go, if you don't want to,' said Conrad. He had jumped onto the sofa and was watching her, his whiskers twitching.

Lulu looked at him and frowned. 'You just read my mind again.'

'You've been deep in thought since we left the restaurant,' he said. 'And I can see that what she is asking you to do puts you in a difficult position.'

'It does, doesn't it?' She opened her fridge and took out

the bottle of Pinot Grigio and a bottle of Evian water. There was just about a glassful left in the wine bottle. 'I mean, what if I think he's a liar and a scoundrel but he isn't? Or worse, what if I think he's marvellous and it turns out he is only after her money? Either way, it puts our relationship on the line, doesn't it?'

'I think she just wants you to confirm that she isn't making a mistake.'

Lulu poured the wine into a glass and water into a bowl. She put the bowl down in front of Conrad. 'Exactly. She's using me as a test. That's a lot of responsibility.'

'She trusts your judgement,' said Conrad. 'And you were a police officer for many years, which means you are a good judge of character.'

Lulu sipped her drink, but frowned when *The Lark* shifted slightly. It wasn't the sort of movement caused by a passing boat, it was somebody climbing onto the rear deck. She looked at Conrad, whose ears had pricked up.

The boat went still and Lulu realized she was holding her breath.

'Do you think . . .?' began Conrad, but he was cut short when the doors to the stern were thrown open.

It was the man from the *Blue Moon*. His hair was unkempt and his cheeks were flushed. He came down the steps and Lulu felt her breath catch in her chest.

'Where are they?' he snarled.

'What are you talking about?' said Lulu. Her hand was trembling and her wine was slopping around the glass, so she put it on a shelf.

'You know damn well what I'm talking about!' he said. 'The figurines that you stole from my boat.'

Lulu frowned. How could he possibly have known that she had been on the *Blue Moon*?

Conrad got to his feet and hissed at the man, his ears back. The man ignored him. 'I'm not fucking about,' he said. 'You need to give me those figurines back.'

'And you need to leave, now,' said Lulu.

'Not until you tell me who you are and why you were on my boat,' said the man.

'I've no idea what you are talking about,' said Lulu. She picked up her phone. 'I'm serious, I'm going to call the police.'

'No idea what I'm talking about? Lady, I have CCTV on my boat, so I damn well know that you and that bloody cat were there. And that you took my figurines.'

'Your figurines? They belong to a very sweet lady by the name of Jessica, and they mean a great deal to her. You broke her heart when you took them and I'm giving them back to her.' She held up the phone. 'Last chance: you get off my boat now or I'll call 999.'

'Put the phone down!' shouted the man. He reached into the pocket of his trousers and pulled out a white-handled knife. He pressed a chrome button and a large blade flicked out and locked into place. 'Put the phone down now!'

Conrad arched his back and hissed again, but the man kept his attention fixed on Lulu.

'Okay, okay, you need to stay calm,' said Lulu. She placed the phone on a shelf and held up her hands. 'I won't call the police, but you need to leave my boat immediately. You're trespassing.'

The man's eyes darted towards her left hand. 'Take your rings off,' he said. 'And that watch. I want that watch.'

'My husband gave me that watch,' Lulu said coldly. 'It has great sentimental value.'

The man jabbed the knife at her. 'Give me the fucking watch, now!' he shouted.

Lulu shrieked and took a step back. There was a blur to her left. It was Conrad. He had launched himself off the sofa, front paws outstretched and his ears back. The man swung the knife towards Conrad but he was too slow and Conrad's claws raked his face. Conrad's rear legs came up and then hit the man's chest. He raked his rear claws down, ripping the man's denim shirt. The blue material turned red.

Conrad twisted and jumped back towards the sofa as the man swayed on his feet, his face and chest glistening with blood. Lulu reached out for the frying pan and walloped the man. The dull thud of the pan connecting with the side of his head echoed around the galley and he fell to the floor. Lulu raised the frying pan again but the man lay still, face down.

'Quick, tie him up,' said Conrad, from the sofa.

'He's unconscious,' said Lulu.

'We've both seen enough movies where the bad guy wakes up to create more havoc,' said Conrad. 'And you should move the knife. Put it out of his reach.'

The knife had fallen from the man's hand and was lying on the floor by the fridge.

Lulu slipped on an oven glove and used it to pick up the knife and place it on the draining board. She looked around for something to tie the man up with.

'His shoelaces,' said Conrad.

Lulu opened her mouth to ask how he knew exactly what she was thinking, but she changed her mind. Conrad did have the uncanny ability to predict what was going through her mind, but he always had a logical explanation. She knelt down and took the lace from the man's left boot and used it to tie his wrists behind his back. 'Satisfied?' she asked.

'You'll thank me if he wakes up,' said Conrad. 'You don't know how long the police will take to get here.'

'You think we should call the police?'

'Don't you?'

Lulu frowned. 'How would we explain the fact that he's on *The Lark*?'

'He's got a knife. He was trying to rob us.'

'What if he tells them we were on his boat? That we went through his things?'

'Things that he had presumably stolen. He's a thief, Lulu. A thief who threatened us with a knife. Even if we tell them the complete story, that's all the police will be interested in.'

Lulu frowned. 'I hear what you're saying, but the police always try to be even-handed. They're not allowed to make judgement calls any more. If he accuses us of breaking into his boat, they will have to take the allegation seriously.'

Conrad wrinkled his nose. 'Well, what other options do we have? I presume you don't want to throw him over the side?'

'Of course not.' She sat down on the sofa next to Conrad and stroked his back.

'So you want to carry him back to his boat?' He held up his left paw. 'Because, you know, the lack of opposable thumbs means I'm not a great help when it comes to carrying. Plus he's a fully grown man and I'm, you know, a regular-sized cat.'

Lulu forced a smile. He was right, of course. She doubted

that she would even be able to lift the man, never mind carry him off *The Lark*. She really only had two options. She could wait until he woke up and try to talk to him, but the fact that he had pulled a knife on her meant that a conversation would probably be pointless. No matter what he said, there was every chance he would try to attack her again if she released him. That left only the second option – to call the police.

'You know I'm right, don't you?' said Conrad.

'You usually are,' said Lulu.

Conrad softly butted his head against her side. 'You'd better believe it,' he said.

9

Lulu took a drink of her coffee and nodded her approval. Generally, police coffee wasn't good, but the one they had given her was rich and flavourful and definitely not instant. She looked around the four bare walls. There was a window high up in the wall to her right, through which she could see the sky. There were four plastic chairs around a square table. The door was closed, but the constable who had given Lulu her coffee hadn't locked it when he left.

'Are we in trouble?' asked Conrad. He was sitting on the chair next to her with a bowl of water in front of him. He had sniffed it but not had a drink, so Lulu figured it was probably tap water. Conrad wasn't really a fan of tap water.

'No, I don't think so,' she said. 'This isn't an interview room, there's no CCTV or recording equipment. It's just a regular waiting room. And we're the injured party, remember that.'

Conrad chuckled. 'But we're not the ones with our cheek slashed, are we?'

'You saved me, again.'

'Anyone who pulls a knife on you gets to see my bad side,' said Conrad.

'You have a bad side?'

'It's been said,' he said.

'You reacted so quickly,' said Lulu.

'Like lightning,' said Conrad.

'Yes, exactly. It was a blur.'

'To you, maybe. To me, it seemed to happen in slow motion. You know we cats react almost twice as quickly as dogs? And way, way quicker than humans.'

'Which is why you always land on your feet.'

'Exactly,' said Conrad. 'Most cat reactions take between twenty and seventy milliseconds. But the average human reaction takes two hundred milliseconds. Even a human reflex action, where the thinking part of the brain isn't involved, takes eighty milliseconds. So cats are always going to react more quickly than humans.'

'It certainly worked out well today. Thank you.'

'You're welcome,' said Conrad. 'The man said that he had CCTV of us on his boat.'

'Yes, he did.'

'Do you think he was telling the truth?'

'I'm sure of it. It's the only way he would know that we were on his boat.'

'And the police didn't check his CCTV?'

'Well, why would they? He attacked us on *The Lark*, so that was the crime scene. They could check his boat, but it wasn't a crime scene, so there'd be no need to look at his CCTV footage. I hope.'

'How did he find us?'

'Well, if he had us on CCTV he knew what we looked like. He could have asked around, you know: did you see the lady with the handsome cat, what boat were they on, something like that?'

'Handsome cat?'

Lulu laughed. 'No need for modesty, Conrad. We both know how handsome you are. But the point I was making was that once he knew what we looked like, we wouldn't be hard to find.'

The door opened. It was Detective Sergeant Colin Morris. He was the officer who had taken her statement. Two uniformed constables in high-vis jackets had arrived at *The Lark* and taken the man with the knife into custody. They had called a van which had taken the man away, and the constables had driven Lulu and Conrad to Greater Manchester Police Headquarters, a six-storey blue and grey building on what appeared to be a large industrial estate to the north of the city centre.

DS Morris was a big man with grey hair and round glasses, wearing a dark blue suit and a red and blue striped tie. He had made a big fuss of Conrad and told them about his own cat, a ginger, so Lulu had known straight away that he was one of the good guys. Lulu had immediately told him that she was a former police officer, but she hadn't mentioned that she had taken the figurines from the *Blue Moon*. The story she had told him had been simple enough – that she and Conrad were on *The Lark* when the man had come aboard and waved a knife. They had defended themselves and called the police. It was a simple story and simple was best. Whether or not DS Morris believed it would come down to what the man with the knife had told him.

The detective closed the door and sat down opposite them. 'Well, we're pretty much done here,' he said. 'It seems you both had a lucky escape. Your attacker's name is Brendan May, like the month.'

'No relation to Brian May, I hope.'

DS Morris smiled. 'Are you a Queen fan?'

'Oh yes.'

'Freddie Mercury loved cats,' said DS Morris. 'He had ten, I believe.'

'All the best people love cats,' said Lulu. 'Sorry, I didn't mean to interrupt.'

He nodded. 'Yes, well, no relation. He's local. Manchester born. He was released from prison last year after serving four years of an eight-year sentence for knifepoint robbery and is still on probation. The mere fact that he was in possession of that flick knife means he'll be recalled to prison to complete his sentence. We're just running fingerprint and DNA checks on the knife, but assuming they match his biometrics, he'll be back inside by tonight.'

'That's good to know,' said Lulu. 'That he'll be back in prison, not that he's a violent robber, I mean.'

'It makes it a lot easier all around,' said the detective. 'This way we avoid a trial, you don't have to give evidence, we just revoke his parole. Unless you want to press charges? That's totally up to you.'

'I think we're okay,' said Lulu. 'It's not as if we were hurt.'

'Thanks to Conrad, from what you said,' said the detective. 'Mr May needed three stitches, which is actually six fewer than his last victim, so no one is shedding any tears over that. And he just jumped at Mr May, you said? As he was about to stab you?'

'He was fearless,' said Lulu. 'I was frozen with fright but Conrad jumped at him without a second thought. My hero.' She reached over and rubbed the back of Conrad's neck and he purred.

'And you hit him with a frying pan, is that right?'

'Yes, it was the first thing that came to hand.'

'It knocked him right out, apparently.'

'It was a Le Creuset.'

'Ah, that explains it. They're heavy.'

'They are, yes. So did Mr May say why he was on my boat?'

DS Morris shook his head. 'He's not said anything other than to ask for a solicitor. He's been through the system before, so he knows how to play the game. He knows that possession of a knife means he goes back to prison. He'll just keep quiet and try to get parole again down the line. The more fuss he causes, the worse it'll be for him.'

'I suppose that makes sense,' said Lulu. In a way she was glad that she didn't have to explain in full what had happened, because that would mean telling the detective that she had broken into the *Blue Moon* and that Conrad had sneaked through the window in the first place.

'The thing is, we found a bag full of what appear to be stolen items on his boat,' said DS Morris. 'Including some quite valuable jewellery and some very distinctive miniatures that were reported stolen last month. It seems that he made a habit of stealing from narrowboats. That's possibly what he was doing on your boat, looking for something to steal.'

'He tried to steal my watch and jewellery,' said Lulu. 'We had a lucky escape, that's for sure.'

'Do you need a lift back to your boat?' asked DS Morris. 'We're a bit off the beaten track here. Between you and me, I think the powers that be didn't want members of the public dropping by.'

'Oh, that's okay,' said Lulu. 'I feel like a walk.'

'It's not a pretty walk, to be honest, and it's five miles,' said DS Morris. 'GMP will be happy to run you back – it's the least we can do for you helping to get a vicious criminal back where he belongs.'

10

Lulu climbed out of the back of the police car. She gathered Conrad up in her arms and then lifted him onto her shoulders. 'Thank you so much for the lift,' she said. The driver was a sergeant in her forties, the front passenger a constable who looked to be only just out of his teens.

'Stay safe!' said the sergeant.

Lulu closed the door and the car drove off. They were standing outside a pretty cafe. Two ladies were sharing an ice cream sundae, four large orbs of chocolate ice cream topped with cream, chocolate shavings and a chocolate-dipped cherry. 'Oh, that looks good,' said Lulu. 'I know I've only just had lunch, but I haven't had ice cream for ages. I recall cats don't react well to dairy, but would you mind?'

'Go ahead,' said Conrad.

Lulu sat down at an empty table. Conrad jumped down and sat on the chair. The man at the table next to them looked over the top of his copy of the *Manchester Evening News*. He didn't appear to be happy at having a cat in the vicinity, but Lulu smiled brightly at him. 'Lovely afternoon, isn't it?' she said.

He raised his newspaper without replying and Lulu shrugged at Conrad. 'I guess not everyone is a cat lover,' whispered Lulu.

'Their loss,' he whispered back.

A young waiter with shoulder-length curly blond hair

came over and Lulu ordered a latte. 'And one of those,' she said, pointing at the chocolate sundae.

'The A-Lotta-Chocca,' he said. 'Good choice.'

'Do you by any chance have a bowl that my plus one could drink from?' Lulu asked. 'He'd love some Evian water.'

'Of course we do,' said the waiter. 'Would he like ice with it?'

'Meow!' said Conrad.

'No ice,' said Lulu.

'He talks!' said the waiter. 'How cool is that?'

'Very cool,' said Lulu. The man with the newspaper lowered it, glared at them, and raised it again.

'I love cats,' said the waiter.

'Who doesn't?'

'My mum,' said the waiter. 'But she's allergic, so I guess she has an excuse. I'll be right back.'

Lulu sat back in her chair. 'Well, this is lovely,' she said.

'Meow,' said Conrad, looking pointedly at the man with the newspaper. 'Quite right,' she said. Lulu was the only person who knew that Conrad could talk, and it was best to keep it that way. There was a diagram on the front page of the paper. She squinted at it. She frowned as for the first time she read the headline of the main story. SERIAL KILLER STRIKES AGAIN. 'Oh, my goodness me,' she said. She leaned forwards to try to read the story.

The man lowered the paper. 'Can I help you?' he asked.

'No,' she said, her cheeks flushing. 'Sorry.' She smiled sheepishly. 'I was just interested in the front-page story, that's all.'

He turned the paper around to see what she was talking about. 'Sensationalist claptrap,' he said. He put the paper down on the table and picked up a brown leather briefcase. As he stood up, Lulu leaned towards him. 'Are you going? Can I be a real nuisance and ask if I can have your newspaper?'

The man smiled coldly. 'You're welcome to it,' he said. 'I've read it.'

'Thank you so much,' said Lulu. She practically snatched it from the table and began to devour the front page.

The man frowned and walked away. 'Some people,' he muttered under his breath.

'That was a bit rude,' whispered Conrad.

'Shhhh!'

'As was that,' said Conrad huffily.

Lulu's eyes widened as she read the front-page article. Eventually she put down the newspaper. 'We have to go back to the police station.'

11

The driver of the Uber was called Marko and he was Ukrainian. He had fled the Russian invasion of his country and now lived with his wife and four children in Manchester. He hadn't known where the police headquarters were, but Lulu had helped him input the destination into his satnav.

'You want to know something funny?' he had said once they were on their way. 'My name is Marko, which in my language means warlike. But because Putin is warlike, I have to flee my country.'

'I think that's ironic rather than funny,' said Lulu. 'And rather sad.'

'Life is sad,' said Marko, nodding in agreement. He kept looking at Conrad in his rear-view mirror. 'Your cat is so beautiful,' he said.

'Yes, he is,' said Lulu.

'Does he go everywhere with you?'

'He does. Yes.'

'You are so lucky. I had to leave my cats in Ukraine.'

'That's a pity.'

Marko nodded. 'We were ready to leave and we couldn't find them. We looked everywhere but then we had to go. That was almost two years ago.'

'I'm sorry.'

'The black one was called Vuhillya, which means coal. And the white one was called Snihovyy.'

'Snowy?'

The driver's eyes widened in surprise. 'You speak Ukrainian?'

Lulu laughed. 'Not a word, but I could see where you were going. Maybe they will be there when you go back.'

Marko shook his head. 'We will never go back. Manchester is our home now. Our life here is much better than it was in Ukraine.' He shrugged. 'But I miss my cats.'

'I bet you do,' said Lulu.

The Prius pulled up in front of the police building. Marko twisted around in his seat. 'It has been a pleasure driving you,' he said. 'Please remember, Marko, five stars.'

'Definitely,' said Lulu. She gathered up Conrad and climbed out of the car. She held Conrad in her arms as the car drove away.

'So basically he abandoned his cats in a war zone,' said Conrad. 'Good to know.'

'He had to make a choice, I suppose.'

'Exactly. I hope Coal and Snowy are okay and that they found more worthy owners.'

Lulu lifted him up so that he could sit on her shoulders. 'I would never abandon you,' she said.

'Oh, I know that. And please don't give him five stars.'

'I won't, if that's what you want.'

'I do,' said Conrad. 'Can you imagine how his cats must have felt, being abandoned like that?'

'I can, yes.'

'Well, there you are then. No stars.'

'Well, I have to leave at least one.'

Conrad sniffed. 'That's one too many, in my opinion.'

Lulu walked into the police HQ, went over to the reception

desk and asked to see DS Morris. A bored civilian worker pointed at a line of white plastic chairs and told her to wait. Told, not asked or suggested; it was an order issued the way a headmaster might talk to an unruly child. Lulu didn't express her displeasure, she just smiled sweetly and thanked the woman. In Lulu's experience, confrontation never stopped a person being rude, it just made the situation worse.

She had the copy of the *Manchester Evening News* with her so she read through it while she waited for DS Morris. Conrad was curled up on the seat next to her. He was snoring softly when DS Morris eventually arrived. 'Mrs Lewis, I am so sorry to have kept you. I was briefing the CPS on a case and it took for ever.'

'Not a problem, DS Morris. I know how busy you all are these days.'

Conrad uncurled himself and sat up, his ears swivelling around.

The detective smiled at Conrad, then looked back at Lulu. 'How can I help you? Did you forget something? Or remember something?'

'It's about this, actually,' said Lulu. She held out the newspaper. 'This lead story, about the serial killer.'

DS Morris took it and scanned the article. He wrinkled his nose. 'Ah, yes. Journalist Dickie McNeil. The bane of our lives. He's always poking his nose where it isn't wanted.' He gave the paper back to her. 'If you're going to suggest that your Mr May is the serial killer, I can tell you that we did check but he wasn't in Manchester during the time of the first murder.'

'No, it's not that,' said Lulu. 'The thing is, I might have some information about the case.'

'Really? You said you only arrived in Manchester yesterday.'

'That's right. But the cases that this Dickie McNeil is writing about are similar to ones that I came across in London. I ran Major Investigation Teams for a time, initially as a chief inspector and later as a superintendent. And after I retired, I went back occasionally as a consultant.'

'I didn't know that,' said DS Morris.

'Well, the last thing you want is a retired detective telling war stories,' she said.

'It sounds like you had an interesting career,' said DS Morris.

'Oh, I did,' said Lulu. 'The thing is, could I possibly speak to the SIO on this case? I might be able to help.'

DS Morris nodded. 'Let me see who the senior investigating officer is,' he said. 'Just wait here for a moment, please.' He walked away and took his mobile phone from his pocket.

'He seems nice, doesn't he?' said Conrad.

'Most police officers are,' said Lulu. 'Despite what you read in the papers. You always hear about the bad apples, but the vast majority of men and women who join the police sign up because they want to help people. They certainly don't join for the pay.'

'He has an especially good aura.'

'Really?'

'There's a lot of orange in it. People with orange auras tend to be creative problem-solvers who aren't scared of taking risks. And his aura absorbs the colours of the people around him.'

'Like empathy?'

'Yes, a bit like a chameleon. It has a calming effect on those around him. He's the sort of person that cats are naturally drawn to.'

'Oh Conrad, you're not going to leave me, are you?'

Conrad walked over to her and gently butted her arm with his head. 'Of course not.'

DS Morris made one call, then another. Then he put his phone away and came back to her. 'We're in luck,' he said. 'DI Julie Friar is SIO and she's up in the canteen as we speak. She'd be very happy to have a chat.'

'Excellent,' said Lulu. She bent down so that Conrad could jump onto her shoulders, then stood up and followed the detective over to the lifts. They rode up to the third floor and then walked along a corridor to a set of double doors that led to the canteen. It was like police canteens the world over, a counter with various items of food on display, a board with prices and a list of specials, and a bored cashier. There were a couple of dozen people eating, a mix of uniformed officers, detectives in plain clothes and civilian workers.

DS Morris took Lulu over to a table by the window. DI Julie Friar was in her mid-thirties. She had short black hair and elf-like ears and was wearing a white linen shirt with the sleeves rolled up. There was a dark blue blazer hanging over the back of her chair. Sitting opposite her was a young man in a grey suit and a blue tie. DI Friar was working her way through a plate of fish and chips while her companion was pecking at a salad.

'DI Friar, this is Mrs Lewis. She used to be a superintendent with the Met. She came in with regard to an attempted robbery at Castlefield Basin. The perp was on probation and will be back behind bars soon, but Mrs Lewis has some information to share with you regarding the murder cases that you're investigating.'

DI Friar looked up and nodded. 'Sorry to be eating, but it's the first chance I've had all day. Please, sit down. And help yourself to a chip.'

'That's fine, I had lunch earlier,' said Lulu. She held up the newspaper. 'Then I saw this.' She sat down.

'I'm sorry, but I'm going to have to love you and leave you,' said DS Morris. 'I've a statement to take and the witness is at the Royal, so I have to get my skates on. Mrs Lewis, I'll leave you with DI Friar. It was nice meeting you again.' He smiled at Conrad, who was still sitting on Lulu's shoulder. 'Nice seeing you again, too, Conrad.'

As DS Morris headed out, Lulu sat down next to DI Friar. Conrad jumped off her shoulder, landed softly on the floor. 'I hope you don't mind,' said Lulu, gesturing at Conrad.

'I'm fine,' said DI Friar. 'But Pete here is a dog person.'

'No, I'm fine with cats,' said her companion.

Conrad jumped up onto the chair next to the man and he reached over and stroked him behind the ear. Conrad purred with contentment.

'Thank you so much for agreeing to see me,' said Lulu.

'I'll take any help I can get on this case,' said DI Friar. 'All the leads I've chased up so far have proven to be dead ends.' She nodded at the young man in the suit. 'This is DC Peter Townsend. Pete, to his friends.'

'As in The Who?'

'The what?' he said, frowning.

'The rock group. The Who. Roger Daltrey, Pete Townshend, John Entwistle and Keith Moon.'

DC Townsend shook his head. 'Sorry.'

'You've never heard of The Who? "Pinball Wizard"? "My Generation"? *Quadrophenia*?'

DC Townsend laughed. 'Before my time, I guess.'

Lulu was about to ask him how old he was, but realized that might imply criticism. 'The Rolling Stones?'

'Oh, yes, I've heard of them,' he said.

'That's a relief,' said Lulu. 'I was starting to feel like a dinosaur. So you're the bag carrier?' A bag carrier was a senior investigating officer's shadow; everywhere the SIO went, the bag carrier went too. Every decision the SIO made was recorded in the Book 194, also known as the key decision log. At any point in the investigation a senior officer could examine the Book 194 to check that all protocols were being followed.

'I am, yes. Though in Manchester we call them scribes. Would you like a coffee or tea? The coffee is quite good here.'

'Yes, I had some earlier today. Coffee would be lovely. And if Conrad could possibly have some Evian water, that would be great.'

DC Townsend nodded approvingly. 'He knows his water.'

'He's not a fan of tap water,' said Lulu. 'He doesn't like the taste of chlorine.'

'Who does?' DC Townsend looked at DI Friar. 'Skinny latte, no sugar, extra shot?'

'Perfect,' she said.

DC Townsend went to the counter. 'In my day, one of my main tasks was to keep my SIO supplied with cigarettes,' said Lulu. 'I suppose that's also a thing of the past?'

DI Friar smiled and pushed up her left shirtsleeve. There was a nicotine patch just above her elbow. 'Pete makes sure there's always one of these in his wallet.'

Lulu chuckled. 'Times have changed.'

'And I didn't want to say anything, but I'm a huge Who fan. Always have been. Way better than the Stones. But he's Townsend without the "h". I loved it when they used "Won't Get Fooled Again" as the theme tune for that CSI show.'

'That show changed the public's perceptions of how the police work, didn't it? They expect every case to be wrapped up within an hour by just taking DNA samples and tapping a few keys on a computer.'

DI Friar nodded. 'The number of times I've been told that all I have to do is to run the DNA sample through the database. If only it was that simple.'

DC Townsend returned with two coffees, which he placed on the table, then he took a bottle of Evian water from his pocket. 'Ah,' he said, as he realized that Conrad could hardly drink from the bottle. 'I'll be right back.' He went over to the counter and returned with a saucer. He poured Evian water into the saucer and placed it on the chair next to Conrad before sitting down.

DI Friar finished her fish and chips and pushed her plate to the side. She nodded at the newspaper. 'So, you have information regarding the so-called serial killer as featured in the *Manchester Evening News*?'

'Is the story true?'

'The lurid headline is down to Dickie McNeil, the reporter who wrote the story. Well, I say reporter, he's a pain in the arse, he really is. He used to be a cop but left under a bit of a cloud. He wrote a book that basically slagged off the Manchester Police, then reinvented himself as a crime reporter. He's still got a lot of friends on the force, and they feed him stuff.'

'But the story is basically true?'

DI Friar shifted uncomfortably in her seat. 'Nothing he says is untrue,' she said. 'It's the way that he spins it that's the problem. I mean, yes, we have had two similar deaths three weeks apart. That is a fact. But does that mean we have a serial killer in Manchester? I don't think it does.'

'You're right,' said Lulu. 'Two killings isn't a serial. The usual definition of a serial killer is a person who murders three or more people, with a cooling-down period between killings.'

'Exactly!' said DI Friar. 'But serial killers sell newspapers, so Dickie gave one to the *Manchester Evening News* and they ran with it.'

'And what he says about the special nautical knot. Is that true?'

'That's what is so annoying,' said DI Friar. 'We were keeping back the information about the knot that was used. We figured that was something only the killer would know, so we could use it down the line. The fact that Dickie knew about it means that he has access to someone on our team. Or someone in the coroner's office.'

'It says in the paper that the knot was a round turn and two half hitches.'

'That's right. It's a very specific knot, apparently. And it was used in both murders.'

Lulu smiled thinly. 'I've come across that knot before. In a series of London murders that were never solved.'

DI Friar's eyebrows shot up and she looked across at DC Townsend. He was just as surprised. DI Friar looked back at Lulu. 'Well now, you definitely have my attention. Tell me more.'

'I headed up a number of murder investigation teams in the city. After I retired, I consulted on a serial-killer case for the best part of two years and sadly never got anywhere. The killer's victims were all middle-aged white men, killed by strangulation. All were strangled with rope tied in a round turn with two half hitches, a common nautical knot. Sailors use it to tie their vessels up to posts or rings. Basically, the rope goes twice around the post and is then tied off. Very secure, and very tight. I use it myself on my narrowboat.'

DI Friar nodded. 'Snap,' she said. 'Same knot.'

'Our victims were all dumped naked, with the rope in place. No DNA, no fibres, no forensics. Almost certainly killed somewhere else.'

'Snap.'

Lulu nodded. 'So it looks as if it could well be the same killer.'

'Either that or it's one heck of a coincidence,' said DI Friar. 'There was no sexual activity linked to our murders.'

'Snap,' said Lulu. 'We were working on the theory that they were hate killings. The fact they were naked was to minimize forensics rather than because there was a sexual component.'

'That's interesting,' said DI Friar. 'But if that's the case, why didn't we hear anything from SCAS?'

The Serious Crime Analysis Section was set up following an inquiry into the Yorkshire Ripper investigation. The prolific serial killer would probably have been caught much earlier if there had been a national database holding details of serious sexual offences committed across the UK. SCAS was established to be such a database, and it was later expanded to include sexually motivated and motiveless murders. There were SCAS contact officers based in all the UK's police forces whose job was to funnel pertinent information to the database. The data was then fed into the Violent Crime Linkage Analysis System, which was available to police forces around the country. One of the first things the Manchester Police would have done early on in the investigation would be to have put details of their murders into the SCAS system to see if there was a match with previous cases.

'SCAS should certainly have all the details.'

'Nothing came back,' said DI Friar.

She looked over at DC Townsend and he nodded. 'No matches,' he said. 'Did you have any suspects at all?'

'Initially we had lots of suspects,' said Lulu. 'Nearly four million adults take part in boating activities every year, and there are more than a million boats owned by UK households.'

'So you assumed that the killer was a sailor?' asked DC Townsend.

'It's a very specific knot,' Lulu said. 'Anyway, nothing came of it. But after the third murder we were able to use CCTV footage to give us a few possibilities. I remember we had three names that we were very interested in – they were referred to as the Three Little Piggies.' She grimaced. 'All three suspects were overweight – what can I say?'

'But you didn't charge any of them?'

'No. It was a few years ago now, so I'm a bit fuzzy on

the details. But I can probably get one of the detectives up here with the file, if you'd be interested.'

'I think we'd be very interested,' said DI Friar.

She looked over at DC Townsend and he nodded. 'It couldn't hurt,' he said.

12

The sun was going down when Lulu and Conrad arrived outside Jane's house. She lived in Salford, a twenty-minute drive from where they had moored *The Lark*. This Uber driver's name was Marcus and he was a student at Manchester University. 'Have a fun night,' he said as Lulu and Conrad climbed out of the car.

'We intend to,' said Lulu. As the Uber drove away, she looked up at the house. It was red-brick and detached with a garage at the side, and a neatly tended rose garden at the front. There was a white Audi sports car parked outside the garage. A curtain twitched in one of the upstairs windows. Lulu looked up. Was that Jane? The twitching stopped. Perhaps it had been the wind.

She walked up the driveway and rang the doorbell. Jane opened it almost immediately, so it couldn't have been her at the upstairs window. 'Lulu! You made it! And Conrad!'

Conrad meowed and jumped down off Lulu's shoulders. He brushed against Jane's legs, his tail straight up in the air.

'Welcome to my humble abode,' said Jane, ushering them into a hall and closing the front door. 'Let me take your coat.'

Lulu slipped off her coat and Jane hung it on a Victorian coat stand. Conrad was already walking down the hall. There were stairs ahead of them and doors to the left and right. 'Jeremy is in the kitchen,' said Jane.

Conrad turned to look at Lulu. He had obviously had the same thought – if Jeremy was in the kitchen, who had been watching them from upstairs?

'So you used an Uber?' asked Jane.

'It's so easy,' said Lulu. 'We use them all the time. Is that your sports car outside?'

'The Audi?' Jane laughed. 'No, that's Jeremy's. His boy toy, I call it.' She took them through to the kitchen, a large room with marble worktops and stainless-steel appliances and a pine-cladded island with four stools around it. There were glass sliding doors that led to a conservatory, and beyond it a garden dotted with flower beds. 'Oh, where's he gone?' asked Jane.

'Sorry, darling, I just popped to the bathroom,' said a voice behind them.

Lulu turned to find Jeremy standing in the doorway, and her first thought was that yes, he did very much have a George Clooney vibe, though he was several inches shorter and a few pounds heavier. He had gelled black hair, a carefully cultivated five o'clock shadow and eyes that crinkled when he smiled. He was wearing a pink linen shirt with the sleeves rolled up, to reveal a Rolex watch on his left wrist and a thick gold bracelet on the other, and tight-fitting jeans that looked as if they might be Versace.

'You must be Lulu,' he said, his voice treacly smooth with just a hint of an Irish accent. 'I've heard so much about you.' He stepped forward, took her hands in his and kissed her softly on both cheeks. 'It's so lovely to finally meet you.' He looked down at Conrad. 'And this must be Conrad,' he said. 'The cat who goes everywhere with you.'

'Yes, he does. My constant companion.'

'Well, he's a charming fellow,' said Jeremy. 'Though I have to say I've always been a dog person myself. You know where you are with a dog. If they're happy they wag their tails, if they're sad they look sad. Cats have such blank eyes, don't they? You can never tell what a cat is thinking.'

'Oh, I usually have a pretty good idea of what's going through Conrad's mind,' said Lulu.

He finally let go of her hands and went over to the stove. 'Well, I hope you like lamb,' he said.

'Love it,' said Lulu.

Jeremy bent down to peer through the glass door of the oven. 'We're having lamb tagine,' he said. 'A friend of mine has a villa outside Marrakesh and we used to eat at a little place in the local village. I had to force the woman who cooked there to give up her recipe. The secret is to leave the lamb marinating overnight in cayenne, black pepper, paprika, ginger, turmeric and cinnamon. But it's the saffron and honey that make it special. The great thing about it is that no matter the quality of the lamb, it comes out tasting delicious. I got ours from the local butcher so it's tip-top, but you can use any old bit of scrag end and still get great results. Jane doesn't have a real tagine but she has a cast-iron pot that does the job.'

'Well, it smells absolutely delicious,' said Lulu.

'How about some wine?' asked Jane.

'Lovely,' said Lulu.

'I'll get it,' said Jeremy. 'You girls make yourselves comfortable in the conservatory.'

Jane took Lulu through to the conservatory while Jeremy opened the large stainless-steel fridge. Conrad padded behind them, his tail in the air. 'This is lovely,' said Lulu. The conservatory had a terracotta floor and the furniture was white wood with colourful jungle-pattern cushions. There was a large wooden-bladed fan turning slowly overhead and huge ornate urns containing spreading green plants. Jane sat on a sofa and patted the cushion next to her. Lulu joined her and Conrad settled down at her feet.

'You've been here before, right?'

'Yes, years ago. But I don't remember a conservatory.'

'Oh, that's right. We had it built five years ago. It was all done to Clive's design but he never really had the chance to enjoy it.'

'Life can be like that sometimes,' said Lulu. 'You keep putting things off and then one day it's too late.'

'That's exactly what Jeremy says. *Carpe diem*. Seize the day, because you never know when it could be your last.'

'Your last what?' said Jeremy, appearing at the door carrying a tray with a bottle and three glasses.

'Last day,' said Jane. 'You have to enjoy life when you can. Treat every day as if it was your last.'

'Exactly!' said Jeremy, putting the tray down on a table in front of them. 'It's like John Lennon said: life is what happens to you while you're busy making other plans.'

He sat down on a chair and used a stainless-steel corkscrew to open the bottle. 'So, where do you stand on corks, Lulu?' he asked.

Lulu frowned. 'Corks?'

He held up the bottle. 'Corks or screw-top. I can't abide screw-tops.'

'I always think it depends on the wine,' said Lulu. 'I must admit I do love to hear a cork pop on a bottle of champagne or Prosecco, but as long as the wine tastes good, I don't think the stopper matters much.'

'I can see why you and Jane are best friends,' he said. 'That's exactly what she says. But for me, it has to be a cork. It's the tradition. There's something almost sexual about the uncorking; it's all tactile, about touch and pressure. Then the cork slides out ever so slowly and you smell the bouquet for the first time.'

'You make it sound like foreplay,' said Jane.

'Exactly!' said Jeremy. 'That's what it is, it's the foreplay before the partaking of pleasure. And where's the foreplay in twisting off a cap and pouring? Wham, bam, thank you, ma'am. I mean, you might as well drink wine from a can.'

'I have done,' said Lulu. 'And it was actually okay. Better than okay, Simon and I had canned rosé on a picnic once. It was delicious.'

Jeremy shuddered theatrically. 'If I had known you were such a heathen I would have brought in a Marks and Spencer ready meal and forgone three hours in the kitchen.'

Lulu laughed. 'I am a huge fan of M&S ready meals. I live on a narrowboat, remember? Very small kitchen.'

'And Simon was your husband?'

Lulu nodded.

'Jane said he passed away a year after she lost her husband. She says you were the merry widows.'

'I don't remember much merriment, I have to say. Not at the time.'

'But we do okay now,' said Jane. 'Don't we?'

'Of course we do,' said Lulu.

'Time is a great healer,' said Jeremy. 'That's what they say.'

'What about you, Jeremy? Have you ever been married?' Jane had said that he had never married, but Lulu wanted to hear it from the horse's mouth.

He shook his head. 'I came close a few times, but the sticking point was always that I never wanted children. I never had the time, or the inclination, I suppose.' Jeremy poured wine into a glass and handed it to her, then gave another glass to Jane. He raised his own glass in salute. 'Great to finally meet you, Lulu. Jane talks about you all the time, so it's wonderful to finally be able to put a face to the stories.'

They all tasted their wine. Lulu nodded her approval. It was good, and perfectly chilled. 'You know, Jane has told me almost nothing about you,' said Lulu.

'I think she wants to keep me for herself,' said Jeremy. He looked over at Jane and winked.

'You're from Ireland?'

'I live in Ireland. And my business is based there. Irish corporation tax is almost half what it is in the UK.'

'And what sort of business is it?'

'Well, I say business. It's a company, but all it does is hold assets. Investments that I have acquired over the years. All I do is take the dividends, really. Jane says you were a police officer. That must have been challenging, especially in London.'

'It had its moments.'

'You were a superintendent?'

'When I retired, yes. I was a super for almost five years.'

'So no glass ceiling?'

'Plenty of women were being promoted by the time I left.'

'Was Cressida Dick commissioner when you were there?'

'She got the top job after I retired. But she was very much around when I was there. She was the first woman assistant commissioner in 2009 when she was put in charge of the

Specialist Crime Directorate. And of course she was in charge of security for the 2012 London Olympics. Things were different when I joined, but by the time I left there were plenty of women in top jobs.'

'As it should be,' said Jane.

'No question,' said Jeremy. He took a drink. 'What sort of policing were you involved in?'

'Everything, really. I started walking a beat, I worked serious crimes and homicide. I had spells in New Scotland Yard.'

'You never wanted to be commissioner?'

'Me? No. I enjoyed police work, but I couldn't be bothered with the politics.'

'You just wanted to catch villains?'

'I did, yes.'

Jeremy laughed. 'Get your trousers on, you're nicked. *The Sweeney* was a great show.'

'It was, but nothing like the real thing,' said Lulu.

'Television drama rarely is,' said Jane.

'And what about you, Jeremy?' asked Lulu. 'What was your job?'

'Jack of all trades, and master of none,' said Jeremy.

'You must have done something,' said Lulu.

'Oh, I did. Lots of things.'

'Did you go to university?'

'The university of life,' he said.

'And he graduated with honours,' said Jane, raising her glass to him.

Lulu smiled and drank with them. Jeremy wasn't avoiding her questions, but his answers were nebulous at best. He was charming – no question – and he was good fun. But he was also being evasive, albeit with good humour. 'But you must have had a job, before you retired,' she said.

'I did, lots of jobs. But none of them as interesting as yours.' He savoured a mouthful of wine, but she held his look and didn't say anything. Eventually he lowered his glass. 'I bet you were a first-class interrogator,' he said eventually.

'I had my moments,' said Lulu. 'But usually people want to tell you the truth, they really do. Lying is bad for the soul.'

'You believe in souls?'

He was very good at getting out of answering questions, Lulu realized, forever leading the conversation away from revealing personal details. 'Of course,' said Lulu.

'What about animals?' said Jeremy, waving his glass at Conrad. 'Do they have souls?'

'Oh, I think so,' said Lulu. 'So, let me guess. I think you have the look of an accountant about you.'

Jeremy clasped a hand to his heart. 'Oh my God, kill me now,' he said. 'Really? A bean-counter? That's what you think about me?'

'Well, let's be honest, you don't have the look of a ditch-digger, do you? Your hands are soft, there's a nice glow to your skin that suggests top-of-the-range toiletries and you definitely have the appearance of a man who enjoys the finer things in life.'

Jeremy laughed and slapped his thigh. 'My goodness, you really do have a detective's instincts, don't you?' He looked at Jane. 'Lulu is delightful, she really is. I can see why you'd want her as a friend.' He looked back at Lulu and grinned. 'The thing is, you couldn't be more wrong,' he said. 'I mean, yes, I definitely do enjoy the finer things of life now, but way back when I started . . .' He shook his head. 'I was a labourer, Lulu. Working on building sites. Sweating like a pig as I hauled bricks up a ladder in the summer, standing in freezing mud up to my knees in the winter. I left home when I was sixteen. My parents had died and my brother and sister and I were living with our grandparents. They never let us forget what an imposition we were and, as soon as they were old enough, my siblings ran away to Australia. My plan was to follow them, so a mate got me a job on a building site; the idea was to make a bit of cash before I left for Oz. It was hard work but I enjoyed it, and I began picking up skills. If a plasterer needed help he'd call me over; if a chippy needed a hand, then I'd be there. I never did an apprenticeship but I soaked up skills like a sponge. Plumbing, electrical, joinery, roofing, plastering; I wasn't kidding when I said I was a jack of all trades.'

'He is very good with his hands,' said Jane, then blushed as she realized what she had said. 'That's not what I meant,' she said to Lulu. 'I mean he is really good around the house. My dishwasher was leaking and he fixed that. I had a couple of loose slates on the roof and before I could say anything, he'd taken out the ladder and was up there sorting it out. My dimmer switch broke and he replaced it. He really can do anything.'

'Impressive,' said Lulu.

'Anyway, after a few years I gave up on the idea of moving to Australia and started my own building company. I was actually quite good at it, mainly because I worked so hard. All the hours that God sends. Evenings, weekends, public holidays. I took a couple of younger lads under my wing and the business grew. Then I moved into property development: buying old buildings, doing them up and then renting them out. I made some good contacts within a couple of banks and they started throwing money at me. I never looked back.' He grinned. 'And that, Lulu, is the story of my life. But an accountant, never. I mean, don't get me wrong, I know my way around a company report and accounts and I can read a profit and loss statement, but I've never been a number-cruncher.' He held up his hands. 'And you're right, I do use lotions and I have manicures and I take care of my hands. But if you look closer you'll see the scars and callouses from years working outside.'

'I stand corrected,' said Lulu. 'And really, what a fascinating life you've led.'

'You don't know the half of it,' he said. He took a quick look at his watch. 'Time to check on the tagine.'

He headed for the kitchen, taking his glass with him.

'Isn't he lovely?' asked Jane.

'He is, yes. Did he tell you about his building site days?'

Jane nodded. 'He did, yes. Why?'

Lulu shrugged. 'I don't know. It just felt like a story that he was used to telling, that's all. A well-polished anecdote.'

'Well it's his life story, Lulu. I'm sure he's told lots of people over the years. We all polish our stories, don't we?'

Lulu smiled. 'Yes, I suppose we do.'

13

Dinner was amazing; Jeremy was clearly a talented cook. The lamb tagine was cooked to perfection, as was the dessert. Jeremy had made a baklava, layered filo pastry filled with chopped nuts, syrup and honey. He said he had got the recipe from another restaurant in Marrakesh, this one a favourite of Tom Cruise. 'I never actually met him, but his photograph is on the wall,' Jeremy had said as he served Lulu a second helping.

After they had finished, Jeremy cleared the table and opened another bottle of wine.

'How did you learn to cook so wonderfully?' Lulu asked. 'That really was delicious.'

'Oh, I've owned a few restaurants over the years,' said Jeremy, sitting back in his chair. They were in the dining room, sitting at a table large enough for eight. There was a skylight above them. It was a clear night and there was a half-moon, its craters clearly visible. Conrad had curled up on an armchair by the door. He wasn't a fan of lamb, apricots even less so.

'I didn't know that,' said Jane.

'Didn't I mention it? I had one in Temple Bar in Dublin years ago. I'd bought the building and done a refurb. The tenant was an Italian guy and he put in a pizza oven and decent fridges and a cooking range, then six months into the contract he did a runner and cleaned his bank accounts out before he went. He owed me thousands and the only way I could get any of it back was to start running the restaurant as a going concern. For the first three months I did almost all of the cooking but then I hired a couple of decent chefs to help. We ended up being voted as one of the best restaurants in Dublin.'

'Well done, you,' said Lulu.

'The funny thing is, I've never been a great fan of Italian food.'

'But you do the most wonderful spaghetti carbonara,' said Jane. She looked over at Lulu. 'And he doesn't use cream.'

'Italians never put cream in a carbonara – it would be sacrilege,' said Jeremy. 'You use eggs, pork cheek, pecorino cheese and pepper. And a splash of extra virgin olive oil.' He picked up his glass. 'I much prefer Turkish food. Or Spanish. I'll do you my paella next time you're here.'

'His paella is to die for,' said Jane. 'He has this way of making the rice crunchy at the base. I love it.'

'I do it the traditional Valencian way, and they make them dry with socarrat, where the rice goes crunchy because of the heat,' said Jeremy. 'I always prefer to use prawns, squid and langoustines, but I can do chicken paella if pushed.'

Lulu sipped her wine. 'You seem to succeed at everything you do,' she said.

'When I was younger, I couldn't afford to fail. I didn't have a safety net. It wouldn't be an exaggeration to say that I'd die if I didn't succeed. So succeed I did.' He picked up the bottle and poured more wine into their glasses. 'At least those days are behind me. I don't have to worry where my next meal is coming from.'

'Because you can cook it yourself,' said Jane.

'You know what I mean, darling,' said Jeremy. 'Once you feel secure you can start really enjoying life.'

'And that's what you're doing now?' asked Lulu.

'Enjoying life? Of course. What else is there? You start off working to live. Then you live to work. Finally, if you're lucky, you simply get to live. You of all people must surely understand that?'

'Why me of all people?'

'Because you travel by narrowboat. That's not in any way cost effective, in terms of time or money, but you do it because you enjoy the journey. Right?'

Lulu nodded. 'I can't argue with that.'

'I imagine you take pleasure in slowly motoring through the scenery, breathing in the fresh air, hearing the birds sing. Living in the moment.'

'I do, yes. Very much so.'

'That's what life is all about, Lulu. Enjoying the moment.'

There was a thoughtful silence while they all sipped their wine. 'So, Jane says you met on the internet?' said Lulu.

'On a dating app. Yes. I think that's how most people meet these days, isn't it?'

'You used it a lot, this app?'

Jeremy tilted his head on one side. 'Didn't Jane tell you? It was a total one-off.' He looked over at Jane. 'I can't believe you didn't tell her.' He put his glass down. 'I was in Dublin, dinner at the Unicorn with an old mate. He was heading to London for a few days and was looking for a date. He showed me the app. To be honest, I thought it was ridiculous, and I told him so. I figured it was probably just a way for hookers to pick up clients.'

'Well, thank you very much for that,' said Jane, pretending to be shocked.

'That's what I thought, but when he showed me the type of people on there, I changed my opinion. They seemed to be real profiles, mainly. Real people. And Jane's profile was among the first half-dozen he showed me. My pal wasn't interested because he was going to London, not Manchester, but I was fascinated by her profile. So later that night I downloaded the app, opened an account and went looking for Jane.'

'Oh my God, you were a stalker,' said Jane.

'No, I wasn't stalking at all. My profile was genuine, you know that. But the only profile I was interested in was yours. I found you and we started chatting.'

Jane nodded. 'We chatted online for a couple of days and then we exchanged phone numbers and we spoke for an hour or so a day. For weeks.'

'She took her time,' said Jeremy. 'I had to ask a dozen times for a face-to-face meeting.'

'Well, because it was a bit strange, you being in Dublin and me being in Manchester. What if you had flown over and we hadn't got on?'

'That was never going to happen,' said Jeremy. 'Anyway, a few months after we met online, I had a business meeting in Manchester. So I was flying over anyway. That's when she agreed to meet me for lunch.' He held up his glass. 'And the rest is history.'

'That's a lovely story,' said Lulu.

'I knew what I wanted and I went for it,' said Jeremy. 'Faint heart never won fair lady.'

'Well I'm glad you persevered,' said Jane. She leaned over and clinked her glass against his.

They drank and smiled at each other, then Jeremy looked over at Lulu. 'So did Jane tell you that I asked her to marry me?'

'Yes, she did.'

'And how do you feel about that?'

Lulu raised her eyebrows. 'It hardly matters what I think, does it?'

'You're a close friend; of course your opinion matters. I want to make an honest woman of her, but she's hesitating.'

'I'm not!' said Jane.

'Then let's set a date,' said Jeremy.

'You're in such a rush,' said Jane, shaking her head.

'I'm not getting any younger,' said Jeremy. 'When I see something I want, I go for it. He who hesitates is lost, as they say.'

'You know, I always think that should be "He who hesitates is last", because taking your time doesn't automatically mean that you get lost,' said Lulu. 'But you might be last.'

'Good point,' said Jeremy. 'But last or lost, I want to marry Jane and I don't know what else I can do to persuade her.'

'Did you go down on one knee?' asked Lulu.

'No, I didn't.' He looked over at Jane. 'Would that do the trick? Down on one knee and offer up a ring?'

'Do you have a ring?' asked Jane.

'I was thinking we could choose it together,' said Jeremy. 'But maybe you're right: the romantic thing would be for me to get a ring and go down on one knee.' He grinned. 'Duly noted.'

'Now you're putting words into my mouth,' said Jane. 'There's just such a lot to consider.'

'But there isn't,' said Jeremy. 'I don't have kids, neither do you. We're free agents.'

'Aren't you happy with the way we are now?' asked Jane. 'I know I am.'

'Of course I am,' said Jeremy. 'I'm having the time of my life, and I want it to continue that way. But I'd like to continue as Mr and Mrs Jeremy Connolly rather than Jeremy Connolly and some bird he met on the internet.'

'Bird!' said Jane. 'Is that how you see me? Some bird?'

Jeremy chuckled and shook his head. 'Of course not, it's just an expression. You're the love of my life, darling. You can't fault me for wanting to make it permanent, can you?'

'But marriages aren't permanent these days, are they?' said Lulu. 'The average marriage lasts just eight years.'

'Well, I intend for ours to last a lot longer than that,' said Jeremy.

'But marriages do fall apart,' said Jane. 'And when they do, well, life gets difficult.'

Jeremy frowned. 'In what way?'

'In every way. And where would we live, for instance?'

'Up to you. I'd be very happy here. I doubt that you'd want to move to Ireland, but I'll happily move to the UK. We could live here or we could buy a new place together. Spain, maybe?'

'And what if it went wrong? Who would get the house? Divorce is so messy.'

'Why on earth are you thinking about divorce when we aren't even married? That makes no sense.'

'We need to think ahead. If we were teenagers then maybe we could act without thinking, but we're not teenagers. There are – oh, I don't know – financial implications.'

'You think I'm after your money?' He shook his head and laughed. 'Oh darling, listen to yourself.'

'No, I don't think that at all. But getting married means that our lives become entwined and if anything does go wrong, it can become very complicated. And expensive.'

'Would a prenup make you feel more relaxed?' asked Jeremy.

Jane looked uncomfortable and she shifted in her chair. 'I'm not sure,' she said. 'Maybe.'

'The thing is, I don't have anyone else to leave my money to. I certainly wouldn't want my siblings in Australia to get it. So if I die, I'd want you to have everything. Not that I'm planning on dying anytime soon, but if I was in a plane plummeting towards the ground I'd be happier knowing that you'd be better off.'

Jane laughed. 'That's crazy,' she said.

'I'm serious.'

'Yes, I can see you are.'

'Look, darling, if you want me to sign a prenup, of course I will. But I have no intention of divorcing you. This is for ever. My last chance at happiness. True happiness.'

Jane leaned over and kissed him. 'You are such a sweetie.'

'Right back at you.' He looked over at Lulu. 'Sorry, you probably hate these PDAs.'

'PDAs?'

'Public displays of affection.'

'No, not at all. It's sweet.'

'For people of our age?'

'For people of any age,' said Lulu. 'So, if you do get married, who would be your best man?'

'Now, that's a good question.'

'Maybe the chap who got you into the dating app. What was his name again?'

'I didn't tell you his name,' said Jeremy. 'But it was Seamus. Seamus Gannon.'

'So maybe Seamus could be your best man. It would certainly be a great story for the reception.'

Jeremy looked at Jane. 'Would we want a reception? I was thinking of something small, cosy, just a few close friends. A register office and a nice meal afterwards. But whatever you want, darling.' He smiled at Lulu. 'And of course you and Conrad must come.'

'Jeremy, I haven't even said yes yet,' said Jane. 'You really are counting your chickens.'

'But you will think about it?'

Jane laughed. 'Yes. I will.'

Lulu looked down at Conrad. He was staring at Jeremy, his ears up and his whiskers twitching.

14

Lulu ordered an Uber just after eleven o'clock and a grey Skoda arrived within ten minutes. 'Can you remember what life was like before Uber?' asked Jane. 'Frantically ringing minicab companies, only to be told there was no one available?'

'Smartphones have changed our lives so much,' said Jeremy. 'A gift and a curse.'

'I feel the same way,' said Lulu. 'I was saying to Conrad, the smartphone has made narrowboating so much easier, with GPS showing exactly where you are and where the nearest facilities are.'

Jeremy frowned. 'You were talking to Conrad? Your cat?'

Lulu laughed. 'I talk to him all the time. As I said, he's my constant companion. I tell him everything, pretty much. Anyway, the downside of smartphones is that you can always be contacted. You're never out of range.'

'You can always switch it off,' said Jane.

'Do you?'

Jane laughed. 'Of course not. Who does?'

'And don't get me started on social media,' said Lulu. 'Even when I was a police officer, the amount of work generated by social media was soul destroying. And it's gone from bad to worse.'

'Yes, but it's swings and roundabouts, isn't it?' said Jeremy. 'Social media has raised the police's workload, but at the same time smartphones have made the police's work so much easier, surely. You can track where the criminals are, what they're saying to each other, who they're talking to. I heard that you can use phones as bugs, too, and listen in even when a call isn't being made.'

'Is that true?' asked Jane.

'I think it's technically possible, but I've never heard of the police being allowed to use it. MI5, maybe.'

'It's a whole new world,' said Jane.

Lulu stood up and hugged Jane. 'It's been delightful, really. Thank you so much.' She looked over at Jeremy. 'It's been a real pleasure meeting you, Jeremy. And thank you so much for a wonderful meal.'

Jeremy held her hands and kissed her on both cheeks. 'It was great to meet you, too. I'm sure we'll meet again. At the wedding, I hope.'

'He's not going to give up,' said Jane.

'Damn right I'm not,' he said. 'I'm in for the long haul.'

Lulu bent down, scooped up Conrad and put him on her shoulders.

'And it was a pleasure meeting you, Conrad,' said Jeremy. 'And I won't hold it against you that you turned up your nose at my lamb tagine.'

'Let me see you to your taxi,' said Jane, and she took Lulu down the hall to the front door. 'Thank you so much for coming,' she said.

'I had a lovely time,' replied Lulu.

They walked out of the house and along the driveway. The Uber was waiting for them on the road. 'So what do you think?' asked Jane, linking her arm through Lulu's. 'Does he have your seal of approval?'

'He's lovely,' said Lulu.

'His offer of a prenup took me by surprise.'

'I think he realized that you were worried about the money thing.'

'But it's good, right?'

'I guess so,' said Lulu. 'But let me sleep on it. I'll phone you tomorrow.'

'Please do, yes. And thank you again for coming.' They hugged and Jane headed back to the house. Lulu took her phone out of her handbag and snapped a photograph of the number plate of the Audi.

'He's watching you from an upstairs window,' whispered Conrad.

Lulu turned her back to the house. 'Did he see me take the photograph?'

'I'm not sure.'

Lulu slid the phone back into her handbag. 'Fingers crossed,' she said.

'Cats can't cross their fingers,' said Conrad.

'What do you do for luck?'

'We try to avoid walking under ladders. And cracking mirrors.'

'Good to know.'

The Uber driver was called Ahmad and he had the disconcerting habit of constantly looking over his shoulder to talk to them as he drove. Lulu listened and nodded politely, though several times she felt the urge to shout at him to keep his eyes on the road.

'Ahmad, five stars if you please,' he said as they climbed out of his car.

'Definitely,' she said, though she had already decided not

to give him a review. She never liked giving bad ratings to Uber drivers because she knew it could affect their livelihood, but travelling with Ahmad hadn't been a pleasant experience, so best just to say nothing. She closed the door and scooped Conrad up onto her shoulders.

She walked along the towpath towards the Staffordshire arm. There were more than a dozen narrowboats moored there now, with only a few spaces left. Two young women in jeans and pullovers were sitting on their boat, sharing what was clearly a cannabis joint. Their boat was painted a deep green and they had called it *Reefer Madness*, the name printed in gold capital letters above a painting of a marijuana leaf. They waved at Lulu and she smiled back.

'We love your cat!' one of them shouted.

'Thank you!' replied Lulu.

A young man was sitting on the rear deck of the next boat, playing a flute. He was good and Lulu stopped to listen. She actually recognized the tune: it was the second movement of Mozart's Flute Concerto no. 2. The man seemed oblivious to the fact that he had an audience, and played with his eyes half closed. It was only when he finished and put down the flute that he noticed Lulu and Conrad. He smiled and wished them a good evening. 'That was lovely,' said Lulu. Conrad meowed. 'Conrad enjoyed it too,' said Lulu.

'Cats love the flute; they can hear frequencies that we humans can't,' said the man. 'They must hear a very different tune to the one we hear.'

'I'd never thought of that before,' said Lulu. She smiled at the man and walked on to *The Lark*. She stepped carefully onto the rear deck, unlocked the doors and went down into the cabin. Conrad jumped onto the sofa and Lulu put the kettle on before pouring some Evian water in a bowl for him. She put the bowl down in front of him and he thanked her.

'You haven't said anything about Jeremy,' said Lulu.

Conrad lapped at the water, then sat down and wiped his whiskers. 'I was waiting for you to ask.'

'That sounds ominous.'

Conrad tilted his head on one side and stared at her with his unblinking green eyes. 'His aura was confusing.'

'Really? Confusing?'

Conrad nodded. 'There was a strange energy to it. There was lots of dark, dirty, avocado green.'

'Didn't you once tell me that a green aura meant the person was starting a journey, a meaningful journey or a healing journey?'

'That's light green. And vibrant. Jeremy's was dirtier and much darker. Like I said, the dull green of an avocado. And that is the energy of deceit. People who are being honest and truthful radiate a deep blue aura, topped by a white crown of energy. I didn't see any of that in his aura, I'm afraid.'

'So Jeremy was lying?'

'Maybe not lying, but certainly embellishing the truth.'

'Well, the Irish are said to be great storytellers.'

'The more he spoke, the dark green energy got stronger and was absorbed by Jane's aura. She was accepting his lies. I could see it happening.'

'That's not good,' said Lulu.

'No, it isn't. He had a lot of magenta, too. That's what you see with people who put their own needs above everyone else's. They don't need validation from anybody but themselves.'

'That sounds like a sociopath.'

'Well, yes, maybe. But he is charming.'

'Oh, he is definitely that. He could charm the birds from the trees.'

'Now that is a skill I could do with,' said Conrad.

'But other than the aura, what did you think?'

'I thought he was a bit smarmy. A bit full of himself. Sometimes it felt as if he was talking down to you and Jane. But he tells such good stories, doesn't he?'

'He does, yes. Though sometimes it was like we were watching a performance. As if he was playing a part.'

'Yes, he'd obviously told those stories before.'

'So what should I tell Jane?'

'Do you have to tell her anything?'

'She wants my advice.'

'She has to make her own decisions in life, surely?'

Lulu nodded. 'That's true. But sometimes it's difficult to see the wood for the trees. Sometimes you need to see a situation from a different perspective.' She sighed. 'I've no idea what to say to her, frankly.'

'Because you liked him, too?'

Lulu laughed. 'Yes, I did.'

15

Lulu was at Piccadilly Station just after nine o'clock in the morning, and Detective Inspector Phil Jackson stepped off the train from London a few minutes later. He waved as he walked along the platform towards her. He was in his forties and his hair was already turning grey, a good-looking guy who in some photographs was the spitting image of Denzel Washington in the film *The Pelican Brief*. His skin, the colour of burnished mahogany, came from his Barbadian father but the twinkle in his brown eyes definitely came from his Irish mother. He was wearing a dark blue suit and carrying a battered leather briefcase and had an Adidas holdall slung over one shoulder.

'Trouble seems to follow you, boss,' he said.

'Trust me, it was the last thing I wanted to happen,' said Lulu. 'Come on, we'll need to get a taxi to their HQ. We can check you in to your hotel later.'

'And nice to see you again, Conrad,' said Jackson.

Conrad meowed at him and he laughed. 'I just love the way he talks.'

'Me too,' said Lulu. She headed towards the taxi rank.

'So you brought your boat up to Manchester?'

'Yes, I wanted to see a friend of mine here and I was at a loose end in Maida Vale so I thought I'd give it a go.'

'How long did it take you?'

'Almost three weeks.'

He laughed. 'You know it took me two hours and sixteen minutes.'

'I can believe that. Narrowboats aren't about speed.'

Phil laughed. 'Clearly not.'

'That's what makes life on a narrowboat so enjoyable,' said Lulu. 'It's a slower pace of life. You feel more in touch with the landscape around. For you, travelling from London to Manchester is just two hours watching fields flash by. For me, it was a true journey. I met people on the way, I visited places I've never seen before. I have a real understanding of just how far apart the two cities are.'

'I can imagine telling my bosses that I've got to look at a case in Manchester and that I'll be back in six weeks.'

'That's exactly what travel was like back in the seventeen hundreds,' said Lulu. 'Most people were born, lived and died in the same village. Now look at you. Mum from Galway, dad from Barbados, living in London, and you've holidayed in the US, France, Spain, Thailand.'

He grinned. 'I was in Vietnam last year.'

'How was it?'

'Hot.'

They reached the taxi rank and climbed into a black cab. 'I didn't realize they had black cabs in Manchester,' said Phil after Lulu had told the driver where they wanted to go.

'They do. Along with flushing toilets and central heating.'

Phil chuckled. 'That's not what I meant and you know it. I mean I always thought they were a London thing.' He lowered his voice and leaned towards her. 'So you think the Choker is back?'

That was the nickname that the investigators had given to

the serial killer they had been pursuing, though it had remained firmly within the ranks.

Lulu nodded. 'There have been two killings here and the killer used the same knot. Both victims were male.'

'Gay?'

'Not sure. Certainly one of the victims had a wife. The investigators took him at face value but they might have to take another look at his private life.'

'We came up against that in London, remember? The parents of two of the victims swore blind that their sons weren't gay, but it became obvious that they were – they were just hiding it.'

'And there have been no other cases in the past . . . How long has it been?'

'Since the last killing? Five years. The killings just stopped. Then your consultancy came to an end and the investigation was gradually wound down.'

'And there's been no cold case follow-up?'

'There was no evidence, boss. No fingerprints, DNA or fibres; nothing that would get a conviction, anyway. And we'd run out of leads. To be honest, the only way he would have been caught would be if he had started killing again. We were just happy that the killings stopped.'

'Obviously you need to brief the investigators on our cases. I was a bit rusty, I'm afraid.'

Phil patted his briefcase. 'I've got all the latest here, but nothing substantial has changed since you left.'

'How long can you stay for?'

'Well that's the good news. There's a cold case budget which is flush with funds at the moment so they've said I can stay for at least two or three days, maybe longer if there's an indication that we might solve our cases. They've even sprung for a decent hotel. I'm booked into the Midland. That's where Mr Rolls is said to have met Mr Royce, according to Google.'

'And we all trust Google, don't we?' said Lulu.

The taxi pulled up in front of GMP headquarters. Lulu took out her wallet but Phil shook his head. 'I'm on expenses, remember,' he said. He paid and asked for a receipt.

They climbed out of the cab. Phil looked around. 'Not exactly in the middle of things, are they? I suppose they don't want passing trade. And I can't see beat bobbies setting off from here.'

'Beat bobbies?' said Lulu. She laughed. 'What century are you from?'

'I walked a beat, boss. And so did you. And we're better police because of it.'

Conrad sat contentedly on Lulu's shoulders as she took Phil into the building and asked for DI Friar at reception. Within a couple of minutes DC Townsend came down to meet them. Lulu introduced him to Phil and the two men shook hands. 'DI Friar said you should brief our team straight away, if that's okay with you,' said DC Townsend.

Phil held up his briefcase. 'I've come prepared.'

'Excellent,' said DC Townsend. He nodded at the holdall. 'Are you staying?'

'My bosses say I can stay for a couple of days, at least.'

'Even better,' said DC Townsend. He took them to the lifts and up to the second floor, then along a corridor to a door with a sign that read 'MIT 2' which Lulu figured stood for Murder Investigation Team 2.

'What's MIT 1 working on?' she asked.

'Three drug dealers were killed earlier this month,' said DC Townsend. 'An Albanian gang is trying to take over the cocaine market in the south of the city and they don't seem to care how many people they have to kill on the way.'

'We're having a similar problem in London,' said Phil. 'The Albanians are in a whole different league.'

'And getting intel on them is next to impossible,' said DC Townsend. 'They only deal with their own people.' He pushed open the door and a couple of dozen expectant faces looked in their direction. DI Friar was standing between two large whiteboards which were plastered with photographs and printouts. She smiled at Lulu and waved, and then waggled her fingers at Conrad. Lulu waved back.

DI Friar walked over to them. Lulu introduced her to Phil. Phil put down his briefcase and holdall and they shook hands. 'Thanks so much for coming up for this,' she said.

'This case has always bugged me,' said Phil. 'If the Choker is still active, I want to help.'

'The Choker?'

'That's what the team called him,' said Lulu.

'I hope Dickie McNeil doesn't get hold of that,' said DI Friar. 'I wouldn't want that splashed over the *Manchester Evening News*.'

DI Friar looked at her watch. 'Superintendent Dennis Knight is on the way. It'd be great if you could wait until he's here. He's in overall charge and I know he's keen to hear what you have to say.'

'Not a problem,' said Phil. He picked up his holdall and briefcase and put them on a table. 'Sorry,' he said. 'I'm just off the train, I haven't had time to check in to my hotel.'

'We'll get a car to take you to your hotel when we're

done,' she said. 'In the meantime, let me run our two cases by you.' She took them over to the nearest whiteboard. 'This was the first. Three weeks ago. Forty-two-year-old Derek Sawyer's body was found on Heaton Park golf course in the north of the city.' She tapped a photograph of a length of white rope, similar to the picture that had been on the front page of the *Manchester Evening News*. 'The knot was very unusual, at least to our eyes. But then we found out that it is commonly used by sailors. The body was naked and had been washed, so there was no forensic evidence at all.'

There were several post-mortem photographs, including shots of marks on the victim's neck, wrists and ankles. Phil looked at the photographs and his eyes widened. 'I know him.'

'You what?' said DI Friar.

'He's a cop.'

'Yes, with the GMP. A sergeant.'

Phil shook his head. 'No, he was with the Met. We were at Hendon together. More than twenty years ago.'

DI Friar looked over at DC Townsend. 'Did we know this?'

'We knew he had done five years with the Met before he transferred here. It's in the file. But it was never considered significant.'

'We might be reconsidering that now, obviously,' said DI Friar.

'But if he left London, what, at least fifteen years ago, that would be long before the Choker was active,' said Lulu. 'Maybe it's a coincidence.'

'How well did you know him?' asked DI Friar.

'Not at all, really,' said Phil. 'We were just there at the

same time. I played football against him a couple of times, and I remember seeing him around. But our paths didn't cross again after we graduated. Back then there must have been close to thirty thousand cops in London.'

The double doors opened and a uniformed superintendent walked in. He was in his late forties, tall and thin with the dour expression of an undertaker. His hair was receding and he had dark patches under his eyes. He walked over to DI Friar and greeted her with a curt nod.

'Superintendent Knight, can I introduce you to former superintendent Lulu Lewis of the Met, and DI Phil Jackson.'

'Good of you both to come,' he said. 'We're hoping you'll provide some insight.'

'DI Jackson was just telling us that he knew the first victim.'

'That's right, Sawyer was with the Met for a few years, wasn't he?' said the superintendent. 'Do you think it's relevant?'

'I was just saying that it could be a coincidence, and he did leave London before our killer started killing, but it'd definitely be worth looking into,' said Lulu.

The superintendent spotted Conrad sitting on a chair and he frowned. 'Why is there a cat in the incident room?'

'He's with me,' said Lulu.

The superintendent smiled for the first time. 'He's very well behaved.'

'He is,' said Lulu.

'It's unusual to take a cat around with you.'

'Conrad is a very unusual cat,' said Lulu.

The superintendent smiled again. 'I'm sure he is.' He looked back at DI Friar. 'So what's happening now?'

'I was just briefing DI Jackson and former superintendent Lewis on our two killings, and then DI Jackson will tell us about their cold case killings.'

'Then I'll sit in, if that's okay with you.'

'Of course, sir.' As the superintendent dropped into an empty chair by the windows, DI Friar went back to the Sawyer whiteboard. 'So, as I was saying, Derek Sawyer's body was found on Heaton Park golf course three weeks ago, naked, and the body had been washed. Sergeant Sawyer was married, no children, no financial problems, no ongoing disputes. He was last seen leaving for work on the day he died, and his car was parked not far from North Manchester Division Police Station, where he was based. He didn't report for duty that day so the assumption was that he was abducted on the way in to work. No CCTV coverage of the area where he parked, and no eyewitnesses. As of today, we have no active leads to pursue.'

'Did any of his cases bring him into contact with anyone who might do something like this?' asked Lulu.

'Sergeant Sawyer was office based, nine to five, working for the Youth Engagement Team. They work full-time with universities and students in Manchester, basically keeping young people safe. So, no. He wasn't up against violent criminals.'

'Do you think he was targeted, or was it random?' asked Lulu.

'A very good question, and one we haven't found an answer to,' said DI Friar. 'We haven't been able to find a reason why he would have been targeted, but if it was random, why take a police officer? Surely they would have chosen an easier target if it was random.' She walked over to the second whiteboard. There were half a dozen photographs on display. Two were head-and-shoulder shots of a middle-aged man with thinning blond hair and a sprinkling of freckles across a snub nose. 'Fraser Robinson, thirty-five years old, worked in a city centre barber's. Lived with his parents, left work five days ago and his body was found the following day by a man walking his dog on Stretford Meadows. It's a seventy-acre park to the south-west of the city.'

'Thirty-five is a bit old to be living with his parents,' said Lulu.

'He had his own business, but it went bust during Covid,' said DI Friar. 'He lost the business and his house, his wife divorced him and he moved back in with his mum and dad.'

'How far from where the first body was found?'

'Eight or nine miles as the crow flies. But it's on the other side of the city. A half-hour drive, probably.'

'And was any attempt made to conceal either of the bodies?'

DI Friar shook her head. 'They were both dumped. Not in plain view but not concealed.' She tapped at a photograph of a section of knotted rope. 'An identical knot was used. A round turn and two half hitches. And again, there was nothing in Mr Robinson's background to suggest a reason why he might have been targeted. No recent problems at work or at home. No conflicts that we know about. Never been in trouble with the police.'

'Drug use?' asked Lulu.

'Occasional marijuana user,' said DI Friar. 'His parents had asked that he didn't smoke inside the house and he stuck to that arrangement. Obviously the body was only discovered four days ago so the investigation is still very active, but we appear to have a second random victim with no forensic or CCTV evidence.'

'Did you find any connection between the victims?' asked Phil.

'None. But we are still looking.'

'I read in the paper that Sergeant Sawyer had a wife. Was there any suggestion at all that your other victim was gay?'

DI Friar frowned. 'No, Fraser Robinson also had a wife – although they did get divorced. Why?'

'Of the four victims in our cases, three were gay,' said Phil. 'Two were killed after visiting gay bars in Soho. It was a very strong line of inquiry, but sadly it didn't lead anywhere.'

'Perhaps you could start your briefing,' said DI Friar, gesturing at the empty whiteboard. 'And I'm sure there'll be a lot of questions.'

'No problem,' said Phil. He went over to his briefcase and took out a file. He walked over to a table close to the whiteboard, opened the file and took out a photograph. 'We had four victims, their deaths occurring over an eighteen-month period,' he said.

DI Friar passed him a pack of Blu-tack and Phil nodded his thanks. He stuck the first photograph onto the board, a head-and-shoulders shot of a middle-aged man, then added another three photographs. Then he picked up a marker pen and began writing names under the pictures. 'Ian Pettigrew. Nick Hurst. William Eccles. John Dunne.' He then wrote a series of dates below the photographs. 'The victims were all gay, with the exception of the third victim, William Eccles. Mr Eccles had a wife and a young child. We suspected, but were never able to prove, that he had something of a double life.'

'Bisexual? Having affairs?' asked DI Friar.

'We could never prove it,' said Phil. 'We knew for sure that Hurst and Dunne had been active in the Soho gay bar scene. As part of the investigation we would visit the bars at various times of the day and night and show patrons photographs of the victims. Several men said they thought they remembered seeing Mr Eccles but we could never find corroborating CCTV, and generally there was a lot of drinks and drugs involved, so memories could be hazy.'

'But you think the killer was targeting gay men?'

'That was one of our main theories,' said Phil. 'Mr Hurst and Mr Dunne were openly gay and were regulars in Soho. Mr Pettigrew was less open about his sexuality, but his laptop was checked after his death and there were videos on there that told the true story.'

'What story, exactly?' asked DI Friar. 'What sort of videos were they?'

'Gay sex, generally of a violent nature. And some bondage.'

'Bondage? Similar to the method used to kill our victims?'

'Similar, yes. But not identical.'

'The thing is, so far as we know, neither of our victims were gay,' said DI Friar.

'Well, we didn't know that Mr Pettigrew was gay, or at least liked gay porn, until some time into the investigation. And we never proved for a fact that Mr Eccles was gay. Or bisexual. So it might be worth you having another look at your two victims.'

He took a map from his briefcase, unfolded it and stuck it to the whiteboard. There were four red circles on the map.

'The bodies were dumped in different areas across London. Always on parkland, always under or close to trees. Never closer than fifty yards to a road. We believed that the bodies were carried some distance and then dumped. So either the killer was quite strong, or he had help.'

'So you considered the possibility of two killers working together?' asked DI Friar.

'We had no evidence that there were two, but the method of disposal suggested that two would have been able to do the job more efficiently than one. But we never found footprints and there was never any CCTV footage.'

He stuck another four photographs on the board. Crime scene pictures. Naked bodies with ropes around their necks.

'All were found naked and with ropes still around their necks. All the lengths of rope came from the same source, but it was a common brand and sold in literally hundreds of stores across the country. Three-strand nylon rope, made by a company called Marlow.'

'Ours were both three-strand nylon rope, but the brand was Kingfisher,' said DI Friar. 'Very common.'

'In all four cases there were marks on the wrists and ankles which had been caused by the same type of rope,' continued Phil. 'According to our pathologist, each victim had been bound with their hands behind them and placed face down on the ground. A noose was then placed around the victim's neck and the other end of the rope tied to the ankles. The victim would then slowly strangle themselves, their legs would drop and pull the noose tighter.'

DI Friar nodded. 'Snap.'

'We never made that public,' said Lulu.

'We hadn't planned to either,' said DI Friar. 'But Dickie

McNeil published it in the *Evening News*. So it was torture, right?'

'We think the killer wanted them to suffer,' said Phil. 'It wouldn't have been a quick death.'

'That's the conclusion our pathologist reached,' said DI Friar. 'Either because it gave the killer sexual gratification, or because there was a personal angle. Revenge.'

'But the victims were never sexually abused?'

Phil shook his head. 'No. No evidence of that.'

Superintendent Knight stood up. 'This is all very interesting,' he said. 'Fascinating, in fact. There's no question that there are many, many similarities between the two sets of killings. So it's almost certainly either the same killer, or a copycat. But here's what's worrying me, DI Jackson. If all that detail was passed on to the Serious Crime Analysis Section, why wasn't it passed on to us when we registered our cases?'

'I can't answer that,' said Phil. 'Yet. But I will find out.'

'DI Friar and I have discussed this and we definitely kept in touch with the SCAS,' said Lulu. 'So yes, we need to find out what went wrong.'

'I have a contact at the National Crime Agency,' said the superintendent. 'I'll take it up with her, see if we can work out what happened. And did you turn up any suspects at all during your investigation?'

'We did,' said Phil. He looked over at DI Friar. 'Do you have another whiteboard?'

16

Phil took a manila file from his briefcase and laid it on the table. He flicked it open. 'During the investigation we had three main names in the frame. We called them the Three Little Piggies.' He looked sheepish. 'Not my idea, I hasten to add.'

He took a photograph from the file and stuck it onto the whiteboard. It was a head-and-shoulders shot of a man in his twenties, with small eyes and a snub nose, his cheeks pockmarked with old acne scars. It had been years since Lulu had seen the photograph, and yes, he did look a bit piggish. 'This is Jack Butler,' said Phil. 'He was our first real suspect. He was a taxi driver and he picked up two of the victims in his car. Not on the days that they died – that would have been too easy. But he drove the first victim about a month before he died and he drove the third victim six days before he was killed. The big red flag, though, was when his DNA was found on the third victim. Specifically under a fingernail. We had him in for questioning and he had a solicitor right from the start. The solicitor pointed out that Butler's DNA could have been transferred from his vehicle, and his vehicle had a dozen or so people a day in it, more at weekends. We argued that he couldn't have got skin cells under his nails by sitting in a taxi, but Butler stuck to his story. In fact, he didn't say a word, he let his solicitor do his talking for him.'

'Which is a red flag in itself,' said DC Townsend.

'Well, it is and it isn't,' said DI Friar. 'People do have the right to silence. And some people really don't trust the police and prefer not to say anything. Silence can never be considered a sign of guilt. We all know the words of the caution: You do not have to say anything. But it may harm your defence if you do not mention when questioned something which you later rely on in court.' She looked at Phil. 'And it never went to court, I assume?'

'Mr Butler died not long after our first interview,' said Phil. 'Killed in his taxi during the course of a robbery. He was lured to a pick-up on an industrial estate and stabbed. His wallet and watch were taken. He had a camera in his cab but it didn't show the killer's face. The fourth murder was not long after Mr Butler's death, which effectively ruled him out as a suspect.'

'But the DNA is still a worry, presumably?' asked DI Friar.

'It's never been explained,' said Phil. 'But DNA is a funny thing, as we all know. Yes, you can say with a very high degree of certainty that two DNA samples came from the same source. But sometimes there can be a perfectly reasonable explanation of how a DNA source got onto a person. If Butler's DNA had been on the rope around the victim's neck, then we would have been on firmer ground.'

'But under the victim's fingernail? That has to be conclusive, right?' said DC Townsend.

'Well, you'd think so,' said Phil. 'But suppose I'm sitting in a Wetherspoons enjoying a pint and a steak. And suppose I'm sitting on a fabric chair. I run my hands over it, I'm shedding skin cells and hair, my DNA is everywhere. The longer I sit there, the more DNA I leave behind. And suppose after I've gone, you sit down in the same place and order a pint and a burger. Now you're sitting in a pile of my DNA. And if for any reason you scratched the fabric chair, well as sure as eggs are eggs my DNA would be under your nails.' He held up his hands. 'Now, I'm not suggesting that Mr Butler and the victim ate at the same Wetherspoons, but DNA is not the definitive proof that it's often portrayed as.'

Phil stuck a second photograph onto the whiteboard. It was also a head-and-shoulders shot of a man in his twenties, overweight and with flushed cheeks. 'Gordon Wallace,' said Phil. 'It was ANPR that led us to him. He's a freelance courier, working for various courier companies when they're short-handed. His registration number was spotted near two of the disposal sites on the days that the bodies were dumped. He was pulled in for questioning both times and, like Mr Butler, he spoke only through his solicitor. His explanation was that he was out on deliveries both days and so was criss-crossing the city all day. He was a firm favourite for several months, and for a while we had him under twenty-four-seven surveillance.'

'Did you check his vehicle?'

'We did, yes. And it was spotless. Too clean, according to the SOCO team that examined it. The interior had been cleaned with bleach. Who does that? Okay, I get that deep cleaning became a thing during Covid, but this was way before that. Mr Wallace's solicitor said that he had a germ phobia and liked to keep his van clean.' Phil shrugged. 'Other than that, he kept his mouth shut.'

'And where is he now?' asked DI Friar.

'Mr Wallace was a drug user and while the investigation was ongoing he got behind the wheel while high and killed a mother and her two kids on the M25,' said Phil. 'He fled the scene but left his van, and the whole thing was captured on CCTV, so it was open and shut. He went down for nine years after pleading guilty to three counts of causing death by dangerous driving. While he was inside, there was another murder in the same style. The fourth murder. So he was no longer a suspect.'

'Nine?' said DI Friar. 'So is he still in prison?'

'I did check, and no, he was released last year. He was remorseful and joined Narcotics Anonymous while he was inside. But he's no longer a person of interest in the serial cases because of the final murder. He had the perfect alibi.'

He stuck a third photograph onto the whiteboard. 'And last, but not least, Mr Edward Parker. It was CCTV footage that put him on our radar. Two of the victims – Mr Hurst and Mr Dunne – were out drinking in Soho the nights before their bodies were found.' Parker was also in his twenties, chubby with slicked-back hair and black-framed spectacles.

'At the same bar?' asked DI Friar.

'That's right. The two victims both visited the same bars on multiple occasions. There was quite a lot of bar-hopping involved in the Soho gay scene at the time, so it didn't seem unusual. But while we were checking footage from various bars for Mr Hurst and Mr Dunne, we realized that Mr Parker would often appear in the same bar, usually within an hour or so of each of them arriving.'

'But Parker didn't leave with the victims?' asked DC Townsend.

'No, and there was no interaction between him and either Mr Hurst or Mr Dunne. He was just there around the same time. We had him in for questioning but – you've guessed it – he let his solicitor talk for him. It was a coincidence, the solicitor said. There are a lot of bars in Soho and a lot of bar-hopping goes on.'

'Is Mr Parker gay?' asked DI Friar.

'He refused to comment on his sexuality. In fact he refused to make any comment at all.'

'Was there any other reason to focus on him, other than the bar-hopping?' asked DI Friar.

'Ah yes, sorry, I should have mentioned that we had phone intel on him, too,' said Phil. 'The second victim was dumped on Wimbledon Common and Mr Parker's phone pinged off a cell phone tower at about the same time as the body was dumped. Admittedly several hundred other phones pinged off the same tower, but he was the only one who also visited the Soho bar where they were last seen.' He held up a hand. 'But yes, circumstantial. As the solicitor kept saying.'

'But you still believe he's the killer?'

'Well, unfortunately, at the time of the second killing, he was speeding on the M1. Caught on camera. Once we realized he had an alibi for the second murder, we stopped trying to connect him to the rest. So no, eventually we reached the conclusion that he couldn't be the Choker.'

'And where is he now?'

'Not long after the fourth killing, he moved to Spain.'

'Is he there now?' asked DI Friar.

'I've put in a request with our team on the Costa del Crime,' said Phil. 'The thing is, the killings stopped five years ago. By then, Mr Parker had left the UK, Mr Wallace was in prison and Mr Butler was dead.'

'Do you think they knew each other?' asked DI Friar. 'The Three Little Piggies?'

'We tried to connect them, but we never found a link between them.'

'I'm sure you've thought of this, but doesn't the fact that the killings stopped when Parker was abroad and Wallace was behind bars suggest that one or both were involved?' said DI Friar.

'Well, as I said, we ruled out Mr Parker when we saw the CCTV of him speeding. He couldn't have committed the second murder. And the final murder occurred when Mr Wallace was in prison. So that ruled him out.'

'They could have been working together,' said DI Friar. 'Wallace could have committed the first murder, they could all have done the second and third together, and then Parker could have done the final murder on his own.'

'We did look at that possibility,' said Lulu. 'But, as Phil said, we could never find a connection between them. We checked their phone records and they never called each other. Wallace lived north of the river in Barking, Butler lived out west in Wandsworth and Parker lived in south London. They never worked at the same jobs, didn't support the same football team, had no similar hobbies or interests.'

'Universities? Schools?'

'None of them went to university, and they attended different schools.'

'Criminal records?'

'Minor shoplifting from Wallace, schoolboy stuff, and then some drug use. Nothing on Parker apart from speeding and parking offences.'

Superintendent Knight got to his feet. 'I guess the question now is, where do we go from here? It looks as if Dickie McNeil was right, we do have a serial killer. And one who has been inactive for five years.'

'Either that or a copycat,' said Lulu.

'But they couldn't have copied the knot from our cases, because that information was never made public,' said Phil. He frowned and looked at the whiteboard. 'Unless the knot is a complete coincidence.'

'I think that's unlikely, but yes, it is a consideration.' The superintendent sighed. 'What we need, obviously, is access to your HOLMES data.'

HOLMES was the Home Office Large Major Enquiry System, actually HOLMES 2, the second version of a computerized case management system originally set up around the United Kingdom in 1985. (Lulu had always thought that the use of Large Major Enquiry was obviously tautological and served no other function than to call to mind the great detective, Sherlock Holmes.) All evidence in a case – including documents, witness statements and CCTV footage – would be entered into the HOLMES database. Detectives could then search the database using sophisticated algorithms, which could often uncover patterns and similarities that the human eye might easily miss. All the data collected as part of the Choker investigation was on the team's HOLMES system in London. DI Friar and her team would be working on their own HOLMES set-up in Manchester. The problem, Lulu knew, was that the two networks were not connected.

'I'm assuming that it's possible to connect our two systems, but does anyone here know for sure?' The superintendent looked around and was faced with blank looks and shaking heads. 'I'll talk to our IT people and see what can be done,' he said. 'Obviously, if we can have access to the Met's HOLMES system, it will make our lives a lot easier. In the meantime, we need to locate both Mr Parker and Mr Wallace and see where they were at the times of our murders. And in view of what DI Jackson has said about the gay connection, we need to take another look at the personal lives of our two victims. We need to tread carefully there, obviously.' He looked over at DI Friar. 'Any thoughts?'

'I'd like to keep a Q&A running here with DI Jackson and Mrs Lewis for a while,' she said. 'I think we have a lot of questions, and in the absence of the HOLMES data I think a Q&A will be helpful.'

'I agree,' said the superintendent. 'I'll leave you to it. I have back-to-back meetings ahead of me.' He smiled and nodded at Lulu. 'Thank you so much for bringing this to our attention, Mrs Lewis,' he said. 'And thank you, DI Jackson, for your time and insight. Hopefully together we can move this forward.' He headed for the doors.

Phil looked around the room. 'Right,' he said. 'Fire away.'

17

The briefing and Q&A session took almost three hours in total. Several of the detectives used their phones to photograph the pictures that Phil had stuck onto the whiteboards. Lulu followed their example and took snaps of the two Manchester victims. Once the briefing was over, DI Friar and DC Townsend took Phil and Lulu along to the canteen. Conrad jumped down off Lulu's shoulders and found sanctuary under a table while they went over to the counter to collect their food.

They all had coffee, and Lulu took a bottle of Evian water and two saucers for Conrad. DI Friar insisted she paid for their food, and they carried their trays over to the table that Conrad had selected. Lulu poured some water for Conrad and put a piece of her fish on the other saucer.

'I didn't want to mention it during the Q&A because I didn't want to muddy the water, but there was a case like this in London in the nineties, wasn't there?' said DI Friar. 'The Gay Slayer?'

'That's right,' said Lulu. 'Colin Ireland. He killed five men, all gay, and there was bondage involved. He was jailed for life in 1993, back when I was still in uniform.'

'I joined some time after, but I remember reading about the case in the papers at the time,' said Phil. 'He died in prison, in 2012.' He looked over at Lulu. 'We did actually look at the case, didn't we?'

'We did, yes. I think for a while we considered that the Choker was copycatting Ireland. We ruled out the idea pretty quickly, but there were definite similarities. Ireland used a noose to strangle his victims, but not the knot that we found. He was meticulous about cleaning up any forensic evidence too. But he didn't dump the bodies, he would leave them where he killed them.'

Superintendent Knight arrived as they were finishing their food. He came over to their table and grimaced. 'Bad news on the SCAS front, I'm afraid,' he said. He pulled over a chair from a neighbouring table and sat down. 'I spoke to my NCA contact and she checked the SCAS data on your four murders. The murders are on file, but there is no mention of the rope or the knot. The cause of death was given as strangulation and there was a note to the effect that a hate crime was a possibility. So when our two killings were put into the database, the London killings weren't shown as having connecting factors.'

Lulu frowned. 'That doesn't make sense,' she said. She looked over at Phil. 'Who would have been responsible for liaising with the NCA?'

'It would have been a junior member of the team,' he said. 'Tommy Cox, maybe.'

'Yes, Tommy Cox. He was desperate to join CID, wasn't he? So we took him on attachment. He wasn't that impressed, I seem to recall. He thought he'd be out chasing villains but he spent his shifts tapping on a keyboard.'

'He actually wanted to be in the Arts and Antiques Squad,' said Phil. 'His degree was in fine arts or something. Last I heard, he was working for the Anti-Corruption Command.'

'Oh my goodness. Well, I can imagine he's worked off his

feet at the moment.' The Anti-Corruption Command's mission was to proactively root out corrupt and abusive officers and staff in the Metropolitan Police. 'I don't suppose you still have his number, do you?'

'I think I do,' said Phil.

Lulu looked at the superintendent. 'Let me talk to him and I'll get back to you.'

'It's not a big issue: we've linked the two sets of killing ourselves so we got there eventually. It would just be nice to know what went wrong.' He forced a smile. 'Better news on the HOLMES front. I've spoken to our IT people and there's no problem linking the two databases. They're working on it now. I'm not exactly computer literate, but from what I understand they can take all the case details on your HOLMES system at the Met and add them to our system here. Then any search on a terminal here will have access to everything on your cases. It's one-way, you won't be able to access our data from London. And anything you enter into HOLMES in London after today won't appear on our terminals. But from the sound of it, you're unlikely to have any new information.'

Phil nodded. 'That's true. We've no open leads at the moment.'

The superintendent stood up. 'Right, I'll leave you in the capable hands of DI Friar.' He nodded and walked away.

Phil finished his pie and chips and took out his phone. He scrolled through his address book and grinned. 'Yeah, I've got Tommy Cox's number. Detective Sergeant Cox now, I might add. Shall I give him a call?'

'It might be better if I do it. You're still in the job so he might assume it's an official complaint.'

'That makes sense,' said Phil. He showed her the screen and Lulu tapped the number into her phone.

The ringing tone sounded and within a few seconds DS Cox answered.

'Tommy, long time no talk,' said Lulu. 'It's Lulu Lewis. Detective Superintendent Lewis. Retired.'

'Boss, yes, how are you?'

'All good, Tommy. Sorry to call you out of the blue, but I've got a question that needs answering about four murders we worked on, back in the day.'

'The Choker?'

'Exactly. It's now a cold case and I'm in Manchester with DI Jackson on what might be a lead. Tommy, when you were on the team, you liaised with the NCA regarding the Serious Crime Analysis Section, right?'

'Absolutely, yes. Is there a problem, boss?'

Lulu could hear the tension creeping into Cox's voice; he was obviously expecting the worst. She kept her voice soft and light. 'No, no, it's not a problem. I'll tell you what it is. There have been two similar killings in Manchester involving a similar sort of rope and the same knot, but the Manchester cops didn't get a hit on SCAS. We've checked and SCAS doesn't have the rope and knot details.'

DS Cox went quiet for a few seconds, and then he made a humming noise. 'I'm pretty sure I was told not to make the details of the rope and the knot public, boss,' he said eventually. 'The plan was to withhold the details so we could use them if and when we had a suspect.'

Lulu immediately realized what had happened. 'Ah, okay,' she said.

'That's what you wanted, right?'

Clearly Lulu's instructions had been misinterpreted. Yes, details of the rope weren't to be made public, but they very much should have been shared with SCAS. But it was a long time ago and a lot of water had passed under the bridge since then. 'That's fine, Tommy. I just wanted to check what information they had been given.'

'Everything but details of the rope and the knot,' said DS Cox. 'So do you think it's the same guy?'

'There are a lot of similarities,' said Lulu.

'Well a copycat isn't likely because we withheld the rope details.'

'Exactly.'

'I hope you get the guy, boss.'

'Me too, Tommy. Thanks for the info.'

'Give my best to DI Jackson.'

'I will.'

Lulu ended the call and put the phone into her handbag. 'Tommy didn't pass the rope details on to SCAS,' she said to DI Friar. 'That explains why you didn't get a hit.'

'Why didn't he pass them on?' asked Phil.

Lulu smiled tightly. 'I think there was some confusion about what "going public" meant. He assumed that we were keeping the information totally to ourselves. To be honest, I should have checked that he'd done as asked.'

'You can't second-guess everybody, boss.'

'Well, he was young and inexperienced.' She held up a hand. 'But it's not a problem. We've linked the cases now; at most it's cost us a few days.'

DI Friar finished her meal and moved on to her coffee. 'What do you two want to do for the rest of the day?' she asked.

'I hate to ask, but would you mind if I looked through the decision log, just to get a feeling of how far you've got?' Lulu asked. 'I'd quite understand if you said no – I don't want you to think I'm looking over your shoulder.'

'I'd be delighted,' said DI Friar. 'It'd be useful to have a fresh pair of eyes looking at the investigation. And you should both start looking at what we have on HOLMES.' She looked across at DC Townsend. 'I'm wondering if it would help if Mrs Lewis and DI Jackson had a look at the places where the victims were dumped.'

'I could run them out tomorrow,' said DC Townsend. 'I could pick them up at their hotel first thing.'

'Oh, we're not staying together,' said Lulu. 'I'm on my narrowboat, moored at Castlefield. But I can get to the Midland bright and early. Also, I wondered if there was any way you could allow DI Jackson and me to talk to the relatives of the two victims?'

DI Friar grimaced. 'Much as I appreciate your input, you're a civilian now.'

'Very much so. But you could introduce me as a consultant. The Met used me as a consultant after I retired – including on the Choker case – so it's not my first rodeo, as they say. And if you get any pushback, I can leave. I just think it might be helpful to know where the victims came from. I'd be looking for similarities with the victims we had in London.'

DI Friar nodded. 'Yes, I get it. And I'm not against the idea, not in principle. But I'd have to clear it with Superintendent Knight first.'

'Of course you would,' said Lulu. 'I'd do exactly the same if I was in your position.'

DI Friar sat back in her chair and folded her arms. 'What's your gut feeling about this?' she asked. 'Is it the same killer, picking up where he left off? Or is it a copycat?'

'Five years is a long time for a hiatus,' said Lulu. 'Most serial killers are driven by the urge to take lives, and over time the urge gets stronger. So usually the time intervals between killings gets shorter. Or they stop completely. I mean, Jack the Ripper was never caught. He just stopped. And there was a serial killer they called Bible John in Glasgow during the sixties. Bible John killed three brunette women and then stopped. There are lots of examples of serial killers in the US who killed and then stopped. The Zodiac Killer, for example. They probably either die, or they end up behind bars for something else. But what has happened here is very unusual. To stop suddenly and then restart years later in a different part of the country – I've not heard of that happening before.'

'Me neither,' said DI Friar.

'Maybe he was sick, and recovered,' said DC Townsend. 'Or was in prison and has recently been released. I like the sound of this Gordon Wallace. The killings stopped when he was in prison and now that he's out, the killings have started again.'

'He's definitely got to be looked at,' said DI Friar.

'And this Edward Parker, the guy who moved to Spain,' said DC Townsend. 'It'd be handy if we could find out if there were any similar killings in Spain while he was there.'

'Oh, that's a good thought,' said Lulu. She looked at DI Friar. 'How easy is that to do, post-Brexit?'

'Not as easy as it used to be,' said DI Friar. 'But the NCA still cooperates with Europol so we can definitely check that out. But I don't want to focus on those two just yet. For a start, as DI Jackson said, each of them can be ruled out of at least one of your killings. And there are loads of reasons why a killer might start and restart. An illness. An injury that temporarily affects mobility. Marriage to a spouse who keeps a close eye on him. Financial reasons. Loses his job so he can't afford to run a vehicle. Maybe it's job related.'

'Could be a soldier who gets sent overseas,' said DC Townsend. 'An engineer who gets sent on a large project in another country.'

'He could be a journalist,' said DI Friar. 'Maybe he worked for a newspaper in London, so that's where he killed. Then he starts work for a newspaper overseas and drops off our radar. Maybe he kills wherever he is, but we don't hear about it. Then he moves to Manchester to work for a newspaper here, and starts killing again.' Her face broke into a grin and she looked over at DC Townsend.

'Dickie McNeil,' they both said at the same time, and they laughed.

DI Friar waved a hand at Lulu. 'Obviously it's not Dickie, although I love the idea that it might be. But I don't want to narrow down our list of suspects at the moment; I'd be happier keeping an open mind.'

'I take your point,' said Lulu. 'There are a whole host of reasons why a serial killer might stop killing and then start again. If we knew why, we'd be a lot closer to knowing who.'

18

The taxi pulled up in front of the Midland Hotel. The massive Victorian building sat like a faded aristocrat amid the bustling city streets. A grand testament to a bygone era. Its red-brick facade had been professionally cleaned but it was weathered by the passage of time; Lulu could easily imagine men in top hats and women in fur-trimmed coats popping in for afternoon tea while their horse-drawn carriages waited outside.

'Do you want to come in for a bite to eat, on my expense account?' asked Phil. 'It's the least the police can do for you tipping them off about this case.' DI Friar had offered a car to run them home, but Phil had explained that he was on expenses and more than happy to use a minicab.

They had spent the afternoon and a good part of the evening going through DI Friar's decision log and the HOLMES data. The decision log had been pretty much faultless, a textbook example of how to run a murder investigation, from the initial preservation of the murder scenes and the identification of the victims through to the investigation phase and the case management phase. DI Friar had done everything by the book but still had no suspects. A canvass for witnesses and CCTV footage hadn't produced anything useful and the murders appeared to be motiveless. Random killings were always the hardest to solve, as Lulu knew from experience.

'I'm not sure they'll allow Conrad into the restaurant,'

said Lulu. Conrad was lying in her lap. His eyes were closed but she could tell from his breathing that he wasn't asleep.

'I'll flash my warrant card and say that he's a police cat,' said Phil.

Lulu looked at her watch. 'Well, I suppose it is wine o'clock,' she said.

'Let's have a drink and maybe a bite and then I'll walk you home. Where did you park?'

Lulu laughed. 'I moored at what they call the Staffordshire arm of the Castlefield Basin, between the Bridgewater Canal and the Rochdale Canal. I can stay there for seventy-two hours. It's a short walk from here.'

'Perfect, then. A drink, a bite and a walk.'

'You've talked me into it,' said Lulu, smiling.

Phil paid the driver and asked for a receipt.

'What shall I make the receipt out for?' asked the driver.

'The fare,' said Phil. 'That'll be fine.'

'Suit yourself. Most people like to turn a profit,' said the driver. He scribbled out a receipt and handed it to Phil.

A tram rattled past as they climbed out of the cab and walked into the hotel, with Conrad sitting on Lulu's shoulders. Phil was carrying his briefcase and holdall. 'You could have arrested him for conspiracy to commit fraud, right there and then,' said Lulu.

'I held myself back,' said Phil.

The reception desk was to the right and there was a champagne bar to the left, with wicker seats and potted plants giving it a Mediterranean feel. 'Oh, this looks nice,' said Lulu.

'Let's grab a seat and order drinks, then I'll check in,' said Phil. They found a free table at the far side of the bar. There was a group of middle-aged men in suits at the table to their left, drinking cocktails, and two elderly women sipping martinis to their right. Conrad jumped down onto one of the chairs and settled down, nose to tail. A young waiter in a white shirt and black trousers and waistcoat came over and Lulu ordered a glass of Chardonnay. Phil asked for a pint of Guinness.

The waiter shrugged apologetically. 'I'm sorry, sir. No Guinness.'

'A pint of bitter will be fine, then.'

'No draught beer, I'm afraid. We do have bottled Peroni.'

Phil managed to smile politely. 'Maybe bring me two,' he said.

'And if it's not too much trouble, a bowl of Evian water for Conrad,' said Lulu. 'He really doesn't like the taste of tap water.'

'Who does?' said the waiter. He leaned towards Lulu and lowered his voice. 'Hotel policy is that animals aren't allowed in the bars or restaurants,' he said in a soft Irish accent. 'My policy is that if they stay out of sight, they're grand.' He winked and walked away.

'Sorry about this, Conrad,' said Lulu. She picked him up and put him under the table. He meowed but curled up into a ball again.

'In my experience, most animals are better behaved than many people,' Phil commented.

'You are preaching to the converted,' said Lulu. She looked around the bar. 'This is nice,' she said.

'It is,' agreed Phil.

'And this is where Mr Rolls met Mr Royce?'

'Allegedly. There are two commemorative plaques outside the building saying that, so it must be true.' He gestured at his holdall and briefcase. 'Why don't you wait here while I check in and freshen up? Then we'll get something to eat.'

'Go ahead,' said Lulu. Phil picked up his bags and headed to reception.

As he left, the waiter returned with their drinks on a tray. He put the two bottles of Peroni in front of Phil's seat, gave the glass of Chardonnay to Lulu, then bent down and slid a bowl of water under the table. 'Out of sight, out of mind,' he whispered to Lulu.

Lulu was halfway through her glass of wine when Phil came back. The businessmen at the next table were discussing sales targets, and Conrad had stayed quiet, curled up on the floor next to the bowl of water. 'All done,' said Phil, as he dropped down into his chair. He picked up one of the bottles and toasted her. 'First today,' he said and took a swig.

'How's the room?'

'Very nice,' he said. 'I won't complain if they tell me to stay for a week or so.'

'Do you think that's likely?'

'The powers that be would really like to catch the Choker,' said Phil. 'And that won't happen without new evidence. Plus we've got the fact that one of the latest victims is a former Met cop.'

'Have you told the Met that yet?'

Phil shook his head. 'The super will be off home already and he doesn't like being phoned out of hours. I'll talk to him first thing.'

'And you're okay if I accompany you with DC Townsend tomorrow to check out the crime scenes?'

'Of course. You visited all the London crime scenes – they need your experience.'

'I'm just very conscious that I'm a civilian, Phil. And retired. They can justify having you around – you're a serving officer – but they could get into trouble involving a civilian in active cases. Especially with that journalist sniffing around.'

'They need your insight, boss. No question. I might even be able to swing a consultancy fee for you, same as we did when we brought you back last time They really want this guy caught. It's not exactly a "money no object" situation, but the fact that they've put me up in the Midland suggests that they're not counting the pennies.'

'I don't want paying, Phil,' said Lulu. 'But I really do want to catch this guy. I put hundreds of hours of my life into the investigation back then and it all came to nothing. Be nice if we could get a result after all this time.'

'We'll give it our best shot, boss,' said Phil, and he took another pull on his bottle. He grimaced. 'I've never been a fan of Italian beer,' he said. 'But I suppose beggars can't be choosers.'

Lulu sighed and settled back in her chair. 'I don't need the money, Phil, but I do need a favour.'

He raised his bottle in salute. 'Ask and you shall receive, boss.'

'It's personal, but I suspect there may be a crime involved. Just so you know.'

'We're well past the stage of you having to explain yourself,' said Phil. 'What do you need?'

Lulu had to fight the urge to reach over and hug him. He was such a good-hearted man, so dependable and reliable. She had been lucky to work with him and she was luckier still that they had remained friends. 'A friend of mine is being courted by a guy she met on a dating app, and there's something not right about him,' she said. 'He says he's got investments, mainly in Ireland, but he's light on details. And he's pressing my friend to marry him.'

'You've met him?'

'Last night. He cooked an amazing lamb tagine.'

'With apricots?'

'Oh, yes.'

'Yummy. I love a good lamb tagine. So what's the problem?'

The problem was that Conrad had seen Jeremy's aura and decided that he was up to no good. But Lulu could hardly tell Phil that. 'Copper's intuition,' she said.

'Your instincts have always been good, boss. Remember that guy who killed his landlady in Kilburn? Butter wouldn't melt in his mouth, he was so shaken up, remember? Said he'd found the body when he came back from a night in the pub. You said right from the start that he'd done it but there was no forensics and he had alibi witnesses for the time we thought the lady died. Three weeks later and we found out that you were right.'

'He just seemed off,' said Lulu. 'Especially when he thought we weren't watching him. It was like he was performing for an audience. Jeremy is the same. It's an act, I'm sure. A good act, but an act nevertheless.'

'What's his full name?'

'Jeremy Connolly.'

'Have you googled him?'

'Yes, and there's nothing. Nothing on social media, either. There are nine Jeremy Connollys on LinkedIn but none are him. A few more on Facebook but most of them are in America. This guy is a ghost.'

'What about family members attending the wedding?'

'He has a brother and sister in Australia – allegedly – so they wouldn't be able to make it.'

'Friends?'

'Mostly in Ireland or overseas. He mentioned a friend by the name of Seamus Gannon in Dublin. And he doesn't want to make a fuss, he says. He just wants to put a ring on her finger. A small, quiet, low-key ceremony at a register office.'

'And you're worried about what? Bigamy?'

'She's quite well off, Phil. Her husband worked for the BBC for many years, so there's a decent pension. Plus he was good with money and made a few shrewd investments over the years. He also bought a villa in Spain and inherited a cottage in Norfolk. Jeremy knows what she's worth, but she has no idea what – if anything – he has.'

'So she's worried that he's after her money?'

Lulu nodded.

'Not much of a basis for marriage, is it?' said Phil. 'Trust is pretty much the prime requisite, I would have thought. Not that I'm an expert, of course.'

'You reach an age where these things matter,' said Lulu. 'She loves him, I'm sure of that. But she knows she has a lot to lose. If he marries her and they divorce later, she could lose half of everything. More than a million pounds in assets.'

'So get him to sign a prenup.'

'He's okay with that. In fact, he suggested it.'

'So what's the problem?'

'His idea of a prenup is that if they get divorced they each take what they brought into the marriage. But in the event of him dying, he wants Jane to inherit everything. He says he wants to make sure that she's provided for.'

'Well, that's sweet of him.'

'That's one way of looking at it. The other way, of course, is that if there's a quid pro quo and she dies, he'll get everything.'

Phil's eyes narrowed. 'You think that's his plan?' He grimaced. 'That's cold, boss. Ice cold.'

'I don't know what he's thinking, Phil. That's why I need your help. It might be that he is head over heels in love with Jane and wants to spend the rest of his life with her. That's what she hopes, and she worries that by doubting him now she might spoil things. So she's asked me to do the doubting for her, and unfortunately when I met him, I wasn't convinced that he's genuine. At times we felt he was acting.'

Phil frowned. 'We?'

Lulu nodded at Conrad. 'Conrad didn't seem to be taken with him. And he's a very good judge of character.'

'One sure way of finding out is to insist that he signs a prenup that guarantees he gets nothing in the event of her death.'

'Indeed, yes,' said Lulu. 'But first of all that's tantamount to saying that she suspects him of planning to kill her. And second of all, what if she does insist on that and he walks away? If he really is planning to kill for money, what's to say that he won't target someone else? And maybe next time the victim won't have a friend who was a superintendent with the Met.'

'What did you think when you met him? Did he look like a murderer to you?'

'No, of course not. But they never do, do they? Ted Bundy was charming and presentable. And I'm sure most of Harold Shipman's patients thought he was simply lovely right up until the point he injected them with diamorphine.'

'But you think he's not right?'

Lulu nodded. 'You can see where we're going with this. Guy meets a lonely widow on a dating app, weaves his spell on her, and a few months later . . .' She forced a smile. 'It's probably nothing, but to put my mind at rest I'd like you to run some checks.'

'I will, Lulu. I'll run him through the Police National Computer and any other databases that come to mind.'

'You're a star, Phil.'

'Least I can do, boss.' He drained his bottle. 'And I promised you food.'

'Yes, you did.'

19

It was only a fifteen-minute walk from the Midland Hotel to *The Lark*, most of it down the city's main thoroughfare, Deansgate. Phil insisted on walking her back, even though Lulu had told him that Manchester was much safer than London and she walked everywhere in London. He smoked a cigarette as they walked. Conrad rode on her shoulders and attracted lots of looks and smiles.

'So do you think this really is the Choker?' asked Phil.

'I wouldn't have asked you to come up to Manchester if I didn't,' said Lulu. 'That knot is just so specific.'

'It is, but as we both know, it's a knot used by hundreds of thousands of sailors every day.'

'But the fact that the victims were dumped naked, with rope marks on their wrists and ankles, is another similarity that really can't be a coincidence. And it can't be a copycat because we never released details of the knot.'

Phil nodded. 'If it is, I really want to get him this time.'

'We really wanted to get him last time,' said Lulu.

'I know. But now we have a second chance.'

'We did everything right last time, Phil. We covered all the bases and ticked all the boxes. We didn't miss anything. I worry that DI Friar might do all the right things, too. And still not catch him.'

'The more victims we have, the more likely we are to find something that identifies the killer.'

'That is certainly true. When I first spoke to DI Friar and realized it was almost certainly the Choker, my first thought was that we had been given a second chance and that we need to grab it. But then I wondered whether we are any more likely to catch him this time.'

'Let's try to stay optimistic, boss,' said Phil.

'I'll do my best. What's your take on DI Friar?'

'First-class detective. Good people skills. Good instincts. She reminds me of you.'

'No need to sweet-talk me, Phil. I've retired, remember?'

'I'm serious, boss. She's very like you were. Driven, but knows when to cut her people some slack. And she's not afraid of advice or criticism. She had no problems at all letting us look through her decision log. A lot of SIOs don't like outsiders looking at their logs. And whenever either of us makes a suggestion, she listens and takes it on board. She never seems threatened.'

'DC Pete Townsend hadn't heard of The Who.'

Phil laughed out loud. 'Well, the policemen are getting younger,' he said. 'It's the way of the world.'

They reached the towpath and stopped to let a man with two pit bulls walk by. Lulu could feel Conrad stiffen at the sight of the two muscular dogs and she gave him a reassuring pat.

They walked along to *The Lark*. Lulu climbed on board and unlocked the door to the cabin. 'Thanks so much for walking us back, Phil,' she said. Conrad jumped down onto the rear deck seat and meowed at him. 'Conrad thanks you, too,' said Lulu.

'You're both very welcome,' said Phil. 'So what's the plan for tomorrow? I feel I should be in bright and early, make a good impression.'

'I'm hoping that Superintendent Knight will let us talk to the relatives of the two Manchester victims,' said Lulu. 'And maybe check to see if there's a gay connection. Do you think he would allow me to get involved?'

'I don't see why not. You worked on the London murders; your expertise has to be useful. If you're with me I can show my warrant card and identify you as a consultant.' He grinned at Conrad. 'I'm not sure how we explain away your constant companion, but I'm sure we'll manage.'

Lulu nodded at the door. 'Fancy another nightcap?'

He laughed and put up his hands. 'I'd love to, boss. But I want to make an early start in the morning. I'm told the Midland does a superb full English so I want to give that a try. Why don't you meet me at the hotel and we'll cab it to the HQ?'

'Perfect,' said Lulu. 'And thank you again for escorting us home.'

Phil threw her a mock salute. 'All part of the service, boss,' he said. He turned and walked back along the towpath.

Lulu and Conrad went down into the cabin. Lulu locked the door behind them. Conrad jumped up on the sofa and looked at her. 'You've never done that before,' he said. 'You always used to leave the door open.'

'Better safe than sorry.'

'The police have arrested him. He's going back to prison.'

'I know. And you're right. But he got onto *The Lark* and barged in, no pun intended. So I'll sleep easier with the doors locked.'

'I'll protect you.'

Lulu smiled. 'I know you will.' She bent down and stroked him behind the ears and he purred contentedly.

'Phil is a lovely man,' he said.

'One of the best.'

'Is he married?'

'No. He has girlfriends, though. Women love him, he's just not the sort to settle down and has never wanted children. And he was focused on his career for the longest time. Not so much these days, but the habit is engrained.'

Lulu took a bottle of Evian water out of the fridge, poured some into a bowl and placed it in front of him. 'Chamomile tea,' he said.

Lulu frowned as she replaced the bottle in the fridge. 'Excuse me?'

'You were wondering if you should open a bottle of wine or make some chamomile tea, and I think the tea would be better for you. It'll help you sleep.'

Lulu's frown deepened. 'So you read my mind?'

Conrad chuckled. 'I read your body language. When you took the bottle of Evian water from the fridge, you looked at the bottles of wine there, and you hesitated. Then when you went back to the fridge, you looked at the jar where you keep your chamomile teabags, and you hesitated again. You were weighing up your options.'

'You have very keen eyes.'

'What can I say? I'm a cat.'

'Yes, you are. A very insightful cat. And, as usual, you are quite right.' She switched on the kettle and placed a chamomile teabag in a mug.

'I remember you talking about the reasons that people commit murder,' said Conrad. 'There was a top ten list, you said.'

'There was, and is,' said Lulu. She sat down on the sofa

next to him. 'There's nothing new under the sun.' She frowned. 'Who said that?'

'It's in the Bible,' said Conrad. 'In the Book of Ecclesiastes. "The thing that hath been, it is that which shall be; and that which is done is that which shall be done: and there is no new thing under the sun." It's nonsense, of course. There are always new things being created. Mobile phones. Facial recognition systems. DNA testing. Investigating crime is changing all the time, isn't it, because of new technologies?'

'That's true,' said Lulu. 'Things change, but people and the way they behave tend to stay the same.'

'And did you run the top ten motives through the killings you had in London?'

Lulu nodded. 'I did. We ruled out the number-one motive, sex or love, because the victims had no romantic or sexual connection to their killers; not that we could find, anyway. Number two is greed, and so far as I remember no one benefited financially from the deaths. The victims might well have been robbed, because we never found their clothes or wallets, but it would be unusual to go to all that trouble over a simple mugging.'

'Which brings us to number three,' said Conrad. 'Revenge.'

'You have a very good memory,' said Lulu.

'Yes, I do,' said Conrad. 'And catlike reflexes.'

Lulu chuckled. 'We couldn't find anyone that any of the victims had been having problems with,' she said. 'They all lived quietly, no disputes with anyone that we could find.'

'And number four. To hide a secret. The victim knows something damaging about the killer, or maybe has been blackmailing him. The killer knows that the secret dies along with the victim.'

'Again, could four totally separate men have known the same secret? They weren't friends, we couldn't find any connections between them.'

'You checked their phones?'

'Of course. And social media. They weren't connected.'

'So number five. Hatred.'

'Yes, that seemed to be a possibility. Three of the victims were gay and there was some doubt about the fourth. But perhaps the killer thought that he was gay. So then we would have had a serial killer targeting gay men.'

'The two victims here in Manchester weren't gay.'

'Well, that's what DI Friar said. But both victims could have been concealing their sexuality. They could have had double lives. I'll raise it with DI Friar tomorrow.'

'So you're definitely working on the case?'

'I wouldn't say that,' said Lulu. 'I'm retired, remember? But I might be able to help. Anyway, that brings us to number six: a crime of passion. An argument develops, someone loses their temper and lashes out and someone dies in the heat of the moment. These weren't crimes of passion, these were well planned and thought out.'

'Number seven, to protect someone you love,' said Conrad.

'We had no evidence that any of our victims were a threat to anyone,' said Lulu. 'None of them had a criminal record, they were all just regular citizens. Okay, so, number eight, killing a family member. Not in these cases: all the family members checked out.'

'Most people are killed by friends or family, right?' said Conrad.

'Certainly in the vast majority of cases, the victim knows their killer, that's true.'

'So if the killer knew all four victims, they would have known him. Which means that the victims would have been connected.'

'But they weren't, so far as we can see. And how likely is it that they were also connected to the two victims here in Manchester? That's one of the things I can probably help with. We need to find a link between the four men murdered in London and the two victims here in Manchester.'

'And motive number nine was status, you said.'

Lulu nodded. 'That's right. Someone kills a colleague so they can get his job; by killing the person, they move up in the world. But that didn't appear to apply to the London murders.' She smiled. 'Which brings us to number ten,' she said.

'Crazy people.'

'Yes, crazy people,' Lulu said. 'Motiveless killings. Senseless violence. The mentally ill are usually the easiest to catch because so little thought goes into what they do. But as I said, these killings seem to have been well planned. And that can be the hardest sort of killer to catch. An intelligent, efficient, organized crazy person.'

'Is that an official term?' asked Conrad. 'Organized crazy person?'

Lulu chuckled. 'No, it isn't. Sociopath or psychopath would be the technical terms, I suppose. Someone who can kill without empathy, perhaps someone who gets pleasure or sexual gratification from killing, and they are often the hardest killers to catch. More often than not they continue to kill until they get caught. Killers like the Yorkshire Ripper or Fred West.'

'But if this is the same killer, he did stop,' said Conrad. 'For five years.'

'Yes, and if we could find out why he stopped and started again we'd be a lot closer to identifying him.'

'I'm sure you'll work it out,' said Conrad. 'I have faith in you.'

Lulu smiled. 'That's such a nice thing to say.'

'I mean it.'

'I know you do, that's what makes it so nice.'

20

Lulu woke at sunrise. She pulled on a sweatshirt and jeans and made herself a cup of coffee. Conrad sat on the sofa and watched her. 'So what's the plan for today?' he asked.

'We have to move *The Lark*,' she said. 'We're only allowed to moor here for seventy-two hours and this is our third day here.'

'What happens if you don't move? Do they clamp you?'

Lulu chuckled as she poured milk into her coffee. 'No, but I'd receive a strongly worded letter from the Canal and River Trust. And if I continued to flout the rules, they could take away my licence.'

'But how would they know?'

'Oh, they check. They have people patrolling all the time, checking that boats have valid licences and that they aren't abusing the mooring restrictions.'

She took her mug of coffee out onto the rear deck and started the engine. A cloud of grey smoke billowed from the exhaust and then the engine settled into its comforting phut-phut-phut sound, like the resonant heartbeat of some giant mythical creature. Conrad followed her. The *Bee Happy* had moved and two other narrowboats had moored on the right-hand section. There were four boats and plenty of spaces on the left-hand section.

'Can't you just move over there?' asked Conrad.

Lulu looked at him in surprise. 'You just read my mind again.'

Conrad sighed. 'I read your body language,' he said. 'You looked at where the *Bee Happy* was, then you looked over at the boats on the right-hand side and frowned. It wasn't hard to follow your train of thought.'

Lulu laughed. 'You do read me like an open book,' she said.

'So can we do that? Just move *The Lark* over there?'

'I'm really not sure,' said Lulu. 'You're not allowed just to move back and forth between mooring spots, that much I do know. And I know that the Canal and River Trust have to be satisfied that you are continually cruising. But their guidance is that you must travel at least twenty miles over the duration of your licence. Obviously *The Lark* has done way more than that.' She sipped her coffee. 'I can't moor in the basin because that's only for permanent licences. I suppose I could take her back down the Bridgewater Canal, but it is so convenient here. And there are plenty of moorings – it's not as if we'd be taking someone else's space.'

'Plus you are here for a very good reason,' said Conrad. 'You're trying to catch a killer.'

'The Canal and River Trust doesn't take things like that into consideration,' said Lulu. 'But I don't see that we'll have a problem. If they do check, they'll see that at least I made the effort to move.'

She put down her mug of coffee and jumped off *The Lark* to untie the lines. It took her less than three minutes to move the boat to the left-hand section and another minute to tie up the lines again. 'Job done,' she said, stepping back onto the rear deck.

'I wish I could help,' said Conrad.

'Oh, you help me in lots of ways,' said Lulu. She looked

at her watch. 'Right, I'll shower and change, then we can go and have breakfast with Phil.'

'Sounds like a plan,' said Conrad. 'I shall have a cat wash while I'm waiting.'

Lulu spent a few minutes tidying up the saloon and bedroom, then she showered, towelled herself dry and pulled on a Ted Baker dress that she used to wear when she was a detective chief inspector. She took pride in the fact that it still fitted perfectly. She topped the dress with a Burberry jacket.

'Well, you look amazing,' said Conrad when she went back onto the rear deck.

'Why, thank you, kind sir,' said Lulu. 'I thought I should try to look as professional as possible.'

Lulu locked the doors and stepped off the boat, then bent down so that Conrad could jump onto her shoulders. She walked to the Midland and joined Phil in the hotel's restaurant. They both had the full English and coffee and chatted about the Choker case. Lulu's memory was generally razor-sharp, but it had been five years since she'd had any involvement with the case, so she had quite a few questions for Phil, some of which required him to dip into his briefcase. Conrad lay under her chair and Lulu slipped him a saucer with a piece of sausage and a strip of bacon on it. They were just finishing when Phil's mobile buzzed. 'DC Townsend is outside,' he said.

'I thought we were cabbing it,' said Lulu.

'Sorry, he sent me a text earlier saying that he'd pick us up and show us the sites where the bodies were dumped. Superintendent Knight has given us the green light.' He signed the bill and they headed out. DC Townsend was waiting for them in a white Toyota Corolla. Phil climbed into the front passenger seat and Lulu got into the back with Conrad.

'So how is it, the Midland?' asked DC Townsend as he pulled away from the kerb.

'Perfect,' said Phil. 'You know it's where Mr Rolls met Mr Royce?'

DC Townsend laughed. 'I'm afraid that might be apocryphal,' he said as he braked to allow a tram to go by.

'There are two plaques to that effect.'

'Yes, I've seen them. But if you do a little digging it seems not to be as clear cut as that. The man who originally went public with the meeting was a friend of Rolls and he actually said they went to Great Central Hotel. No one mentioned the Midland Hotel by name. But there never has been a Great Central Station in Manchester. So people assumed that he had meant the Midland. But, as we all know, assumptions can often be wrong. The man who relayed the story said that Mr Rolls caught the morning train from London, which would have arrived at what we now call Piccadilly Station. Traffic back then was way worse than it is now; it would have been a half-hour taxi ride from there to the Midland. But across the road from the station was the Great Central Refreshment Rooms, so it's much more likely he met Mr Royce for lunch there and that the guy who told the story just mixed up the names.' He grinned. 'But who knows?'

'You seem to know an awful lot about this,' said Lulu.

DC Townsend chuckled. 'I did it as a history project at school,' he said. 'I was car-mad in those days and heard the story about Rolls and Royce and decided to do it for my history project. It made me realize that just because someone says something is true doesn't mean it's necessarily so.'

'That's very true,' said Lulu. She smiled. 'Though of course I see the irony in my saying that.'

'But you know what I mean, right?' said DC Townsend. 'Eyewitness testimony is the most unreliable of all. People believe that something happened but often there is no way that it could have taken place in the way they remember. It happens all the time with road traffic accidents. Eyewitnesses will swear blind that a white car crashed into a blue van but in fact it was a white van hitting a green minibus. It's actually what made me become a police officer.'

'The search for the truth?'

'I know, it sounds ridiculous when you say it that way. But, yes, looking at the whole Rolls Royce thing was like an investigation and I had so much fun doing it that I began to think about becoming a detective.'

'And now, here you are,' said Lulu.

DC Townsend nodded. 'Yes, indeed. Here I am.'

'Is this your first murder investigation?'

'Gosh, no. My fifth, actually. Well, fifth and sixth, since we have two bodies. We have more than ninety homicides a year in Greater Manchester, more than half of them in the city itself. Not far behind London and about the same as Birmingham.'

'Most of it gang- and drug-related?' asked Phil.

DC Townsend nodded. 'Unfortunately, yes.' He stopped at a red light. 'So, we'll drive south to Stretford Meadows, where the first body was dumped. Then I'll take you to Heaton Park golf course. I'm not sure there'll be much to see: our forensics people are finished with both scenes. Then DI Friar said I should run you back to HQ and we'll see how they're getting on with the HOLMES data dump.'

'What I'd really like to do is talk to the relatives of the victims,' said Lulu. 'Ideally the ex-wife of Fraser Robinson and the wife of Sergeant Sawyer.'

'Widow,' said DC Townsend.

'Yes, right. Of course. His widow.'

'I'd have to check that with DI Friar.'

'Of course, yes. It's just that, as we're out and about, it might make sense to get everything done on the one day.'

'I'll call her,' said DC Townsend.

They drove for fifteen minutes, heading south on the M60. When they left the motorway, they drove for almost a mile, then pulled into a parking area. DC Townsend stopped the car and switched off the engine. 'So, here we are,' he said. 'We're actually in Stretford now, which is in the borough of Trafford, but it's still Greater Manchester. We've got the River Mersey to the south and Stretford to the north. The park covers about fifty hectares and has meadows, woodland and wetland.'

'What is fifty hectares in old money?' asked Lulu.

DC Townsend frowned. 'Old money?'

'Acres,' said Lulu. 'I still think in acres.'

'Fifty hectares is about a hundred and twenty acres, boss,' said Phil, twisting around in his seat.

'The park is popular with birdwatchers, walkers and cyclists,' said DC Townsend. 'It was a dog walker who found the body.' He climbed out of the car and Lulu and Phil followed him. Conrad jumped out too and padded behind them. It felt as if they were in the countryside; they were surrounded by high hedges and trees and the ground was muddy underfoot, but they could hear the hum of traffic on the motorway behind them. Phil lit a cigarette and blew smoke up at the clouds. 'First today,' he sighed.

'I thought you were giving up,' said Lulu.

'Cutting back rather than giving up,' he said. 'I'm down to ten a day. I was on two packs a day when I was working with you.'

'Working with me was that stressful, was it?'

Phil laughed. 'Nah, they were just a lot cheaper then. Six or seven quid a pack. Those were the days.'

'My dad was a smoker,' said Lulu. 'Park Drive. A pack of twenty used to cost five bob. He'd send me to the corner shop to buy them when I was a kid.' She laughed. 'Can you imagine doing that now? Sending your kids to buy cigarettes. You'd have the long arm of the law knocking on your door before you could say "exploitation of minors". The world was different back then.'

'Yeah, lung cancer rates were a lot higher, for one thing,' said Phil. He held out his cigarette. 'But smoking makes me feel good. It just does.'

'Five bob?' said DC Townsend.

Lulu chuckled. 'Five shillings. That's twenty-five pence in new money.'

'And they really let kids buy cigarettes?'

'If they knew your parents, sure. As I said, it was a different world back then.'

'I'd say so,' said DC Townsend. He gestured ahead. 'This way,' he said. He took them through a gap in a hedge and along a path that led through a grassy field. In the distance was a clump of trees. Lulu began silently to count off her footsteps and she had reached fifty-eight by the time they arrived at the trees. DC Townsend stopped and pointed. 'The body was found here,' he said. 'We had crime scene tape up for a couple of days but the forensic team didn't find anything so it was reopened to the public.' He pointed at a dozen or so bunches of wilting flowers leaning against a tree. There were cards on several of the bouquets. *RIP Fraser. Gone But Not Forgotten. Taken Too Soon.* 'Those are from well-wishers.'

'Did you check them out?' asked Phil.

'We send someone up every evening, and if there's a card we try to find out who left it. We did have the area under surveillance for a couple of days in case the killer came back to reminisce, but nothing came of it.'

'And is there anything special about this bit of the park?' asked Phil. 'Anything happen here before?'

DC Townsend shook his head. 'Nothing.'

Lulu looked around. The road and the parking area were out of sight but she could still hear the traffic. 'So this is, what, fifty yards or so from where their car would have been parked?'

DC Townsend nodded. 'That's right.'

'And was Mr Robinson a big man?'

'I'd say average. Eighty kilograms. Eighty-five maybe.'

Lulu looked over at Phil. He grinned. 'A hundred and eighty-five pounds, boss. Give or take.'

'So about thirteen stone, in old money,' said Lulu. She grinned at DC Townsend. 'Do you know what a stone is?'

He pulled a face and shrugged. 'Sorry.'

'A stone is fourteen pounds, two stones make a quarter and four quarters make a hundredweight.'

'I have no idea what any of that means,' he said.

'And don't get me started on threepenny bits,' said Lulu. She looked at the grass between the trees and the car park. 'Were there any drag marks?'

'No,' said DC Townsend. 'We think he was carried here.'

'That's a long way to carry a body weighing a hundred and eighty-five pounds,' said Lulu.

'I agree, but it's possible. What about your victims? How far were they carried?'

'About the same,' said Lulu. 'And we did wonder if there might be two people doing the carrying.'

Phil nodded. 'In all four cases it was doable,' he said. 'Remember, we had one of the PCs do a fireman's lift to see if it could be done?'

'That's right,' said Lulu. 'I'd forgotten that. Ricky Landers. Who did he carry?'

'Joe Carter. Joe was about the same build as the victim. It was at Wimbledon Common, remember? Ricky managed it but he was complaining about a bad back for weeks afterwards.' He looked over at DC Townsend. 'Any footprints?'

'It was drier than it is today. No prints that we could see. We think the body was under the trees for twelve hours, so any grass that was disturbed was back in place.'

'Were you one of the first out here?' asked Lulu.

'Yes, the case was assigned to DI Friar and I was her scribe. The dog walker who found the body called 999 and a patrol car came out. As soon as they saw the condition of the body they cordoned off the area and called CID.'

'So the body hadn't been disturbed by the time you got here?'

'No.'

'And the crime scene photographs I saw on HOLMES, they were exactly as the body was when you arrived?'

DC Townsend nodded. 'Yes.'

'The body was on its back, and no attempt had been made

to conceal it? And the rope was around the neck and lying next to the body?'

'That's right.'

Conrad began walking around, sniffing the ground as his tail swished from side to side.

'It was the same with our four killings,' said Lulu. 'The bodies were dumped almost carelessly. A lot of effort went into cleaning the bodies to make sure there was no forensic evidence, and they were dumped well away from any roads, but there was no attempt made to hide them.'

'The killer wanted them to be found, you mean?'

'Or he just didn't care. It was all about the killing. Once that was done he just wanted the body out of the way. And the fact that he made no attempt to cover their faces suggests that there was no personal connection. The killer didn't care about how they were found.'

'I couldn't understand why he left the rope on,' said DC Townsend. 'That's forensic evidence, isn't it?'

Phil nodded. 'We wondered that too. In all cases the knot was really tight. Maybe it was just more convenient to leave it on.'

'We wondered if it was a message, maybe,' said DC Townsend. 'He dumps the bodies where he knows they'll be found, and the rope is – I don't know – some sort of warning.'

'You think that someone might recognize the knot?' asked Lulu. 'It might mean something?'

'It was just a thought.'

'No, it's a good thought. It's a common knot among the boating fraternity, but perhaps it does have a special meaning to someone.'

Conrad had his head up now and was sniffing the air.

'There's nothing to connect this parkland with the area where Sawyer's body was dumped?' asked Lulu.

'Heaton Park golf course? No, nothing.'

Lulu nodded. 'That was the same with our disposal sites. The killer never used the same area twice, and there was nothing to connect them other than that there was always a safe place to park a vehicle and the area was secluded, with grass and trees.'

'The grass because it would make it difficult to find footprints?' said DC Townsend.

'Exactly.'

'And the trees?'

'We never worked out why he always left the bodies under trees,' said Phil. 'Are there trees at the golf course?'

'There are,' said DC Townsend.

'Let's have a look, then,' said Lulu. She gathered Conrad up and put him on her shoulders and they walked back to the car.

21

Heaton Park golf course was a half-hour drive from Stretford Meadows. They left the motorway on a slip road, drove by a Sainsbury's to a pay-and-display car park. There were already several dozen cars lined up. Lulu frowned. 'This is a bit public,' she said. 'Do you think he parked here?'

'It's much quieter at night,' said DC Townsend. He pointed at a clump of trees in the distance. 'The body was dumped about sixty metres away. But it's possible he left his vehicle further down the road.' They climbed out. DC Townsend went over to a sign and used his phone to pay for parking. 'An hour should be enough, wouldn't you say?' he said.

'I think so,' said Lulu. 'We just want to get the lay of the land.' They walked across the grass to the trees. Conrad rode on Lulu's shoulders, a soft breeze ruffling his fur.

It was a grey day, with most of the sky obscured by thick cloud. There were golfers off in the distance, brightly coloured figures in groups of four. 'I've never seen the point of golf,' Lulu said to Phil as they followed DC Townsend across the grass. 'I get the walking part, I love a good walk, but hitting that tiny ball with a piece of metal on the end of a bendy stick? Why?'

'I prefer cricket,' said Phil. 'But then I guess I've always preferred team games.'

'Oh, I love cricket. Watching it, anyway. But golf? Half

the time you can't even see the ball. I've no idea why people would want to watch it. But I get the exercise angle, I do.'

'Except that most of the punters I see playing golf are way overweight,' said Phil, 'and don't get me started on the clothes they wear.'

'I'm assuming they don't play in the dark,' said Lulu, looking around. 'So it'd be emptier then.' She looked down. 'The grass is thick and springy, so no prints.'

DC Townsend's mobile rang and he took the call. When he'd finished, he nodded at Lulu. 'DI Friar says she thinks it best if she went with you when you visit the relatives. It makes sense; she has built up quite a rapport with them, so they'll probably be more accepting of strangers if she's there.'

'That's absolutely fine,' said Lulu.

'So the plan is I'll take you from here back to the station, and she'll drive you.'

'That works for me,' said Lulu, with a smile.

They reached the trees. 'Sawyer's body was there,' said DC Townsend, pointing to a spreading oak tree. 'Two dog walkers found it.'

'Is this a regular dog-walking area?' asked Lulu.

'It is. There's a path running around the perimeter of the course. There's no way a golfer would have seen the body here, but anyone who knew the area would know that there'd be dog walkers.'

'He wants the bodies to be found, that's for sure,' said Lulu.

'Or he just doesn't care,' said Phil.

'Why not just dump the body in the car park?' said DC Townsend. 'Or leave them anywhere, by the side of the road? Why go to the trouble of carrying them, just to dump them?'

'If he left the body at the side of a road, there's a chance it could be discovered quickly,' said Lulu. 'By dumping them in a quiet place, he has plenty of time to get away, clean his vehicle, maybe establish an alibi. If he does it late at night, he has seven or eight hours to get away.'

'And this is similar to where the Choker dumped his victims?'

Phil nodded as he looked around. 'Wimbledon Common, Hampstead Heath, Clapham Common, Oxleas Wood. All near places where people walked their dogs.'

'Do you think the killer has a dog?' asked DC Townsend.

'Now that's a thought,' said Lulu. 'You mean he walks a dog in the area, looking for a place to dump the body?'

'That would explain the dog-walking connection.'

Lulu nodded. 'It might.' She looked over at Phil. 'What do you think, Phil?'

'Most serial killers don't own pets,' said Phil. 'In fact, isn't torturing pets one of the early signs of a potential serial killer? That and bed wetting?'

'There are always exceptions,' said Lulu. She looked over at DC Townsend. 'Did you have any thoughts on the vehicle the killer uses?'

'No CCTV or eyewitness statements, and no tyre tracks. It's all supposition. But we're thinking probably a van. Something that can be driven late at night without attracting attention. Probably with no windows at the back. A sliding door, perhaps. Getting a body out of a boot is no easy feat.'

'We thought the same,' said Lulu. 'But yes, with no CCTV it was just guesswork.' She looked up at the clouds. 'It looks like rain.'

DC Townsend smiled. 'It's Manchester, it always looks

like rain,' he said. 'We get rain on close to a hundred and eighty days a year. Wettest place in the UK, pretty much.'

'Were you first on the scene?' asked Lulu.

'DI Friar and I came together. The call came in just after nine and we were both at the station. One of the dog walkers called 999. The PCs that attended weren't as forensics savvy as the ones at the Stretford Meadows scene. They moved the body and one of them tried to loosen the noose. I think they thought they could try CPR even though he'd been dead for almost twelve hours by then. They trampled around the grass and their DNA was everywhere. Though, to be fair, the grass was dryish, so there wouldn't have been any decent prints anyway.'

'But the body hadn't been posed? Or covered?'

'Naked, with the noose in place. Marks on the wrists and ankles.'

'We wondered if he wrapped them in something, a sheet maybe, when he carried them,' said Phil. 'Otherwise there'd be fibres and DNA on the body.'

DC Townsend nodded. 'We wondered about that. Plastic sheeting, maybe. He covers the body until he's dumped it, then takes the plastic sheet away and burns it.' He waved his arm around the area. 'So what do you think?'

Lulu nodded. 'There are definite similarities with our disposal sites, yes.'

'So it's the same killer, right?'

'It certainly looks that way.'

22

DC Townsend drove them back to GMP HQ, where DI Friar was waiting for them. DC Townsend headed for the lifts while DI Friar took Lulu and Phil back out to the car park. 'How did it go?' she asked Lulu.

'There are definitely similarities to where our bodies were dumped,' said Lulu.

'So we could be looking at the same killer?'

'It certainly looks like it,' said Lulu.

DI Friar stopped by a dark blue Vauxhall Corsa and they all climbed in. Phil took the front passenger seat and Lulu and Conrad sat in the back. 'We'll go and see Mrs Sawyer first,' said DI Friar. 'I've told her that two colleagues from London want a word and she's okay with that. But if at any time she shows any reluctance, we leave straight away.'

'I quite understand,' said Lulu.

Conrad settled in her lap and Lulu stroked him gently as DI Friar drove them out of the car park and onto the A56.

'Where do they live?' asked Phil.

'Sale,' said DI Friar. 'About five miles away.'

'Oh, we came through Sale on the Bridgewater Canal,' said Lulu.

'How long did it take?'

'From Sale to Manchester? About an hour and a half.'

'And how long from London?'

Lulu chuckled. 'Eighteen days.'

'Eighteen days!'

'I can go twenty miles on a good day,' said Lulu.

'You could fly to Australia in twenty hours.'

'You could, but it wouldn't be as much fun.'

'And you'll take another eighteen days to go back.'

'I was actually thinking of heading to the West Country for a while,' said Lulu. 'Maybe take *The Lark* to Bath.'

'I know this is a stupid question, but what do you do bathroom-wise?'

'Oh, I have a bathroom. It's small but has a shower and a toilet and a washbasin. There's enough water for two or three weeks and the waste stays in a capsule that needs emptying when it's full.'

'And you have electricity?'

'Indeed. Whenever the engine runs it charges the batteries, and many moorings have electrical sockets you can plug into.'

'A home from home.'

'Oh, *The Lark* is my home. It has been for a while now.' She stroked Conrad behind the ear and he purred softly.

Mrs Sawyer lived in a small red-brick semi-detached house with a slate roof. There was a little garden to the front and a single garage to the side. DI Friar parked in the road and they walked to the front door. Mrs Sawyer had obviously heard them pull up because she had the door open as they walked up the path. She was in her forties, her bleached blonde hair tied back in a ponytail, her face devoid of make-up. She was wearing a baggy pullover that Lulu thought had probably belonged to Mrs Sawyer's late husband. Her eyes were red from crying and she was holding a pillow.

'I'm so sorry to be bothering you, Sue,' said DI Friar.

'It's not a problem,' said Mrs Sawyer, holding the door open.

They filed into the hall and Mrs Sawyer closed the door. 'This is Detective Inspector Jackson from London and Mrs Lewis, who was a superintendent in London. As I said on the phone, they would like to ask you a few questions.'

'Come on through,' said Mrs Sawyer. She took them into the front living room, where a young woman in a pink jogging suit was sitting on a low sofa. 'This is my neighbour, Jenny,' said Mrs Sawyer. 'She's been keeping me company.'

'What about the family liaison officer?' asked DI Friar.

'She only stayed for a few days. She was doing her best, but she was just a stranger and she really wasn't much help so I sent her away.'

'I'm sorry.'

'No, she was fine. But really all I need is some company and Jenny has been a rock.' She flashed her friend a watery smile.

Jenny indicated the seat next to her. 'You sit yourself down and I'll make everyone a cup of tea,' she said.

Mrs Sawyer sat down and hugged her pillow.

'Will you be all right, Sue?' asked Jenny.

Mrs Sawyer nodded. Jenny patted her on the shoulder and headed to the kitchen. Lulu looked around the room. There was a large TV on one wall, facing the sofa, and two armchairs in a matching houndstooth pattern. There was a low brass and glass coffee table in front of the sofa on which was a box of Kleenex tissues and a copy of the previous day's *Manchester Evening News*. There was a collection of framed photographs on a sideboard in front of the window. Most of them were of Sergeant and Mrs Sawyer, including several of their wedding. He was wearing an ill-fitting black suit, but Mrs Sawyer looked radiant in a flowing white dress.

Mrs Sawyer looked up at Lulu and for the first time noticed Conrad. 'There's a cat on your shoulders,' she said.

'Yes. His name is Conrad.'

On cue, Conrad jumped down onto the carpet and padded over to Mrs Sawyer. He looked up at her, meowed, and jumped up onto her lap. Mrs Sawyer beamed with delight. 'Oh, he's lovely.' Conrad curled up and began to purr. Mrs Sawyer gently stroked him.

DI Friar sat down on the sofa next to her; Lulu and Phil took the two armchairs. 'Mrs Lewis and Inspector Jackson have a few questions for you, Sue.'

'They're from London, you said?'

DI Friar nodded. 'There were similar murders in London some time ago,' said DI Friar. 'It might well be that they are connected to Derek's death.'

'I was at Hendon with Derek,' said Phil. 'Do you know why he moved to Manchester?'

'He said he didn't like London. It was too expensive and he'd had too many bad experiences.'

'Was he from London?' asked Lulu.

Mrs Sawyer nodded. 'He was born in the East End. A real Cockney, he always said. Born within the sound of Bow bells.'

'So why Manchester?'

'I'm not sure. I don't think he ever said, really. I met him after he'd been here for a while.'

'Did he ever talk about having any problems in London? Issues with anyone who might want to harm him?'

'He didn't talk about London much.'

'It was a big move, though,' said Lulu. 'Change of city, change of job, a whole new life, really. When a person does that, there's usually a good reason.'

'I think he just wasn't happy there,' said Mrs Sawyer, her eyes on Conrad. 'As I said, we didn't really discuss it.'

'Does he still have any friends from London? Anyone he was in regular contact with?'

Mrs Sawyer shook her head. 'He never mentioned anyone.'

'Did he go back to London?' asked Lulu.

'Never.'

'What about his parents?'

'His father left when he was a baby and his mum died when he was quite young. He was in a children's home until he was seventeen and he joined the police when he was nineteen. He had a rough childhood, which is why he didn't like talking about it.' She looked up, her brow furrowed. 'Why are you so interested in London?'

'We had four very similar murders in London, about five years ago. Inspector Jackson and I wondered if the same person was responsible.'

'You think someone from London killed Derek?'

'It's possible, yes.'

'But why?'

'The killer might have moved from London and started killing in Manchester.'

Mrs Sawyer's frown deepened. 'You mean that the killer followed Derek? After five years?'

'Not necessarily,' said Lulu. 'It could have been random. That's why we wanted to talk to you.'

'Random? I don't know if that's better or not,' said Mrs Sawyer.

'Why do you say that?' asked Lulu.

Mrs Sawyer dabbed at her eyes. 'I've been racking my brains trying to think who might want to hurt Derek. Family, friends, his co-workers, you start to suspect everybody. Maybe he had offended someone, maybe one of our neighbours was bearing a grudge. Maybe someone from a case he'd worked on. It's all I can think of. I've been looking at everyone with suspicion. Everyone.' She blew her nose. 'But now you tell me it could have been a complete stranger, that it was totally random. Derek was killed for no other reason than that he was in the wrong place at the wrong time. That means if he had changed his routine just a bit he might still be alive. If I'd just taken the time to give him a good morning kiss or made him finish his coffee, his path might never have crossed with the path of his killer and he'd still be alive.' She was talking so fast that she began to hyperventilate.

'Please try to stay calm, Mrs Sawyer,' said Lulu. 'There's no need to rush. We have time.'

Mrs Sawyer nodded and took several deep breaths.

'You need to think about the future rather than dwell on what might have happened,' said Lulu softly.

Mrs Sawyer's eyes narrowed. 'What would you know about it?' she snapped. 'Your husband isn't the one who died.'

Lulu smiled sympathetically. 'You are quite right, Mrs Sawyer. And I wasn't trying to tell you what to do – you have to process your grief in your own way.' She shrugged. 'And my husband died a couple of years ago, in what we thought was a hit-and-run accident. For a long time afterwards I kept trying to rewrite history. If I had just gone to meet him, if he'd come home earlier or later, if he'd done anything else other than cross that road at that particular time . . .'

'I'm sorry,' whispered Mrs Sawyer.

'No, I'm the one who should apologize,' said Lulu. 'I wouldn't have wanted anyone else to try to tell me how to handle my grief and it was wrong for me to do that to you.'

'I just miss Derek so much.'

'I know you do.'

'I don't know how I can live without him.' Mrs Sawyer sniffed.

DI Friar moved over and put her arm around the crying woman. 'I think perhaps we should go,' she said to Lulu.

Lulu nodded. 'Of course.' Conrad eased himself off Mrs Sawyer's lap. Lulu picked him up, slid him onto her shoulders and stood up. 'I'm so sorry to have bothered you, Mrs Sawyer. And again, I am so, so, sorry for your loss.'

Phil stood up. 'We'll see ourselves out,' he said. He and Lulu left the room and walked down the hall. Phil opened the front door and they stepped outside. Phil closed the door and lit a cigarette. 'It's never easy, talking to the relatives of the deceased,' he said.

'It has to be done,' said Lulu. 'But it's never pleasant.'

'She's clearly distraught.'

'I don't think there was ever a question of her being a suspect,' said Lulu.

'I didn't mean that.' He blew smoke up at the sky. 'The marriage seemed rock solid, she obviously loved him.'

'So not gay, is that what you mean?'

'Everything I saw suggested they were a happily married couple.' He took another draw on his cigarette.

The door opened and DI Friar appeared. She closed the door behind her. 'She's obviously still fragile.'

'Understandably so,' said Lulu. 'I'm sorry if I upset her.'

'You didn't say anything wrong. She's just in a sensitive state at the moment.' She headed towards the car and Phil and Lulu followed her. 'I don't get the feeling that Sergeant Sawyer led a double life,' said DI Friar.

'Phil and I had come to the same conclusion,' said Lulu.

'So we have a killer using the same method but with a changed victimology,' said DI Friar. 'That is unusual.'

'Everything about this case is unusual,' said Lulu.

Phil threw away the remains of his cigarette and they all climbed into the car. DI Friar started the engine.

'Where to now?' asked Lulu.

'Back to Manchester,' said DI Friar, 'to see Fraser Robinson's parents.'

23

Mr and Mrs Robinson lived in a terraced house in Gorton, five miles to the east of Manchester. DI Friar parked in the street, a short walk away. The houses were almost identical, weathered brick with a door and a single window facing the pavement, and two bedroom windows upstairs. Most of the cars parked in the road were more than five years old but the houses were well cared for.

DI Friar walked along to a black door and pressed the bell. After a few seconds a grey-haired woman in a floral apron opened the door. She blinked her eyes behind thick-lensed glasses, and then smiled when she recognized DI Friar.

'Hello, Mrs Robinson. This is Detective Inspector Jackson and Mrs Lewis. I told you about them on the phone.'

'Come in, come in,' said Mrs Robinson, and she took them through to a small sitting room. 'Please sit,' she said. 'I'll get my husband. He's in his shed.' She smiled ruefully. 'It's his refuge. He always hides away in his shed when he's unhappy. Would you like tea?'

'Tea would be lovely,' said DI Friar.

Mrs Robinson went back into the hallway. Lulu looked around the room. There was no television, just an old-fashioned radio on a table by the window. There were two armchairs either side of a Victorian fireplace. There was a pile of knitting next to one of the chairs and an ashtray and a pack of tobacco next to the other. Facing the fireplace was a high-backed three-seater sofa in a floral pattern that matched the chairs. There were packed bookshelves to the right of the fireplace. Lulu went over to look at the books. They were mainly romance novels – Barbara Cartland, Jilly Cooper, Nora Roberts and Danielle Steel. All were well-thumbed paperbacks that had clearly been read several times. There were three framed photographs on one of the shelves. A black-and-white wedding photograph of a much younger Mrs Robinson with a tall, good-looking man with a killer smile, a young Fraser Robinson wearing a brand-new school uniform, and finally a picture of their son in his thirties, standing in front of a barber's shop and holding a giant pair of scissors. Next to him was a pretty young woman wearing a tight T-shirt and jeans. There was a logo of flaming scissors across her shirt and below them the name of the shop – A CUT ABOVE. Lulu smiled. Fraser was grinning at the camera and his chin was up proudly, clearly pleased with himself. He had the world at his feet, he was his own boss and had a pretty wife by his side. Little did he know that in a few short years it would all be over. Covid would steal his dreams and a serial killer would take his life. She shuddered at the thought and turned back to look at DI Friar, who had walked over to the window and was looking at the radio.

'How long had Fraser been living back home?' Lulu asked.

'About two years,' said DI Friar. 'When his company folded, the bank took his house, and the ex-wife took the car and the furniture. He still owed money to the bank, so most of what he earned went to pay off the debt.'

'And where was he last seen?'

'He went to a pub a short walk away from here. The

Lamb and Flag. The landlord remembers seeing him but doesn't remember him leaving.'

'CCTV?'

'Some footage, but two of the cameras weren't working, so all we have is him buying drinks at the bar.'

'Drinks plural? So he was with someone?'

DI Friar nodded. 'Two pints of lager. We're assuming that he was drinking with another guy.'

'Women drink pints,' said Phil.

'They do, yes. But we have no footage to confirm either way.'

'And the parents didn't worry that Fraser didn't come back from the pub?'

'They go to bed early,' said DI Friar. 'Fraser had his own key, it wasn't unusual for him to stay out late. It's not as if he had a curfew.'

'A curfew?' said a voice at the door. Lulu turned to look at the man who had spoken. He was in his late sixties, grey-haired and wearing a tweed jacket and baggy grey trousers and holding a polished wooden pipe.

'Hello, Mr Robinson,' said DI Friar. 'I'm sorry to bother you again.'

'It's no bother,' said Mr Robinson. 'Now what's this about a curfew?'

'I was just asking DI Friar whether it was unusual for Fraser to be out late at night.'

'He was a night owl,' said Mr Robinson. 'Always was, even when he was a schoolboy. We'd have to shake the boy awake some mornings.' He walked stiffly over to his chair and slowly lowered himself down. He eased himself back with a grimace that suggested he suffered from a bad back, then looked over at Lulu. He waved for her to sit on the sofa. She sat down and Phil joined her. 'My wife says you are from London?' said Mr Robinson.

Lulu nodded. 'Inspector Jackson and I worked on several cases in London that were similar to what happened to your son. Can I say how sorry I am for your loss? And thank you for agreeing to see us.' Conrad jumped up onto the sofa and sat next to Lulu.

Mr Robinson's eyes narrowed as he looked at Conrad, but then he switched his attention to Lulu. 'I'll do whatever's necessary to catch the bastard,' he said. He frowned. 'I didn't read anything in the papers about murders in London.'

'It was some time ago,' said Lulu.

Mr Robinson's frown deepened. 'I read the papers every day. And there was nothing on the radio.'

'Our cases were five years ago.'

Mr Robinson tilted his head on one side and squinted at her. 'So whoever killed my son was killing five years ago? In London?'

'The killings we investigated were similar, so yes, we think it is possible that it's the same man.'

DI Friar held up her hand. 'It's a possible line of inquiry, Mr Robinson,' she said. 'We are still pursuing local leads, obviously.'

'You told me last week that you didn't have any leads,' said Mr Robinson.

'Well, we're still looking for CCTV footage, and canvassing for witnesses.'

Mr Robinson made a soft snorting noise. He looked back at Lulu. 'Did you have any suspects?'

'We did, but nothing concrete. Can I ask you – did Fraser often stay out late at night?'

'I told you, he's a night owl.' He grimaced and corrected himself. 'He was a night owl.'

'And where did he go? At night?'

'The pub, I suppose.'

'Did he have many friends?'

'Some.'

'He wasn't with any of his friends the night he disappeared,' said DI Friar. 'We spoke to them all.'

'What about girlfriends? Did he have anyone special?'

Mr Robinson shook his head. 'Not that we knew about.'

'Was he still upset about his divorce?'

Mr Robinson frowned again. 'What do you mean?'

'I just wondered if he perhaps wanted to get back with his ex-wife. Or if he was looking for someone else.'

'Debbie is gone for good,' said Mr Robinson. 'She had another fella before the ink was even dry on the divorce. As soon as Fraser's business went under, she was off.'

'And no children?'

'That's right. No children.'

'Was that Debbie's idea, or your son's?' Mr Robinson's eyes hardened and Lulu realized she had touched a nerve. 'They are such a financial responsibility, children,' she added hurriedly. 'I really don't know how young people manage.'

Mr Robinson opened his mouth to say something but he was interrupted by the arrival of his wife, bearing a tea tray.

'Let me help you with that,' said Phil, hurrying over to her. He took the tray and placed it on the coffee table. 'I've brought some biscuits, just in case anyone is peckish,' said Mrs Robinson.

'Could I possibly use your bathroom, Mrs Robinson?' asked Lulu.

'Of course,' said Mrs Robinson. She pointed at the door. 'Up the stairs, second on the right.' She began pouring tea into cups. Phil leaned forward and helped himself to a Hobnob.

Lulu stood up. 'Thank you so much.' Conrad jumped down off the sofa.

'Oh, does he go everywhere with you?' asked Mrs Robinson.

'He does, pretty much,' said Lulu. 'You don't mind, do you? Conrad gets nervous if he doesn't know where I am.'

'Conrad can go wherever he wants,' said Mrs Robinson. 'He seems so well behaved.'

Lulu opened the door and went up the stairs. Conrad ran ahead of her and waited for her at the top. 'I don't get the least bit nervous,' he said.

'Well, of course you don't,' whispered Lulu. 'But I needed a reason for you to be coming with me, didn't I?'

There were three doors leading off the landing. Lulu eased the first one open. There was a large double bed and two heavily varnished dark oak wardrobes. A faded cotton nightdress lay on the bed, and three bottles of tablets sat on one of the bedside tables. It was obviously the Robinsons' bedroom. She closed the door, passed by the toilet and opened the door to the bedroom at the rear of the house. Conrad slipped in first. Inside was a single bed and a suitcase on top of a chest of drawers.

Lulu closed the door and tiptoed over to the suitcase. She opened it. There were clothes inside, a couple of pairs of training shoes and a washbag containing toiletries. At the bottom of the case were half a dozen books of hairstyles and cutting techniques. They were well thumbed and spotted with yellow and pink Post-it notes.

'What are we looking for?' asked Conrad, who had jumped onto the bed.

'I'm not sure.'

'Evidence that he led a double life?'

'That would be too easy,' said Lulu. 'But Mr Robinson suggested that Fraser's wife left him when the money dried up.' She frowned and rubbed her chin.

'Do you think she had another reason?'

Lulu shrugged. 'I don't know. Perhaps.'

'Maybe we could talk to her.'

Lulu nodded. 'I'll ask DI Friar.'

'Covid ruined a lot of lives,' said Conrad, looking around the room.

'It certainly did.'

'He can't have been happy, losing his wife and his business and having to move back in with his parents.'

'I suppose not.' She raised her eyebrows as she pulled out a small plastic bag filled with cannabis buds.

'I don't suppose that's catnip,' said Conrad.

Lulu found a pack of Rizla cigarette papers and a cigarette lighter. 'It doesn't mean anything, of course,' said Lulu. 'Lots of people smoke cannabis these days.' She put the cannabis, cigarette papers and lighter back into the suitcase. There were socks, underwear and folded shirts in the chest of drawers. She knelt down and checked under the bed, but there was nothing there.

'Well, it doesn't look as if he's hiding anything,' said Lulu as she straightened up.

'If there was anything, it would probably be on his phone,' said Conrad.

'That's a good point,' said Lulu as she headed for the door. 'I wonder why DI Friar didn't mention it.'

Lulu went downstairs. 'Sorry about that,' said Lulu as she went back into the sitting room. 'I think I drank too much coffee this morning.' She dropped down on the sofa next to Phil.

Mrs Robinson was now sitting in her armchair, facing her husband. He was drinking his tea. Phil was on his second or third Hobnob and DI Friar was still standing by the window. Mr Robinson slowly lowered his cup, his eyes fixed on Lulu.

'So, let me ask you a question,' he said. 'Do you think the killer knew Fraser when he was in London? You think he followed him back to Manchester?'

Lulu's eyebrows shot skywards. 'Fraser used to live in London?'

'For two years. Not long after he finished hairdressing college. He said he wanted to make it big in London, that Manchester was too small for him. But he only lasted two years before coming back with his tail between his legs.'

'You didn't tell me that Fraser used to live in London,' said DI Friar.

'You never asked,' said Mr Robinson tersely.

'Did he ever talk about his time there?' asked DI Friar. 'Who he met? Any problems he might have had?'

'I think he was too embarrassed to talk about it,' said Mr Robinson.

'He thought he was a failure,' said Mrs Robinson. 'He had a couple of jobs, but the pay wasn't great, and it costs an arm and a leg to live in London. He stayed with us for a few weeks but then he got a job at a barber's in Deansgate and after a couple of years he had saved enough to open his own place. He and Debbie got a house together and I really thought he had his life sorted. Then we had the Covid, and everything changed. He lost his business and the house, and then Debbie left him.'

'Why didn't they have children, do you think?' asked Lulu.

'I think they were trying, but you don't like to pry, do you? We would have loved a grandchild, obviously, but Fraser never reacted well to pressure.' She forced a smile but there were tears in her eyes. 'I hear that Debbie's pregnant now. So that's nice, for her.'

DI Friar took a step forward. 'I really think we've taken up enough of your time, Mr and Mrs Robinson.'

Lulu and Phil got to their feet. 'And again, I am so very sorry for your loss,' said Lulu. She bent down so that Conrad could jump up onto her shoulders.

'Just get the bastard who killed Fraser,' said Mr Robinson through gritted teeth. 'That's all we ask.'

'We will do,' said Lulu.

'You promise?'

The question caught Lulu by surprise. She knew that making a promise like that went against all policing rules. You could promise to do your best, you could promise never to give up, but you could never promise to get a result, because that was often in the lap of the gods. She looked over at DI Friar, who was staring at her anxiously. DI Friar's eyes narrowed and Lulu got the message, loud and clear. There was no way that she could promise to catch the killer, but she knew that just then it was what the Robinsons needed to hear. She looked back at the couple and nodded. 'I promise,' she said.

Mrs Robinson dabbed at her eyes with a tissue and her husband nodded grimly. Lulu could feel DI Friar's eyes burning into the side of her head but she ignored the sensation and walked into the hallway with Phil.

Mrs Robinson let them out. Her husband stayed in his chair.

DI Friar spent a minute or so talking to Mrs Robinson on the doorstep, before joining Lulu and Phil at her car. 'Well, that took me by surprise,' said DI Friar.

'My promise, or the fact that Fraser was in London at the time of the killings?' said Lulu.

'Both.' She smiled thinly. 'I understand why you felt the need to promise, but it does make you a hostage to fortune.'

'We're going to catch him, I'm sure of that.'

'You can feel it in your bones?'

'Sort of, yes. We will catch him. I know we will.'

'I certainly hope so.' DI Friar wrinkled her nose. 'So we now know that both the victims here, Sergeant Sawyer and Fraser Robinson, were in London at some point. That can't be a coincidence. But they had both left London long before the killings started.'

'Mr Robinson asked the right question, didn't he? Did the killer follow them to Manchester?'

'If he did, it changes everything, doesn't it? It means that they weren't chosen at random. They were targeted.'

'We never found a connection between the London victims,' said Phil. 'They lived in different parts of London, no common interests, no work connections, different schools.

They appeared to have been chosen at random. Other than the possible gay connection.' He nodded. 'You're right – if the killer did target Sergeant Sawyer and Fraser Robinson, then there's every chance he also targeted the victims in London. Which means we're missing something.'

DI Friar unlocked the car and they all climbed in.

'Suppose that, despite all the evidence to the contrary, Sergeant Sawyer and Fraser Robinson were leading double lives,' said Lulu. 'Suppose they were gay, or bisexual. How might that work in Manchester?'

'The same as anywhere else in the world, I suppose,' said DI Friar. 'Linking up on the internet. Grindr and such. Swipe right, swipe left.'

'Did you find Mr Robinson's phone?'

'We didn't. Or any of his clothes. Even his watch was gone.'

'The same with Sergeant Sawyer, obviously.'

DI Friar nodded. 'Just the body and the rope.'

'I don't mean to try to teach anyone to suck eggs, but did you get the records of the phones from the phone companies?'

'We did. Sergeant Sawyer's phone went off shortly after pinging the cell phone tower near where he worked. Mr Robinson's phone was last active at the pub down the road. That was where he was last seen.'

'So do we think the killer switched off the phones after he abducted the victims?'

DI Friar nodded. 'I think most people know that they can be tracked through their phones these days,' she said.

'Yes, it's a brave new world, isn't it? Mobile phones and CCTV have transformed the way the police conduct inquiries.

Back when I was a PC, you'd be knocking on doors and speaking to people. These days it's all technology-led.'

'We did do a fair amount of door-knocking, too,' said DI Friar. 'But it gave us no leads. Both men disappeared into thin air.'

'And there was nothing untoward in their phone messages or social media.'

'Neither were on Facebook, Twitter or Instagram,' said DI Friar. 'And there was nothing in their text messages to cause concern.'

Lulu nodded. DI Friar had clearly covered all the bases. 'In the London cases, two of our victims frequented gay bars in Soho,' said Lulu. 'Is there a similar area in Manchester?'

'There is,' said DI Friar. 'It's down on Canal Street. Though these days you're as likely to see a hen night or stag night there.'

'I wonder if it would be worth canvassing the area, showing photographs of the two of them and seeing if anyone remembers seeing them.'

DI Friar wrinkled her nose. 'I think that might well backfire on us,' she said.

'How so?'

'If word got out that we suspected a gay link in the murders, we might start a panic. Dickie McNeil would be sure to find out and the story would be splashed all over the *Manchester Evening News*. It could do more harm than good. And for what? A hunch?'

'More a line of inquiry than a hunch,' said Lulu. 'But I take your point. What if Phil and I did it off our own bat? We could say we were trying to find our friends.'

'Lie, you mean? I'm not sure that would be a good idea.

You're attached to my inquiry, which does give you some sort of official status. It wouldn't reflect well on the force.'

'We could go in the afternoon, and just speak to the staff. We'd be careful, I promise.'

DI Friar grimaced. 'I wish you hadn't asked me,' she said. 'If you'd just gone ahead and done it, I wouldn't have been involved.'

'Don't ask, don't tell?'

'Exactly.'

'Then just forget I ever mentioned it,' said Lulu.

'I already have,' said DI Friar. She smiled. 'So can I drop you somewhere?'

24

DI Friar brought the car to a stop on an almost empty Canal Street. 'I thought it would be busier,' said Lulu as she looked around. There was a line of buildings to her right, facing a narrow pedestrianized road and the Rochdale Canal beyond, a sliver of a waterway with barely enough room for two narrowboats to pass. A couple of tourists were taking selfies in front of one of the bars.

'It doesn't really get busy until the evening,' said DI Friar.

They had stopped close to the New Union Hotel. It was a two-storey Victorian building with a brick facade. The ground floor was painted white and dotted with giant cartoon bees and there was a painted rainbow arch around the door.

'The New Union has been here since 1865, back in the days when Canal Street was the heart of the cotton trade,' said DI Friar, gesturing at the building. 'Something like a third of the world's cotton came through Manchester. When the cotton trade died, Canal Street became a red-light area and the New Union became a pub. Then in the fifties it became popular with the gay community – that's why the windows on the ground floor are all frosted glass, so that nosy parkers couldn't look in. It's been a major part of the whole Gay Village area ever since.'

'And why the bees?' asked Lulu.

DI Friar laughed. 'It's one of the best-known symbols of

Manchester,' she said, 'and has been the city's emblem for more than a hundred and fifty years. It's supposed to illustrate our hard work ethic and the fact that the city is a hive of activity. London doesn't have an emblem, does it?'

'Not that I know of,' said Lulu.

'A broken-down donkey on its last legs,' said Phil. 'Beaten, shackled, but unbowed.'

Lulu's jaw dropped. 'That's a bit pessimistic, Phil.'

'What would you choose?' he asked.

'As London's emblem? A lion, I suppose.'

'That's because you're a cat person,' said Phil.

Conrad meowed and they all laughed. 'It's true, I am,' said Lulu.

Lulu and Phil climbed out. Lulu scooped Conrad up and placed him on her shoulders. They waved as DI Friar drove off. Phil nodded at the hotel. 'What do you think?'

'As good a place to start as any,' said Lulu.

They walked in. There were two young men sitting at a corner table. They both had rucksacks with maple leaf flags on them. Canadian backpackers. Other than the Canadians, the only other person in the pub was a burly bearded barman in a tight black T-shirt who grinned at them when he saw Conrad on Lulu's shoulders. 'Now that's a neat trick,' he said. 'Does she ever fall off?'

'She's a he,' said Lulu. 'And no, he's a very well-balanced cat.'

'My apologies for the sexual misidentification,' said the barman. 'He is a very handsome cat indeed. What can I get you?'

'A cappuccino for me. And some Evian water in a bowl for Conrad.'

The barman smiled at Phil. 'Would you like ice and lemon with that?'

Phil laughed. 'Conrad is the cat,' he said. 'I'm Phil, and I'll have a cappuccino as well. Just plain water for Conrad.'

The barman shook his head. 'Apologies again, it's obviously my day for misidentifying,' he said. He went over to a coffee machine and began making their cappuccinos.

Phil leaned against the bar. 'Bit of a faux pas that the Manchester cops didn't spot the London link,' he said.

'To be fair, both Sergeant Sawyer and Fraser Robinson lived locally and had families here. They knew Sawyer had been in the Met but didn't see any significance in it. Hindsight is always twenty-twenty.'

'What we need to do is to look for any links that Sawyer and Robinson had with our victims.'

'We never found a connection between the London victims,' said Lulu. 'Other than that they were middle-aged white men who were possibly gay or bisexual.'

'It can't be a coincidence that the two victims here both spent time in London.'

'Coincidences do happen, Phil.'

'Do you think it's a coincidence?' He stared at her with unblinking brown eyes. 'Do you?'

She smiled. He was always such a good interrogator. He had the knack of connecting with anyone, no matter their background, and he was able to fake sincerity better than anyone she knew. She had watched him get close to murderers, rapists and career criminals from across the offending spectrum, win them over and then get them to open up, even when opening up meant they faced a long prison sentence. She had always thought that Phil would have made a great priest. Or a psychologist. He was definitely a superb detective, one of the best. She knew that he wasn't faking sincerity with her – Phil was one of her closest friends and he had been a staunch ally when she had been a detective. He had never let her down, and she was confident that he never would. 'It can't be, can it? Which means that there has to be a connection between the victims. All of them.'

'And a connection between the killer and the victims. They're not random killings. The killer hasn't targeted them just because of their sexuality. There's something else going on, something that we missed.'

The barman returned with two frothy cappuccinos that he placed on the bar in front of them. He had drawn hearts in the froth. Lulu and Phil thanked him. He bent down behind the bar and reappeared with a ceramic bowl with cartoon bones around it and a bottle of Evian. 'No cat bowls, I'm afraid, but this has been through the dishwasher.'

Conrad jumped down onto the floor with a dull plopping sound. The barman unscrewed the cap from the bottle and poured water into the bowl before handing it to Lulu. Lulu bent down and placed it in front of Conrad, who lapped at it gratefully.

Phil took out his phone. 'You haven't seen this guy in here, have you?' he asked, holding out the phone so that the barman could see the screen. It was one of the photographs of Fraser Robinson on the whiteboard in the incident room.

The barman peered at it and shook his head. 'Doesn't ring a bell. Do you think he drinks here?'

'Maybe,' said Phil. 'I was hoping you could tell me.'

'It's possible,' said the barman, shrugging. 'We're heaving over the weekend; it's hard to remember faces.'

Phil took back the phone and flicked through to a photograph of Sergeant Sawyer. 'What about this guy?'

The barman screwed up his face as he peered at the screen. 'I know him,' he said. He looked up at Phil. 'He's that cop who died. Killed by that serial killer.'

'And you saw him in here?'

'No, I'm saying I recognized him from the paper. That's him, isn't it?'

Phil nodded and put the phone away. 'Yeah, it's him.'

'And you think he was in here?'

'We're covering all bases at the moment,' said Phil. 'Just trying to see where he went before he was killed.'

'He went missing on his way to work, didn't he?'

'That's right,' said Phil.

'But now you think he might have been in Canal Street? Are you cops?'

'I am,' said Phil.

The barman looked at Lulu. 'I used to be,' she said. 'We're just trying to see if Sergeant Sawyer or Fraser Robinson were down this way before they were killed. There are lots of lines of inquiry being followed up.'

'What about the Canal Pusher? Are you looking at him?'

Lulu frowned. 'The Canal Pusher?'

The barman grinned. 'You're not from around here, are you? The Canal Pusher is our local serial killer. There have been almost eighty bodies pulled from the canals in the past twenty years. And a lot of them have been gay men.'

'This is the first I've heard of it,' said Lulu.

'Oh, it's a thing, all right. No one knows for sure if it's a serial killer doing it for kicks or a mugger who mugs and kills, but the bodies keep coming.'

'Sergeant Sawyer and Fraser Robinson weren't found in a canal,' said Lulu.

'But they were killed by a serial killer, right?'

'Well, strictly speaking, there have to be three murders before it's a serial killer,' said Lulu.

One of the Canadians walked over to the bar and the barman went to serve him. Lulu and Phil finished their coffees, then Lulu bent down so that Conrad could jump up onto her shoulders. Phil paid for the drinks and collected a receipt, then they walked out of the pub and along Canal Street. About half the bars hadn't yet opened. Waiters were arranging tables and umbrellas outside some of them. They walked over to the nearest. The facade was painted white with a vibrant rainbow arching over the main window, below a large sign that read RAINBOW BAR. There were posters in the window advertising drag queen cabarets and cheap cocktail hours.

'Can I get you anything?' asked a balding waiter who had tied back what was left of his hair into a limp ponytail. He was wearing a white linen shirt and tight trousers with rainbow braces.

'I think I'll have a white wine,' said Lulu. She looked at Phil. 'We're done for the day, aren't we?'

'I could definitely do with a pint,' said Phil. 'And my clock has stopped running.'

'In or out?' asked the waiter.

Lulu looked up at the sky. 'Do you think it's going to rain?'

The waiter laughed. 'It's Manchester, love. It's either just finished raining, or it's about to rain. Unless it's already raining.'

Lulu laughed too. 'Outside it is,' she said.

The waiter pulled two chairs over to a table and erected an umbrella over their heads. 'I have a very nice Pinot Grigio,' he said.

'Perfect.'

'And what beer would you like?' the waiter asked Phil.

'Surprise me,' said Phil. He sat down and took out his cigarettes. Conrad curled up under the table as Lulu sat down opposite Phil.

The waiter disappeared inside the bar. Phil was just about to light his cigarette when his mobile phone rang. He fished it out of his jacket pocket and held it to his ear. The call lasted just over a minute and consisted mainly of Phil saying 'okay' and 'right'. Then Phil thanked the caller and put his phone down on the table. 'That was a pal of mine in the Garda Síochána,' he said. 'She can't find any trace of a Jeremy Connolly between the ages of forty and sixty. There's a guy in his seventies with a boatload of speeding tickets who has that name and a teenager with minor drug-dealing convictions, but that's it.'

'Did she check birth certificates and passport applications?'

'Yes and yes. And no joy.'

'So it's a fake name?'

'Not necessarily. His name could be genuine but he might not be Irish. Or he could be Northern Irish, of course. Then his details would be on the UK databases.'

'Do you think you could check for me?'

'Of course. If this guy is saying he's Irish – Irish Irish – then he's lying. Either about his name or his citizenship. Either way, it's a red flag.' He lit a cigarette. 'What about getting his prints, or his DNA?'

'I suppose I could, yes. But . . .' She left the sentence unfinished.

'But what?'

Lulu frowned. 'It's a big step, isn't it? It's an out-and-out declaration that we don't trust him. If he found out . . . he wouldn't take it well, would he?'

'If we catch him out in a lie, does that matter?'

'If he's lying, then no, of course, it's better that we have the facts. But what if he's not? What if he was adopted or changed his name by deed poll? What if he was born overseas but his parents were Irish? What if there is a perfectly reasonable explanation, and he finds out that we've been treating him like a criminal?'

Phil exhaled smoke. 'He wouldn't be happy.'

'No, and it might destroy any chance of them having a future together. I wouldn't want to be responsible for that, Phil.'

'To be fair, your friend is the one who asked you to help. She can't blame you if she finds out something upsetting.'

'I don't want her shooting the messenger,' said Lulu. 'Plus, what if she tells him what I did? There are data protection issues and I'm just a civilian these days.'

'I'll be the one accessing the databases, not you,' said Phil. 'If he is planning to marry her under false pretences, that's a crime. I'm well within my rights to make inquiries.'

'Thanks, Phil.'

He flashed her a smile. 'Just doing my duty, boss.'

Lulu took out her phone. 'I'm going to send you a picture of the car that Jeremy is driving. A white Audi.'

'You want me to check the plate?'

'If you would.' She sent the picture and Phil's phone

beeped. He picked it up and checked the picture. 'Nice motor.'

'A bit flash, don't you think?'

'A midlife crisis, maybe,' said Phil, putting his phone away.

The waiter reappeared, carrying their drinks. He put the white wine in front of Lulu and gave Phil his pint. 'Let me know if you need anything else,' he said.

'You could do one thing for me and tell us if you've seen this guy here,' said Lulu. She took out her phone and showed him the photograph of Fraser Robinson.

The waiter peered at the screen and then nodded. 'Yeah, maybe. He looks familiar. What's your interest?'

Phil took out his warrant card and showed it to the waiter. 'We're just trying to plot the whereabouts of a couple of people,' he said.

'I didn't think you could drink on duty.'

Phil laughed. 'We've just clocked off,' he said.

The waiter looked at the picture again. 'I'm pretty sure I've seen him a few times,' he said. 'On his own usually. Late at night. But I wouldn't want to swear on a Bible. We get a lot of guys his age.'

Lulu flicked through to a photograph of Sergeant Sawyer. 'What about this chap?'

The barman took the phone from her to get a better look. He wrinkled his nose. 'I don't think so.' He flicked his finger across the screen, shook his head and repeated the action.

'That's okay,' said Lulu. 'It was just those two I wanted to know about.'

'This guy I saw,' said the waiter, handing the phone back to Lulu. 'About a week ago.'

Lulu's mouth fell open when she looked at the screen.

The photograph was of Gordon Wallace, one of the Three Little Piggies, the one who was released from prison last year.

'Are you sure?' She held the phone out to Phil so he could have a look.

'Very sure,' said the man. 'That's an old photograph, but it was him.'

'Why so sure?' asked Phil.

'Because I had a bit of an argument with him,' said the man. He pointed at the railings next to the canal. 'He was standing over there with a bottle of beer. I told him that vertical drinking isn't allowed. And he wouldn't have it, despite the fact there are signs everywhere.'

'Vertical drinking?' said Phil.

The man grinned. 'You're not locals, are you? Basically the law is that you can't stand and drink. You have to be sitting down.'

'To stop people falling in the canal?' asked Lulu.

The man laughed and shook his head. 'No, it's a way of stopping antisocial behaviour,' he said. 'It's in effect across the city. Groups of drunk guys milling around with glasses is asking for trouble.'

'Was he with anybody?'

'Not that I remember. I had a bit of back and forth with him and I don't remember anyone else joining in.'

'How did it end?'

'I threatened to call the police and he chucked his bottle into the canal and left. I don't know where he went.'

'He wasn't by any chance here when the other guy was?'

The man frowned and then nodded. 'Yeah, it's possible. But they weren't together, they weren't talking or anything.'

Lulu showed him the screen again. 'And it was definitely him?'

'One thousand per cent.'

'Do you recall what day it was last week?'

The waiter shrugged. 'Wednesday. Thursday maybe.' He shook his head. 'I'd be guessing. All I remember is the argument. And the homophobic abuse.'

'Really? What did he say?'

'It was nothing. Water off a duck's back. Called me a dirty poofter and a few other even less imaginative insults.'

'That's a strange way for someone to behave after they've chosen to visit a gay venue,' said Phil. 'So you didn't think he was gay?'

'He was just an ignorant twat,' said the waiter. 'His sexuality didn't come into it.' He gestured at a stack of chairs by the railing. 'Sorry, but I've got to get back to work.' He went over to the chairs and began arranging them around tables.

'Well, I didn't expect that,' said Phil. 'It looks as if we have a suspect.'

'I agree,' said Lulu. 'But we ruled him out, remember? He was in prison at the time of the fourth murder.'

'But he was very much in the frame for the first three.' He took a gulp of beer.

'Remind me again why we didn't consider that there might be two killers working together.'

'We did. But we could never find a connection between the Three Little Piggies. Different schools, different occupations, lived in different areas of the city. No phone traffic connecting them. I suppose we might have kept looking if the killings had continued, but they didn't. The cases went cold.'

'Well, they're obviously not cold any more,' said Lulu.

'Assuming that our friend is right and Wallace was here. The picture he saw was ten years old.'

'We should check the CCTV,' said Lulu.

'Definitely, but that'll be down to DI Friar. We don't have any jurisdiction here.'

Lulu sipped her wine. 'Do you think it's possible that the killings are random? That Wallace is just a serial killer who has moved location?'

'It's possible,' said Phil. 'Anything's possible. But is it likely? Now that we know that both Sawyer and Robinson were in London at some point, we have to start considering the fact that these killings were never random. Wallace – if it is Wallace who is committing the murders – must have an agenda.'

'Which means that we missed something.'

Phil nodded slowly. 'It's starting to look that way, boss. But we did everything by the book. And at least two senior officers went through your decision logs after your consultancy ended and they never raised any issues. It was a textbook investigation.'

'Except we never caught him. And if he does have an agenda, we missed it.' She ran her finger round her wine glass. 'We need to find him, obviously.'

'And then what? We had him in last time and he played the "no comment" card to perfection. We still don't have any physical evidence.'

'CCTV, phone tracking and ANPR has come a long way in the past five years. Once we have his details we can start plotting his movements.'

'That's still only circumstantial, boss. And we still have

to deal with the fact that he was behind bars at the time of the fourth London murder.'

Lulu nodded. 'True. Which means we need to locate Edward Parker, ASAP.'

'DI Friar said she'd been in touch with Europol, but I've got a decent contact there too, so I'll chase them up tomorrow. I'll also run Jeremy Connolly by them. See if there's any trace of him in Spain. Or anywhere else in Europe for that matter.' He picked up his glass. 'So we could try running the pictures by a few more barmen, then how about dinner at the Midland? Then I'll walk you home.'

Lulu raised her glass in salute. 'Sounds like a plan.'

25

Lulu's phone rang, waking her from a dreamless sleep. She picked up the phone. It was half past seven. She blinked and sat up. Conrad was lying at the bottom of her bed, his eyes open. 'It's for you,' he said.

Lulu laughed. 'Of course it's for me – whoever heard of a cat using a phone?' She took the call. It was DI Friar. 'There's been another murder,' said the inspector. 'A body has just been found on Stretford Meadows.'

'Stretford Meadows? The same place where Fraser Robinson's body was left?'

'The very same.'

'That doesn't make sense, does it? The killer has never used the same place before.'

'The body is naked and there's a rope noose around the neck. A couple of PCs have preserved the area and I'm meeting DC Townsend out there. I can have him pick you up, if you'd like.'

'Oh my goodness, yes. How about I meet him at the Midland Hotel with DI Jackson? I'm only a ten- or fifteen-minute walk away.'

'That'll work,' said DI Friar. 'I'll see you at Stretford Meadows.' She ended the call.

Lulu phoned Phil, explained what had happened, and arranged to meet him in reception. She pulled on a blue and white Ted Baker dress and grabbed her blazer and handbag.

'No make-up?' asked Conrad.

'Really?'

'I bet DI Friar will be wearing make-up.'

Lulu laughed. 'Yes, you're probably right. Thank you.' She went into the bathroom and spent five minutes on foundation, mascara and a touch of lipstick before presenting herself to Conrad for his approval.

'Perfect,' he said.

'Cats are so lucky,' said Lulu.

'Fur does cover a multitude of sins,' said Conrad. Lulu bent down so that he could jump onto her shoulders. She climbed the steps onto the rear deck, locked the doors and stepped onto the towpath.

She arrived at the Midland just before eight, where Phil was sitting in reception with a cup of coffee in front of him. 'This is a turn-up for the books,' he said. 'Usually there are long gaps between the killings. It's been less than a week. Do you want a coffee?'

Lulu's phone rang. It was DC Townsend, telling her that he was outside. Phil gulped down his coffee and they headed out. They climbed into DC Townsend's white Toyota Corolla and he waited for a tram to go past before they headed west.

'So what do we know?' asked Phil, who was sitting in the front passenger seat.

'Just that a body has been found, not far from where Fraser Robinson's body was found last week.'

'Dog walkers again?' asked Lulu.

'Apparently,' said DC Townsend. 'There's a forensics team on the way, and a doctor.'

'And no idea who the victim is?' asked Phil.

DC Townsend shook his head. 'Just that it's a man.'

It took just under twenty minutes to reach Stretford Meadows. Lulu and Conrad peered out of the window as they drove by the same Sainsbury's that they had seen on their last visit, pulling up in the parking area.

'It's fairly close to the previous spot,' said DC Townsend, 'but not as far to walk this time.'

'But the killer would have parked here again?'

'I assume so.'

They pulled up next to DI Friar's Corsa. There were several other vehicles nearby, including an ambulance and two GMP patrol cars.

DC Townsend got out of the car and opened the boot. 'I have spare foot covers and gloves,' he said.

They all rolled blue plastic covers over their footwear and put on latex gloves. DC Townsend used his smartphone to pay for parking, then headed through the hedge. Conrad jumped up onto Lulu's shoulders. 'There's no way our killer uses the same place twice,' said Phil, as he and Lulu followed the detective.

'Not unless he's changed his way of operating,' said Lulu.

'Why would he do that, when he's been so successful in the past?'

'That's a very good question, Phil.'

As they passed through the hedge they saw a group of people gathered in the field, about fifty feet away. There were four uniformed officers in high-vis jackets standing guard around the crime scene. DI Friar was with a middle-aged Asian man in a heavy overcoat with a bright red scarf wrapped around his neck. Three SOCOs in full forensic gear were walking around, one of them snapping away with a digital camera.

Lulu and Phil stayed by the hedge as DC Townsend went over to DI Friar. He spoke to her and then she waved them over. As they got closer they saw the body on the ground and the length of rope around the neck.

'This is Dr Patel. He's putting time of death at about midnight, maybe an hour or two either way,' said DI Friar.

Dr Patel nodded at them. His eyes widened when he saw Conrad. 'There's a cat on your shoulders,' he said.

Lulu smiled brightly. 'I know,' she said. She looked down at the body. It was never easy to look at a corpse, and it didn't get easier over the years, especially when violence was involved. It was lying on a bedsheet, pale blue, the lifeless eyes staring up at the sky. The rope was around the neck and Lulu immediately recognized the knot as a round turn and two half hitches.

'Was the body found like this?' asked Lulu.

'It was actually on its side,' said DI Friar. 'But wrapped in the sheet. We moved it so that Dr Patel could get a better look at the neck.'

'Who found it?'

'Two dog walkers. They didn't touch anything; even with the sheet over it they could see what it was. A patrol car came and the officers moved the sheet but then preserved the crime scene.'

Lulu looked over at Dr Patel. He was in his fifties; his hair was jet black, but his beard was greying. 'What do you think, Dr Patel?'

'He was certainly killed elsewhere and dropped here,' said the doctor. 'Lividity suggests that he was on his back for several hours after death.'

'But the noose wasn't the cause of death, was it?'

The doctor raised his eyebrows. 'You have a keen eye,' he said.

Lulu smiled thinly. 'I've seen more than my fair share of strangulations over the years,' she said. 'The thumb marks around the trachea suggest that he was manually strangled. From the size of the bruises on the sides of the neck the killer had large hands, so it's more likely it's a man.'

The doctor nodded his approval. 'Exactly. There are marks from the rope, of course, but they are abrasions that were almost certainly made post-mortem.'

'Someone wanted it to look as if he had been strangled with the rope,' said Lulu. She looked at DI Friar. 'So not our killer, then. Other than the knot, nothing else matches. The sheet, the way the knot is loose around the neck, the closeness to the car park, the type of rope – it's all different.'

DI Friar nodded. 'Someone is trying to pass off the murder as the work of the serial killer.' She scowled down at the body. 'This is down to Dickie McNeil going public with the details of the knot.'

'Didn't he used to be a detective?' asked Dr Patel.

'He did,' said DI Friar. 'And he should know better.'

Dr Patel looked at his watch. 'I have to go,' he said. 'I'll email you my report and death certificate.'

'Thank you, Dr Patel,' said DI Friar. The doctor smiled and nodded at Lulu and Phil, then walked back to the hedge.

Lulu looked up at the clouds that were darkening overhead. 'It looks as if it's going to rain.'

'We're almost done here,' said DI Friar. 'I'm hoping that the sheet will help us.'

'The fact that the body was covered suggests that the killer knew the victim,' said Lulu. 'The killer wanted the face covered, which points to a personal connection.'

'Perhaps,' said DI Friar. 'But it might have just made it easier to carry. We'll do a full DNA check on it.'

They began walking back to the hedge. Phil took out his pack of cigarettes and lit one. DI Friar looked longingly at the cigarette as he blew smoke up in the air. 'Get thee behind me, Satan,' she said.

Phil held the cigarette behind his back. 'Sorry,' he said.

'I forgot to put a patch on this morning.' She looked over at DC Townsend.

He checked his pockets and grimaced. 'I'm sorry, boss, I'm out. I could pop to the chemist.'

'Not on police time, you can't,' said DI Friar. She smiled ruefully. 'I'll survive.'

Phil took out his pack of Lambert and Butler and offered it to her. 'One wouldn't hurt,' he said.

'Oh, you are a bad man,' she said.

He grinned. 'You're just swapping one nicotine delivery system for another.'

DI Friar stared at the pack for several seconds, then sighed. 'Just the one,' she said.

Phil tapped a cigarette out of the pack and she took it. He clicked his lighter and she cupped her hand around the flame as she lit her cigarette. She took a deep drag and then blew a tight plume of smoke up at the gathering clouds. 'Oh, that's good,' she said.

As they reached the car park, they spotted Dr Patel driving away in a blue BMW. He waved at DI Friar and she waved back. She looked at her watch. 'We should get back to the incident room and get the details entered into HOLMES.'

'How long does it usually take your lot to identify a body?' asked Phil.

'It depends if they have been reported missing or not,' said DI Friar. 'Sergeant Sawyer was identified almost immediately because his wife had been frantically phoning all evening when he hadn't come back from work. Fraser Robinson's parents didn't report him missing, so it took longer.' She looked over at DC Townsend. 'We identified him through his dental work, didn't we?'

DC Townsend nodded. 'He had a missing back tooth and some distinctive bridgework, so we got a hit within forty-eight hours.'

'We'll check the missing persons lists for this latest victim, and run his DNA and fingerprints through the databases and if we're lucky we'll get a hit. If not, we'll go the dental route.' She bent down and extinguished her cigarette on the ground, then wrapped it in a tissue and popped it into her handbag. 'Best not to contaminate the crime scene, obviously,' she said, before unlocking her car and climbing in.

'Can we come with you?' asked Lulu.

'Of course you can,' said DI Friar. 'I'll need you and Inspector Jackson around when we eventually identify him.'

'In case there's a London link?'

'Exactly.'

26

Lulu and Phil followed DI Friar and DC Townsend into the GMP building. Conrad was sitting on Lulu's shoulders and his ears pricked up when a tall, dark-haired man in a long, black trench coat stood up from a chair and walked towards DI Friar. 'What the hell is he doing here?' she muttered.

The man was in his late forties, his hair slicked back behind his ears, his face creased into a beaming smile that showed brilliant white teeth. There was a light blue double-breasted suit under his trench coat, along with a crisp white shirt and a black and yellow striped tie with crests on it. 'Julie, lovely to see you,' he said.

'Who let you in, Dickie?' The man was blocking her way to the lifts, so she stopped.

'And DC Townsend, faithful scribe and bag carrier. I hear you were both out on Stretford Meadows bright and early this morning.'

'Who told you that, Dickie?'

'Investigating another murder, is that right?'

'Where are you getting your information from?'

The man ignored her and flashed his gleaming smile at Lulu. He was well over six feet tall and Lulu had to tilt her head back to look into his eyes, which were a piercing blue. 'Sorry, I didn't get your name,' he said. He offered his hand. 'Dickie McNeil of the *Manchester Evening News*.'

Lulu shook his hand. The skin was soft and the nails

glistened as if they had been polished. There was a faint smell of sandalwood and citrus around him and a minty aroma to his breath. 'Nice to meet you, Dickie.'

McNeil continued to smile at Lulu, but his pale blue eyes were as hard as ice. 'Are you involved in this serial killer case?' he asked.

'Goodness gracious, no,' said Lulu. 'I'd lost my cat and DI Friar helped me find him.' She patted Conrad, who purred loudly.

McNeil grinned at DI Friar. 'From serial killers to lost cats! Is there no end to your talents, Julie?'

'I'm going to have to ask you to leave, Dickie.'

'You're throwing out a card-carrying member of the fourth estate, are you, Julie? A story like that deserves to be on the front page.'

DI Friar sighed. 'What do you want?'

McNeil looked at Phil. 'And what about you, sir? Are you involved in the case of the missing cat? Or are you on the hunt for the Strangler?'

'Please don't give him a nickname, Dickie,' said DI Friar. 'That's the last thing we need.'

McNeil grinned. 'So you are admitting that you are chasing a serial killer? Looks like I have my splash.'

'That's not what I said, Dickie. Please don't make things up.'

McNeil turned his attention to Phil. 'You have the look of a cop, sir,' he said. 'But I haven't seen you around. Are you from another force?'

Phil smiled amiably. 'I'm just a friend of the family,' he said. 'We've been looking everywhere for Conrad.' He patted Conrad, who purred again.

'How do you know about the body, Dickie?' asked DI Friar. 'Who told you there was a body at Stretford Meadows?'

'Julie, darling, you know you never ask chefs or journalists about their sources.'

'Was it someone in GMP? Or a member of the public?'

'I can't say.'

'Was it someone who saw the body? A dog walker?'

McNeil just smiled and shrugged.

'This is important, Dickie. I need to know who told you. Not their name, necessarily, but their situation.'

'And I need a story, Julie. The information I have is that a naked body complete with noose around its neck was found on Stretford Meadows this morning. Can you confirm that?'

'We'd like to keep quiet about the rope, but yes, there is a body.'

'A man in his forties?'

DI Friar nodded. 'Yes.'

'Have you identified him yet?'

'No.'

'So the Strangler has claimed his third victim?'

'Please don't use that name, Dickie. It glamorizes him. And it frightens the community.'

'But you can confirm there have now been three victims?'

'Quid pro quo, Dickie. Who tipped you off?'

'I cannot reveal my source – you know that.'

'I don't need a name, I just need to know the circumstances.'

'And you'll answer my questions if I tell you? Quid pro quo?'

'I'll answer some of them. It's an ongoing investigation

so there are limits to what I can say. Much of the information we have is operationally sensitive. Now who called it in?'

'Just a member of the public. They said the cops were out at Stretford Meadows and that there was the body of a naked man there with a noose around his neck.'

'Had the caller seen the body? Or just the police activity?'

'I didn't ask.'

'Was the caller a man or a woman?'

'A woman. Middle-aged, maybe. Local.'

'And what time was this?'

McNeil pulled a notebook from his pocket and flicked through it. 'Twenty past nine.'

'And was the call to your mobile or to the office?'

'The office. So, who found the body?'

'It was found by dog walkers early this morning. Just after seven.'

'And you can confirm there was a rope around the neck?'

'I already did, Dickie. Yes.'

'With the same knot that was used before?'

'The knot that you so helpfully went public with? Yes.'

'And no sexual activity?'

'We won't be able to confirm that until after the postmortem. Did the woman say anything else?'

'All she said was that there was a body and that the police were there. We sent a photographer out but the area was cordoned off and the cops wouldn't let him near the body.'

'Did the woman leave her name?'

McNeil shook his head. 'No.'

'So she didn't want a tip-off fee?'

'Just a member of the public doing her civic duty. So you are now confirming that you are hunting a serial killer who is targeting middle-aged men?'

'No, of course not. Please don't put words in my mouth, Dickie. Especially when I don't know where they've been.'

'But you're okay with me running the story?'

'I'd rather you didn't, but I don't see that I can stop you.'

'I'd really like to quote you, Julie. To add authenticity.'

'Any quote will have to come through the press office, you know that.'

'How about I quote a police source close to the investigation?'

'"A source familiar with the investigation",' said DI Friar. 'The body is on the way to Manchester Royal Infirmary mortuary as we speak. I'm sure you've got a contact there. Please, Dickie, remember that everything I've given you is off the record. We never spoke.'

McNeil grinned. 'Understood, Julie.' He looked at Lulu and Phil. 'Pleasure meeting you, mysterious strangers. I'm so glad you got your cat back.' He winked at Conrad and made a clicking sound, then walked away, his long coat flapping behind him.

DI Friar narrowed her eyes as she stared after him. 'That man is just so annoying.'

'I don't think he believed me about my missing cat,' said Lulu.

'I'm sure he didn't,' said DI Friar. 'I just hope his contacts within the GMP don't tell him why you and DI Jackson are here. That could get very complicated.'

Lulu nodded. 'Yes, we don't want the killer knowing that we've linked the two sets of murders. And I gather you didn't want to tell him that the third killing probably isn't related to the first two?'

'Whoever disposed of today's body with the rope around the neck is obviously hoping that we will blame our serial killer,' said DI Friar. 'It will probably work to our advantage if he thinks we are doing just that.'

'So in a way, you're using Dickie McNeil.'

DI Friar smiled grimly. 'Yes, I suppose I am, in a way.'

27

DI Friar took Phil and Lulu up to the canteen. 'I missed breakfast,' she said. 'Didn't even have time for coffee.'

'You and me both,' said Lulu. They lined up at the counter and ordered full English breakfasts, with toast and coffee. Conrad jumped down off Lulu's shoulders and stuck close to her heels.

'I'll get these,' said Phil, taking out his wallet.

'He's on expenses,' explained Lulu.

'I never turn down a free meal,' said DI Friar.

DC Townsend arrived and joined the queue at the counter. Lulu and DI Friar went over to a table by the window while Phil used a debit card to pay for their food. Conrad slipped under Lulu's chair and curled up there.

'So how did it go in Canal Street?' asked DI Friar as she tucked into her breakfast.

'Better than we expected,' said Lulu. 'We found someone there who remembers seeing Gordon Wallace. Recently.'

DI Friar frowned. 'One of the Three Little Piggies?'

'The very same. A waiter in a place called the Rainbow Bar is sure he saw him a week ago. They had an argument over drinking outside. What is it they call it? Vertical drinking?'

DI Friar nodded. 'You have to sit if you want to drink outside in most places these days. And this guy is absolutely sure it was Wallace?'

'He seemed to be. But obviously it's an old picture. I didn't get the waiter's name but he's quite recognizable: balding with a ponytail. There seemed to be plenty of CCTV cameras around. We didn't ask to see it – not our jurisdiction, of course.'

'I'll get it checked,' said DI Friar. She buttered a slice of toast. 'What about Sergeant Sawyer and Fraser Robinson?'

'We found a few serving staff who thought they might have seen Fraser Robinson, but none of them was certain. And several people recognized Sergeant Sawyer from the newspapers but none remember him being in Canal Street. But the guy who saw Wallacc is fairly sure that Wallace was there at the same time as Fraser Robinson, a few days before Robinson died.'

'That makes interviewing Gordon Wallace a priority, obviously.'

Phil arrived at their table and sat down.

'I was just telling DI Friar about our Wallace sighting,' said Lulu.

'It's a game-changer, that's for sure,' said Phil.

'So what we've got – potentially – is a serial killer from London pursuing victims who have moved from London to Manchester. It can't be random.'

'That's the conclusion we came to, yes,' said Phil. He reached for a bottle of ketchup and poured a liberal amount over his sausages and bacon. 'But it's all circumstantial.'

'We don't know where Wallace is, or if he's working, do we?' asked DI Friar.

'He's probably on probation, so let me check,' said Phil.

DC Townsend appeared at their table and sat down opposite DI Friar. He had a bowl of muesli and another bowl of blueberries, strawberries and raspberries on his tray, and a glass of orange juice. 'I picked up some nicotine patches on my way back,' he said.

'You're a star,' said DI Friar.

'Tell me about the Canal Pusher,' said Lulu.

'What?'

'The Canal Pusher.'

'Who's been filling your head with that nonsense?' asked DI Friar, stabbing her fork into a sausage.

'Just something we heard.'

'Down on Canal Street, I assume.'

'We were told that there have been eighty or so bodies fished out of the canal.'

'Canals, plural,' said DI Friar. 'And yes, that's true. But it's over the past twenty years or so. How many bodies are fished out of the Thames?'

'I don't know.'

'Well, I do. Fifty or so. Every year. And I don't see the Met looking for a serial killer. The Canal Pusher is an urban legend, the sort of story that Dickie McNeil would write.'

'So there's nothing to it?' said Phil.

'I'm not saying that there haven't been murders where the body has ended up in the canal. Or that people don't get mugged and then thrown in. That does happen. But a serial killer . . . no.'

'But most of the victims are gay men?' asked Lulu.

'Men, yes. But then most murder victims are male. Last time I checked the stats, it was about seventy per cent, across the country. Yes, some of them were gay, but not the majority.'

'So what do you think is happening? Eighty is a big number.'

'It's a handful each year, about the same as you'd see in Amsterdam. Why does it happen? There are canals close to pubs and bars throughout the city. Drunks get too close to the edge and fall in. Maybe they stand on the edge to pee. Maybe they get depressed while drunk and throw themselves in. We investigate each and every case and more often than not there's no suspected foul play. It's just bad journalism, trying to sell papers by preying on the community's fears.'

'Do you think Dickie McNeil is going to write that the serial killer has claimed a third victim?' asked Phil.

'I'd put money on it,' said DI Friar.

'And what's your game plan?'

'Identify the victim, that has to be our priority. And then look at who might have wanted him dead. The fact that they went to all the trouble of trying to blame it on our serial killer suggests that he – or she – is close to home.'

'Will you handle the investigation, even though you're sure it's not the same killer?'

DI Friar nodded. 'I'll ask my boss if we can use the same MIT,' she said. 'We can't yet rule out that it isn't the same killer, and it makes sense to run the three cases together. But I'll brief the team accordingly. I'll get someone down to Canal Street to check the CCTV at the Rainbow Bar. Did your waiter say what day he saw Wallace?'

'He wasn't sure. A week ago, maybe. Wednesday or Thursday, he said. But he might remember if pressed.'

DI Friar nodded. 'Once we know the date and time, we

can start checking other bars. I'd love to know if Wallace was definitely following Fraser Robinson.'

'You and me both,' said Lulu.

28

DC Townsend put a fresh whiteboard on an easel and stuck a photograph of the face of the latest murder victim at the top. He took a marker and wrote UNKNOWN in blue capital letters. Then he stuck a map of the Stretford Meadows area below the photograph. The spot where the body had been found was marked with a red X.

It was still early, so there were only a dozen or so people in the MIT room, including three civilians who were inputting data into HOLMES terminals.

There were four male detectives wearing near-identical grey suits drinking coffee by the window, chatting about football, and a much older detective in a tweed jacket and corduroy trousers who was munching on a Danish pastry while reading through his notebook. Two uniformed officers were on the phone and two more were sitting at the back of the room studying CCTV footage. Phil and Lulu were sitting at a table by the door. Conrad was on Lulu's lap, curled up but with his eyes open.

DI Friar went over to the whiteboard. 'If you could just give me your attention for a couple of minutes,' she said, loudly enough to get everyone's eyes on her. 'We have a new victim, a middle-aged white man found naked on Stretford Meadows with a noose around his neck, and with a similar knot to our previous two victims. We will be investigating this killing, but at this stage we are not convinced that it is the same perpetrator. Early indications are that it is someone trying to pass the murder off as the work of the killer who we're looking for. But let's keep an open mind.' The detective in the tweed jacket raised his hand. 'Yes, Ron?' she said.

'Why don't you think it's the same killer, boss?'

'There's a number of things. The body was dumped in a sheet, the noose was loose around the victim's neck and there are marks that suggest the noose was applied after the victim had been strangled.'

'So we're looking for a copycat?' said one of the young detectives.

DI Friar shook her head. 'No, we think that the killer of the latest victim added the noose to divert attention elsewhere,' she said. 'I am fairly sure this is a one-off. But until we know that for sure, we'll keep the details on the board here.'

DI Friar's mobile phone rang and she stepped away to answer it. 'We have a possible ID on our latest victim,' she said when she returned. 'Robert Pearson. His wife reported him missing just after midnight. Thirty-eight years old and his description matches our victim. His wife is on the way to Manchester Royal Infirmary to identify the body. DC Townsend and I will meet her there.'

She put her phone away and headed for the door, with DC Townsend in her wake.

'Can we come?' asked Lulu.

'It's not our killer. We're pretty sure of that. I'm not sure that we can justify your involvement in the case.'

Lulu forced a smile. 'I understand.'

'I'll keep you informed, obviously. But I wouldn't want to jeopardize the case by having you involved before anyone has been charged.'

'It's quite okay,' said Lulu.

DI Friar picked up her handbag and she and DC Townsend left the room.

'That's a pity,' said Phil. 'I'd have liked to hear what Mrs Pearson had to say.'

'Me too, but DI Friar's right: it's almost certainly not our killer and a good defence lawyer could well make capital out of two outsiders being involved. Our presence could easily taint the investigation.'

'So what do you want to do today?' asked Phil.

'I'm really not sure,' said Lulu. 'I've been out of the loop for so long that I don't think I'll be of much help. You need to be here, obviously, but I think that Conrad and I will just get in the way. I thought we might as well go back to *The Lark*. I might go and see Jane.'

'Are you sure?'

'I really don't think I have anything to offer, not until we know for sure whether Gordon Wallace is our killer. Plus I've got work to do on *The Lark*.'

'I'll call you if anything happens,' said Phil. 'Oh, by the way, I heard back from my DVLA contact. That white Audi, the one that Jane's boyfriend is driving, it's leased.'

'To him?'

Phil shook his head. 'To a local company. An IT firm.'

'Here in Manchester?' She frowned. 'That doesn't make sense, does it?'

'Well, it makes sense that he wouldn't own a car here if he spends most of his time in Ireland. But you'd expect him to hire one at the airport.'

'Does he work for this IT company?'

'I had a look at their website and he's not mentioned on

it. It's mainly young techie types. And I checked the listing at Companies House and he's not listed as a director.'

'But they've given him a car to drive around in? That's very strange.'

'There might be a simple explanation,' said Phil. 'He could be working as a consultant, or he may be friends with one of the company bosses and they lent it to him as a favour. I'll keep looking at the company. The bulk of the shares are owned by another IT company in London. Again, Jeremy isn't listed as a director but there's a holding company above that, which I'll check on. It's like one of those Russian doll things, except that the dolls keep getting bigger.' He smiled. 'I suggested this before, but you knocked me back. Why not get me a DNA sample or a fingerprint? Ideally both. Get a glass that he's drunk out of and I'll get it to a lab.'

'That's a big step, Phil.'

'You've done it before, boss. Remember the time you gave that skinhead a can of Coke? We needed a DNA sample and we needed it quick, and he was already at the "no comment" stage. So you gave him the Coke and a burger and then you had us pull him out for an identity parade. When he got back the can had gone and he knew that the jig was up.'

'That was a bit different, Phil. We knew for sure he was guilty, we just needed the evidence. The problem with Jeremy is that we don't know for sure that he's done anything wrong. We're on a fishing expedition. And if he ever finds out that we took a sneaky sample . . .' She grimaced. 'Well, he's never going to trust me or Jane again, is he? I feel bad enough doing database searches on him, but running a DNA profile on him would take it to a whole different level. I mean, by doing that, or by running his fingerprints, we're saying that we think he's a criminal. We're doing it because we think his prints and DNA are on file.'

'That is sort of the point,' said Phil.

'If we truly believe that, then we should just tell Jane to run a mile.'

'But he might be innocent.'

Lulu smiled. 'Exactly. He might be. And if he is, he'd have every right to be furious at her, and us.' She sighed. 'We're in an impossible position. Damned if we do, damned if we don't.'

'We could just do nothing. Just let it play out.'

'And if he really is a conman planning to take all her money? Or worse?'

'You know what this reminds me of? Schrödinger's cat. You know, the cat is both alive and dead until you open the box.'

Conrad meowed on Lulu's lap and they both laughed.

'Sounds like Conrad has heard of it,' said Phil.

'So you're saying that Jeremy is both innocent and guilty, but it only becomes clear which it is by us looking at him?'

'I'm not sure how good an analogy it is. It was just a thought. Shall I see if I can get you a car to run you back?'

'Oh no, I'll call an Uber,' said Lulu.

'How about we have dinner at the Midland tonight?'

'On expenses?'

'Exactly.'

29

The Uber driver dropped them in front of the Museum of Science and Industry and Lulu walked across the road towards the Staffordshire arm with Conrad on her shoulder. There were three new arrivals moored in her section, two about fifty feet long and the third a new-build that was closer to seventy feet, its roof covered with solar panels. A young woman in denim dungarees was cleaning the panels and she waved as Lulu went by. 'Lovely day, isn't it?' she said. She had a Birmingham accent and a sunny smile.

'It is,' said Lulu. The name of the boat was *Cloud Nine* and Lulu smiled as she recognized the pun. 'Oh, so you're on cloud nine. I do like that name.'

'It was Sean's idea,' she said. 'My husband.'

'Is he with you?'

'He's in the cabin, working. He's a website designer; he can work anywhere.'

'That must be lovely.'

'It beats working in an office,' said the girl, 'but it's strange how often he has a deadline when there are chores to be done. I'm Brianna, by the way.'

'I'm Lulu, and this is Conrad.'

'He's a lovely boy.'

'Yes,' said Lulu. 'He is.'

Brianna pointed over at *The Lark*. 'Is that your boat?'

'It is, yes.'

'Just to let you know, there was a man hanging around earlier. He went away when we moored.'

'Was he on the boat?'

'No, he was walking up and down, looking through the windows.'

'What did he look like?'

'I didn't get a good look at him. He was quite tall, dark hair, and he was wearing a big coat.'

'I wonder who it was,' said Lulu.

'Maybe he was just interested in your boat,' she said. 'We get people peering in through our windows all the time. It can be like living in a goldfish bowl sometimes.'

She resumed cleaning the solar panels as Lulu walked over to *The Lark*. She climbed onto the rear deck and Conrad jumped off her shoulders and landed on the seat. Lulu checked the lock and chain. The doors were secure.

'Who do you think it was?' asked Conrad.

'Probably just a curious passer-by,' said Lulu. 'Only Phil and DI Friar know that we're here.' She unlocked the padlock and opened the doors. She went down into the galley, filled the kettle and used a match to light one of the rings on the hob. 'Evian?' she said.

'See, you're a mind reader, too. You knew I wanted a drink.'

Lulu chuckled as she took a bottle of water from the fridge and poured some into a saucer. 'So you know about Schrödinger's cat?' said Lulu as she put the saucer on the floor. 'You meowed when Phil mentioned it.'

'Of course. It's horrible. Truly horrible.'

'Why do you say that?'

'You know what happened, right? He put a cat in a box

with a radioactive substance that was connected to a vial of poison. When the substance decayed, it triggered a Geiger counter that allows the poison to be released which then killed the cat. How horrible is that?'

'Oh Conrad, Schrödinger didn't actually carry out the experiment. It's what's called a thought experiment. All in the mind.'

'That doesn't make sense.'

'It's not a real experiment. He never set out to actually hurt a cat. It was all hypothetical. He wanted to show that because the box was locked, there was no way of knowing if the radioactive substance had decayed and released the poison, so there was no way of knowing if the cat was alive or dead. There was a fifty-fifty chance, either way. He argued that until the box was opened, the cat was both alive and dead. It's only when you open the box that you know either way.'

'Well, why use a cat? Scientists use rats, don't they? Why isn't it Schrödinger's rat? Or Schrödinger's dog? Or why didn't he put himself in the box if it was only hypothetical?'

'I don't know,' said Lulu.

'Because Schrödinger hated cats, clearly,' said Conrad.

'Well, I'm not sure that's true.'

'He could have chosen any animal for his hypothetical experiment,' said Conrad. 'The fact that he chose a cat says a lot about the man.'

'But you understand the point that Phil was making? At the moment Jeremy is neither guilty nor innocent.'

'Maybe it's better it stays that way,' said Conrad. 'If Jane finds out that he has been lying to her, she'll be hurt.'

'Better to know the truth, surely?'

'Don't they say that ignorance is bliss?' asked Conrad.

'They do indeed. But "they" aren't always right.' She put a teabag in a mug. 'I do hope it works out all right for them. She seems to be happy when she's with him. And he is charming. Smarmy, perhaps, but with charm.'

'That reporter seems charming, too.'

'Dickie McNeil? Yes, he's quite charming. Reporters often are.'

'And sharp.'

'Yes, sharp enough to cut himself. What was his aura like?'

'A lot of white,' said Conrad. 'That's the sign of a quick mind, but also nervous energy. And it shows an inclination for perfectionism.'

Lulu laughed. 'In my experience, journalists are rarely perfectionists: they write what they think will sell papers. Very few of them are to be trusted.'

'Maybe Dickie McNeil is different,' said Conrad. 'I didn't see anything untrustworthy about his aura.' He tilted his head on one side. 'It was interesting that a woman phoned with the tip-off. You think the killer is a man, but a woman made the phone call.'

'Yes, I wondered about that,' said Lulu. 'But just because she made the call doesn't mean she's the killer.'

'But she wanted publicity, obviously. She wanted to be sure that Dickie knew about the body so that he would link it to the other killings.'

'That's possible, yes.'

'So maybe she was involved in the killing. Maybe she is the killer and she wants to throw the police off the track.'

'I'm not sure a woman could have carried the body to where it was found.'

'That's sexist, Lulu. She could have been a strong woman.'

Lulu laughed. 'Yes, you're right.' The kettle began to boil and she poured hot water into the mug.

'And if she wants to throw the police off the track, that must mean there is a track.'

Lulu frowned. 'Now you're confusing me.'

'The woman must know that if the police look in the right direction, they will find her. Which is why she wants them looking elsewhere.'

'So the woman has a motive?'

'Exactly,' said Conrad. '*Cherchez la femme.*'

They both froze when they heard a voice shouting outside. 'Permission to come aboard!'

Lulu and Conrad both looked at the window. It was a man's voice. A Manchester accent.

'Hello! I can hear you in there! Permission to come aboard.'

Lulu went up the stairs and out onto the rear deck. Dickie McNeil was standing on the path at the side of the boat. He had his hands in the pockets of his trench coat as he grinned up at her.

'Mr McNeil,' she said. 'This is a surprise.'

'Call me Dickie,' he said. 'So, can I come aboard?'

'I'm not sure that's a good idea,' she said. 'But I am sure DI Friar wouldn't want me talking to you. Didn't she say everything needs to come through the press office?'

'She's a stickler for the rules, is Julie, I'll give her that. But surely you and I can chat. Professional courtesy, what with us both being former police. Former superintendent Lulu Lewis, late of the Metropolitan Police.'

Lulu's eyes hardened. 'How did you find me, Mr McNeil?'

'Please, Lulu, call me Dickie.'

'How did you find me, Dickie? You didn't follow me, did you?'

McNeil tilted his head. 'No, I didn't.'

'So how did you know where I was?'

'I'll tell you what, Lulu. You invite me on board and I'll tell you.'

Lulu looked at him for several seconds, then nodded. If he knew who she was and what she used to do, then he almost certainly knew about the Choker investigation. She turned and went back into the cabin. McNeil stepped onto *The Lark* and followed her.

He had to stoop as he came down the stairs. He looked around. 'Isn't there someone else here?' he asked.

Lulu nodded at Conrad, who was still sitting on the sofa. 'Just Conrad.'

'I heard voices.'

'I was on the phone.'

'Two voices.'

'Speakerphone,' said Lulu. 'I worry about the radiation, don't you? I can't see that it's healthy to hold a piece of electrical equipment against your head for long periods of time.'

'I suppose you're right,' he said. 'Do you mind if I sit down? There really isn't enough headroom for me.'

Lulu waved at the sofa. 'Please.' McNeil sat down next to Conrad. 'Can I get you a drink?' she asked.

'Not a drink drink,' he said. 'I've been sober for almost twelve years. But a glass of water would be nice.'

'Evian?'

'I'm a big fan of Evian.'

Lulu smiled. 'So's Conrad.'

'Cats have a favourite water?'

'Conrad does. Actually, I'm just making tea.'

'Tea would be nice.'

'I have some chamomile teabags from Fortnum and Mason, or regular tea if you'd prefer.'

'Chamomile would be fine, thank you.'

Lulu put a teabag into another mug and poured in hot water. McNeil sat on the sofa and Lulu gave him the mug. He thanked her and looked around, nodding his appreciation. 'This is nice,' he said. 'Really nice.'

'Thank you.'

'My parents loved canal boats. We went on quite a few canal holidays when I was a kid. I really enjoyed it.' He grinned. 'I'm too tall these days,' he said. 'I'd be banging my head on the roof all day and my feet would be sticking out of the bunk.'

'Luckily that's never been a problem for me,' said Lulu. 'So how did you find me, Dickie?'

'Dogged police work,' he said, and tasted his tea. 'Oh, this is lovely. Thank you.'

'Specifically?'

'I started wondering if the Strangler had come out of the blue, or if he'd killed before. He seems very well organized, very professional, so it didn't feel like he had come from nowhere. I've got a pal who works for the National Crime Agency and he contacted the Serious Crime Analysis Section.'

'That's very enterprising of you,' said Lulu. 'And almost certainly illegal under the 2018 Data Protection Act.'

McNeil put up a hand. 'You got me,' he said. 'But everything we're talking about here is off the record.'

'I hope that works both ways,' said Lulu. 'I wouldn't want to see my name in the *Manchester Evening News*.'

'You won't,' said McNeil, lowering his hand. 'This is just a couple of former detectives chewing the fat.' He sipped his chamomile tea. 'According to my pal, until recently there were no matches for the three killings in Manchester, at least no matches for the type of knot and rope used. But SCAS was updated two days ago, and now we have a match.'

Lulu smiled thinly, but didn't say anything. There was nothing she could say: she had a pretty good idea which way the conversation was heading and all she could do was to let it run its course.

'Four matches, in fact. All of them in the London area. And the SIO in the first two London murders was assisted by a consultant whose name was . . .' He paused for effect, but Lulu kept her face impassive. 'Former superintendent Lulu Lewis.' He smiled.

'That doesn't explain how you found me here,' said Lulu.

'I've got pals who worked in the Met and you're very highly regarded. A good, honest cop who isn't afraid of a hard day's work and who cracked a fair number of difficult cases over the years. You retired to live on a canal boat called *The Lark*. From their description it was clear that it was you I met with Julie, so I put two and two together. There aren't too many places in Manchester where you can moor a narrowboat.' He looked around. 'I was expecting to see DI Jackson here.'

'He's at his hotel,' said Lulu. She didn't want to give

him the satisfaction of asking him how he knew Phil's name.

'He's equally well regarded,' said McNeil.

'I'm sure he'll be delighted to hear that,' said Lulu.

McNeil grinned. 'So obviously you and DI Jackson are here to help with the investigation.'

She flashed him a tight smile. 'Well, that's your inference.'

'Oh, come on, Lulu. I can call you Lulu, can I? Or would you prefer retired Detective Superintendent Lewis?'

'Lulu is fine. Dickie, you seem to know all there is to know. So why are you here? Surely it's not just to show me how clever you are.'

'I want the story.'

'From the sound of it, you already have the story.'

'So you can confirm that you and DI Jackson are here to help with the investigation?'

'I can't confirm anything, Dickie. This is all off the record, remember?'

'I would prefer to quote you, that's all.'

'But you can't. If it was down to me, then I would probably say yes, but it isn't. DI Friar has been very clear that she doesn't want you talking to us, she wants you to go through the press office.'

'The GMP Press Office is as much use as a chocolate teapot,' said McNeil. He put his mug down. 'How about this, Lulu? Can you answer questions about the London murders? You worked on those investigations. DI Friar didn't. So she can't really object if we talk about them.'

Lulu sighed. 'What do you want to know, Dickie? And we're still off the record.'

'They were listed on SCAS as gay hate crimes.'

'Possible gay hate crimes. One of the victims had a wife and children.'

'Yet the three victims in Manchester aren't gay.'

'So far as we know.'

McNeil frowned. 'So you're suggesting that they might be gay? Or bisexual? Leading double lives?'

'I thought we agreed that we'd only talk about the London cases.'

McNeil nodded. 'Yes, okay, right. Do you have any idea why your killer stopped killing in London and then five years later started killing in Manchester?'

'We're not sure that it is the same killer,' said Lulu. She saw McNeil open his mouth to reply and she stopped him with a wave of her hand. 'But if it is, there are a number of possible reasons.'

'Prison, incapacity, moving overseas?'

'Exactly.'

'And would that have applied to any of the suspects you had?'

'Who said we had any suspects?'

McNeil smiled. 'An experienced copper like you? You'd have some names in the frame.'

Lulu sighed. 'You don't have to keep soft-soaping me, Dickie. Yes, one was in prison and another moved overseas. To Spain. We're trying to track them down at the moment. But please, that's not for publication.'

'And why would the killer move from London to Manchester?'

'No idea.'

'And did you ever come up with a motive? Other than the gay hate crime scenario?'

'We couldn't find motives for any of the killings,' said Lulu.

'The victims weren't connected in any way?'

'No. Their lives never intersected. As you know, HOLMES is very good at spotting links and connections and there weren't any.'

'So they were killed because they were gay?'

'That was what we thought, yes.'

'Which means that the three victims here must be gay. Or bisexual.'

'That's a jump, Dickie.'

'But is it? If it's the same killer, and if said killer targets gay men, then that means the victims here have to be gay.'

'You can't print that, Dickie.'

'I can if I can confirm that they were gay.'

'And how would you do that?'

'I can talk to the relatives.'

'I've already done that.'

'And?'

'Now we're back to talking about the Manchester cases.'

McNeil held up a hand again. 'I hear you. Sorry. But it's hard to separate the two sets of killings.'

Lulu looked thoughtful. 'I would have thought that the job of a journalist was to report what was happening. It seems to me that you're more interested in solving the case than writing about it.'

McNeil grinned. 'Once a copper, always a copper. Sure, yes, I'd love to solve the case, but we both know that lone wolves don't crack cases. Murder investigation is a team sport, despite what you see on television.' He sighed. 'So, you don't mind if I write that two detectives from London are helping GMP with their inquiries, and that said detectives were involved in similar cases in London?'

'You clearly know that, so how could I stop you? I have to say that I'd prefer that you didn't name me or Phil, but again I can't stop you. You'd just be reporting the facts.'

'What I'd really like is a photograph of the two of you.'

Lulu laughed and waved her hand. 'Well, that's not going to happen.'

'I didn't think so. But is there anything that you can tell me, off the record? Anything my readers should know?'

Lulu drank her tea and looked at him over the top of her mug. Part of her wanted to tell him that the third murder didn't match the rest. That would have been the fair and honest thing to do, but Lulu knew that making the knowledge public would put the most recent killer on the defensive. Far better that he believed his ruse had worked, and that meant keeping Dickie McNeil in the dark. 'You seem to be on the right track,' she said.

He pulled out his wallet and handed her a business card. 'If you ever do have something to share with me, please give me a call,' he said. 'I won't insult you by saying that we pay for tip-offs, but we do pay for tip-offs.'

'Can I ask you a question, Dickie?'

'Of course.'

'Is there anything to this Canal Pusher that I keep hearing about?'

McNeil grinned. 'Are you asking me as a former cop, or as a journalist?'

'Is there a difference?'

'Heck, yes. As a journalist, every time a body is fished

out of a canal it gives me a front-page story – is it the work of the Canal Pusher? Even if it clearly isn't, the question can be asked. And when it is answered a day or two later, well, I still had my splash, didn't I?' He chuckled. 'No pun intended.'

'And your view as a former police officer?'

He shrugged. 'The Canal Pusher is an urban myth, nothing more. More often than not it's just a drunk or druggie falling in and drowning. The occasional suicide. You do get the odd murder, but it's usually the result of a drunken brawl or a mugging gone wrong. There's none of the attention to detail that we're seeing with the Strangler.'

'DI Friar really hates it when you give him a nickname.'

McNeil smiled mischievously. 'Yes, I know.' He stood up and put his mug in the sink. 'And with that, former superintendent Lewis, I shall love you and leave you.' He looked over at Conrad. 'And it's been a pleasure seeing you again, Cecil.'

'Conrad,' said Lulu.

'I apologize,' he said. He put his hand over his heart and bowed to Conrad. 'It has been a pleasure seeing you again, Conrad,' he said. 'I'm so pleased that you were never actually lost.'

He headed up the steps and out onto the rear deck. *The Lark* swayed as he stepped off the boat and they heard his shoes crunching on the rough path as he walked away.

'He's tenacious,' said Conrad.

'Yes,' said Lulu, 'he is. Dogged, you might say.'

'You might,' said Conrad. 'I wouldn't. It's a pity that you have to lie to him.'

'Yes, it is. But needs must.'

'So sometimes lying is okay?'

Lulu sighed. 'Well, it's never okay, is it? Not really. But there are times when one really doesn't have a choice.'

30

Lulu was trying to decide if she should open a bottle of Chardonnay or make another cup of chamomile tea when her phone rang. It was Phil. 'Are you still up for dinner at my hotel?' he asked.

'I'm not really dressed for the Midland right now – I've been doing boat maintenance.'

'There's a Marks and Spencer food hall not far away. I could bring nibbles.'

'Perfect,' said Lulu. 'But I only have wine, so bring beer if you prefer.'

'I'll be there within half an hour.'

Phil ended the call and Lulu smiled at Conrad, who was sitting next to her on the sofa. 'Phil's coming, with nibbles.'

'I heard. I hope he brings some salmon. I do love Marks and Spencer salmon.'

'Who doesn't?'

Phil arrived exactly thirty minutes later, smoking a cigarette and holding a Marks and Spencer carrier bag. He finished his cigarette before boarding. 'You've moved *The Lark*,' he said as he climbed on board.

'I had to. You're only allowed seventy-two hours in one spot.'

'So you have to move every three days?'

'On this part of the canal, yes. In most places you can

stay for two weeks. And of course in Little Venice I have a permanent mooring.'

He held up the carrier bag. 'I come bearing gifts.'

Lulu took the bag from him. It contained a bottle of Pinot Grigio, two bottles of lager, a baguette and a selection of deli items, including tempura prawns, mozzarella sticks, sausage rolls, quiche, coleslaw and potato salad. The last item was a cooked salmon fillet. Lulu showed it to Conrad. 'There you go,' she said.

Conrad meowed and licked his lips. Lulu put half the salmon on a saucer and set it down in front of Conrad, who immediately tucked in. 'This is really good of you, Phil,' said Lulu as she laid the food out on the small table.

'Pleasure, boss,' said Phil.

Lulu put plates and cutlery on the table, then opened a beer for him and poured wine for herself. She sat down on the sofa and sipped her wine. 'So, how are things progressing?'

'No joy finding Wallace. He has a probation officer and he's supposed to be at an address in Bermondsey, but the probation officer went round and there's no sign of him. He had fixed himself up with a courier job, but he walked out on that last month.'

'So he's in breach of his probation?'

'Definitely. But that doesn't get us any closer to finding him. We're not even sure if he's in Manchester.'

'And what about Edward Parker? Did you hear back from your Europol contact?'

Phil nodded. 'Parker was on the Costa, working as a handyman in a place called Fuengirola. But he hasn't been seen for a few months. He didn't apply for permanent residence after Brexit; he could well be back in the UK now.'

'So he could have linked up with Wallace?'

'It's possible. But we had no evidence that they knew each other when we investigated them back in the day, and nothing has changed.'

'Maybe we didn't look hard enough. And we need to start looking at connections between Wallace, Parker, Sawyer and Robinson.'

'If there were any connections, HOLMES would have spotted them. That's what HOLMES does.'

'Yes, but HOLMES can only make connections if the information is in the database.'

'So we're missing something?'

'There has to be a link between Wallace and the two victims here. And if we throw Parker into the equation, there must be something that links them all.'

'That's assuming that Parker and Wallace are working together.'

'I take your point – it could be a coincidence that Parker vanished from the Costa about the same time that Wallace was released from prison.'

'DI Friar is checking hotels and guest houses, but if they're savvy they'll be using fake names and paying in cash. And there are several thousand Airbnb rooms. He could even be on a canal boat.'

'Presumably Wallace's probation officer has a phone number for him.'

Phil nodded. 'The phone's been off for a month. It was last used in London.'

'He clearly knows how to cover his tracks.'

'That's why we never caught him in London. And, to be honest, everything we have now is circumstantial. Even if we find him, we don't actually have anywhere near enough to charge him.'

'I'm getting a terrible feeling of déjà vu,' said Lulu.

'You and me both. DI Friar is doing everything by the book, but she's no closer to making an arrest than when she started.'

Lulu sighed, then took a sip of wine. 'And what about this latest victim? It's definitely Robert Pearson?'

Phil nodded. 'The wife identified him. Got very emotional, of course, and ended up fainting.'

'Did she know of anybody who might want to harm her husband?'

'She said everyone loved him. Not an enemy in the world.'

'What did he do for a living?'

'He was a home energy surveyor. One of those guys who tells you how energy-efficient your property is and what you need to do to improve. Lots of travelling, a fair amount of work in the evenings when people are home.'

'So he was often out at night?'

'That's right. But he was always home by ten. When it got to midnight she phoned the police. They took it seriously because his absence was out of character, but there wasn't much they could do that late at night.'

'His phone was off?'

'It was. And his appointments were all on his laptop, which is missing.'

'What about his car?'

'The police are looking for it and DI Friar is getting ANPR data.'

Like all UK cities, Manchester had hundreds – if not thousands – of cameras linked to the Automatic Number Plate Recognition system. Cameras across the country fed number plate details to the National ANPR Data Centre in Hendon, north London, from where they could be accessed by police forces around the country. Billions of ANPR hits were recorded every year and the system had become one of the police's most effective crime-fighting tools.

'Do they know where his last appointment was?' asked Lulu.

'Unfortunately not. His company gives him a list of properties that have to be surveyed but he arranged his own schedule.'

'Did you see the wife?'

Phil shook his head. 'She's at home with a family liaison officer. DI Friar plans to talk to her again tomorrow.'

'Is she a suspect?'

'Boss, she's less than five feet tall and probably weighs forty kilos dripping wet.' He smiled. 'That's ninety pounds in real money. There's no way she could have dropped the body where it was found, and she wouldn't have been able to strangle him.'

'The marks on his neck were made by large hands.'

'Exactly.'

'Still, we need to look into Mrs Pearson in more detail. When a husband or wife is killed, the obvious suspect is the spouse, right? Could she have been having an affair?'

'I'm sure DI Friar is looking at that. But it could be that the killer is totally unrelated to Pearson. It could have been the last job that he did. Something happened, they fight and the guy kills Pearson. In an attempt to throw the police off the scent he copies the knot as detailed in Dickie McNeil's newspaper article.'

'I suppose so.'

Phil narrowed his eyes. 'You think that the wife was involved?'

'It was a woman who tipped Dickie off about the body,' said Lulu.

'*Cherchez la femme*?'

Lulu smiled as she reached for a mozzarella stick. 'Exactly.'

31

When Lulu and Phil arrived at the MIT room the next morning, DI Friar was in a glass-sided cubicle with Superintendent Knight. He was pacing up and down and gesticulating with both hands, his face contorted with anger. 'That doesn't look good,' whispered Lulu.

'He's not a happy bunny,' said Phil.

'Let's keep out of the way,' said Lulu. They headed to the back of the room and sat down in front of a HOLMES terminal. Lulu peered over the top of the monitor. The superintendent had stopped pacing and was standing in the centre of the cubicle, jabbing his finger at DI Friar as he continued to rant at her. DI Friar's cheeks were flushed and she had her arms folded. Most of the time she stared at the floor and occasionally she nodded her head.

Conrad dropped off Lulu's shoulders and stood on the desk. He stared at the superintendent, his tail twitching.

There were a dozen or so detectives and civilians in the MIT room and they were all watching what was going on.

The superintendent began pacing again. DI Friar opened her mouth to speak but the superintendent stopped her with a wave of his hand and she stared at the floor again.

'What do you think has happened?' whispered Lulu.

'Your guess is as good as mine,' said Phil. 'But he's definitely reading her the Riot Act.'

The superintendent turned and yanked the door open,

then stormed out of the MIT room, his brow furrowed. DI Friar stood stock still for several seconds, then took a deep breath before walking out of the cubicle.

Lulu stood up and hurried over to the inspector. 'Is everything all right?' she asked, even though it was clear there was a problem.

'No, everything is not all right,' DI Friar snapped, then she exhaled slowly before smiling at Lulu. 'I'm sorry. I've just had the mother of all bollockings thanks to Dickie bloody McNeil.'

'What on earth happened?'

'Apparently he went round to speak to Sergeant Sawyer's widow and Fraser Robinson's parents last night, raising questions about their sexuality.'

'Oh no.'

'Oh yes,' said DI Friar. 'They were all on the phone first thing to file complaints.' She gritted her teeth. 'Damn him.'

'The superintendent can't blame you, surely?'

'He's got to blame someone and he has no authority over McNeil.' She took out her phone, scrolled through her address book and made a call. 'Voicemail,' she said. 'He probably knows the trouble he's in.'

'Is he, though?' asked Lulu. 'He's a journalist and journalists ask questions. He's just doing his job.'

'No, he's upsetting the families of the deceased. And jeopardizing our investigation. The superintendent has promised to put uniforms outside their houses to make sure it doesn't happen again.' She called the number again and this time left a curt message. 'Dickie, it's Julie Friar. Call me.' She ended the call and put the phone away. 'What's the betting he doesn't call me? I'll have his guts for garters when I get hold of him.'

One of the detectives raised his hand to get DI Friar's attention. 'Boss, we've got the data from the victim's phone. And his wife's.' The detective was young, still in his twenties but growing a moustache to make himself look older.

DI Friar walked over to him. Lulu and Phil followed. She put her hand on the detective's shoulder. 'Do we have the GPS details of Mr Pearson's phone?'

'We do. The system is showing that it was last seen at his house.' The man stared at the screen. 'There's nothing after nine o'clock yesterday morning, which is presumably when the battery died.'

'That's interesting,' said DI Friar. 'What about calls and messages?'

The detective tapped on the keyboard. 'He made twenty-odd calls during the day that he went missing, the last at six-thirty in the evening. The GPS shows him arriving at his house at just before eight o'clock in the evening, the day before yesterday. There were thirty texts sent during the day, mostly work-related, and forty-odd received.' He leaned towards the screen. 'The last five are from his wife. She texted "What do you want for dinner?" at nine-thirty, then "Where are you?" at ten o'clock. "Are you ok?" at eleven. "Is something wrong?" at eleven forty-five. The last one says "Right, I'm calling the police", and that was just before midnight.' He sat back in his chair and looked up at DI Friar. 'So the wife is texting him asking where he is some three hours after he arrived home?'

'His phone was home – it doesn't necessarily mean that he was,' said DI Friar. She frowned and rubbed the back of her neck. 'Right, I want all CCTV footage checked in the vicinity of the Pearson house. Let's see if we can find him driving back to his house.' She looked at DC Townsend. 'What does he drive?'

DC Townsend took out his notebook and flicked through it. 'A blue Ford Focus.'

'Has it been found yet?'

DC Townsend shook his head. 'No. We're actively looking and there's a request in with the ANPR centre but apparently they've got a backlog.'

'Get on to them again and make it clear this is a murder inquiry.' She patted the detective on the shoulder again. 'Okay, Simon, good work. Now I need you to go through every call and text she sent and received over the past month. Let's see if Mrs Pearson has a male friend with big hands.'

'Will do, boss.'

A phone rang on the far side of the MIT room and a female detective went over to answer it. She listened for a few seconds, nodded, and then waved to get DI Friar's attention. 'Call for you, boss!'

DI Friar went over to take the call. Lulu saw the colour drain from her face as she listened to the person on the end of the line. She bit down on her lower lip and then grabbed a chair and sat down. She replied to the caller and then replaced the receiver. Lulu hurried over to her. 'What's wrong?' she said.

DI Friar looked up at her, tears welling in her eyes. 'They've just found Dickie McNeil,' she said, her voice a hoarse whisper. 'They found him in an alley in Rusholme, the back of his head smashed in.'

Lulu's jaw dropped. 'Oh, no, that's awful.' She sat down next to DI Friar. 'Truly awful.'

Phil stood up and walked over. 'Do they know what happened?'

'There's a homicide team out there now,' said DI Friar. 'His wallet and watch are missing, so possibly a mugging.'

'Do you get violent muggings like that in Manchester?'

'We have muggings, yes, but they usually involve knives and occasionally firearms. This sounds . . . unusual. Oh, poor Dickie.' A tear trickled down her cheek and she dabbed at her face with the back of her hand.

Phil produced a handkerchief from his pocket and gave it to her.

'When was the last time you spoke to him?' asked Lulu.

'When he ambushed us in reception.' She frowned. 'Why do you ask?'

'We saw him yesterday afternoon. On my boat.'

DI Friar's frown deepened. 'We?'

Lulu shook her head. 'Sorry. Conrad and I. He came to *The Lark*.'

'How did he know where to find you?'

'That's the exact same question I asked him. Dogged police work, he said. He heard that I lived on a boat called *The Lark* and went looking for it.'

'And what did he want?'

'Confirmation that Phil and I were helping you with your inquiries. I said I couldn't comment but he already had the information. He knew about the Choker investigations, too. He's got a contact within the NCA.'

'Typical Dickie,' said DI Friar, wiping her eyes.

'He seemed a genuinely nice man.'

'He had his faults and he could be a nuisance, but his heart was in the right place.'

'Why did Dickie leave the police? You said he left under a cloud.'

'We had a fourteen-year-old girl go missing and Dickie was sure that her uncle was involved. We had the uncle in a few times but we couldn't get him to talk. Dickie went round to his house and things got a bit physical. The uncle went to hospital and a few days later the girl turned up in Blackpool with her boyfriend.'

'So the uncle was innocent?'

'Sometimes we get it wrong. Dickie went with his gut, which is never a good idea. The uncle ended up in ICU. There were no witnesses so no criminal charges, but Dickie was told if he resigned he'd keep his pension, so he went.'

'So Dickie beat up the uncle?'

'Dickie said no. He said the uncle attacked him with a knife. The uncle's fingers got broken when Dickie took the knife off him, and his spleen was ruptured after Dickie pushed him away and he fell over a chair. No one saw it, so it was difficult to prove either way. It was a mess.'

'What do you think? Did Dickie set out to hurt the uncle?'

'Hand on heart, I don't think he did. He's a genuinely nice guy who really does believe in law and order. I know he was very frustrated that the powers that be didn't back him. And they really didn't. They hung him out to dry. Eventually Dickie just said "Sod it" and handed in his papers.' She looked at her watch. 'I'm going out to the crime scene.'

'Are you SIO?'

'No, DI Howe is in charge. He's out there now. But he won't mind if I turn up. He knows that Dickie and I have a history.'

'A history?'

She took a deep breath. 'There was a time when I was thinking about becoming the third Mrs McNeil.'

'The third?'

'Dickie was married twice and divorced twice. He married civilians both times and neither of them enjoyed competing with the job for his attention.'

'I'm so sorry, Julie.'

'Oh, water under the bridge. It was a few years ago. We're good friends now.' She paused and corrected herself. 'We were good friends,' she said. She picked up her handbag and phone.

'I'd like to come with you,' said Lulu.

'Me too,' said Phil.

'Meow!' said Conrad.

DI Friar looked at Conrad in astonishment. 'Did he just talk to me?'

'He did,' said Lulu. 'He wants to come too.'

32

DI Friar parked her Vauxhall Corsa next to a skip overflowing with rubbish. There was an ambulance parked on the other side of the street and two paramedics were standing at the rear of the vehicle, smoking. 'Where are we?' asked Lulu.

'Wilmslow Road in Rusholme. They call it the Curry Mile,' said DI Friar. 'We're a five-minute drive from the city centre and it has the largest concentration of Indian restaurants in the UK.'

'I've heard of it,' said Phil. 'I love a good curry and I was planning to pay it a visit.' He grimaced. 'Not like this, obviously.'

They climbed out and DI Friar opened the boot so they could all put on protective footwear and gloves. She locked the car before heading to the entrance of an alley which was being guarded by a uniformed constable in a high-vis vest. He recognized her, nodded and lifted the police tape so that she could duck under it. 'They're with me,' she said, and Lulu and Phil followed her into the alley. The constable frowned when he saw Conrad curled around Lulu's neck but didn't say anything.

There were plastic rubbish bins and skips either side of the alley, and doors that led to backyards behind the restaurants that lined the street. Air-conditioning units and ventilation ducts were peppered across the rear of the buildings.

A white-overalled forensics team was taking samples from the ground while two detectives watched. The body was about fifty feet away, on its back, the face a white blur. A SOCO photographer was snapping away with her camera.

The detectives turned as DI Friar approached them. One was in his forties, wearing a long sheepskin jacket with the collar turned up. The other was a decade younger with a black North Face fleece over a dark blue suit. Both had blue plastic covers over their shoes and were wearing latex gloves. 'You think this is connected to your murders, Julie?' asked the older of the two.

'Not sure,' said DI Friar. 'Dickie ruffled a lot of feathers, as you know.'

The detective nodded. 'That series he did on the Albanian heroin gangs didn't win him any friends, that's for sure. But we don't think this is gang-related. More likely a mugging.' He looked over at Phil and Lulu, and his eyes widened when he saw Conrad. 'That's a cat,' he said. 'On her neck.'

'Sorry, yes. This is Lulu Lewis, former detective superintendent with the Met. And Inspector Phil Jackson. They're assisting on our serial case.'

The two detectives nodded at Lulu and Phil.

'DI Paul Howe,' said the older of the two.

'DC Max Wilkinson,' said the younger one.

'When did it happen?' asked DI Friar.

'The pathologist thinks time of death looks to be yesterday evening, around six p.m.,' said DI Howe. 'The body was hidden by bins, so it wasn't discovered until this morning when a chef came out for a crafty smoke.'

They walked slowly over to the body. The SOCO photographer had moved away and was taking photographs of the ground. Lulu had seen a lot of dead bodies in her time, but it still affected her. And it was always worse if she knew the deceased. She had only met Dickie McNeil a couple of times and found him a bit pushy, but he clearly cared about his work and he didn't deserve what had happened to him.

DI Friar shook her head sadly as she looked down at the body. 'Poor Dickie,' she whispered. 'What the hell happened?'

Lulu looked at the ground around the body. There were no footprints to be seen, and as far as she could tell, no blood spatter, just a few drops of dried blood that one of the SOCOs had circled with chalk.

'So the body was here overnight?' said DI Friar. 'And no one saw it?'

'We moved the bins to get to the body,' said DI Howe. 'You could easily have walked past it. It looks like he was mugged, then when the mugger or muggers realized he was dead they hid the body and did a runner.'

'Was it definitely a mugging?' asked DI Friar.

'Wallet and watch have gone,' said DI Howe. 'And his phone.'

'He was wearing a cheap Casio the last time I saw him,' said Lulu.

DI Howe raised an eyebrow. 'That's interesting,' he said. 'Most muggers wouldn't bother.'

Conrad jumped down off Lulu's shoulders and walked slowly along the alley. Lulu turned to watch him. He was looking left and right, his ears up and his whiskers twitching.

'Why would he be in the alley in the first place?' asked Phil.

'It's a short cut,' said DI Howe.

'Yes, but late at night?'

'Well, if time of death was around six p.m., it would still have been light. And Dickie's a big guy, he can . . .' He grimaced. 'I was going to say that he could take care of himself, but clearly not.'

'Do you get a lot of muggings here?' asked Phil.

'It's no worse than the city centre,' said DI Howe, 'but there are easy pickings here, plenty of drunks around. The Curry Mile is where you end up after a night's drinking.'

'Dickie didn't drink,' said Lulu. DI Friar turned to look at Lulu, frowning, clearly wondering how she knew that. 'I offered him a drink when he came to my boat and he asked for water,' she explained. 'I gave him tea. Chamomile tea.' She stopped when she realized that she was talking too much. Seeing a dead body sometimes affected her that way.

'I didn't mean that Dickie was a drunk,' said DI Howe. 'I just meant that most muggings here would be late at night, after dark. But mugging is a twenty-four-seven business, obviously.'

Lulu turned to look at Conrad. He had stopped and was sniffing the ground, his tail swishing from side to side.

'He was hit from behind, you said?' asked DI Friar.

DI Howe nodded. 'Caved the back of his skull in. Dickie was hit hard. The only blessing is that he wouldn't have seen it coming.'

'So what do you think?' asked DI Friar. 'Somebody stopped him and then someone else hit him from behind?'

DI Howe nodded at the ground. 'No footprints, so no way of knowing for sure,' he said. 'But Dickie was street smart – I doubt he'd let someone run up behind him and cold-cock him. Much more likely that one or two guys blocked his way and another came up behind him. Maybe the attacker was hiding behind a bin. But that's all conjecture.'

DI Friar looked around. 'No CCTV?'

'Not in the alley. There's some coverage on the roads at either end and most of the restaurants have CCTV covering the front of their premises, but nothing here. We'll get the cameras checked, but I wouldn't hold your breath.'

'And no witnesses, obviously?'

'Unfortunately not.'

Conrad had stopped sniffing at the ground and was now looking at Lulu, his tail upright and his ears erect. Lulu walked over to him. He looked at her, then down at the ground. Straight away she saw what he was looking at, three small rust-coloured patches on a piece of slate. She bent down and looked at them. 'It's blood,' Conrad whispered into her ear.

'You're sure?'

'I'm a cat, I know what blood smells like.'

'Well done,' Lulu whispered. She straightened up and waved over at the detectives. 'DI Howe, you might want to look at this,' she said.

DI Howe and DC Wilkinson walked over, followed by DI Friar and Phil. Lulu pointed at the spots of dried blood. DI Howe bent down for a better look. 'Could be blood,' he said. 'But there's no way of knowing how long it's been there.'

'It was raining the night before last, so it has to have been since then,' said DI Friar.

'I hear you,' said DI Howe. 'But this can't be his. He wouldn't have been moving around, not with a wound like that.'

'No,' said Lulu. 'But he could very well have been moved into the alley, after death.'

DI Howe scratched the back of his neck. 'That's a stretch,' he said. 'This alley is the perfect place for a mugging. In fact we had two here last month. No fatalities, fortunately. But a woman was slapped and a man was threatened with a knife. They were both robbed. But sure, we'll get this checked out. Obviously if it's Dickie's blood, it changes everything.' He grimaced. 'But I just don't see it.'

Lulu gestured at McNeil's body. 'A wound like that, there'd be blood spatter,' she said.

'There is,' said DI Howe. 'All down the back of his jacket.'

'Yes, but none on the ground,' said Lulu. 'No substantial spatter that I could see, anyway. Just a few drops that could have happened when the body was dropped here. And it was a cold night last night. When I saw him he was wearing a trench coat. He was wearing the same trench coat when DI Friar and I saw him at HQ. The fact that he isn't wearing it now suggests that he was inside when he was attacked, doesn't it?'

DI Howe nodded. 'That makes sense.' He looked over at DC Wilkinson. 'We'll need to start checking all CCTV in the area, council and private, for a vehicle that could have dropped the body off.'

'The pathologist puts the time of death around six?' said DI Friar.

'Approximately, yes,' said DI Howe.

'That would have been a long time for the body to have been here without being seen, so it makes sense that he was killed elsewhere,' said DI Friar. 'More likely it was dumped in the early hours when there was no one around.'

'I hear what you're saying, Julie. But if it wasn't a mugging, what are we looking at?'

'Well it's probably not gang-related,' said DI Friar. 'They would almost certainly use a gun and they wouldn't hide the body behind a skip in an alley. They'd either leave it where it was or they'd bury it where it'd never be found. And, as you said, the fact that he was hit from behind suggests that there was more than one person involved. And hitting him with a blunt object suggests it wasn't planned. An argument, maybe. Certainly an amateur. Dumping the body here is also the sort of thing an amateur would do.'

'You knew him pretty well, Julie,' said DI Howe. 'Can you think of anyone he knew who would want him dead?'

'I know of a lot of people who've said they'd swing for him, but no one ever meant it seriously. His heart was in the right place, and while some of the stories he wrote pissed a lot of people off, I doubt anyone seriously wished him harm.' DI Friar forced a smile. 'Superintendent Knight said some pretty nasty things about him this morning. Including that someone needed to teach Dickie the error of his ways.'

'In what context?' said DI Howe.

DI Friar shook her head. 'I'm not putting the super up as a suspect,' she said. 'Dickie had been talking to the relatives of the victims in our serial-killer case. They didn't like the sort of questions that Dickie was asking, and the super wanted him to stop.'

'Could one of the relatives have killed Dickie?'

'I seriously doubt it. Sergeant Sawyer's wife is quite a slight woman and Fraser Robinson's parents are elderly. I don't think any of them would be capable of beating Dickie to death and then dropping the body here.'

'Maybe, if Dickie was talking to the relatives, he tracked down Mrs Pearson as well,' said Lulu.

DI Howe frowned. 'Mrs Pearson?' he repeated.

'The wife – I'm sorry, the widow – of the man they found at Stretford Meadows yesterday.'

'That's one of your serial-killer victims, right?' DI Howe asked DI Friar.

'It's complicated,' said DI Friar. 'When you're done here, why don't you come to the MIT room and I'll bring you up to speed?' She took a deep breath. 'Look, I already have a team in place – would you mind if I get my people to start looking at Dickie's phone records?'

DI Howe's eyes hardened. 'Do you want to take over the investigation, is that what you're saying?'

DI Friar held up her hands. 'No, absolutely not. But we know that Dickie was speaking to the relatives of our victims, so there might be some crossover. It just might save some time if I put my phone people on the case.'

'What about his vehicle?' asked DI Howe.

'Dickie didn't drive,' said DI Friar. 'He always used public transport. Or walked.'

DI Howe nodded. 'Okay.' He rubbed his chin thoughtfully. 'Dickie had been writing a lot of stories about your serial killer,' he said. 'Is it possible that the serial killer did this?'

DI Friar wrinkled her nose. 'Our serial killer always uses

a rope and a particular knot,' she said. 'He's never used a blunt object before.' She shrugged. 'But I suppose there's a first time for everything.'

33

Lulu spent most of the afternoon revisiting the London cold cases on the HOLMES system. It had been five years since she had looked at the cases, and while she remembered many of the details, there was still much that felt as if she was reading it for the first time. That was why HOLMES was such an invaluable investigative tool – memories faded and even changed over time, but the database was irrevocable and always available.

She read through the interviews that she had done with the Three Little Piggies. All three suspects had stuck religiously to 'no comment', but the questions that she had asked showed her line of thinking. The evidence against all the men was purely circumstantial, so the interrogations were really nothing other than fishing expeditions. In a successful interrogation, you only asked questions to which you already knew the answers. Then, when you were lied to, you could produce the evidence to show that you had been lied to and the more lies a suspect told, the guiltier he or she became. The problem with the Three Little Piggies interrogations had been that she really had no idea of what their motive might be. She had never been able to find a link between any of the suspects and the four victims, which could only mean that they had been chosen at random. If they had at any point started answering Lulu's questions, she might have been able to catch them out in a lie, but that had never happened.

'No comment.'

'No comment.'

'No comment.'

At about four o'clock, DI Howe and DC Wilkinson arrived and DI Friar took them into a side office. A few minutes later, DC Townsend joined them with a tray of canteen coffees. They talked for the best part of half an hour, after which they were joined by Superintendent Knight. The superintendent seemed to be in better humour than he had been that morning, but he was still stern-faced and did a lot of pacing. Lulu would have loved to have known what was discussed but she knew better than to intervene – she was only a guest in the investigation. The superintendent stayed in the side office for ten minutes, then left, his head down and his brow furrowed.

DI Friar then took DI Howe and DC Wilkinson out of the side office and sat down with them at a HOLMES terminal. She began showing them files. DC Wilkinson took notes.

Phil came to sit down next to Lulu.

'What do you think's going on?' she asked.

'I think DI Friar thinks that Mrs Pearson had something to do with Dickie McNeil's murder,' he said.

'What's the thinking? That Dickie went round to see her to ask her about the death of her husband?'

'Well, he was definitely on the story, wasn't he? And the guy wasn't afraid of turning up where he wasn't wanted. Or expected.'

Lulu frowned. 'So what theory do you think she's working on? Dickie goes to see Mrs Pearson and she kills him?'

'That would be possible.'

'Possible, but not likely. I think it'd be hard to get the drop on a former cop like Dickie.' She paused. 'But if Mrs Pearson did have a male friend – a lover or whatever – who killed her husband for her, what if the man was at the house when Dickie turned up unannounced? If Dickie saw her with a man, he'd put two and two together quicker than you could say front-page story.'

'She might have invited him into the house. Faced with a tearful widow, he might just have let his guard down. Guy comes up behind him and cracks him over the head.' He shook his head. 'But thinking that and proving it are two very different things. They'll be tracking McNeil's phone, for sure. So they'll know where he was when he died. Do you know if they found anything else in Mrs Pearson's phone records? Was she talking to anyone on a regular basis?'

'I don't want anyone to think I'm being nosy,' said Lulu. 'It's not connected to our investigation.'

'Well, it is in the sense that whoever it is, they're copying our killer.'

'But that's the only connection, so I haven't stuck my nose in.'

At just after five o'clock, DC Townsend grabbed his coat and headed out.

Phil went up to the canteen to get them coffees. While he was away, DI Friar came over. She looked tense and had tied her hair back. 'Busy day?' said Lulu.

'One of the busiest I've ever had.'

Conrad walked out from under Lulu's chair and looked up at the detective.

'Well done on noticing those drops of blood, Conrad,'

said DI Friar. 'They were indeed from Dickie, so he was definitely killed somewhere else and dropped in the alley.'

Conrad tilted his head to one side, then sat down.

'I guess he's not in a talking mood today,' said DI Friar. She smiled at Lulu. 'Seriously, it was a good spot. As was your realization that he wasn't wearing his coat when he was attacked.'

'So you agree he was killed inside?'

DI Friar nodded. 'Absolutely, and now that we've accessed Dickie's phone records, we've a pretty good idea where that was.' She looked at her wristwatch. 'DC Townsend is bringing Mrs Pearson in as we speak.'

'It's a bit late, isn't it?'

'I want to strike while the iron's hot,' she said. 'At the moment she doesn't realize that she's a suspect so we're hoping we'll catch her on the back foot.'

'So you think she did it?'

'Why don't you watch the interview?' she said.

'I thought having an outsider there wouldn't be a good idea, especially a civilian.'

'I didn't mean in the interview room,' said DI Friar. 'There's an observation room where you can watch via CCTV link. If you'd like.'

Lulu beamed. 'Oh yes, I'd like. I'd like very much.'

34

Mrs Pearson was sitting at a table with a bottle of water in front of her. DC Townsend was standing by the door, his arms folded. There was a slight smile on Mrs Pearson's face, but it was a sign of nervousness more than anything. She was a small woman, a couple of inches below five feet, with close-cropped black hair and slightly pointed ears that gave her a pixie-ish look. She was wearing pink lipstick and heavy mascara that appeared to have been freshly applied, which struck Lulu as strange considering that only the previous day she had learned that her husband had been murdered. She was wearing a denim shirt and had a pink pullover draped over her shoulders. 'Can I smoke?' she asked.

'I'm afraid not,' said DC Townsend.

The interview room was on the ground floor but the room that Lulu and Conrad were sitting in was on the second floor, just down the corridor from the MIT room. There were half a dozen plastic chairs facing two monitors. One feed was from a camera facing Mrs Pearson; the other was a view of the other side of the table, where there were two empty chairs.

On the wall by the table in the interview room was the audio recording system, which operated the old-fashioned way with two cassette recorders.

Lulu and Conrad were alone in the observation room and were sitting on the two seats closest to the monitors. As they watched the monitors, the interview room door opened and DI Friar walked in, carrying a pale blue folder and two cassette tapes.

'Thank you so much for coming in at such short notice, Mrs Pearson,' said DI Friar as she closed the door behind her.

'Has something happened? DC Townsend wouldn't tell me what was going on.'

'We just need to confirm a few things with you, for the record,' said DI Friar. She sat down and handed the two cassettes to DC Townsend. He slotted them into the deck and then sat down next to DI Friar.

DI Friar smiled brightly. 'So, it's just after six o'clock in the evening on 12 May. This is Detective Inspector Julie Friar and I am with . . .'

She nodded at DC Townsend. 'Detective Constable Peter Townsend,' he said.

'We're here to interview Mrs Tanya Pearson. If you could say your name for the tape, please, Mrs Pearson.'

'Tanya Pearson,' she said, gripping her water bottle tightly.

'She's nervous,' said Conrad.

'What does her aura look like?' asked Lulu.

'I can't tell on screen,' said Conrad. 'I have to actually see the person. You can't capture the vibrations with a camera. But just look at the way she's squeezing that bottle. She feels trapped.'

Lulu nodded as she stared at the screens. Mrs Pearson definitely looked worried.

'So, Mrs Pearson,' DI Friar continued. 'There are a few things that we need to run by you. You reported your husband missing two days ago, at midnight.'

That's right.'

'And prior to that you had sent your husband a number of text messages, asking where he was.'

Mrs Pearson nodded. 'Yes, he's usually back by ten o'clock at the latest. He does a lot of surveys in the evenings, but people have to sleep, so ten o'clock would be the latest.'

'And you called several times, starting at nine o'clock?'

'No, I didn't call. He doesn't like being called when he's working. I sent texts. The first one was to ask him what he wanted for dinner.'

And when did you send that text?'

'About half past nine, I think. He didn't reply, so I sent him another text at ten. He didn't reply to that either. Sometimes when he's working he can't reply right away, so I wasn't worried, but then it got to midnight and I was worried so I called the police. Not that they were any help. They said they wouldn't be able to do anything until the following day.'

DI Friar nodded. She opened the folder and took out a black-and-white photograph of a Ford Focus passing through a set of traffic lights. She gave it to Mrs Pearson. 'That's your husband's car, isn't it?'

Mrs Pearson narrowed her eyes. 'I suppose so.'

'Surely you recognize the registration number? Is it or is it not your husband's car?'

'It's our car. We both drive it.'

'Can you explain why your husband was seen driving home just before eight o'clock on the night he died?'

Mrs Pearson screwed up her face. 'That's not possible. He didn't come home that night. And you've been to our house. You know that the car isn't there.' She pushed the photograph back towards DI Friar. 'Maybe he was on the way somewhere else. Or maybe someone had stolen his car. Maybe the person who killed him.' She tapped the photograph. 'You should be looking for whoever was driving, because it can't have been Robbie.'

The door opened and Lulu jumped – she had been so engrossed in what was happening on the monitors. It was Phil, carrying two coffee mugs, a bowl and a bottle of Evian water. 'Have I missed much?' he asked as he sat down next to Lulu.

'DI Friar's showing her photographs of her husband's car, heading home about eight.'

'Ouch,' said Phil, handing her one of the coffee mugs.

On the monitor, DI Friar smiled thinly and took another sheet of paper from the file. 'We accessed your husband's phone records, and according to the GPS data he arrived home just after eight o'clock. The phone stayed there for another fifteen hours, after which it went dead. Presumably the battery died. So, Mrs Pearson, can you explain why you phoned the police at midnight to report your husband missing when he in fact arrived home at eight o'clock?'

Mrs Pearson grimaced and didn't reply.

Phil poured some water into the bowl and placed it on the floor in front of Conrad. Conrad jumped down off the chair and began to lap at the water.

DI Friar reached into the folder again and took out a second photograph of the Ford Focus, this one taken by a motorway camera. 'And perhaps you can explain why your car was then photographed being driven along the M60 towards Stretford Meadows just before eleven o'clock that night.'

Mrs Pearson squinted at the photograph. 'You can't tell who's driving.'

'That's true. But we are sure it isn't your husband at the wheel, because the post-mortem suggests that he had been dead for more than two hours at that point. Were you driving the car, Mrs Pearson?'

'No, of course not.' She sighed and slumped back in her chair. 'Am I under arrest?'

'Not at the moment, no. At the moment you are just helping us with our inquiries. You don't have to say anything. But it may harm your defence if you do not mention when questioned something which you later rely on in court. Anything you do say may be given in evidence. And of course this conversation is being recorded. So this is really your best opportunity to tell us the truth. If you do decide to lie, there could be repercussions down the line.'

'I didn't kill my husband,' she said quietly.

'And I believe that,' said DI Friar. 'Your husband was strangled by hands much bigger than yours.'

'He was killed with a rope.'

'No, he wasn't. He was strangled and the rope was put around his neck afterwards. So I don't believe that you strangled your husband. And I don't believe you would have had the strength to carry his body out onto Stretford Meadows. The question I want answering is, did you help carry the body? Or did you drive the car?'

She shook her head. 'I stayed at home.'

'And who took the body to Stretford Meadows?'

'How would I know? The killer, obviously.'

DI Friar opened her folder and slid a sheet of paper across the table. 'When we checked your phone records, it became clear that you were having an affair with a man by the name of James Millington.'

Mrs Pearson swallowed nervously. Her eyes darted from side to side like a trapped animal looking for a way out.

'You do know Mr Millington?' asked DI Friar.

Mrs Pearson stared at the sheet of paper.

DI Friar took a photograph from the file and pushed it across the table. 'Mr Millington works with your husband. Sorry, worked. Past tense.'

Mrs Pearson closed her eyes.

'Please look at the photograph, Mrs Pearson. For the tape, I am showing Mrs Pearson a recent photograph of Mr James Millington. Do you know this man, Mrs Pearson?'

'Yes, of course I do.'

'And were you having an affair with Mr Millington?'

'If you've seen my text messages, then you know I was. You've snooped at my messages and seen the photographs.'

DI Friar nodded. 'Yes, we have.'

'Did it turn you on? Seeing those pictures? Got you all wet, did they?' She glared at DC Townsend. 'What about you? Did you get a stiffie looking at them?'

'I haven't actually seen them,' said DC Townsend.

Mrs Pearson looked back at DI Friar. 'Do I need a solicitor?'

'That's up to you, Mrs Pearson. You can call a solicitor if you want, or we can get you a duty solicitor. But at the moment you are simply helping us with our inquiries. Things might get a bit more adversarial if there is a solicitor in the room. At the moment I'm trying to help you make the best of what could be a pretty bad situation. As I said, I don't think you killed your husband, and I don't think you disposed of his body. The question is, were you an accessory before or after the fact, and were you involved in a conspiracy to kill your husband?'

'There was no conspiracy!' said Mrs Pearson. 'Robbie came home early. He caught me and Jim and went crazy. He grabbed a knife and tried to stab Jim. Jim was only defending himself.'

'So Mr Millington strangled Mr Pearson?'

'You make it sound worse than it was. Robbie attacked Jim, Jim grabbed him by the throat to make him stop. He only had Robbie by the throat for a few seconds, then Robbie collapsed. We just thought he'd passed out but . . .' She shook her head. 'It was an accident.'

'If it was an accident, why didn't you call the police immediately?'

'Jim said they wouldn't believe us. Then he had the idea of making it look like the serial killer had done it. There was a story in the *Manchester Evening News* about the knot the killer used and Jim had some rope in his car.'

'What about your husband's clothes, and his phone?'

'We put them in the attic. Jim said he'd dispose of them later. You have to believe me, it was an accident.'

'Would you like a cup of tea?' asked DI Friar. 'Or coffee? Maybe a sandwich?'

Mrs Pearson shook her head. 'My stomach is churning, I can't eat. But maybe a cup of tea.'

DI Friar looked at DC Townsend. 'Could you get Mrs Pearson a cup of tea, please? And a cup of coffee for me.'

'Milk and one sugar, please,' said Mrs Pearson.

'No problem,' said DC Townsend. He left the room.

DI Friar leaned across the table. 'Are you okay?' she asked.

Mrs Pearson shook her head. 'Not really,' she said. 'I just want to go home.'

'Just a few more questions,' said DI Friar. 'What can you tell me about Dickie McNeil?'

Mrs Pearson frowned.

'Dickie McNeil. Richard McNeil, but he's always gone by Dickie.'

Mrs Pearson shook her head. 'The name doesn't ring a bell.'

'Maybe a picture would help.' DI Friar opened the file and slid out a head-and-shoulders shot of McNeil. She looked at it wistfully, then pushed it across the table. Mrs Pearson turned her head away.

The door to the observation room opened. It was DC Townsend. 'I thought you were on a tea run?' said Lulu.

'DI Friar wanted to be on her own for a while,' said DC Townsend.

'Good cop, bad cop?' said Lulu.

'It's funny how often it works,' said DC Townsend. 'They think that because one of the detectives has left the room, the interrogation has stopped. They forget that the tape and the cameras are still running.' He sat down on the chair next to Phil. 'She does this quite a lot, with considerable success.'

On the monitors, DI Friar tapped the photograph. 'So, what time did Mr McNeil visit your house last night?'

'I didn't say that he did,' said Mrs Pearson.

'No, but the GPS on his phone tells us all we need to know. It also told us where you dumped Mr McNeil's phone. In a skip between your house and Stretford Meadows.'

'I didn't dump any phone. I was at home all night.'

'So you were there when Mr McNeil called?' DI Friar

leaned across the table. 'I'm trying to help you here, Tanya. I'm on your side. You're a mere slip of a thing, I know you didn't hit Mr McNeil. According to the pathologist who carried out the post-mortem, Mr McNeil was hit from behind by someone who was bigger and stronger than he was.'

Lulu looked across at DC Townsend. 'Has the post-mortem taken place already? That was quick.'

DC Townsend smiled. 'It hasn't. She's winging it.'

Lulu smiled and shook her head. 'Naughty, naughty.'

On the monitor, DI Friar smiled at Mrs Pearson. 'You see, Tanya, I think Mr McNeil was talking to you when Mr Millington came up behind him and hit him with what we police like to call a blunt object. Almost certainly something that you already had in the house.'

Mrs Pearson shook her head but didn't say anything.

'You probably didn't even realize what was happening. It was so fast, right? One minute you're talking to Mr McNeil, the next he's on the floor. And there was a lot of blood, I'm sure. You must have been shocked. And terrified.'

Mrs Pearson bit down on her lower lip. Tears were welling up in her eyes.

'I'll go and get the tea,' said DC Townsend. 'She'll be needing it.' He stood up and left the room.

'And it was Mr Millington who took the body away, wasn't it? He probably used his own car. But we'll know for sure soon enough.'

Mrs Pearson frowned.

'We have a forensics team checking his car now,' said DI Friar. 'And another forensics team is inside your house as we speak. If there's a single speck of Mr McNeil's blood in the car or in your house, that'll be all the proof we need.'

'I didn't kill anyone.'

'I believe you, Mrs Pearson. As I said, whoever killed Mr McNeil was big and strong. And whoever carried your husband out onto Stretford Meadows, well, they had to be big too.' She reached over and tapped the photograph of James Millington. 'Jim is a big man, isn't he? Big hands.'

Tears were running down Mrs Pearson's face now and DI Friar reached into her pocket and brought out a small packet of tissues. She held out the packet and Mrs Pearson took one. 'Thank you,' she said and dabbed at her eyes.

'I'm on your side, Tanya. We women have to stick together, don't we?'

Mrs Pearson blew her nose and nodded. 'Yes. Yes, we do.'

'We're also talking to Mr Millington, and I am sure he has his own view of what happened two nights ago. And I'm sure he'll present himself in the best possible light. Was it his idea to say that your husband attacked him with a knife?'

Mrs Pearson sniffed and nodded.

'Tanya, this is your chance to tell me what really happened. We need to get this straight now so that there's no misunderstanding down the line. If you are the innocent party here, now is the time to make that clear. I can see how upset you are. I realize that you are not the sort of person who would set out to commit two murders.'

'I didn't want Robbie dead,' she said. 'It just happened so quickly. They were fighting in the bedroom and then they were on the floor and Jim was on top of Robbie and he had his hands around his throat. I shouted for Jim to stop but he was crazy and he kept strangling him until he went still.'

'And then Mr McNeil came to talk to you yesterday evening about Robbie's death?'

Mrs Pearson nodded. 'Jim was in the house when he called. He said he had information about Robbie's death, and I let him in. We went into the kitchen and he said he had heard that Robbie was gay, which was stupid. Robbie wasn't gay. Then he saw Jim's jacket and asked if there was someone in the house. I said no, I was alone, and then he asked me whose car was parked in the driveway. It was Jim's, but I said it was mine. He said he knew what car we had and it wasn't mine and he said it was the easiest thing in the world to get the owner's name and address. Then he saw the rope that Jim had used to make it look like the serial killer had killed Robbie. The rest of the rope was on a chair with Robbie's clothing. Jim had put it all in a pile; he was going to get rid of it all – that's why he'd come round to the house. Then Jim came up behind and hit him with a fire extinguisher. There was blood everywhere. I screamed at him, asking him what he'd done, and he said he had to do it because if the police knew he was there then they might suspect him. He said it was the journalist who had been writing about the serial killer. He told me to clean the floor and that he'd get rid of the body.'

'And Mr McNeil had taken his coat off while he was in the house?'

Mrs Pearson nodded tearfully. 'Jim took the coat along with Robbie's things. He said he was going to burn them.'

'And you knew who Mr McNeil was when he called at your house, didn't you?'

Mrs Pearson shook her head.

'You did, because you'd phoned Mr McNeil to tell him about your husband's body being at Stretford Meadows.'

'Oh. Yes. I suppose so.'

'Was that Jim's idea, to call McNeil?'

Mrs Pearson nodded. 'Yes. He said the sooner they found Robbie, the sooner they would connect it with the other killings and stop looking for someone else.'

'How did you get his number?'

'Jim had it. It was in the paper.' She blew her nose. 'Can I go home now?' she asked.

'I'm afraid not. At this point I am arresting you for the murder of Robert Pearson and for the murder of Richard McNeil. And I will read you your rights again for clarity. You do not have to say anything. But it may harm your defence if you do not mention when questioned something which you later rely on in court. Anything you do say may be given in evidence.'

Mrs Pearson burst into tears and buried her head in her hands.

'Gotcha,' said Phil.

'That was a textbook interrogation,' said Lulu. 'DI Friar is a first-class detective.'

'Takes one to know one, boss.'

Lulu smiled. 'Why, Phil, you always say the nicest things.'

35

The Uber dropped Lulu and Conrad in front of the Museum of Science and Industry. Conrad rode on Lulu's shoulders as she crossed the road and walked down the steps to the Staffordshire arm. There were several groups of teenagers sitting on the concrete steps of the Castlefield Bowl and the sickly sweet smell of marijuana wafted in their direction.

Lulu had shared fish and chips with Conrad in the police canteen. Phil had joined them and tucked into sausages and mash. He had decided to work late, making his way through the HOLMES files, trying to find a link between Sergeant Sawyer and Fraser Robinson and the four men who had died in London.

Lulu walked along to *The Lark*. Brianna was sitting on the rear deck of *Cloud Nine* with a young bearded man who was presumably her husband, Sean. They both waved as she approached their boat.

'Finished your chores?' asked Lulu.

'You're never finished on a boat, you know that,' said Brianna. 'It's never-ending.' She introduced Sean, and he smiled at Conrad.

'I love the way he rides on your shoulders,' he said. 'We had a cat once, a tabby. She was lovely but one day she just upped and went.'

'That's a pity,' said Lulu.

'It was the strangest thing,' said Brianna. 'We were just

outside Liverpool and she just jumped onto the towpath and walked away. Not even a backward look. We ended up staying for two weeks but she never came back. We put posters up but no one ever called.' She sighed. 'It was the not knowing that was worst. Not knowing what happened. We assume she got hit by a car, but she never really went near roads.'

'I'm so sorry,' said Lulu. She reached up and patted Conrad. 'I know I'd be distraught if I lost Conrad.'

Sean held up his glass of beer. 'Would you like a drink?'

'I've had a long day, so I think I'll have an early night. Maybe tomorrow?'

'We're leaving tomorrow,' said Brianna.

'Oh, that's a shame,' said Lulu. 'Safe travels, anyway.'

'You too, Lulu,' said Brianna.

Lulu walked over to *The Lark* and climbed on board the rear deck. Conrad jumped down onto the seat and watched as she unlocked the door.

'I think I'll have some chamomile tea before I turn in,' she said. 'Would you like some water?'

'Please,' said Conrad. He followed her down the steps into the cabin.

Lulu put the kettle on to boil and poured Evian water into a bowl for Conrad. 'Do cats do that?' she asked. 'Just walk away without a backward look?'

'They can't be expected to leave a note, can they?' said Conrad. 'And they can't use phones, obviously.' He lapped at the water.

'You know what I mean,' said Lulu. 'You never hear about dogs leaving to live somewhere else, do you? A dog is yours for ever. Someone might steal them – I know that happens –

but generally they stay home, no matter how badly they're treated.'

'Dogs are dogs,' said Conrad. 'They're not very bright.'

'But I have known people whose cats have just gone to live in someone else's house. Sometimes they pop back and forth between the two homes but sometimes they never come back.'

'Cats choose where they want to live,' said Conrad. 'Dogs pretty much do as they're told.'

'Well, I hope you don't leave me,' said Lulu.

'I'm very happy with you,' said Conrad. 'I couldn't be happier.'

'What about before me? Who did you stay with? That day you walked along the towpath in Little Venice. Did you have an owner then?'

Conrad snorted. 'I have never had an owner, Lulu. I've never been owned.'

'I'm sorry, I didn't mean to offend you. What's a better word than owner?'

'Companion works for me,' said Conrad.

'Then that's the word I shall use,' said Lulu. 'Did you have a companion then?'

Conrad sat down and looked at her, his head tilted to one side. 'I was alone when I met you. I had been for several months.'

'Okay. I didn't mean to pry.'

'No, it's a fair question.'

'And what happened to your previous companion? Did you leave?'

Conrad sniffed. 'He died.'

'Oh, Conrad, I'm sorry. It's none of my business, and I'm sorry I asked.'

'No, it's perfectly reasonable for you to ask.' He shrugged. 'Sometimes humans die and he died. So I was alone for a while and then I found you.'

'All's well that ends well.'

'That's what they say.'

'Really, I'm sorry that I pried.'

The kettle began to boil and Lulu was grateful for the interruption. She made herself a cup of chamomile tea and then sat down on the sofa. Conrad jumped up to join her. 'How long do you think we'll stay in Manchester?' he asked.

'With any luck, until we solve the case,' said Lulu. 'But to be honest, we don't seem to be making much progress.'

'DI Friar has charged Mrs Pearson and her boyfriend with the murders of Mr Pearson and Dickie McNeil.'

'Yes, but they were never our cases; they were collateral damage, really. Nothing to do with the killer we're looking for.' She smiled. 'And well done finding those blood spots in the alley.'

'Oh, I think you'd already realized that Dickie had been killed somewhere else.'

Lulu sipped her tea. 'I suppose so.'

'And you were fairly sure that Mrs Pearson had killed her husband.'

'Well, I knew that it was someone who was close to Mr Pearson. That was why they wanted to throw suspicion on our serial killer.' She sighed. 'It's so frustrating. I'm sure the key to solving this is on HOLMES somewhere.'

'Phil seems to think so, too.'

'He does, that's why he's still there.'

Lulu had left Phil sitting at his HOLMES terminal, drinking coffee. His boss had been on the phone, asking Phil how much longer he'd be in Manchester. His expenses had started working their way through the system, and while there was money in the cold case budget, bed and breakfast at the Midland was burning through it at a fair pace. Phil had been told that if he hadn't made any progress over the next two days, it might be time to call it a day and leave the job to DI Friar and her team.

'Did you have many unsolved cases?' asked Conrad.

'Not many,' said Lulu. 'But some, yes.'

'It must be frustrating.'

'It is. Very. But I really hoped that the two murders in Manchester would help us solve our case. Instead, it's just made it all the more confusing. We thought we were on the trail of someone who was targeting gay men. Hate crimes. But it doesn't look like Sergeant Sawyer and Fraser Robinson were gay. And assuming it is the same killer, he followed them from London, which means they were targeted. And if he targeted his two victims in Manchester, there is a very good chance that the victims in London were also targeted.'

'That makes sense,' said Conrad.

'But that means there must be a connection,' said Lulu. 'Something that connects the victims to the killer. And probably something that connects the victims. But we didn't find anything.'

'Well, back then it probably looked like a series of random killings. Like you said, hate crimes.'

'We did think they were random killings, yes. But HOLMES is able to spot any connections there are, even when we're not looking for them. If a white car is spotted at several crime scenes, HOLMES will tell us. If the victims frequented the same bars or worked at the same company,

HOLMES will flag it. It's doing that all the time, behind the scenes. Looking for connections. And in this case, it didn't find any. Not one.'

'Well, I can see connections, even from the little I know.'

'I'm listening.'

'As you've pointed out, all the victims are men. And now it seems that all the victims were in London at the same time. Before the killings started, yes, but at the same time nonetheless.'

Lulu nodded but didn't say anything.

'They're all white, and none of them was bald.'

'Okay.'

'And the victims in London were all middle-aged.'

'That's true.'

'Now, the victims here in Manchester were what?'

'Sergeant Sawyer was forty-two and Fraser Robinson was thirty-five.'

Conrad wrinkled his nose. 'Ah. So Fraser Robinson definitely doesn't fit the pattern, does he? Sergeant Sawyer would have been in his late thirties when the killer was active in London and Fraser Robinson would have been barely in his thirties when the murders started. But both were in Manchester by then.'

'True. But I do hear what you're saying. They were all very similar physically.' She smiled. 'Though I'm not sure baldness is a factor. But the thing is, as I said, other than the physical and age similarities, HOLMES didn't find a single connection between the men.'

'Because maybe the connecting data isn't in the system.'

'Everything goes into HOLMES,' said Lulu. 'Every interview, every statement, every step of the investigation.'

'Bear with me for a while,' said Conrad. 'What about connections between your suspects? The Three Little Piggies.'

'Nothing. Believe me, we looked. They lived in different areas of London, had different jobs, went to different schools, supported different football teams. We checked phone records and they didn't speak or text. We even went back through Gordon Wallace's courier deliveries for two years to see if he had ever delivered anything to the other two. He hadn't. And we checked with Butler's taxi firm and he had never picked up either of the other two.'

'But you did say that Butler had picked up two of the victims.'

'Which is why he was on our radar. But he never picked up either of the other two Little Piggies. And now, of course, he's dead. So he's no longer a suspect.'

'He could be a dead suspect. Just because he's dead doesn't mean he wasn't involved in the first three murders.'

Lulu nodded. 'That's true. Fair point.'

'Now, you say there are no connections between the Three Little Piggies, but I can see some.'

'None of them is bald?'

'There's that. And they are all white and male, about the same age. They were all in their early twenties when you were looking at them.'

'That's true. Butler and Edward Parker were both twenty-two, and Wallace was twenty-three.'

'You obviously think that the fact they all had a full head of hair was a coincidence, but what about the age thing?'

'People of the same age tend to hang out together. I'm not sure that counts as a coincidence.'

'Except you said you couldn't find evidence of that. They didn't hang out together, so far as you know. So is the age thing a coincidence? They all three just happened to be in their early twenties?'

'Well, clearly you don't think it is.'

'I'm looking for patterns, Lulu. And I think there is a pattern here. The victims in London were all about the same age, weren't they? Late thirties, early forties. But the Three Little Piggies were in their early twenties in London and would be in their late twenties now. HOLMES looks for connections, and in this case it hasn't found any. No connections between the victims, no connections between the suspects. And the only connections you have between the victims and the suspects are some DNA, which might be circumstantial, and some CCTV evidence, also circumstantial.'

'That's a pretty good summation of the position, yes.'

'Assuming that HOLMES is as good as you say it is, and assuming that there are connections to be found, that can only mean that the data isn't available to the computer.'

Lulu frowned. 'I suppose so.'

'So the question that I would ask is: what connections could there be between a group of middle-aged men and another group of men in their twenties?'

Lulu shook her head. 'I have no idea.'

'Well, if there had been something, you would have found it. So let's move the goalposts.'

'How do you mean?'

'Let's go back in time. Let's go back, say, fifteen years. What connection could there be between a group of ten-year-old boys, and a group of adult men?'

Lulu's mouth opened. 'Oh, my goodness me.'

'You didn't go back that far, did you?'

Lulu shook her head. 'No, we didn't. There would be no reason to.'

'But you see it now, don't you?'

'Yes, Conrad, I do. Oh, my goodness. Of course.'

36

When Lulu and Conrad arrived in the MIT room it was just after seven o'clock in the morning and Phil was already tapping away at a HOLMES terminal. Lulu was holding two Starbucks coffees and she put one down in front of him. 'So this is why we can't have breakfast at the Midland,' she said. 'Did you sleep last night?'

'I got back to the hotel about midnight, grabbed six hours of shuteye and came straight back.'

'That's burning the candle at both ends, Phil.'

'The clock is ticking, Lulu. I really don't want to go back to London with my tail between my legs.'

She took a bag containing a croissant from her coat pocket and gave it to him. 'This should keep you going until the canteen opens and I can do a bacon-roll run,' she said, and sat down next to him. Conrad jumped off her shoulders and landed on the table. 'We had a brainwave last night,' said Lulu.

'We?'

'Conrad and I.'

Phil laughed. 'That's right, Conrad the cat detective. What was the brainwave?' He took a gulp of coffee.

'You still haven't found any links between the victims and our suspects?'

Phil shook his head.

'And no links between the victims here and the victims we had in London?'

'Nope. I've been all through HOLMES and there's nothing.'

'Maybe we're not going back far enough.'

Phil frowned. 'What do you mean?'

'Maybe we're not seeing any connections because they're historical.'

'Why do you say that?'

'Well, it's a hunch. A copper's hunch. But look at their ages. The Three Little Piggies are in their late twenties now. They were in their early twenties when we first looked at them. And the victims were all much older. Ian Pettigrew was fifty-two when he died, Nick Hurst was forty, William Eccles was thirty-eight and John Dunne was thirty-seven. We looked at them and found no connections, but did we go back far enough? What if we had gone back fifteen years or so? To when the Three Little Piggies were children?'

'We checked their schools, remember? They were at different schools in different parts of London.'

'In their final years at school, yes. When they were sixteen or seventeen. But what about earlier, when they were younger? They could have been at primary school together. Or maybe they were in a social group. Cub Scouts or something like that. A youth club, perhaps.'

Phil rubbed his chin. 'So you think something happened to the Three Little Piggies when they were kids? Then for some reason they split up, but get back together ten years later? For what? Revenge?'

'That's what I'm thinking. And whatever it was happened so long ago that the details aren't in HOLMES.'

Phil nodded thoughtfully. 'Then because Butler died and Wallace was in prison, they stopped. And started again when Wallace got out?'

'It makes sense, doesn't it?'

'Yes, boss, perfect sense. So what do we do? How do we fill in the gaps?'

'We need to get the full employment records of all the victims, going back fifteen or twenty years. And we need to speak to the parents of the Three Little Piggies, to find out where they were when they were kids. We need to identify any overlap.'

'Do you want to do Butler and I'll do Parker, and whoever finishes first can do Wallace?'

Lulu grinned. 'So it's a race?'

'Game on,' said Phil, reaching for his phone.

37

Lulu checked the HOLMES files on one of their original suspects, Jack Butler, but there were no details of his parents. There was an address of a flat in Wandsworth. She remembered seeing Butler there, early on in the investigation. She was a consultant at the time, but the DNA evidence had been a major breakthrough and she wanted to do the initial interview herself. DNA had been found under the fingernail of the third victim – William Eccles – and it was an exact match with Butler's. Lulu had gone with Phil, arriving at Butler's doorstep at seven o'clock in the morning to get Butler out of bed.

Butler had shared the flat with two other young men, both of whom had been able to provide alibis for the time that William Eccles had been killed. Butler had refused to cooperate and they had taken him in for questioning. As part of the interview process he had been asked to supply details of his next of kin and he had refused. In fact he had refused to cooperate in any way, and other than to ask for a lawyer he would say only 'No comment'.

Lulu had assumed that the DNA would be conclusive, but the Crown Prosecution Service was reluctant to take the case to trial with just that. They wanted more – at the very least a motive and evidence that Butler had been in the vicinity of the dumped bodies. The interview had been fruitless, and not long after that Butler had been killed in his cab.

There was a copy of Butler's driving licence on HOLMES, using the Wandsworth address. It was a simple matter for Lulu to get Butler's birth certificate. Born in Croydon Hospital. A healthy eight and a half pounds. Father Reginald Butler, mother Anne. Maiden name Butterworth.

She checked the electoral roll but while there were plenty of Butlers there were none called Reginald or Anne. She used her mobile phone to access Google and did a search for Reginald and Anne Butler. Nothing came up.

She put down her mobile and looked over at Phil, who was talking earnestly into his phone, his head down and his left hand pressed against his forehead. It looked as if she had drawn a blank with Jack Butler and she was out of options. She decided to have a go at Gordon Wallace. She tapped his name into HOLMES and flicked through the files. She and Phil had interviewed him twice after ANPR cameras had spotted his van in the vicinity of two of the disposal sites on the days that the bodies were dumped. Like Butler, he had refused to say anything other than 'No comment'. But he had been more forthcoming with his personal details and his next of kin were listed as Eric and Beverley Reeves. Lulu frowned as she read the names. Why the different surname? An uncle and aunt, maybe. There was an address in Ealing but no phone number. She called directory enquiries and they had a listing for the address. Lulu smiled. Finally things were going her way. She rang the number and a woman answered, but Lulu could tell from her voice that she was far too young to be Wallace's mother.

'I'm trying to contact Mrs Beverley Reeves,' said Lulu.

'Who's calling?' asked the woman.

'My name is Lulu Lewis. You're not Mrs Reeves, are you?'

'I'm afraid Mrs Reeves died several years ago.'

'Oh, I'm sorry. Is Mr Reeves there?'

'Can you tell me what it's about, please?'

'Mr and Mrs Reeves are shown as the next of kin of a Mr Gordon Wallace and I'm just trying to ascertain the nature of their relationship, their surnames being different and all.'

'Mrs Lewis, I'm afraid that Mr Reeves isn't really up to answering questions. I'm one of his care workers – we pop in three times a day to make sure he's okay. He has dementia and is very forgetful. It's got worse since his wife passed away and he'll probably be in a home fairly soon.'

'Oh, that's a pity,' said Lulu. 'But could you ask him if he remembers Gordon Wallace?'

'I'll try, but really, he barely remembers if he's been to the toilet.' The woman put the phone down. Lulu smiled at Conrad as the seconds ticked by. He was sitting on the chair next to her and had been reading the HOLMES data with her.

Eventually the woman came back on the line. 'I'm really sorry, but Mr Reeves doesn't even know who I am today.'

'Could I try again tomorrow, maybe?'

'You can, of course, but I can't promise that he'll be any more coherent. He's definitely getting worse. You say it's a next-of-kin thing?'

'Yes, Mr and Mrs Reeves are down on a form as being Mr Wallace's next of kin, but obviously as the family names are different, we needed to check.' Lulu didn't want to explain that the information had been fed into HOLMES as part of a murder investigation.

'You know that they fostered, for years?'

'I didn't know that, no. Ah, that explains it.'

'Hang on, the couple have a filing system here. Mr Reeves used to show it to me all the time and talk about the children they fostered. There were more than a hundred and fifty in all, over the years. What was the person's name again?'

'Gordon. Gordon Wallace.'

'And when might he have been with them?'

Lulu frowned as she did the calculation in her head. If Wallace had been fostered, he would have been under sixteen. 'Fifteen years ago or more.'

'Let me check. They always kept very neat files.'

The woman put the phone down. Lulu looked over at Phil, who was now off the phone and tapping on his keyboard. 'Phil, I've drawn a blank with Jack Butler so I'm looking at Wallace now.'

Phil nodded. 'I'm waiting for someone from social services to get back to me,' he said. 'Edward Parker was adopted. Parker wasn't his birth name. He was born Edward Lawson, but his parents died when he was eight and he was in the care system for a few years. I'm trying to find out where he was before the Parkers adopted him.' His phone rang and he picked it up. 'Fingers crossed.'

The care worker came back on the line. 'Gordon Wallace, you say? Yes, he was fostered here from the ages of thirteen to sixteen. That's quite a long time; they mainly did short-term fostering, which is why so many kids stayed with them over the years.'

'How much information is in the file?'

'It's mainly made up of the monthly reports they submitted to social services. Basically saying how he was getting on.'

'Does it say where he was before he came to the Reeves house?'

'Let me see. Yes, he was at the Horizon Residential Home for Boys. In Islington.'

'Is there a phone number?'

'Yes, there is.'

Lulu picked up a pen and scribbled down the details of the home, then checked the phone number with the woman before thanking her and hanging up. She dialled the number and wrinkled her nose in annoyance when she heard the unobtainable tone. As she replaced the receiver, she looked over at Phil, who was scribbling in his notebook. Her heart began to pound when she realized what he had just written – Horizon Residential Home for Boys.

Lulu stood up and waited impatiently for Phil to finish his call. As soon as he put the receiver down, she showed him what she had written on her notepad and his eyes widened.

'Well, that can't be a coincidence, can it?' Lulu said.

'So Wallace and Parker were in the same children's home? That's the connection we never had. This is big, boss.'

'I'll get on to Islington Council,' said Lulu. 'Can you have another go at Jack Butler? You might see something I missed.'

'Sure.'

It took Lulu almost an hour on the phone with Islington Council to get the information she wanted. She was passed from one department to another and spoke to half a dozen people before she reached a young man in the Children and Young People Directorate. He introduced himself as Martin and he had a soft Irish accent that made her think of rolling green hills and slow-flowing rivers. He looked through a list of council and private children's homes and initially couldn't find one called Horizon, but he found it eventually and told her that it was a privately run boys' home that had shut down years ago.

'Does it say why it closed?' Lulu asked.

'It wasn't up to the council's standards, that's all it says. Let me have a look at the file.' He hummed quietly to himself and Lulu heard the occasional tapping sound. 'Ah, dear me. They had a number of suicides there. Four that I can see. The council ended its contract after the fourth death.'

'Was there an inquiry? Or a criminal case?'

'No, nothing like that, no. It's not unusual for a home's standards to fall. Sometimes the home will up its game, sometimes they'll decide it's not worth it, especially with budget cuts and the like.'

'Does it say what happened to the children who were there?'

'Not specifically, but they would have been dispersed through the system.'

'Within Islington?'

'Not necessarily, no. Initially within the Greater London area, but they could in theory have been sent anywhere in the country.'

'How many children would that have been?'

'Let me see.' He hummed again for half a minute. 'Twenty-six boys were resident when the home closed.'

'How would I go about finding out where the boys went?'

'That would be harder. I could probably locate the individual files of any boys you were interested in, but it would take time.'

'Can I run a few names by you? See if they were at the home at the time of its closure?'

'Sure, go ahead.'

'Gordon Wallace?'

There was silence for a few seconds. 'Yes,' said Martin eventually.

'Jack Butler?'

'Again, yes.'

Lulu's breath caught in her throat. 'Edward Parker?'

There was a delay of almost a minute. 'I don't see an Eddie or Edward Parker, no.'

'Oh, wait, try Edward Lawson.'

'That we have,' said Martin. 'Edward Charles Lawson.'

Lulu's heart was beating faster now. 'What about Derek Sawyer?'

There was silence for almost a minute. 'No.'

'Fraser Robinson?'

Another minute-long silence. 'No.'

'Okay, that's very helpful indeed, Martin. Thank you so much. Just one more thing – who was running the Horizon home at the time it was closed?'

'That should be easy enough to find,' he said. 'Just give me a few seconds. Yes, here we are, it was an Ian Pettigrew. He was the manager. And chief executive. So an owner-manager, I guess.'

Lulu's heart pounded. 'Bear with me for a minute, Martin,' she said into the phone, then she waved at Phil, who was on a call. 'I need you now,' she mouthed.

Phil nodded and ended his call. 'What's up?' he asked as he stood up and walked over to her.

She held up a hand to silence him. 'Martin, I'm going to hand you over to Detective Inspector Philip Jackson of the Metropolitan Police. We'd like names of all the boys who were at the home and a list of the staff, and as there might be data protection issues it might be better handled through him.' She put her hand over the receiver. 'Ian Pettigrew ran the Horizon home, and Butler, Parker and Wallace all lived there. I think we've cracked it, Phil.'

'Awesome, boss,' said Phil, taking the receiver.

'The guy's name is Martin, he's been very helpful,' said Lulu. She reached down and stroked the back of Conrad's neck. 'We're almost there,' she said.

'Almost where?' asked a voice behind her, and Lulu jumped. It was DI Friar.

'I think we might have found our motive,' said Lulu. 'At least for our murders. The Three Piggies were all in the same boys' home at the same time, and the home was owned and managed by our first victim, Ian Pettigrew.'

'What about our victims, Sergeant Sawyer and Fraser Robinson?'

'No connection yet, but they're going to send over a full list of boys and staff.'

'So you're thinking revenge for something that happened in the home?'

'It would make sense, wouldn't it?'

'It would. But we still need to know why they then came to Manchester to kill our two victims.'

Lulu nodded. 'We're working on it.'

38

It was close to six o'clock when the lists finally came through from Martin at Islington Council's Children and Young People Directorate. Phil printed them out and DI Friar and Lulu hurried over to the printer. DI Friar pulled out the first pages, listing the boys who had been at the home when it closed. 'Yes, here they are,' said DI Friar. 'Butler and Wallace. But I don't see Parker.'

'He was Lawson back then,' said Lulu. 'He was adopted after he left the home.'

DI Friar nodded. 'I see him. Edward Charles Lawson.'

The printer ejected another sheet and Lulu took it. It was a list of employees at the Horizon home. Ian Pettigrew's name was at the top. Chief executive. She scanned the rest of the names and her eyes widened. 'Nick Hurst was employed as a manager at the home. And so was William Eccles.' She continued to scan the list. 'And John Dunne was a handyman there.' She looked at DI Friar. 'That's it. That's the connection we could never find,' she said. 'The Three Piggies lived at the home, the four London victims worked there.'

'Something terrible must have happened to those three boys,' said DI Friar.

Lulu nodded. 'Four boys committed suicide. That's why the home was shut.'

'So some sort of abuse? And they set out to get revenge? Were Sergeant Sawyer and Fraser Robinson on staff?'

'No.'

'And they weren't at the home, either. But they were killed in the same way; there has to be a connection.'

DC Townsend came over, and it was clear from the smile on his face that he had good news. 'We've had a break,' he said excitedly. 'We think we've found Wallace.'

'What? Where?' asked Lulu.

'He was parked in a motorhome last night, in Clifton Country Park, about eight miles to the west of us. It's a nature reserve close to the River Irwell. You're not supposed to park there overnight so a patrol car moved him on, but not before checking his details. Tax and insurance were okay and the driving licence was in the name of Gordon Wallace. When the officers got back to their station they realized that we were looking for Wallace. They went back and he'd already moved on, but we got lucky with ANPR and we know where he is now. Parked in a Tesco car park.'

'That's great police work,' said Lulu.

'Well done, Pete,' said DI Friar. 'Right, let's go out and talk to Mr Wallace.' She looked at Lulu. 'You and DI Jackson have interviewed him before – you should come with us.'

'I'd love to,' said Lulu. She looked at Phil. 'Phil?'

'Hell, yeah,' he said.

Lulu scooped Conrad up from under her chair and set him on her shoulders. Phil stood up and grabbed his jacket. 'Let's go,' he said.

DC Townsend was waiting for them by the lifts and they rode down together.

'The motorhome is parked in the Tesco Superstore car

park in Valley Park Road,' he said. 'That's Prestwich. We have it under observation as we speak. There is at least one person inside.'

'What sort of motorhome is it?' asked Lulu.

DC Townsend took out his notebook. 'It's a Chausson, apparently,' he said. 'About twenty feet long and based on a Ford Transit van. Sleeps four. Six years old. Wallace has been the registered owner for the past four months.'

'Just before the first killing here?' said Lulu.

'He bought it from a guy in north London,' said DC Townsend. 'Paid in cash.'

They walked out of the building and climbed into DC Townsend's Toyota Corolla. Conrad sat on Lulu's lap as they drove out of the car park and headed west. They were outside the Tesco Superstore car park in just under twenty minutes. DC Townsend pulled up behind a blue Ford Focus. 'That's our guys,' he said.

They all got out and DI Friar went over to the Focus. Two men wearing leather jackets and jeans climbed out and she had a brief conversation with them. Lulu and Phil waited with DC Townsend. Eventually DI Friar came back. She pointed at a white motorhome streaked with rust parked at the far side of the car park. 'That's it,' she said. 'A man came out and went into the superstore about an hour ago and came back with a full carrier bag. From the description, it sounds like Wallace.'

Lulu looked over at the vehicle. There were empty parking spaces around it, as if shoppers were reluctant to get too close to it. 'Anybody else inside?' she asked.

'They only saw Wallace,' said DI Friar. 'I'm happy just to knock on the door. There's no history of him using a weapon, is there?'

'No, none,' said Phil.

'Obviously this is your investigation, but do we have enough to confront him?' asked Lulu. 'Isn't everything we have circumstantial?'

'The worry is that he just drives off and we lose him,' said DI Friar. 'He could be anywhere tomorrow. You can live off the grid for weeks in one of those motorhomes. Plus, we do have some damning ANPR data that shows the vehicle in the vicinity of Heaton Park golf course when Sergeant Sawyer's body was dumped, and the vehicle was recorded in the area of Stretford Meadows several hours before Fraser Robinson's body was discovered. I'm hoping that means there's DNA or fingerprint evidence inside the motorhome. It'd be difficult to get it spotlessly clean, but we'll know better once we've had a look inside.'

'And we're starting to see a possible motive now that we know about the boys' home connection,' said Phil. 'I think we're ready.'

'I'm worried that he'll go the "no comment" route again,' said Lulu. She smiled brightly. 'But yes, let's see what Mr Wallace has to say for himself.'

DI Friar started walking towards the motorhome. Lulu fell into step beside her and DC Townsend and Phil followed.

There didn't seem to be anyone in the cab and there were curtains drawn across the two small windows in the side of the vehicle. As they got closer, Lulu saw that the wheels and wheel arches were splattered with dried mud.

DI Friar banged on the door and Wallace opened it almost immediately. He glared at DI Friar, then peered at the warrant card she was holding out. 'I'm allowed to park here,' he said.

'It's not about where you are parked, Mr Wallace.'

'Well, what is it about, then?' he snarled. For the first time, he looked at Lulu, then spotted Conrad on her shoulders. 'There's a cat sitting on you,' he said.

'That's right,' said Lulu. 'His name's Conrad.'

He squinted at her, then jabbed a finger at her face. 'I know you,' he said.

'Well, I would hope that you would, considering all the time we spent together.'

'You're with the Met.'

'I'm retired, actually.'

Wallace looked at Phil and jabbed his finger at him. 'And you're that sergeant. I remember you.'

'Inspector now, and please stop jabbing your finger at my face,' said Phil.

'You can all piss off, I've got nothing to say to any of you.'

'We'd just like a chat about where you've been for the past few days,' said DI Friar.

'No comment,' said Wallace.

'What about Mr Parker?' said Lulu. 'Edward Parker?'

Wallace frowned. 'Eddie? What about him?'

'Is he staying with you?'

'No. Why would he be staying with me?'

'Would you mind if we had a look around, just to see if Mr Parker is inside?' asked DI Friar.

'I've just told you, he's not here.'

Conrad jumped down from Lulu's shoulders, landed on the ground and then immediately sprang towards the door of the motorhome. 'Hey!' shouted Wallace. He tried to slam the door shut but Conrad was too quick, dashing between Wallace's legs and into the motorhome. Wallace began to curse, then he turned and followed Conrad inside. 'I'll kill you!' he yelled.

'Don't you dare hurt him!' shouted Lulu.

DI Friar pushed the door open and hurried inside. Lulu followed her.

Wallace had grabbed a broom and he was using it to stab at Conrad, who was hiding under a table with bench seats either side. A metal ladder led up to a bed over the cab and there was a small kitchen at the rear.

'Get out of there, you bastard cat!' shouted Wallace.

'Leave him alone!' yelled Lulu.

Wallace turned around and gripped the broom handle with both hands.

'Put it down, Mr Wallace,' said DI Friar calmly.

'Get out of my home!' Wallace shouted. 'You've no right to be here!'

'Just put the broom down.'

Wallace raised the handle and gritted his teeth, but before he could lash out, DI Friar stepped forward and kneed him in the groin. His breath exploded from his lungs and, as he bent forward, DI Friar took the broom from him. 'Thank you so much.'

Phil had appeared at the door and DI Friar pushed the still-spluttering Wallace towards him. 'I think Mr Wallace could do with some fresh air.'

Wallace tried to protest but Phil bundled him outside.

Lulu knelt down and reached out for Conrad. 'Was that nasty man trying to hurt you?'

Conrad meowed and backed away.

'What's wrong?' said Lulu, then gasped as she saw the

coil of rope under the seat. 'Oh, my goodness. What a clever cat you are.'

'What's happening?' asked DI Friar.

'I rather think that Conrad might have found some actual evidence,' said Lulu. 'Doesn't that look exactly like the rope that you found on your victims?'

DI Friar bent down and looked at the rope. 'It does indeed,' she said. 'I'll get a SOCO crew here right away.'

Lulu smiled. 'I don't think that "no comment" is going to help him this time.' She reached out her arms and picked up Conrad. 'You are one very clever cat,' she said. He meowed as she clasped him to her chest and kissed the top of his head. 'I am so proud of you.'

39

The SOCO team produced a preliminary report for DI Friar and she read it through before grinning at Lulu. 'There's DNA on the rope, which is presumably Wallace's, but it'll take time to get that confirmed. But the rope is a definite match to the rope that was found on Sawyer and Robinson.'

'That's very good news,' said Lulu.

'Isn't it?'

Superintendent Knight walked over. 'Did you say the rope matches?'

'It does. And there are traces of bodily fluids on the carpet, including blood. Again, it'll take time to run any DNA against Sawyer's and Robinson's DNA, but it's looking very hopeful.'

'And what about Eddie Parker?' asked Phil. 'Any sign of him?'

'He's on a flight to Spain as we speak,' said DI Friar. 'Malaga airport.'

'We can have people waiting for him,' said Phil. 'The Met has a team out in Malaga monitoring criminal activity on the Costa.'

'It's already in hand through Europol,' said DI Friar.

'Who will you get to conduct the interview?' asked Superintendent Knight.

'I'll lead, obviously,' said DI Friar. 'And I thought it would be useful to have Mrs Lewis there so that we can raise the four murders that took place in London.'

'And DI Jackson? He's obviously up to speed on the London end.'

'Frankly, sir, I'm thinking that we keep it to women in there. Wallace clearly has issues with men, so a male interrogator might well get his back up from the start. I thought DC Townsend and DI Jackson could watch over CCTV.'

'You think too much testosterone in the room might put him on the defensive?'

'Exactly.'

'Good thinking. I'll watch over the CCTV with the team. Is there anything else you need?'

'I think we're good to go, sir.'

'Right then. Break a leg.' He turned and left the room.

'Is it all right if Conrad comes with us?' asked Lulu.

'Well, considering that he's the one who found the rope, it'd be churlish to say no,' said DI Friar. She looked at DC Townsend and smiled sympathetically. 'Sorry to leave you out of this, Pete. But I really think Mrs Lewis and I will get more out of him.'

'Not a problem, boss. It's the conviction that counts, not the glory.'

'I wish every detective felt like that,' said DI Friar.

'Come on,' said Phil, patting DC Townsend on the shoulder. 'I'd like a front-row seat for this.'

Phil's mobile rang and he took it out and looked at the screen. 'I've got to take this,' he said to Lulu, 'it's about Jeremy.' He looked at DC Townsend. 'Sorry, I'll catch up with you later.'

DC Townsend headed out of the room. DI Friar nodded at Lulu. 'Are you ready?'

'Oh, my goodness, yes,' said Lulu. She bent down so that Conrad could jump onto her shoulders. 'And Conrad is ready, too.'

40

DI Friar and Lulu walked down the corridor towards the interview room. 'You've spoken to him before, so maybe you should do the introduction,' said DI Friar. She was holding a black leather briefcase.

'I worry that if he sees me he'll go straight back into his "no comment" routine,' said Lulu.

'Perhaps,' said the detective. 'But he knows you'll want to talk about what happened in London, and that was five years ago. My cases are much more recent, so he's more likely to be defensive about them.'

'I understand.'

They reached the door to the interview room. DI Friar opened it and stepped to the side to let Lulu go in first. There was a uniformed female constable wearing a high-vis jacket standing with her back to the wall. She nodded at DI Friar. 'You can stay, Sally,' said the detective, and the constable nodded again.

Wallace was sitting at the table with a plastic bottle of water in front of him. They had taken his shoes and clothes away and given him a white forensic suit to wear, and blue shoe covers for his feet. He snarled at Lulu, 'What is it with you and that bloody cat?'

'I'm former superintendent Lulu Lewis,' she said. 'Do you remember we spoke in London? Five years ago, give or take.'

'I remember,' he said. 'But you didn't have a cat then.'

'We've only recently become acquainted,' she said, sitting on the chair opposite him. Conrad jumped off her shoulders and landed on the floor. Lulu looked at DI Friar. 'This is Detective Inspector Julie Friar,' she said.

'No comment,' said Wallace, and he folded his arms.

DI Friar sat down and placed the briefcase on the floor next to her chair. She took two cassettes from her pocket and slotted them into the recorder on the wall. She pressed 'play' and settled back in her chair.

'So, as I said, Gordon, I am former superintendent Lulu Lewis and with me is . . .' She looked across at DI Friar.

'Detective Inspector Julie Friar,' she said.

'Could you say your name, please, Gordon.'

'No comment.'

'We are here to interview Mr Gordon Wallace,' said Lulu. 'He is refusing to comment.'

'No comment.'

'You do have the right to a solicitor, Gordon,' said Lulu.

'I don't need a solicitor because I'm not saying anything.'

'Gordon, we know what happened in the boys' home,' said Lulu. 'The Horizon Residential Home for Boys.'

Wallace's eyes narrowed but he didn't say anything.

'We know it was bad, but obviously we weren't there so we can't comprehend the full horror of it. But we know that four boys committed suicide there.'

'And the rest,' sneered Wallace.

'More boys killed themselves?'

'One or two a year when I was there. And I was there for five years.'

'And they were all suicides?'

Wallace nodded. 'Pettigrew covered it up.'

'Ian Pettigrew, the boys' home manager?'

Wallace frowned, then his face went blank. 'No comment.'

'Gordon, now is your time to tell us your side of the story,' said Lulu.

'No comment.'

'We're here to listen to you, Gordon. We want to hear what you have to say.'

'No comment.'

Lulu looked over at DI Friar. Friar flashed her a tight smile and picked up her briefcase. She flicked open the two locks. 'I understand that you were interviewed at length about what happened in London five years ago,' she said.

'No comment.'

'And I know that you refused to comment at the time. But back then, the police had no real evidence against you. That is no longer the case.' She took out four SOCO photographs. 'This time we have evidence. Hard evidence.' She placed one of the photographs on the table. 'This is the body of Sergeant Derek Sawyer, whose body was found on Heaton Park golf course. She placed a second photograph next to it. 'And this is Fraser Robinson, whose body was found at Stretford Meadows last week. Automatic Number Plate Recognition shows that your vehicle was in the vicinity of both bodies shortly before they were found.'

Wallace shrugged. 'No comment.'

'We are checking the data from the phone we found in your motorhome. Now, it's probably a burner phone that you were planning to ditch at some point, but if your fingerprints are on it and there are incriminating messages between yourself and Eddie Parker, then it's game over for you. We'll also be looking at the phone's GPS. If you left that on and you took it with you when you dumped the bodies, then we will know.'

'No comment.'

DI Friar put a third photograph on the table. It was of the coil of rope they had found, in an evidence bag. 'This coil of rope was found in your motorhome, under the table. It is an exact match to the rope that was found on Sergeant Sawyer and Fraser Robinson. Three-strand nylon rope, Kingfisher brand. We are examining it for DNA, so if you ever touched that rope, we will know.'

'No comment.'

She pushed a fourth photograph towards him. 'And this is a photograph of the carpet on the floor of your motorhome. Those marks you see are from bodily fluids, and we are testing them for DNA as we speak. If that DNA matches to Sergeant Sawyer or Fraser Robinson, or both, then your goose is well and truly cooked.'

Wallace gritted his teeth and snarled at her, but continued to say nothing.

'It's over, Gordon,' said Lulu quietly. 'This isn't like the last time we spoke. This time the evidence will convict you.'

Wallace shook his head.

'You can stay silent, you can refuse to speak, that's your right. But you will still go to prison.' Lulu tapped the photograph of the carpet. 'If either of those two men were in your motorhome, the DNA will prove it. You killed them there and you drove the bodies to dispose of them. But if you have anything to say, anything that might justify what you did, now is the time to tell us. We are here to listen, Gordon. And maybe we can help.'

'It's too late to help,' whispered Wallace. 'That ship sailed years ago.'

'This is all about what happened at the home, isn't it? It's about what Ian Pettigrew did to you.'

Wallace nodded slowly. 'And his team. They were all in on it.'

'What I don't understand is why the local authority didn't take action against them,' said Lulu. 'All they did was close the home and move the boys. No charges were ever laid, were they?'

'Nobody cared,' said Wallace. 'All they wanted to do was sweep it under the carpet. They were scared shitless of it getting in the papers. Pettigrew told me that if I ever said anything about what had happened at Horizon he'd track me down and kill me.' He chuckled. 'That didn't work out too well for him, obviously.'

'And you and Eddie Parker and Jack Butler were all abused?'

'Most of the kids were. The Horizon didn't take older kids. Thirteen was the oldest. We were too young to fight back. And anyone who tried, they were beaten to a pulp. We soon learned not to resist.'

'And you didn't tell anyone?'

Wallace scowled at her. 'You've no idea what it was like. Pettigrew had complete control over what went on there.'

'Didn't you have social workers?' asked DI Friar.

'They didn't care. They just wanted us homed and out of the way.'

'What about the police?' asked Lulu.

'The police?' sneered Wallace. He shook his head. 'They were as bad as the home staff.'

'What do you mean?' asked DI Friar.

'One of the boys wrote a letter to the police and a cop came round to the home. He grabbed the boy and beat him black and blue. We were all made to watch. Pettigrew said that was what happened to anyone who went to the police.'

'This policeman, was it Sergeant Sawyer?' asked Lulu.

Wallace gritted his teeth. 'Constable Sawyer he was back then. He started coming to the home regularly after that. The boy killed himself a few weeks later. And another two boys topped themselves the following year. That was when they closed the home. The council knew there was a problem so we were split up and put in foster homes. Mine was actually okay.'

'But you never told anyone what had been done to you? After you left the home?'

'What would have been the point? Sawyer was a cop. How many other cops were doing the same thing? We had no way of knowing.'

'Someone would have helped.'

'Or we might have been killed. No, we kept our mouths shut.'

'Gordon, I need to ask you about Fraser Robinson,' said Lulu.

'Robbo? He was a few years older than us and he was Pettigrew's enforcer. He used to keep the kids in line when Pettigrew was away.'

'He wasn't a care worker though, was he?'

Wallace shook his head. 'He came to cut our hair. After a few visits, Pettigrew gave him a room and he lived in.'

'And Fraser Robinson took part in the abuse?'

Wallace nodded. 'He loved it. I'm not sure if it was the power he loved or the sex, but he loved it.'

'And of the managers and care workers in the home, how many were abusers?'

'All of them,' said Wallace. 'And if they didn't actually take part, they damn well knew what was going on.'

'But there was no investigation, was there?' asked Lulu.

Wallace shook his head. 'It was all covered up. If there had been an investigation, it would have been our word against theirs. We were all packed off to different foster homes around London. Some of the lads were sent to different cities. I expected the cops or the council to come along and interview us but no one ever did. No one cared about us or what had been done to us, it was all damage control, keeping it out of the papers.'

'So you lost touch with the other boys at the home?'

Wallace grinned. 'They figured, if they split us up, that would be the end of it. But we made a pact, six of us. Me and Parker and Butler, the Henderson brothers and little Alex Watson. A blood pact. The night before they shipped us out, we cut our fingers and shared our blood and promised to meet again, exactly ten years later. No matter what.'

'And you did?'

'I turned up. So did Butler and Parker. The home had been turned into flats but we met outside. Just the three of us. One of the Henderson brothers had topped himself and the other had joined the army and got blown up in Afghanistan. We never found out what happened to little Alex Watson.'

'What sort of reunion was it, when the three of you got together?'

Wallace smiled thinly. 'We were all still angry. Angry like you wouldn't believe.'

'So you decided to get your revenge?'

'Wouldn't you?' Wallace snapped. 'If you had been systematically abused over years? Wouldn't you want revenge?'

Lulu didn't reply. It wasn't a question she wanted to answer, not on tape anyway.

'So, yeah, the three of us decided to get our own back. To give them a taste of their own medicine.'

'And the rope and knot that you used, that was what they did to you?'

'It was Pettigrew's party trick. Sometimes he'd tie up a few of us and then leave us on the floor while he and his mates sat around drinking and smoking dope.'

'It's quite a complicated knot.'

Wallace nodded. 'Sometimes he made us tie each other up. He got a kick out of that.'

'And when you decided on revenge, how did you find them all? The home had been long closed, hadn't it?'

'Pettigrew was easy enough. His name isn't common and he was on social media. It didn't take us long to find him; we followed him for a while. There was no way he could work with children again, not after the home had been shut down, but he managed to get an office job with an insurance company. He still had a taste for young flesh, though. We trailed him to various bars in Soho and we saw him picking up underage rent boys around Piccadilly Circus. Then one night we grabbed him and did it to him.' Wallace grinned. 'I can't tell you how good it felt, seeing him naked and trussed up like an oven-ready chicken. He was so scared and he babbled away. Told us where the other guys had gone, said he was sorry, swore he was a changed man. We just sat there and drank beer and watched him choke himself to death.'

'What about the way you disposed of the body?' asked DI Friar. 'Whose idea was it to leave them naked?'

'Mutual decision,' said Wallace. 'We'd watched enough crime shows on television to know about DNA and hair and stuff. So we stripped them and washed them before we dumped them.'

'And the rope? Why did you leave the rope around their necks?'

Wallace chuckled. 'To put the fear of God into the others. So that they would know that we were coming for them.' He wrinkled his nose. 'But the cops never mentioned the rope back then. They kept it to themselves.'

'What about the second victim? Nick Hurst?'

'Pettigrew had told us where to find him. After the home was shut down he started working as a schoolteacher, of all things. Turns out he had a degree and a teaching certificate and everything. I guess they didn't ask for references, because he shouldn't have been allowed within a mile of young boys. He was a sleazebag, you could tell by just looking at him.'

'And how did it work?' asked DI Friar. 'Were you all involved?'

'For Pettigrew, yes. All for one and one for all, like the three musketeers. But then we decided we'd better be careful. If the cops started looking at us, we'd need alibis. I mean, we were using burner phones and only spoke face to face or on WhatsApp. But we needed more security, so we decided that, with the second one, Jackie and I would do it and Eddie would make sure he got himself a speeding ticket at the time we were killing Hurst. It paid dividends when the cops did start looking at Eddie. They had CCTV of Eddie in a couple of the same Soho bars as Hurst and Dunne. But once they found the speeding ticket and the picture that came with it, they lost interest.'

'And what about William Eccles and John Dunne?' asked DI Friar.

'What about them?' said Wallace.

'Who killed them?'

'Jackie and I did Eccles. Eddie had to take care of Dunne alone. Pettigrew told us where to find Eccles and Hurst knew where Dunne was.'

'And by the time that Eddie killed Dunne, you were in prison and Jack Butler was dead?' said Lulu.

Wallace looked down at the table. 'Yeah.'

'Mr Butler's death wasn't a mugging gone wrong, was it?' she said quietly.

Wallace looked up, his eyes narrowed. 'Why do you say that?'

Lulu smiled. 'A copper's hunch.'

'Are copper's hunches accepted as evidence in trials?'

'Generally not,' said Lulu. 'But Mr Butler's DNA had been found under the fingernail of Mr Eccles, hadn't it? That put you all at risk.'

Wallace grimaced. 'Jackie didn't care. He said we shouldn't even bother trying to hide what we were doing. It's like he had some sort of a death wish. Eddie said we had to do something or we'd all end up behind bars. We tried talking to Jackie but he wouldn't listen. He was smoking weed big-time and it was making him crazy. He started smoking in the home, when he was ten. We all did. It helped dull the pain of what was happening. But it took over his life and he was smoking every day.'

'Even when he was working?' asked DI Friar. 'He was high when he was driving his taxi?'

Wallace nodded. 'Most of the time.'

'Were you smoking, too?' asked DI Friar.

'I stopped when I left the home. My foster parents were strict.' He smiled. 'Firm but fair. They were good people. Hell, compared with what I had before, they were saints. Mr and Mrs Reeves. I had three good years with them. They saved my life.'

'Mrs Reeves died some time ago, didn't she?'

Wallace nodded. 'Cancer.'

'And Mr Reeves isn't well.'

'Dementia. He's only in his seventies. Life sucks sometimes.'

'Yes, it does,' said Lulu. 'So what happened to Jackie?'

'You know what happened. He died.'

'Stabbed in his taxi,' said Lulu.

Wallace raised his palms. 'He was unlucky.'

'Gordon, we know that you killed Ian Pettigrew, Nick Hurst and William Eccles in London five years ago. And we know you killed Sergeant Sawyer and Fraser Robinson in Manchester. Why are you being so coy about Jackie Butler? Is it because he was a friend? Because, like you, he was abused?'

Wallace sighed and sat back in his chair. 'I'm hungry,' he said. 'Do you think I could have some food?'

'What would you like?' asked DI Friar.

Wallace smiled. 'I'd really like a burger,' he said. 'And chips.'

'I'm sure we could get that for you,' said DI Friar.

'And a Coke.'

'With ice?'

'Why not?'

41

Wallace sighed as he pushed the plate away and settled back in his chair. He patted his stomach with both hands. 'Well, that hit the spot,' he said. He had devoured a canteen cheeseburger and chips and drunk most of the Coke they had given him. DI Friar and Lulu hadn't spoken while Wallace had been eating, but the tape had continued to run.

'You know, people complain about the food in prison, but I never found it that bad. The last place I was in, we had burgers and chips every Saturday. Not quite as good as the burger you've just given me, but good enough.'

'So tell us about Jackie Butler,' said Lulu. 'How did he die?'

'He was stabbed. In his cab.'

'By you?'

Wallace shook his head. 'I was in the back seat. Eddie was in the front.'

'It was planned?'

'We didn't want to do it, but Jackie was off his head. He'd stopped caring. The plan was for him to stay away from the fourth one but he kept insisting that he be there. He was starting to get pleasure from it, you know?'

'Well, you all wanted them to suffer, didn't you? That's why you used the rope.'

'We wanted revenge,' said Wallace. 'We wanted them to feel how we felt. But Jackie, he began talking about it all the time. And he was careless. We had to keep telling him to wear gloves and shoe covers, and he wouldn't help us clean the van.'

'You used your van to dispose of the bodies?' asked DI Friar.

Wallace nodded. 'No one looks twice at a courier van,' he said. 'But we always gave it a good clean afterwards. With bleach and everything.'

'But you didn't use the van to dispose of Jackie Butler's body. You left him in his car?'

'We figured people would think it was a mugging,' said Wallace. 'We took his watch and his wallet and both his phones.'

'Both phones?' repeated DI Friar.

'His regular phone and his burner phone,' said Wallace. 'That's how we stayed in touch. WhatsApp messages on pay-as-you-go burner phones. We knew that the longer it went on, the more likely it would be that the cops would look at us. So we used burner phones to stay in contact. And after the first one, after Pettigrew, we made a point of only two of us doing the job. That way the third one would have an alibi.'

'But with Jackie Butler dead, and you behind bars, Eddie had to kill John Dunne alone?'

'Which he did. But me being banged up really put an end to it all. We knew that Sawyer and Robbo had gone to Manchester, and Pettigrew had said that Sawyer was still a cop, so the plan was always to go up north and find them. But there was no way that Eddie could do that on his own. My accident changed everything.'

'Tell me about the accident,' said DI Friar.

Wallace said, 'I was running late with my deliveries. I'd taken some whizz so I guess I wasn't thinking straight.'

'Whizz?' repeated Lulu.

'Speed. Amphetamines. I'd been working twelve hours flat out and I needed something to keep me going. I was on the M25 and I was checking my phone and I hit another car. Killed a mother and two kids.' He grimaced. 'Not a day goes by that I don't regret what happened. If I could turn back time, I would.'

'You fled the scene?' said Lulu.

'I had to. I had my burner phone on me. If the cops had found it, they'd have linked me to Eddie and Jackie. So I did a runner and dumped the phone. I was actually on the way to turn myself in when the cops pulled me over.'

'And you got nine years for that?'

Wallace nodded. 'And I deserved it. No question. I made a bad decision and innocent people died. But I only did five years in the end and, if you ask me, five years wasn't enough.'

'And while you were in prison, after he'd killed Dunne, Eddie Parker went to live in Spain?'

'He's got family there.'

'And when you were released, he came back? To finish what you'd started.'

'He felt the same as I did. We needed to do to them what they did to us.'

'So after you got out of prison, you tracked them down?'

'It wasn't hard, what with social media and all. Found Sawyer first and reached out to Parker in Spain.'

'Didn't he visit you in prison?'

'No, because there would have been a record. There was

no contact at all until I was released. We had unfinished business, but he couldn't do both of them alone. Then as soon as I was out, he came back to the UK and we came up to Manchester together.'

'Did Sawyer say why he'd moved to Manchester?' asked Lulu.

'When they closed the home, Sawyer was worried that there might be an investigation. So he decided to leave London before the shit hit the fan. He knew that Robbo was from Manchester so maybe that gave him the idea. He got married not long after he moved. Like he wanted to start a new life, pretend that he wasn't a monster.'

'They weren't friends in Manchester?'

Wallace shook his head. 'Sawyer said he'd tried to contact Robbo but Robbo wanted nothing to do with him. He said he wasn't sure where he lived but knew he was working as a hairdresser and was a regular in Canal Street.'

'You went looking for him?'

'Found him easy enough. Followed him home. Picked him up a few days later. Did what had to be done.'

'He'd been married, too,' said Lulu.

'He didn't know what he was,' said Wallace. 'I think he knew he was gay when he was younger. Then Pettigrew got hold of him and twisted his mind. He knew what he was doing was wrong, which is why he went back to Manchester. Probably got married to put it all behind him, same as Sawyer. Tried to become something he wasn't. But he couldn't stop cruising Canal Street.'

'Did Pettigrew push him into doing what he did?' asked Lulu.

'Encouraged him, maybe. But he didn't force him, if that's

what you mean.' He leaned forward over the table. 'He deserved what he got, don't think that he didn't.'

'And what else did you have planned?' asked DI Friar.

'What do you mean?'

'You, Butler and Parker killed – or planned to kill – Pettigrew, Hurst, Eccles, Dunne, Sawyer and Robinson. Were there any more names on your list?'

'About a dozen, but faces rather than names,' said Wallace quietly. 'Our abusers came and went. Pettigrew gave us some of their names, but even he didn't know where to find them. He pimped us out. Men would pay money to come to the home and abuse us. I'm guessing most of them used false names.' He gestured vaguely. 'So yeah, we'd pretty much reached the end of the line, revenge-wise.'

'Where is Eddie Parker, Gordon?' asked DI Friar.

Wallace shrugged but didn't reply.

'We know he was in your motorhome,' said DI Friar. 'There were two mugs and two plates and two sets of cutlery in your sink.'

'I'm no grass,' said Wallace.

'We have information that suggests he's gone back to Spain. Is that correct?'

Wallace folded his arms. 'No comment.'

'Do you feel any better, having done what you've done?' asked Lulu.

Wallace looked at her for a few seconds, then flashed her a tight smile. 'I do, yes. It doesn't make my pain any less, but at least now I know they didn't get away with it.'

'Can I ask you something? The knot. Pettigrew used the same knot when he tied up you and the others, didn't he?'

'He had a boat. Moored down at Southampton. He used

to take us down there, if we were good. He'd take us out on it, show us how to sail. He liked showing us how to tie knots. He liked making us tie each other up. It gave him a hard-on.'

Lulu nodded. 'It must have been . . . awful.'

'Awful? Yes. The only thing that stopped me topping myself was the thought that one day I could make the bastards suffer the way they'd made me suffer.'

He picked up his cup and drank the last of his Coke. 'So what happens now?' he asked.

'You'll be formally charged with the murders of Pettigrew, Hurst, Eccles, Sawyer and Robinson, conspiracy to murder Dunne and accessory to the murder of Jackie Butler, I suspect. You'll need a lawyer.'

Wallace shook his head. 'No need. I did it, and I'm glad I did it. Whatever price there is to pay, I'll pay it.'

'You should still get yourself a lawyer, Mr Wallace,' said Lulu. 'A good one.'

'I'm going down, everybody knows I'm going down,' he said, folding his arms. 'I'll plead guilty with pride. I killed them and if I had to do it again, I would. With pleasure. Except Jackie, of course. That I am sorry about. But it had to be done. It was him or us.'

'You need a lawyer to give your side of the story,' said Lulu. 'It's a story that needs to be told.'

'I've been in prison,' said Wallace. 'It's no hardship for me.'

'You're not even thirty years old,' said Lulu. 'You still have most of your life ahead of you. Do you want to spend all those years behind bars?'

'I don't see that I have a choice, do you? Don't you worry

about me – I'm at peace with what I did and what will happen to me. Hand on heart, I'll be happier in prison with them all dead than if I was free and they were alive. It's a fair price. What do you think, that I can claim it was manslaughter? I wanted them dead. We all did. We set out to kill them and that's what we did. End of.'

'I understand that, but the price you have to pay is negotiable,' said Lulu. 'And a good lawyer can help with that negotiation. You were abused as a child, abused in ways that most people could barely imagine. If it wasn't for that abuse, you'd never have done what you did.'

Wallace pulled a face. 'What's done is done. There's no turning back the clock.'

'No, there isn't. But even if you plead guilty, there's every chance you'll spend the rest of your life behind bars. Unless you tell your side of the story. If a good lawyer explains what you went through as a child, maybe your time served comes down to twenty years. Maybe fifteen. You could be out before you're forty-five, with enough time left to live a decent life.'

Wallace nodded slowly. 'Let me think about that.'

'Please do,' said Lulu. She looked over at DI Friar. 'Are we done?'

DI Friar leaned over to the tape machine and switched it off. 'For the moment.'

42

DI Friar punched the air once they'd left the interview room. 'That went so well,' she said. 'Way better than I expected.'

'Did you think he'd deny it?' asked Lulu.

'I thought we'd get the "no comment" routine,' said DI Friar.

'He's done what he'd set out to do,' said Lulu. 'For him, it's over. Yes, by any definition he's a serial killer, but he's no threat to the general public.'

They walked together along the corridor. 'What you said about him getting a lighter sentence because of what happened, was that just talk or did you mean it?' asked DI Friar.

'Oh, I meant it,' said Lulu. 'The abuse he went through as a child was horrific. Unthinkable.'

'But they killed Jackie Butler too, remember? They killed him to keep him quiet. Me, I think they should throw away the key.'

'Cause and effect,' said Lulu. 'If he had never been abused, he would never have killed.'

'That doesn't make it right.'

'No, it doesn't. But surely it mitigates what he did.'

DI Friar forced a smile. 'I think we are going to have to agree to disagree on that.'

Lulu nodded. 'I guess so. Maybe I am being naive. The thing is, I can understand what drove them to do what they did; I'm just so sad that it's ruined their lives. They'll probably spend what time they have left in prison, whether they are or are not still a threat to the public.'

'They are very damaged individuals, that's for sure,' said DI Friar. 'Who's to say they wouldn't pose a threat?'

'I suppose that's down to the psychiatrists,' said Lulu. 'They'll have a better idea of what's going on inside their heads.' She sighed. 'It's such a mess. Such a sad, sorry mess.'

'You didn't pick up that Pettigrew was a sailor during your investigation?'

'He didn't have a boat at the time of his death. He must have sold it after he left the home. Presumably he'd have had money problems; no cash flow for a while after the council ended the contract.'

They walked along to the MIT room. As they went through the double doors a cheer went up. Superintendent Knight was there, a huge smile on his face. 'I saw it on the CCTV link,' he said. 'Well done, Detective Inspector. That was textbook, it really was. I can see them using it on the interrogation course.'

'Thank you, sir.'

'It's not often we get to close four cold cases and two active cases on one day,' he said. 'And thank you for your input, former superintendent Lewis. Still got that cat on your shoulders, I see.'

'Conrad was a big help on the case,' said Lulu.

'I'm sure he was,' said the superintendent. 'Well, again, job well done. My thanks to you, DI Friar, and to your team. You should all be proud of yourselves.'

There was another round of appreciative applause and DI Friar actually blushed.

Phil came over and grinned at Lulu. 'You've still got it, boss. You had him wrapped around your little finger.'

'He wanted to talk, Phil. I could tell. He just needed someone to listen and understand. Can you imagine what they went through as boys?' She shuddered. 'It doesn't excuse what they did, but I do understand.'

'Well, either way, boss, you and DI Friar did a great job. It's not every day that you close that many murder cases.' He grinned. 'Meanwhile, I think I've solved the mystery of Jeremy Connolly.'

Lulu's eyes widened. 'Oh, do tell! Is it good news or bad news?'

'A bit of both, I'd say.'

43

Lulu walked out of the GMP building. An Uber was waiting for them, a dark blue Volkswagen. 'So that's it?' said Conrad. He was wrapped around her neck like a scarf. 'Our work here is done? Back to London?'

'Parker has landed in Malaga and been arrested,' said Lulu. 'Phil can handle the London end from here on in, so I'm pretty much surplus to requirements. I thought we might visit Bath. There's a friend I haven't seen for a long time. But first there's something I have to do.'

'Jane?'

'Yes, Jane. I have to tell her what I've found out.'

'How do you think she'll handle it?'

Lulu shook her head slowly. 'I'm really not sure.'

'Nobody likes being lied to.'

'That's certainly true.'

The Uber dropped them close to the Wharf. Jane was sitting at the same outside table she had been at the first time that Lulu had met her there. She spotted Lulu and Conrad as they walked up the path, and waved. She was wearing a fluffy white cardigan over a canary yellow dress, and had clipped her hair back. There was an ice bucket with a bottle of champagne on the table in front of her. Lulu sat down opposite her. Conrad jumped down off Lulu's shoulders and curled up under her chair.

'Champagne?' said Lulu.

'Well, I figure I'll either be celebrating or drowning my sorrows. Either way, champagne fits the bill.' Jane pulled the bottle from the ice bucket and poured champagne into an empty glass.

Lulu sipped it and smiled. 'Oh, yes, that's lovely.'

'I assume it's bad news,' said Jane as she put the bottle back into the ice bucket. 'That's why you wanted to see me in person.'

'Well, it's good news, bad news, really.'

Jane wrinkled her nose. 'I knew he was too good to be true. Tell me the worst.' She took a big gulp of champagne and then held the glass with both hands.

'Okay, well, the bad news is that his name isn't Jeremy Connolly. It's Jeremy Collins.'

'That's close, I suppose. But it's still a lie.'

'Connolly is his mother's maiden name. He was born in Beckenham, south London. His mother was Irish and he has a British passport and an Irish passport, both in the name of Jeremy Collins.'

'And his parents are alive and well and living in Beckenham?'

'No, what he told you about his family is accurate enough. His parents did die at an early age, and he and his siblings lived with their grandmother. And his siblings did move to Australia.'

'But no wife?'

'I'm afraid he did lie about that, too. He was married, about twenty years ago.'

'Oh my goodness, and he killed her?'

Lulu laughed and held up a hand. 'Don't let your imagination run away with you, Jane. No, they divorced after a year. She remarried and is alive and well and living in Edinburgh.'

'And he took most of her money in the divorce?'

'No, quite the opposite, in fact. The thing is, Jane, Jeremy is rich. Very rich. Richer than anyone I know, probably, and I've met a lot of wealthy people in my time.'

'Rich, how?'

'Well, again, much of what Jeremy told you was the truth. He started in construction, he moved into property development, and he has investments in Ireland. But what he didn't tell you is that his investments there include a castle in Galway, several large industrial estates, and prime buildings in Dublin, Galway and Belfast.'

'Oh, my . . .'

'That's just a fraction of what he owns. He has a huge London property portfolio, and properties in Paris, Milan and Barcelona. Most of his money is tied up in high-tech companies in the US. He got into Facebook very early, and Google, Tesla, Netflix, all the household names. He's what they call an angel investor and owns several incredibly successful venture capital companies.'

'So he's a multimillionaire?'

Lulu shook her head. 'He's much, much more than that, Jane. He's a billionaire several times over.'

'Well, why did he lie?'

Lulu took a drink of her champagne. 'When he divorced, almost twenty years ago, he pretty much lost everything he owned at the time. He didn't really contest the divorce, even though it was his wife who was unfaithful. I'm guessing that he's worried about gold diggers.'

'So he lied about his name? Who does that?'

'Well, a billionaire using a dating app, probably. Remember what he said? He was with a pal of his when he saw your profile and wanted to connect with you. Now you know who, or what, he is, would you expect him to use his real name?'

'I suppose not.'

'And it is his mother's maiden name, along with his real first name. So it's not a huge lie. More just being careful about his identity.'

'But now that we know each other, why hasn't he come clean?'

'You'll have to ask him that. I'm assuming that at some point before the wedding he'll tell you.'

'He's testing me, isn't he? He wants to know if it's him I want, or his money.'

'Someone as rich as he is must be approached by women all the time. And he was badly burned when he was younger, and back then he had much less to lose.'

'How do you know all this?'

'His car was the clue. The Audi. It was leased through one of his subsidiary companies. Even as Jeremy Collins he has a very small internet presence, and he's rarely photographed. But the company that owns the subsidiary is listed on the UK Stock Exchange and that company's website has his photograph. It took some digging to get the details of his divorce settlement, but it's all there in the public record.'

Jane sat back in her chair. 'I've been such a fool,' she said.

'No, you've been careful. And he was lying to you. Small white lies, and with a good reason, but lying is lying. You picked up on it. And it explains his aura.'

Jane frowned. 'His aura?'

Lulu kept smiling, but her mind began to race. She could hardly tell Jane that Conrad had spotted anomalies in Jeremy's aura. 'I've been studying auras recently, and Jeremy's aura definitely suggested that he was being less than honest.'

'You see auras?'

Lulu continued to smile, but her heart fell at the way she was lying to her friend. Jeremy had lied, and Lulu had caught him out. Now she herself was lying to Jane, and it didn't feel good. But what was the alternative? To explain that Conrad spoke to her, that she shared her life with a talking cat? That wasn't a conversation that would end well. 'I'm a mere student. It takes a lot of practice, and squinting.'

'What does my aura look like now?' asked Jane.

Lulu pretended to squint at her over the top of her champagne glass. 'It's a jumble of colours, which I think shows that you're confused.'

'You can say that again. What am I going to do, Lulu?'

'That's your call, obviously.'

'Have I ruined it, do you think?'

Lulu smiled. 'No, I don't think so.'

'But it shows that I didn't trust him. That's no way to start a relationship, is it?'

'To be fair, Jeremy started it by not being truthful with you.'

'Yes, but like you said, he was doing it for the right reasons. Asking you to check up on him shows a lack of trust, and how can we go into a marriage on that basis? Lies and mistrust. It's hardly a foundation for a successful relationship, is it?'

'Well, you're not married yet, are you? There's plenty of time to clear the air and start afresh.'

'You think I should still marry him?'

'Do you love him?'

Jane nodded. 'I do, yes.'

'And do you want to marry him?'

'I've always wanted to marry him, pretty much from the first time we met.'

'Then that answers your question, doesn't it!'

Jane sighed. 'So what do I do? Pretend that I don't know what I know?'

'Can you do that?'

'Maybe. I suppose so. But then I'm lying by omission, aren't I? He's lied to me about who he is, and I'm lying by not telling him that I know. He's pretending to be something he's not, and I'm letting him do it.'

'Then confront him with it.'

Jane shook her head. 'I can't do that. I'd have to tell him that I've been spying on him. How's he going to react to that?'

'You were responding to red flags – there's nothing wrong with that. If he'd been completely honest with you, you wouldn't have raised it with me.'

'He might not see it that way, Lulu. He doesn't trust people, that's why he hid his true identity. He needs to know that he's loved because of who he is, not because of what he has.'

'And you've shown that, Jane. He knows you fell for him without knowing how rich he is.'

'But now I do know. So I've spoiled it.'

'No, you haven't. You just keep your peace. He's asked you to marry him, you can say yes, knowing that he's not going to murder you in your sleep. At some point he'll tell you the truth. He has to, obviously. He'll tell you who he is, then you'll be straight.'

'And what do I do, Lulu. Express surprise? Tell him I'd never have guessed?'

'That would work, I suppose.'

'Then I'd be lying, wouldn't I?' She gritted her teeth. 'I hate this, I hate the fact that he lied to me and I'm going to have to lie to him.'

'A lie told for the right reasons isn't really a lie,' said Lulu quietly.

'Do you believe that?'

Lulu nodded. 'I do, yes.'

Conrad meowed from under the table.

'Conrad says he does, too.'

Jane smiled and picked up her glass. 'Well if Conrad says so, then it must be true.'

44

Lulu loved early mornings on the canal. The air was fresh and clean and there was still a faint mist over the water. She had risen at dawn, put on a pullover and jeans and made herself a mug of coffee before untying *The Lark* and edging out of the Staffordshire arm and onto the canal network. That was an hour ago and they were now on the Bridgewater Canal, heading west.

'So how long will it take us to get to Bath?' asked Conrad, who was sitting beside her.

'Who knows?'

'Really? You don't know?'

Lulu laughed. 'About a hundred and forty hours, I think.'

'In real money?'

'Yes, in real money. So if we drive for six hours a day it'll take us about three weeks, give or take. It depends on the weather, on the locks we go through, how busy the route is. But three weeks sounds about right.'

'It's not as if we're in a rush, is it?'

'Exactly,' said Lulu. She took a thoughtful sip of coffee.

'Do humans find it easy to lie?' asked Conrad.

'I suppose they do, yes,' said Lulu. 'Why do you ask?'

'I was just thinking how easy they make it look. Criminals lie, of course they do, because they don't want to be punished. They'll say anything to escape being sent to jail.'

'Generally, yes. No one wants to go to prison, do they?'

'So as a detective, people usually lied to you?'

'All the time.'

'That means that whenever you interviewed a suspect, you expected them to lie?'

'And I was rarely disappointed. It's one of the reasons police officers become so cynical. They tend to see the worst in people.'

'And Jeremy lied to you, didn't he? He looked you in the eyes and hid all sorts of things about who he was and where he was from.'

'He did.'

'And he lied to the woman he wanted to marry.'

'Yes, but he had good intentions, I suppose.'

There were two narrowboats moored ahead of them and Lulu slowed *The Lark* down. It was still early and the occupants could well be asleep.

'So lying is all right if it's done for the right reasons?'

Lulu chuckled. 'That's a very complicated question, Conrad.'

'Actually, it's quite simple.'

'Well, yes, the question is, true. But answering it . . .' She shrugged. 'Clearly lying is wrong. People always deserve to hear the truth. But whenever I asked my late husband what a new dress looked like, he would smile and say it was perfect. Even when I knew it wasn't. If I asked if it made me look fat, he'd say of course not. Say I wanted to eat Indian food and I asked him if he wanted to go out to an Indian restaurant, he'd say he'd love to even when I knew he didn't really like Indian food.'

'So it's okay to lie to someone you love?'

Lulu laughed again. 'You see, that's why it's such a difficult question to answer. Of course you shouldn't lie to someone you love. You shouldn't lie to anyone. But sometimes you do it to make the other person feel good.'

'And that makes it right?'

'Well, no. Because lying is wrong. But if the truth is going to hurt someone, maybe a lie is better. Oh, Conrad. You're making my head hurt.'

They passed the two moored narrowboats and Lulu increased the throttle.

'Cats never lie,' said Conrad.

'That's good to know.'

'I'm serious. We're incapable of telling a lie. Physically incapable.'

'So you'd tell me the truth, even if it was hurtful?'

'There's no choice in the matter. Cats can't lie.'

'Well, I won't lie to you, either.'

'Ever?'

'Ever,' said Lulu.

He gently butted his head against her side. 'Thank you,' he said.

'You're very welcome.'

The Cat and the Christmas Kidnapper

Read on for an exclusive extract with Lulu and Conrad, as Christmas cheer is threatened by a ruthless kidnapping plot . . .

1

'Are you hungry?' asked Conrad. 'The reason I ask is that I am definitely getting peckish.' He looked up at Lulu, who was holding the tiller of her narrowboat, *The Lark*, as it phut-phut-phutted its way along the Kennet and Avon Canal, heading towards Bath.

Conrad was sitting on the metal seat at the stern, the cold December wind ruffling his fur. He was a good-looking cat, of that there was no question. The right side of his head was mainly black with an uneven white patch around the nose and mouth, and the left side was brown and white. His eyes were a vibrant green and his mouth seemed to form a sly smile, as if he'd just heard something that amused him. His front legs and chest were white, his body and tail were thick stripes of black and brown and his rear legs had white socks. He was a typical calico cat in many respects, but it was his ability to talk that set him apart from all other cats.

Lulu had been shocked the first time Conrad had spoken to her, after he'd jumped onto *The Lark* at her mooring in Little Venice – so shocked that she'd thought she was either dreaming or losing her mind. Neither was the case. Conrad really could talk, but he had made it clear from the outset that he would only talk to her. Lulu had no idea why Conrad had chosen her, but no one else who came across him received anything more communicative than a 'meow' or, if he was in a particularly good mood, a throaty purr.

'I think lunch would be a very good idea,' said Lulu. She was wearing a heavy sheepskin jacket over a thick pullover, blue jeans tucked into Caterpillar boots, and wool fingerless gloves, but she was still feeling the cold. It had taken *The Lark* just over a week to travel the eighty-odd miles from Reading. It was a picturesque journey with almost a hundred locks to be opened and closed along the way. Dealing with locks single-handedly in the winter was challenging, but not over difficult, and Lulu had become adept at opening and closing the gates, opening the sluices and using the centre line to keep *The Lark* in the middle of the chamber as the water rose or fell. Truth be told, operating the locks kept her warm, while standing next to the tiller meant she had no choice but to face the bitter wind that blew along the canal.

She took her iPhone from her jacket pocket and used her left hand to scroll through the app she was using to keep track of their journey. 'There's a cafe about a mile ahead of us,' she said.

'Is it cat friendly?' asked Conrad.

'There's a terrace at the side of the canal, so I assume so,' said Lulu, putting the phone back into her pocket.

'So where are we?' asked Conrad, narrowing his eyes against the wind.

'We're coming up to Bradford-on-Avon,' said Lulu. 'It's about nine miles from Bath.'

Bath was their ultimate destination, and Lulu hoped to get there before dark. *The Lark*'s top speed was about four miles an hour, but generally Lulu kept to about three miles an hour, even slower whenever she passed moored boats. Considerate boaters always slowed down to pass moored boats; there was nothing worse than being tossed up and down by the wake of a speeding narrowboat.

The canal was clear, so she didn't have to slow down as they headed towards the cafe. They passed a couple of boats coming the other way, and like her the owners were well wrapped up against the winter wind. The first owner was a middle-aged man with a flat cap and a red and white scarf wrapped around his neck. He gave a cheery wave and shouted hello as he went by. Five minutes later they passed a compact narrowboat that couldn't have been more than thirty feet long, about half the length of *The Lark*. The boat was in lovely condition, dark blue with brass portholes and a roof decked out with brightly painted planters filled with small conifers. The boater was, like Lulu, a woman in her sixties, wrapped up against the cold with a padded coat and a white fleece beanie pulled low over her ears. She was holding the tiller with her right hand and had a steaming mug of something hot in her left. The woman raised her mug in salute, and Lulu waved.

A young boy on a bicycle passed by on the towpath, travelling at probably three times *The Lark*'s pace. Narrowboats weren't built for speed, and it wasn't unusual for Lulu to be overtaken by joggers or even fast walkers. Like most boaters, she appreciated the journey as much as the arrival. Getting to wherever she was going was half the fun. Probably more than half, to be honest – although on this occasion she was very much looking forward to spending Christmas in Bath with her goddaughter, Amanda, and her family.

Conrad jumped up onto the roof of *The Lark*. 'Is that it?' he asked, gazing ahead.

Lulu narrowed her eyes as she peered into the wind. 'Yes,

I think so,' she said. There was a stone building at the side of the canal with a roofed terrace. Three narrowboats were moored close by. 'You have such good eyesight.'

'Actually, humans have better long vision than cats,' said Conrad. 'Everything gets a bit blurry for me beyond about twenty feet, but you humans can see clearly up to more than two hundred feet.'

'So how did you see the cafe?'

'I can smell the food,' said Conrad.

'Ah yes, of course,' said Lulu. 'Didn't you tell me that your sense of smell is fifteen times better than mine?'

'Fourteen,' said Conrad. 'Cats have more than two hundred million odour sensors in their noses; humans have just five million.'

'And how does the food smell?' asked Lulu, easing back on the throttle.

'Pretty good,' said Conrad.

Lulu went slowly past the moored narrowboats before pulling in and reversing back. She put the engine to idle, grabbed the stern line, stepped off onto the towpath and used the line to gently ease *The Lark* into place. Then she secured the line, tied the bow and centre lines and climbed back onto the rear deck to kill the engine.

'You always make that look so easy,' said Conrad.

'It's the advantage of opposable thumbs,' said Lulu. The cafe overlooked *The Lark*, so she didn't bother locking up. Conrad jumped up onto her shoulders and Lulu stepped back onto the towpath.

'I am so hungry,' said Conrad.

'Yes, you said.'

The Lock Inn was a beautiful stone cottage with an

outdoor terrace under a roof made from plastic sheeting. Lulu peered through a window and saw that most of the tables inside were occupied. A decorated Christmas tree with flashing fairy lights stood in the corner of the room. There were only two men out on the terrace, and they were standing up to leave. The terrace was shielded from the wind, so Lulu decided she would sit outside.

'Lovely day for it,' said one of the men. He was in his fifties with a bushy grey beard and a captain's hat that made Lulu think of Captain Birdseye.

'It is, yes.'

'So you're on *The Lark*?'

'That's right.'

'You're a long way from home.' He had obviously seen 'LITTLE VENICE' on the sign on the side of *The Lark*.

'Visiting friends,' said Lulu.

The other man was a few years younger and could have well been Captain Birdseye's son, though Lulu had long since stopped assuming relationships based on appearance. 'Are you travelling alone?' he asked.

'Just me and Conrad,' said Lulu. Conrad jumped down from her shoulders onto a green plastic chair.

'Well, fair play to you,' said Captain Birdseye. 'My days of dealing with locks single-handed are well behind me.' He gave her a salute. 'Enjoy the rest of your day.'

'You too,' said Lulu, sitting down. The two men walked down to the towpath and climbed onto a green and red narrowboat with solar panels covering its roof. Lulu had never been a fan of solar panels on canal boats. She understood the advantages of having free electricity on tap, but they always looked so unsightly.

'They spoil the appearance, don't they?' said Conrad.

'Yes, they do,' said Lulu. She frowned. 'Did you just read my mind?'

Conrad chuckled. 'I saw you looking at the roof of their boat, and your nose wrinkled just a little. So it was a straightforward deduction. Elementary, my dear Watson.'

'So I'm Dr Watson to your Sherlock Holmes? I'm the one who was a detective, remember?'

'A detective superintendent with the Metropolitan Police, no less.'

'Indeed,' said Lulu.

A young waitress appeared, wearing a Santa hat and carrying a tray. She began to clear the table where the two men had been sitting. 'I'll be with you in a moment,' she said to Lulu in a soft Wiltshire accent. Conrad dropped down from the chair and curled up beneath it as the waitress began collecting the used plates and mugs. The men had left a newspaper behind.

'Do you mind if I have a look at that?' Lulu asked, pointing at it.

'Not at all,' said the waitress, handing her the paper. 'And what can I get you to drink?'

'A glass of Pinot Grigio would be lovely. And water for Conrad.'

The waitress frowned. 'Conrad?'

'I'm sorry – my companion,' said Lulu, pointing at Conrad.

'Oh! I'm sorry, sir, I didn't see you there. Would tap water be okay?'

'Actually, he's quite partial to Evian. If you have it.'

'We most definitely do,' said the waitress. 'I shall be right back.'

Lulu looked at the front page of the newspaper. It was the *Wiltshire Times* and the main headline was FEARS FOR MISSING SCHOOLGIRL. Beneath it was a photograph of a young girl, her hair in braids, holding a schoolbag to her chest. Lulu scanned the story. Ten-year-old Poppy Novak had vanished on her way home from school. She lived just under half a mile from the school and had left at four o'clock. When she hadn't arrived by six o'clock, her worried parents had phoned the police. A full search of the area had found nothing, and police feared she had been abducted.

Conrad emerged from the under the chair. He looked up at the newspaper, then jumped up onto the chair next to Lulu to get a better look. 'That's awful,' he said.

'Yes, it is,' said Lulu. 'I always hated missing children cases. I couldn't help fearing the worst, even though the vast majority turn up safe and sound in the end.'

'Do a lot of children go missing?'

'Oh, more than a hundred thousand children are reported missing every year in the UK,' said Lulu. 'But most are the result of confusion – basically, children not keeping their parents informed of their whereabouts. And sometimes younger children simply get lost and are found after a search. In cases of abduction, it's often relatives who are involved. Mum and dad split up, one parent gets custody and the other parent takes matters into their own hands. Abduction by strangers is quite rare, thankfully.'

'So do you think they'll find her?'

Lulu looked at the masthead. The paper was a weekly and had been published two days earlier. 'She's probably been found already,' she said.

'Can you check?'

'Can I check? Why?'

'I'm worried.'

'I suppose they probably have a website. Let me have a look.' Lulu picked up her phone just as the waitress returned with a glass of wine and a bowl of water. She put the bowl down on the floor and the glass in front of Lulu.

Lulu thanked her and then showed her the paper. 'Did this little girl ever turn up?' she asked.

The waitress peered at the paper and shook her head. 'That's little Poppy. No. There was another search for her yesterday – I was one of the people looking. She only lives ten minutes from the school and she walks along the main road, so no one can understand how anybody managed to abduct her. Her parents were on TV last night. They're in bits.'

'Novak, that's an unusual name, isn't it? Though there was a film star many years ago called Kim Novak.'

'I think her dad is from the Czech Republic. Her mum's a local girl whose father used to run the Queen's Head. That's the pub down the road. He died a few years ago and the pub was sold.'

'What do they think happened to the little girl?' asked Lulu.

'Nobody knows,' said the waitress. 'She seems to have vanished into thin air.'

'I do hope they find her safely.'

'We all do, but it's been five days now, so people are starting to fear the worst.' She handed a menu to Lulu. 'Can I get you anything to eat?'

Lulu studied the menu and smiled. 'Oh, fish and chips,' she said. 'I haven't had fish and chips for ages.'

'Garden or mushy peas?'

'It has to be mushy, doesn't it?'

'And for Conrad?'

'He can share my cod.'

'I'll bring a spare plate.'

'You're an angel, thank you.'

Conrad waited until the waitress had walked away before speaking. 'Children don't just disappear, do they?' he said.

'No, not really. Adults do. They just pack up and go if life gets too much for them. Teenagers sometimes run away, but they usually take their phones with them, so the police can track them down. But this little girl is only ten – and ten-year-olds don't disappear of their own accord.'

'So somebody has taken her?'

'If the police haven't been able to find her within twenty-four hours of her having gone missing, then that's the assumption.'

'That's terrible. Do you think you can help?'

'Me?'

'You were a superintendent. A detective superintendent.'

'That was a long time ago. And Wiltshire has a perfectly good police force. They'll be doing whatever needs to be done.'

Conrad sighed. 'I hope so.'